PRAISE FOR CALLED

"As a biography and history of the complex South American political machinations of the period, Fiol and O'Connor's narrative about John and Clara's extraordinary accomplishments is replete with riveting details."
—Kirkus Review

"*CALLED* is a decades-spanning story that is suffused with emotion. The prose is refreshingly tender and honest."
—BookLife

"I'm impressed by how accurately this book identifies and describes the way a Plautdietsch Mennonite feels, thinks, and does things. This is a history book written as a fascinating adventure story. It's about true love and the whole truth ar   ted both can be."
—Siegfried El
Fernheim Color

D1293920

"*CALLED* tells the amazing story of Dr. John and his wife and Mennonite medical nurse Clara Schmidt and their strong will, determination, and faith to follow God's calling to serve the underserved, especially the leprosy community in the wilds of Paraguay. The historical content of this book is rich with detail and important background information, which I found valuable and enlightening. The evolution of Clara is so beautiful, at first a shy, unassuming Mennonite nurse who blossoms into a strong, fierce wife, mother, friend, and community activist. Clara and John are heroes, but always felt they were just being obedient servants of God. I found this story to be truly amazing and enlightening. I was pleasantly surprised by this read - never expecting to find the depth and important historical content within its pages!"
—Donna Dreeszen, educator, NetGalley reviewer

"*CALLED* is a book well worth reading. It features a newly minted Mennonite doctor John Schmidt and his wife Clara, who accepted the challenge of treating people with leprosy in Paraguay, an often-forgotten land of intrigue. When they were asked to undertake this daunting task, conventional practice was to provide victims of this dreaded disease with palliative care in an isolated colony. There was no known cure. Dr. Schmidt chose instead to pioneer a new and more humane treatment premised on home care surrounded by family. Before there was time to prove the merits of this innovation, he encountered such strong resistance from North American sponsors that it threatened to shut down his work. In the end, John and Clara's revolutionary model became the standard for leprosy treatment around the world."
—Edgar Stoesz, former associate executive secretary, Mennonite Central Committee, and former chairman, American Leprosy Missions

"This book will keep you moving! From Kansas to Paraguay, from WWII to the present day, from certainties to uncertainty, and from old ideas about "leper colonies" to the most enlightened medical and social practices in the treatment of leprosy. As you move, you will also reflect: can love co-exist with childhood beatings, with Platonic passion, with prejudice, with stubborn egos? How much love is sacrificed in the fulfillment of impossible dreams? And how does love always find a way home?"

—Shirley Showalter, PhD, former professor and president, Goshen College; former foundation executive, The Fetzer Institute; and author of *Blush: A Mennonite Girl Meets a Glittering World*

"As the son of John Schmidt, a pacifist who was determined to make this world a better place. I find *CALLED* to be an honest depiction of who he really was. I was intrigued by the colorful thread depicting the calling of an Argentine contemporary attempting to change her world by force and violence. Both my father's life and the Argentine history are amazingly well researched and accurate. There are many touching anecdotes that demonstrate the human side of a tough, no-nonsense crusader. This testimony will be passed to my children and their children for many generations to come to keep us mindful of our heritage."

—Dr. Wesley Schmidt, son of John and Clara, and medical director of Km. 81 1975-1978

"My wife Anni and I knew Dr. John and Clara Schmidt well and held them up as role models for our own mission work. In this book, Marlena and Ed present an unvarnished and accurate accounting of the work and lives of John and Clara. It is a story of how their joint passion helped overcome many obstacles and misunderstandings, ultimately leading to extraordinary outcomes in leprosy and social work, while deepening their own intimacy."

—Dr. Franz Duerksen, plastic surgeon, and medical director of Km. 81 1971-1975 and 1978-1985

"'Dokta Schmidt' was a household name in my family, who lived in the Fernheim Colony of the Chaco of Paraguay. My mother was in the first group of student nurses that John and Clara trained in 1943. And as a young couple, my parents went to Km. 81 for a year of voluntary service at the newly founded leprosy hospital. Decades later,

the Schmidts chose to spend their last years with the old folks of the Fernheim Colony, and to be buried among the very people they once served. John and Clara would have been the last ones to claim sainthood, and yet they were a beacon of light and hope for thousands."
—Gundolf Niebuhr, archivist,
Fernheim Colony, Chaco, Paraguay

"*CALLED* is a fantastic sweeping tale that provides a striking contrast to the intimate memoir from the same author, Nothing Bad Between Us. So happy to be following the story of these incredible people across their lives and times through such different lenses. What a journey! What a pleasure to read."
—Terri Griffith, PhD, Keith Beedie Chair in Innovation
and Entrepreneurship, Beedie School of Business,
Simon Fraser University

"*CALLED* is a story of how a deep and durable faith inspires and sustains a true visionary. But then this inspiring story takes a turn when we read it alongside Marlena's earlier book, Nothing Bad Between Us. Together, they remind us that no matter how holy, visionary, and transformative we may be, we are all mortal. Do yourself a favor and read both books. They will help you grow the confident humility it takes to live well - both with and for others."
—James Walsh, PhD, former President of the Academy of
Management, and professor, Ross School of Business,
University of Michigan

"*CALLED* is a sweeping historical saga depicting the heroic work of two medical pioneers in Paraguay, South America. Having visited the leprosy station they established at Km. 81, and driven on the trans-Chaco highway, I can attest to the enduring legacy of John and Clara Schmidt. But behind the glorious triumphs, the book reveals three under-appreciated lessons. First, while the popular press may glorify "having a calling," true callings involve deep sacrifice not only of those who have the calling, but of those who must live with them. Second,

dramatic change often involves being unreasonable, and even successful change will not necessarily win you friends. Third, there is transformative power in promoting the human dignity of others. Although in this book applied to those with leprosy, this lesson could be easily applied in our polarized times to everyone we consider to be the "other." I recommend the book to anyone wanting to make the world a better place, or to better understand and help those who are."
—Michael G. Pratt, PhD, O'Connor Family Professor,
Carroll School of Management, Boston College

"*CALLED* is a well-researched and well-told story of two very ordinary persons who accomplished extraordinary things. We get to know John and Clara Schmidt in all their humanness, with both strengths and weaknesses. Dr. Schmidt could have accepted the world-wide understanding of how patients with leprosy were cared for, but his heart and mind told him there was a better way more in line with his Mennonite understanding of how humans should be treated. At great costs to themselves, Dr. John and Clara Schmidt pulled together a varied group of people to help them establish a revolutionary system of caring, not for lepers, but for persons with a disease called leprosy. The genius of their approach was that they saw people, not disease; they sought ways to let love and acceptance touch the lives of folks rejected by all of society. This is a very good read!"
—M. Albert Durksen, retired minister,
Mennonite Church Canada

"Against overwhelming odds but armed with a vision and willingness to sacrifice, John and Clara Schmidt promoted the advancement of the Mennonite colonies in the Chaco, provided medical care without reserve to many needy individuals, and created a new model for engaging with leprosy patients, which revolutionized the treatment of leprosy worldwide. Their legacy remains in three regions of Paraguay, building communities and establishing hospitals. And throughout the story, a beautiful picture is created of their strong and enduring love for each other. Truly I categorize *CALLED* as a page turner! I felt pulled

along through the story from the beginning to the very end. I recommend the book as a wonderful option for your Christmas gift list!"
—Anna Beth Birky, Newton, Kansas

"Dr. John Schmidt was a man of integrity—headstrong and determined—and the relationships of those close to him were sometimes strained and difficult. His wife Clara was strong, loyal, haunted by self-doubt while full of compassion and love for others. Together they revolutionized established practices for the treatment of leprosy and reduced the prejudice and fear surrounding the disease. All this, while battling difficult living conditions in Paraguay, anxiety regarding continued funding, constant negotiating with Mennonite colony leaders, and raising a large family. Working through these complications and uncertainties makes John and Clara's story well worth reading."
—Lori Wise, U.S. Records and Library,
Mennonite Central Committee

"I was fortunate to be one of the early readers of this book based on the lives of John and Clara Schmidt. It captures the essence of two selfless but very human folks who made a difference. If you are drawn to historical sagas, as I am, make certain that you do not miss this captivating work. Rudyard Kipling said that "if history were taught in the form of stories, it would never be forgotten. A literary view of the human experience of the past invites readers into a real, living historical moment, so that the experience of lives and moments distant in time and space become their own." He could have been referring to this book. Get it, sit back, and travel to another time and space."
—Thomas M. Stamm, Lebanon, Pennsylvania

ALSO BY MARLENA FIOL, PhD

Nothing Bad Between Us: A Mennonite Missionary's Daughter Finds Healing in Her Brokenness

ALSO BY MARLENA FIOL, PhD
and ED O'CONNOR, PhD

Separately Together

Reclaiming Your Future
Creating Readiness for Change

Working Together While Maintaining Distinctiveness

A True Story

CALLED

MARLENA FIOL
AND
ED O'CONNOR

JRS
BOOKS

JRS Books
P.O. Box 5274
Eugene, OR 97405

Text copyright © 2021 by Marlena Fiol and Ed O'Connor
All rights reserved.

Book cover and interior design by Monkey C Media
Edited by Tom Jenks
Copyedited by Stephanie Thompson
Map by BMR Williams

First Edition
Printed in the United States of America

ISBN: 978-1-7375314-0-1 (Trade Paperback)
ISBN: 978-1-7375314-1-8 (eBook)

Library of Congress Control Number: 2021915243

To two unreasonable pioneers,
Clara and John Schmidt,
whose lifelong, selfless passion for the welfare
of others made this world a better place for us all.

AUTHORS' NOTE

This is the true story of Dr. John and Clara Schmidt, Kansas Mennonites who devoted their lives as medical pioneers in Paraguay, South America. The book was born out of a desire to bring to life the forces that propelled them from one risky service adventure to another and to publicize their extraordinary contributions, among them revolutionizing how leprosy is currently treated throughout the world.

The book's depiction of locales, events, and characters is based on 740 sources, including published books, diary entries, journals, letters, and interviews with people acquainted with the Schmidts. The references to these source materials, as well as photos and other original documents, can be found at CalledASaga.com, an interactive site where we invite you to share your own reflections and/or experiences regarding the Schmidts and their work.

In telling John and Clara's story, we have condensed several characters into a single role and allowed ourselves a measure of invention and interpretation to help illuminate conflicts at play in the story. For reasons of privacy, we have given fictitious names to several of the characters.

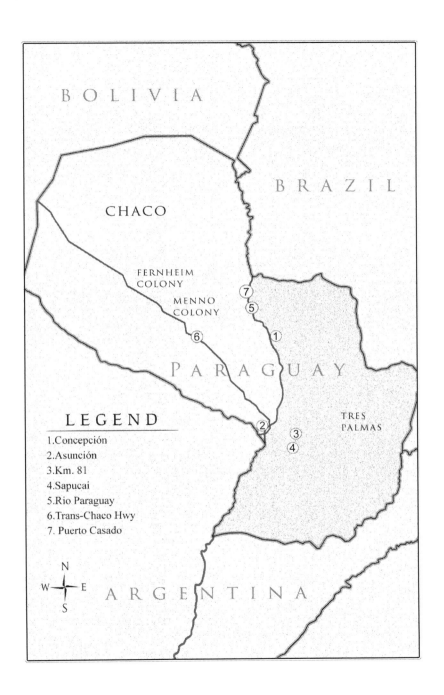

BOLIVIA

BRAZIL

CHACO

FERNHEIM
COLONY

MENNO
COLONY

⑦

⑤

⑥

①

PARAGUAY

LEGEND

1.Concepción
2.Asunción
3.Km. 81
4.Sapucai
5.Rio Paraguay
6.Trans-Chaco Hwy
7. Puerto Casado

②

③

④

TRES
PALMAS

N
W E
S

ARGENTINA

UNWAVERING PURSUIT

1941-1943

"Impossible? The word is a roadblock to progress!"
—Robert H. Schuller

ONE

J ust past midnight on June 7, 1941, John Schmidt boarded the *SS Argentina* in New York harbor. Two years into the second Great War, Germans had overrun much of western Europe, and had advanced deep into the Soviet Union. Given the threat from German U-boats, and because the U.S. was still neutral, two American flags were painted on both sides of the ship's hull. The *SS Argentina* was fully lit, a blazing vessel, carrying 273 passengers, 195 in first class and the rest down below.

The ship's deck shuddered under John's feet. He put down his Army-surplus duffel bag, worn thin with use, and leaned against the rail as the vessel glided out of the harbor past Bedloe's Island. His jaw tightened as he stared into the churning black water, trying to shut out the excited voices of people around him. John gripped the rail with both hands. It was really happening. Less than three weeks ago, he was finishing his medical internship in Baltimore, with no definite plans. And now here he was, traveling to Rio de Janeiro, Brazil, an intermediate stop on his way to landlocked Paraguay, where he was to serve as a pioneering doctor.

An almost full moon cast a glow across the green patina of the Statue of Liberty. But John stared past the statue, out across the harbor into the unknown. He pulled his lanky frame erect and lifted his face into the wind.

Was he doing the right thing? Would the Mennonites in Paraguay accept him as one of their own or would they see him as an interloper? The language wouldn't be a problem. John grew up speaking *Plautdietsch*, their Low-German dialect. But beyond that, he wasn't sure they'd have much in common despite their common heritage. John's people were German Mennonites who emigrated from Russia to Kansas in the late 1800s. Almost five decades later, in 1931, Mennonites from the same Russian ancestry settled in the Chaco of western Paraguay, the vast virtually uninhabitable desert John was soon to call home.

The past few weeks had been hectic, obtaining his draft release as a conscientious objector doing alternative service and acquiring the papers needed to travel to Paraguay. He'd hardly had time to consider the mission that lay ahead. A shiver ran down his spine. Of course he was doing the right thing. It was God's will.

A commotion near the midship stairwell interrupted John's thoughts. He turned from the rail and saw a tall woman emerge from the crowd, her stylish figure contrasting almost absurdly with the two portly men who rushed along behind her. Mesmerized, John watched her glide by not far from where he stood. Her green eyes held his for an instant as she and the two men passed by.

John's gaze followed her, and he momentarily forgot his concerns. He'd always noticed pretty girls. In high school, he'd had a few girlfriends and sometimes he'd needed to get hold of himself, especially when he had to pay his own way through university. His motto was "Profession or marriage, but not both." Now, at thirty, and having finished his medical training, John was freed from his self-imposed vow. But for marriage, he'd have eyes only for the right kind of Christian gal.

He continued to stare into the darkness, the crashing waves reflecting an unfamiliar unease building within him. Something he couldn't name.

"Are you ready for this, John?" A man clad fully in black, wearing thick, black-rimmed glasses, appeared by his side. As leader of the Mennonite Central Committee (MCC), the charitable organization commissioning John's work in Paraguay, Orie Miller was accompanying the young doctor on his voyage south.

John started. Had Orie observed his inner turmoil? "Ready for what?"

"The mission you're on," Orie said.

"Of course I am," John said in a clipped voice. He could have chosen to practice some place around Baltimore, but it was time for him to stop being around women who painted their lips and men who lived in sin. He needed to be back among his own people.

"May God protect us." Orie turned to take the stairs down to their stateroom.

The ship pitched as it sailed into unprotected water. Suddenly a wave of nausea rose in John's stomach, and he followed his travel companion down the stairs.

Orie was folding shirts and placing them in neat piles on shelves lining the wall of their tiny cabin. "You've been to the Paraguayan Chaco colonies before," John said, sitting on the edge of the hard lower bunk bed. "I'm realizing how little I know about those people."

Orie looked up, pushing his glasses farther up his nose.

"I..." John looked around the cabin, as though searching for the right words.

Orie's eyes narrowed. "If this is all too much too soon, we can just pay a visit to the colonies, and then—"

John waved both hands in front of his face. "No. No. Of course it's not too much..." Then, bringing his hands to his mouth, he hurried down the hall to the washroom.

★

For the next two days, John remained in bed, getting up every few hours to retch. When Orie occasionally brought him broth or a piece of toast, John thanked him and then, silent, turned his head toward the wall. He was sure Orie could answer more of his questions about what awaited him in Paraguay. But he didn't know how to ask without sounding like he was weak or afraid. That was most certainly not the case. As a young boy on a Kansas farm, where his parents barely eked out a living for their eleven children, John had learned that it was a waste of time to wallow in fears or doubts. His father's regular beatings and his mother's motto, "You just do what must be done," had taught him well. He knew exactly what he must do now.

By the third evening, feeling better, John ventured out to explore the ship. Aboard this great liner, the opportunities for enjoying a life of perfect ease seemed limitless, even in tourist class. It was like a floating city. He wandered around a swimming pool and stared across to a first-class veranda café where waiters catered to their guests' every whim. There was even a Dorothy Gray beauty salon, and a shop to buy personal items, souvenirs, and ship memorabilia.

John stopped in front of a panel of doors with a sign that read *First Class Only*. Through the glass panel, he peeked into a world like none he'd ever known. People strolled through the wide high-ceilinged corridors, smoking, and chatting with one another. Ornate chandeliers, decorated with fine porcelain roses, spread their elaborate bronze arms across the ceiling. Such excess. If people used only what they needed, there could be an end to poverty in the world.

On the upper deck behind the ballroom, the tennis court between the ship's two stacks had been converted into an open-air cinema. The screening this evening was a newly released short film by Columbia Pictures, *All the World's a Stooge*, starring the Three Stooges. It was a slapstick account of a wealthy man whose eccentric wife wants to adopt a refugee, a trendy thing to do among high society at the time. Her husband, opposed to the idea, concocts a nasty ruse to disabuse his wife of her philanthropic notion by setting up three inept window washers (the Three Stooges) as refugee children.

The deception doesn't go well. About the time the husband began chasing after the Stooges with an axe, John rose from his seat and conspicuously marched toward the stairs.

"Completely immoral," he muttered under his breath. The plight of refugees shouldn't be grist for Hollywood.

"Sorry?" A throaty voice came from the shadows of the stairwell.

John stopped. A woman leaned against the wall, lighting a cigarette. When she inhaled, the glow revealed the full red lips he remembered from the first day of sailing.

"You were saying?" She raised perfectly shaped eyebrows.

"Miss…?" John removed his hat.

"Brighton. Anastasia Brighton," she said, reaching to shake his hand.

"How'd you do," he mumbled. "John Schmidt."

Her lips parted into something bordering on a smile. "Pleased to meet you."

"Excuse me." Still holding his hat in his hands, John rushed down the stairs to his cabin.

He lay on his hard bunk, wondering who she was, still seeing the haze of cigarette smoke and the woman's penetrating green eyes.

In the early morning of June 11, the *SS Argentina* docked in Barbados. Several impressive old forts surrounded the harbor of this tropical paradise. John stood at the railing, watching a large group of swimmers, their black bodies gleaming in the glow of sunrise, making their way toward the ship. He turned to his companion. "You've made this trip before. What do they want?"

"They're hoping for money handouts," Orie said.

"I read that slavery was abolished here thirty years before we got around to it in the U.S.," John said. "And prior to emancipation, the British implemented a four-year apprenticeship program." He frowned and his forehead creased. "Seems like a wise approach, teaching them to work. So why aren't they working now, rather than begging for handouts?"

An old-fashioned work ethic had always prevailed among John's Kansas Mennonites. His family was no exception. John could still feel the sting of his father's leather strap across his buttocks when he slacked off from the expected twelve-hour workdays with his team of horses. His first memory of the whip was when he was seven, when his father caught him picking mulberries in the middle of the day. Slothful behavior was a disgrace.

"My dear John, we don't always know what goes on in another man's life," Orie said.

John pressed his lips into a thin line.

John scanned the crowded dining room that the tourist class shared with the first-class passengers. He'd noticed that Anastasia Brighton usually sat at a corner table with her two companions, engaged in animated conversations. She waved her hands a lot when she spoke.

Tonight, she sat alone, having a drink. Her long legs were casually stretched out in front of her. Her eyes met his, and she signaled for him to join her.

"Miss Anastasia," he said, holding his hat to his chest.

"Oh, do call me Ana. That's what everyone at Yale called me," she said, laughing.

"Yale?" John took a seat across from her.

Ana explained that she was Argentinian, and that she'd been at Yale for a post-JD after graduating from law school in Montevideo, Uruguay. She was returning home to Argentina with two other attorneys.

"And you, Dr. Schmidt? Your name is *German*." She frowned. "Where are you from and why are you going to Paraguay?"

"How do you know I'm going to Paraguay?"

"I've asked about you." She slowly sipped her drink, waiting for him to respond.

"My people are Russian Mennonites," John began. The fact that he grew up in rural Kansas was much less important to his self-identity than being a Mennonite.

"I've heard of *meno-nitas* who live in colonies in Uruguay, but I don't know much about them," Ana said. "I'd like to hear more. But this doesn't explain why you're off to Paraguay?"

John explained that his ancestors who escaped Russia in the 1870s were from the same group that later immigrated to the Chaco of Paraguay. "So you see, Miss Ana, I am going to be a doctor for my people in Paraguay."

"For *your* people?" Ana frowned. "What about the native people in the Chaco that *your* people have displaced? Will you be a doctor for them?"

John's gaze met hers. "I'm going to do God's work, wherever God calls me to do it."

"*God's* work? What makes it God's work?" Ana arched her brows.

Why did her questions feel so challenging? Among John's Mennonite people, no one ever asked what it meant to do God's work. After thinking about it for a moment, he suggested that any work aligned with God's will was God's work. This led her to ask if God's work needed to be religious.

John was silent for a moment. "Why do you ask?"

"My father was British and moved to Buenos Aires in 1913, where he met and married my mother. Because of him, I grew up Anglican. Today I'm an agnostic, I suppose, but an Anglican agnostic, of course. I try to look at the world objectively." She pointed a slender finger at him. "It seems like your kind of people assert that your faith is the right faith, and your work is God's work, often without any supporting evidence. Do you ever stop to ask why?"

John had seldom been challenged to question his belief in God or in God's work. Sure, he'd gone to school with non-believers. But he hadn't had time to pay much attention to the frivolous conversations of his fellow students. To pay for his years of medical school at Kansas University, he'd served food in the cafeteria to his classmates, and he'd shoveled coal to keep their heaters going. And during his residency in Baltimore, he and his fellow residents were focused on their strenuous medical routines. His faith was a given.

Finally, he said, "I just know that the Bible tells us '*Whatsoever you do to the least of your brothers and sisters, you do unto me.*'" Serving his Lord. That's what was important.

Ana shook her head slowly. "I've never met anyone quite like you, Dr. John."

He wanted her to understand. So he told her stories his grandmother Lena had so often recounted about how she and his grandfather Jacob had escaped the persecution in Russia. "If my grandparents hadn't come to the U.S. when they did, I'd be lucky to be a barefoot boy walking behind a plow in Paraguay. For me to help the Paraguayan Mennonites is my expression of thanks to God that I was spared the suffering in Russia."

The dining room had emptied. Waiters were quietly clearing the tables around them and cleaning the floor.

John reached for his pocket watch. "I'm sorry, Miss Ana. It's very late...."

She waved her hand, her head tilted to one side, her eyes flashing. "It's been a pleasure."

As he made his way back down to his cabin, John thought about how strange it was that he felt so at ease around this heathen woman. As though he'd known her for a long time. He changed into his bedclothes and lay on the narrow bed, wide awake. His mind ran back through the evening's conversation. Talking with Ana had awakened excitement in every fiber of his being about his upcoming adventure.

The next few days, John and Ana met regularly in the dining room. He learned that she'd grown up in the affluent northern Buenos Aires district of Palermo, with nannies and a tutor who taught her English.

"You learned English before I did," John said with a wry smile.

"I learned many things from a very early age," Ana said, frowning. She described the high standards her parents imposed on her, from perfect grades in school to social graces in high class society. "I could never live up to their expectations." She sighed. "But enough about that. You didn't speak English?"

"My people speak mostly Plautdietsch, which is a mixed dialect of Dutch, German, and Russian. We were very poor. My father wasn't good at farming and never got out of debt." He lifted his chin. "But he was always generous to those in need. It didn't matter how little we had."

"You seem almost proud of your family's poverty," Ana said.

Not knowing how to respond, he said, "You haven't said what you'll be doing in Argentina, Miss Ana."

Ana pushed herself to the edge of her seat. "Recent correspondence from my father in Buenos Aires suggests that Nazi activists are blanketing South America with German propaganda. I am returning to my beloved Argentina with two other attorneys from Yale to fight the trend toward Nazi support. Like you, Dr. John, I am on an important mission. Only mine is not God's work."

"Any work that serves others and benefits mankind is God's work." Had those words really come out of his mouth? But it had to be true. If the work reflected a desire to do good in the world and be useful, it must be God's work.

Ana said nothing.

"And how do you intend to fight the Nazis?" John asked.

"By force. You can only combat force with equal force and greater cunning," she said.

"I'm afraid I completely disagree," John said. "The application of force only brings about more force." As a pacifist Mennonite, he had a moral duty to *not* engage himself in the physical destruction of others. The goal of any true Christian should be to influence the world in favor of nonviolence.

Ana waved her hands to dismiss his arguments. "Unfortunately, I am unable to tell you more specifically what our plans are to combat Nazism in Argentina. Suffice it to say, nonviolence will *not* be our moral code."

John leaned forward. Argentina was a hotbed of intrigue. How was this impetuous woman involved in the conspiracies? John recognized her passion and commitment. So much like his own.

"I wish you much success with your meno-nitas," Ana said. "I hope to hear from you?"

They exchanged addresses and promised to stay in touch.

The following morning the ship docked in Rio. Orie stood at the doorway of their cabin, bags in hand, watching his travel companion. He took in John's broad shoulders thrown back under a double-breasted black suit, and his white hat worn rakishly off to one side. If Orie hadn't known better, he might have guessed that John was an arrogant swashbuckler off on a grand adventure. But he knew this was the young doctor's only suit. And beneath the stylish hat, John's eyes revealed an almost frightening intensity.

"John, there's something I need to tell you. Please sit down."

John was stuffing his belongings into a bag. "What is it?"

Orie pushed his glasses up against his forehead. How much should he tell John about the seriousness of the situation in the Fernheim Mennonite colony in the Chaco? From everything Orie had heard, Fernheim had become a heated battleground between a majority German Nazi *Bund* (a pro-Nazi organization) and a minority group opposing them. In particular, there was a young schoolteacher who was spreading Nazi fervor throughout the colony. According to reports, over 80 percent of the colonists had joined his Bund. Orie frowned. He should probably assess the situation himself before confronting John with it.

"You'll need to keep your eyes open and watch your back," Orie said. "You're going into pioneering territory." He tried to avoid John's probing eyes.

"I already know that." John yanked on the straps of his duffle bag.

TWO

On Sunday June 15, Clara Regier and her classmates received their nursing caps. The probation period was over. Clara loved the responsibility of working on the hospital floor. Her greatest satisfaction came from connecting with her patients, whether that meant emptying their bedpans, cleaning their wounds, or praying with them.

Clara wanted to be busy. It was the only thing that kept her mind off Franklin Pauls, a science student she'd met during her last year at Bethel College. After they both graduated with bachelor's degrees, she began nurse's training and Franklin left to study science at some fancy college in Lexington, Kentucky. He called it "Transy."

Franklin had just returned for the summer, and Clara couldn't stop thinking about him. Even when Dr. Herb Schmidt, one of the most prominent surgeons at Bethel Hospital, had singled her out from more senior nurses to introduce her to his younger brother John a few weeks ago, her mind had been elsewhere. She already had a boyfriend.

But did Franklin still like her? He called her his girl. But all this time, almost two years, he'd never mentioned anything about a future together. What should a girl make of that? That's not how it played out in the romance novels she read by flashlight late at night. She still occasionally daydreamed about marriage, but things didn't seem to be going that way.

Clara was twenty-six, the oldest of four children. She'd been responsible for her younger siblings at an early age because her mother had "nerve problems." For several years during high school, she stayed home, somehow finishing with correspondence courses before starting college. Her strict Mennonite father had controlled Clara's every move, not allowing her to mingle with young men. He hadn't even allowed her to stay up late in her own room, studying. At age twenty-five, she made the bold decision to stay on campus for her last year of college, working at a farmer's cooperative office to pay her way.

Now that Franklin had returned, Clara had to learn the truth about their relationship. They sat on a bench on the hospital grounds after going for an ice cream soda at the train station diner.

"Franklin, it wasn't really fair to you that I went into training without saying boo," she began. When Franklin hesitated, she turned away, blushing.

"It's all for the best, Clara, because I still have a few years before I'll know what I'm doing or where I'm going," he finally said.

"I feel like you're avoiding talking about our future," she blurted, louder than she'd intended.

Franklin took her hands in his. "I'll be out of town for a bit. But when I return, let's talk. Maybe after your church service next week?"

Franklin belonged to a different branch of the Mennonite denomination than Clara. Their habit was for Franklin to pick her up after her service and go for a Sunday drive together.

Clara sucked in her breath. Maybe finally, they would figure this out.

Clara could hardly get to sleep on Saturday night. Franklin had such an honest and serious look on his face when he'd said he wanted to talk. Maybe tomorrow when they met, he'd stop the car near her favorite willow tree, or maybe he'd ask to drive to her home to speak to her father.

When she woke, her joy and anticipation had vanished. Why had she said what she did? Why had she pushed him into a corner? It wasn't her place to take the lead. Besides, she shouldn't worry or fuss. The Lord would guide them to do the right thing. But still...

She rolled her hair carefully and chose a dress she remembered Franklin saying he liked.

When she left the church after the service, she saw Franklin leaning against his car. She looked down, hiding her flushed face.

"Let's take a walk," he said.

They walked in silence. Clara occasionally glanced at him, but he looked straight ahead.

He abruptly stopped and turned to her. Clara looked up and smiled, but then looked away.

"Clara, it's just not going to work out for us coming from different faiths. What would we do if we had children? Whose faith would they follow? I've asked you before. Please get re-baptized into my church."

Clara jerked back and her shoulders rose. Given how she and Franklin had been raised, this was a significant obstacle. She'd been baptized at the age of seventeen into a branch of the Mennonites referred to as the General Conference (GC) church. Franklin had been baptized into the Mennonite Brethren (MB) church. MBs and GCs were united regarding all substantive Mennonite doctrine, but differed in their views about the true mode of baptism for converted believers. MBs held that baptism by immersion was the only mode that adequately symbolized the death, burial, and resurrection of Christ. By contrast, GCs held that sprinkling was the appropriate mode of baptism. Since each of these Mennonite groups denied the validity of the other's mode of baptism as a genuine sign of Christian faith, the young couple could find no easy compromise.

"Franklin, we've been through this already." Clara's eyes began to sting.

Franklin turned and walked her back to his car. They drove to the nurses' dormitory in silence. Clara thought about her baptism. It had been so serious to her that she'd cried almost the whole day. Baptism had signaled her deep commitment to make her life count for Jesus. She couldn't go back on that and get re-baptized.

When they arrived at the dorm, Clara ran into her room, threw herself onto the bed, and buried her face in the pillow.

In Rio de Janeiro, Orie and John boarded a twin-propeller Panair do Brasil aircraft, which took them across vast mountain ranges and rainforests to the small landlocked country of Paraguay. The plane landed in Asunción on a cold rainy afternoon. At the bottom of the steps of the aircraft, John stood for a moment on the tarmac and breathed in the smoky, pungent air. He pulled down his hat and strode into the terminal building.

A crew of taciturn officers in shabby uniforms fingerprinted Orie and John. Were they marking them as potential criminals? The Paraguayan government, headed by pro-Fascist General Morínigo, expressed unabashed support for the Nazi cause. Widespread propaganda reinforced the view that the German military was superior and that the true threats to the Western Hemisphere were not the Axis powers but Western imperialists.

"What are *you* doing here?" One of the officers squinted at John.

"Chaco," John said, guessing what he was asked without understanding a word of the officer's Spanish.

The officials traded a look. "*No, hombre,*" the man said, shaking his head. "*No se puede vivir en el Chaco.*"

John and Orie walked through the heavy double doors into the airport's grungy waiting room. John scanned the room and spotted an elderly man with a few strands of hair combed back across a bald head. The man held a handwritten sign that read *Miller und Schmidt.*

Their driver took them through the cobblestone streets of Asunción and stopped in front of the Hotel Hamburgo. Orie turned to John. "As you know, I need to head for the Chaco immediately. I've made arrangements for Hans to help you get your medical permit." He nodded to the bald driver, who spoke both Plautdietsch and Spanish.

On July 3, nearly three weeks after landing in Paraguay, John finally obtained his permit. He and Hans began the long trek from Asunción to the Chaco colonies. Just north of Asunción, they boarded a small barge on the Paraguay River. All day, they chugged past miles of uncultivated land and low shrubs. Late that night, they arrived at Puerto Casado, the center of a large tannery. The owner had built a narrow-gauge railroad 145 kilometers into the interior for the shipment of quebracho logs for the tannery.

At 5:30 the next morning, they boarded the small train. Every hour, they stopped to reload the timber that fueled the engine. The train swayed and jolted slowly down the track. John took in the strange, new landscape. It was barren and uninviting, yet something about it sparked a thrill within him. In the evening, as the train shuddered to a stop at "Kilómetro 145," it began to pour.

After a mostly sleepless night in a broken-down shack, lying on the soggy ground next to other smelly travelers, John and Hans continued by oxcart. Without seats or springs, the cart sloshed and bumped through and around muddy puddles and occasional deep waterholes on the narrow wagon trail. Overhanging tree branches and thorn bushes brushed their faces and red-brown dust filled their noses and eyes. John looked in amazement at the masses of low cacti bushes and huge cactus trees. Every growing thing seemed to have thorns.

They stopped in the late afternoon for a bite to eat. Both men huddled underneath the cart for protection from the persistent rain. "*Wot ess dit?*" John asked, poking a finger into a pile of red mush on his tin plate. He gagged when he learned it was raw pork sausage. Didn't these people know about parasites?

Hans had been silent during most of their time together, almost sullen. Finally, John said, "What do you have against me, Hans?"

Hans jerked his head up. "I…I… nothing, *Herr Dokta*," he said. "It's just that you Americans, you don't understand…"

"What is it we don't understand?" John pushed aside his plate.

"*Najo*," Hans began and paused. "When we fled from Russia ten years ago, it was Germany that came to our aid and provided initial refuge, even though they could hardly afford it during that country's dire economic circumstances. Then you Americans got involved and sent us to die in this Godforsaken country."

John frowned. "And you think Germany can help you now?"

"Hitler will defeat communist Russia, and we will be invited to return to our beloved *Mutterland*, our only chance to escape from this hell," Hans said, eyes flaming.

John almost said, "That's nothing but a ridiculous fantasy," but stopped himself, knowing he was at Hans' mercy out in the middle of nowhere. He pinched his lips together and clenched his hands, hardly trusting what he might do to this man who touted the virtues of Nazism. How could Hans call himself a pacifist Mennonite and put his faith in the warlike creed of National Socialism? John threw himself out into the rain and stomped in circles around the cart until Hans was finally ready to ride on. Both men remained mostly silent for the remainder of the day.

That night, they found refuge in a hut along the road. The rough straw mattress poked into John's ribs, and the musty mosquito netting hung down over his face. Despite his exhaustion, he tossed and turned. What was he doing here? Why should he help these people who longed for nothing more than to return to their Russian farms after a Nazi victory? John slapped at the hungry mosquitos that bit him where the net touched his skin.

John had learned what he could from Orie about the Mennonite colonies. The Fernheim group of 3,240 members fled the ravages of communist oppression in the Ukraine and traveled to Germany in early 1930, thanks to the assistance of the pre-Nazi German government. Originally the refugees wanted to continue to Canada, but they were denied entry. The young MCC under the leadership of Orie Miller stepped in to find a way to bring them to Paraguay.

Another group of nearly 7,000 Mennonites had already emigrated from Canada to form the nearby Menno colony in 1927. Paraguay welcomed the immigrants from Canada and Russia, even with their illnesses, hoping they'd develop the vast, nearly uninhabited region of the Chaco, an area of 7,500 km² (2,900 mi²).

Did Hans understand that without MCC's intervention, he and his people would have been shipped back to become victims of terror and repression in Stalin's Soviet Union? Or worse, deported to Siberia, which is what happened to thousands of Mennonites who hadn't escaped?

The next day, John and Hans rode through the Menno colony and continued to Fernheim. Along the way they passed a cluster of dome-shaped huts, about five feet high and ten feet in diameter, made with bent branches covered with straw. Dark-skinned women, wearing only sackcloth wrapped around the waist, sat around a fire. Naked children stared at the cart passing by. They looked just like the Indians John had read about in grade school.

"Who are these people?"

Hans explained that the entire Chaco region was populated by Indians before the Mennonites came. The native tribes had been nomads, living largely on herbs and game found in the bush. But they'd learned to love home-baked bread and other things they could get as payment for odd jobs they did for the Mennonites. Some had even begun to learn words in Plautdietsch.

"They work for us during cotton-picking season, but otherwise we leave them alone," Hans said. "They carry poisonous spears and many of them are known to be hostile."

John stared at them. So these were the natives Ana had referred to.

They rode into Filadelfia at the center of the Fernheim colony before noon. John looked around his new hometown as they trundled along the rutted road, past a lumber mill and a whitewashed adobe building with a tin roof. A small wooden sign that read *Die Kooperative* hung near the door. Much smaller huts with thatched roofs lined the main dirt road running through the village. Pale, listless children sat on the ground in front of the huts, waving flies away from their eyes. The primitive conditions didn't bother John. It wasn't that different than the poor Kansas farm community he was from.

The cart stopped in front of a single-room hut with a sloping thatched roof. Birds had made nests in the roof and the mud brick exterior walls were eroding. The broken-down shutters leaned unevenly from rusty hinges.

"*Welkohme.* We hope it is good for you to live in this house, Herr Dokta," said a stooped man who stood by the door of the hut. "Someone died in it, so people refuse to use it."

"It'll be fine," John said, hardly looking around.

After a short rest, John met Orie and they walked to the Kooperative, the center of the system the colonists had adopted from their Soviet past. They passed a group of young men huddled in a corner. John and Orie stopped when they heard the loud voice of a man at the center of the group. His hair was short, almost shaven, and his dark eyes sank deep into their sockets.

"We asked for a doctor, not a political enemy who will get in the way of our Bund…" When the man saw Orie and John watching him, he quit speaking. Raising his chin, he threw back his shoulders and marched away from them, his followers trailing along behind.

"News travels fast. That's Fritz Kliewer," Orie said quietly when the men had passed. "He's gaining a lot of power. A few years ago, the colony sent him to Germany to study. After earning a doctorate, he returned to Paraguay with his new wife Margarete, a youth leader he met in Berlin. I'm told the German youth movement paid for their return trip. Ever since then, they've been on fire to reform the colony school system to teach principles of Nazism. With youth education as his base, Kliewer has become the de facto leader of the pro-Nazi movement here."

"Don't any of them see the dark side of Nazism?" John asked.

"John, you must understand how it looks to them. Hitler is creating jobs, pulling Germany out of an economic depression, and fighting communism. They believe that if Germany is victorious over Russia, they'll be able to leave the desolation of the Chaco and return to their homeland."

"Ja, I've heard all that," John said, not attempting to hide the bitterness in his voice.

To a neutral outsider, it would not seem surprising that most of the Paraguayan Mennonites signed up for membership in the Bund, given their German heritage and their desire to escape the Chaco. But John Schmidt was no neutral outsider. The matter was quite simple: The principles of the Nazi Bund and Mennonite Christianity could never go together.

The next morning, Orie and John visited the little hospital located across the yard from John's hut. Despite the dirt floor and primitive conditions, the two-room structure seemed clean and orderly. There was only one nurse, *Schwester* Maria, a young woman with blond braids wound around the top of her head.

"Welkohme, Herr Dokta," she said to John in an unwelcoming voice. She reminded them that in prior years the colony was served intermittently by men posing as doctors who stayed for only short periods of time. Many of them were exposed as incompetent imposters.

"The last one flunked his second year of veterinary school before he came and posed as our doctor," she said. "So you must understand that the general health conditions and our expectations here are quite low."

John decided to restrict his office calls to three times per week, reserving Tuesday, Thursday, and Saturday for special work like surgeries and general health screenings. He saw patients until the sun set. In the evenings, after a bite to eat, he sat at his small wooden table by lamplight, creating patient records on filing cards he had purchased in

Asunción. Schwester Maria occasionally stopped by to bring him a cup of tea. Mostly, John spent long hours by himself, carefully reviewing his cases and creating medical records.

One night, after hours of compiling patient notes, John sat back and stared into the flickering flame of the lamp. He thought about the Mennonite student nurse his oldest brother, Herb, had introduced him to just before leaving for Paraguay. Clara Regier. She was the sort of helpmate who could be of great assistance here. But she'd seemed timid and a little nervous. It was preposterous to think that a shy Kansas Mennonite girl like that would want to come to this place. But maybe...?

He pushed aside the piles of filing cards, dipped his pen into the inkbottle, and wrote:

Dear Clara,

I set sail in New York on June 7 at 1:15 AM. I was somewhat seasick but not too much to enjoy the service on the steamer, the vastness of the ocean, and the companionship one develops. There is certain closeness when one is with the same people for twelve days.

John stared out into the darkness. How could he possibly describe this place and these people to someone he hardly knew? He continued to write. About the voyage to Rio, about the Paraguayan people and countryside, about the Mennonites in the Chaco. He left out any mention of the horrific political tensions. John ended the letter with:

Although I have not known you very long, we have friends in common. Bethel College has always been of interest so I would appreciate some news. Let me hear from you.

Besides obstetrics, emergency cases, common colds, and stomach upsets, John treated patients with nutritional diseases (mostly oral abscesses due to vitamin deficiencies), chronic malaria, and typhoid fever. The water was responsible for frequent diarrhea, which the colonists referred to as *Bush Krankheit* (jungle sickness). The most common medical condition was trachoma, an eye disease the immigrants had brought with them from Russia. Over half the people he'd examined needed treatment for trachoma. Also, widespread hookworm infestation led to severe anemia. And there was no iron to prescribe.

"I'm going to the village blacksmith," John said to his nurse. On the farm in Kansas, his dad had heated iron to make farm implements. If he could get the blacksmith to heat the iron, he figured he could grind the red-hot metal with a mortar and pestle into an ingestible powder.

Schwester Maria eyed him in a way that perplexed John, but he had no time to inquire into what it meant.

John had studied internal medicine, so he had minimal surgical training. Since his trunk—which had been shipped separately from Rio—had not yet arrived, he didn't even have his medical books to read about procedures the colonists needed, some of which he'd never seen performed. Nor did he have the required instruments he'd packed in his trunk. He heard from the shipping company that the trunk was in Montevideo and wouldn't arrive for four more months. But sick people needed his help now, so he'd do the best he could under the circumstances.

He created a list of what needed to get done. "We must build a surgical team," he said to his nurse. "For I.V. fluids, we'll make distilled water from collected rainwater. You'll assist me, Schwester Maria, but I'll need an anesthetist."

His nurse stared at him, as she was now prone to do. "We have no one with such training."

"I just need someone who's willing to learn," John said.

"Well, I have a cousin, Horst, who's a grade-school teacher in Schönbrunn (a nearby village). We used to play 'doctor' when we were kids, and..." Her voice dwindled and she looked down, blushing. "He always did want to be a doctor."

"Please take me to him," John said.

They arrived in Schönbrunn and clapped at the doorway, as was the custom instead of knocking. Horst opened the door and shrank back when he saw the doctor.

"Wot ess dit?" he muttered, staring at his cousin.

"I want to teach you how to save lives," John said, reaching to shake Horst's hand. "Can we come in?"

John was persistent. Before long, Horst agreed, and began training with the doctor.

After John's first hemorrhoidectomy, the patient's rectum remained sore and bleeding for weeks. Night after night, John sat in the darkness at his table. Was this normal? Did he need to repeat the surgery? Dropping his head into both hands, John wondered, as he so often did, what his oldest brother, Herb, would do. Of course, *he'd* know what to do.

THREE

In September, Franklin Pauls returned to school in Kentucky. He and Clara had not resolved their differences but had agreed to pray about the matter. She spent less and less time thinking about Franklin. She even put away her late-night romance novels.

Clara had begun training as a surgical nurse and found it exhilarating. She was allowed to assist both the surgeons and the head nurses to ensure a sterile and controlled environment, to have the required instruments available, and to complete the necessary paperwork. Sometimes she even got to assist the surgeon during operations. Clara felt certain she had found her true calling. This was how she would serve her Lord.

In October, an ice storm tore through central Kansas, leaving behind fallen trees, impassable roads, and power outages. Clara worked later than usual in the O.R. and didn't get back to her room until after the cafeteria was closed. Hungry and cold, she wrapped herself in a blanket and picked up the mail someone had placed on her bedside table. The handwriting on one envelope looked familiar. It must be a birthday card from Franklin. She put it aside.

The other was a thin airmail envelope. Clara slit it open. She stared at the loopy handwriting. It was from Dr. Herb's brother John, the man she met just before he left for Paraguay. He'd written the letter over three months ago, in July. It was long and newsy, mostly describing his journey south. Why was he writing to her? Was it possible that he was interested in her? No, he was probably just teasing her. Just to be safe, she'd write him a kind letter, showing Christian gratitude for what he must be doing in that heathen land.

She put aside the airmail letter and reached for the card from Kentucky. She had written Franklin a few weeks ago, saying it was probably best that they call things off, since their differences seemed insurmountable. Maybe this had caused him to rethink his position that she needed to get rebaptized?

She opened the card and read the printed message:

Happy Birthday to a swell GIRL FRIEND

And below the card's message, in Franklin's pinched scribble:

I think of you lots and have my own notions what all might happen in a year if...

Snookums

Why did Franklin sign his letters that way? He meant to be endearing, but it just rubbed her the wrong way. And what did he think might happen in a year if...? She'd been his girl for more than two years, and he still offered no indication of making a definite move. Was the baptism issue just an excuse? She stared out into the icy dark night, silently mouthing the Bible verse, *"I will instruct thee and teach thee in the way which thou shalt go."*

Consistent with what Orie had told John, two clear factions existed in the colony: the *Völkische* Bund (Hitler's ethno-nationalists) was the clear majority group and the *Wehrlose* (anti-Nazi pacifists) were in the minority. John tried to stay out of the political arena, but he had numerous patients who were vocal Bund supporters. The few who did not join the Bund sought out his help. "Promise me that MCC will stick with my family in case we're left here when the majority return to their homeland after German victory," more than one patient had said.

Some were afraid to show their opposition to the Bund and would let him know in roundabout ways. One patient delivered a stool specimen. When John opened the vial to inspect it, a small note was rolled up inside, with the words *Please stand by us if we are left behind* scrawled on it. John stared at the note. These people were desperate.

One evening, several months after arriving in the colony, John finally succumbed to colonists' pressure to attend a Bund meeting. Arriving after the meeting was already in progress, he slipped into a seat in the back. A large portrait of the Führer was posted in the front of the hall, and bold letters declared the National Socialistic motto: *Gemeinnutz vor Eigennutz* (Common Good before Private Good).

The men hunched around the colony's only shortwave radio, donated from Germany. Each announcement about a German victory was greeted with loud cheering. Then a man rose and faced the crowded hall. John recognized the dark eyes buried deep in their sockets. He spoke with messianic fervor. "This is your chance to join the Bund. Eighty percent of our colonists have already joined, including many preachers."

John felt his neck muscles constrict and grabbed the edge of his chair when the crowd in front of him rose and cheered, "Ja Herr Dokta Kliewer. *Heil Hitler!*" A young man rose and stood beside Kliewer, thrusting out a burly chest that was an odd contrast to Kliewer's slight figure. A dark red scar ran like a twisted braid from the left side of the large man's forehead down across his cheek. John had heard about this man, Konrad Wolf, Fritz Kliewer's most loyal follower.

"Our local Bund will wait only ten more days," Wolf snarled, his scar pulsing. "Whoever has not joined us by then will be deserted. When the chance to go back to Europe comes, those of you who have not joined us will be left to your own fate to die here in the Chaco."

Nearly choking with rage, John rose and left the hall. He thought he'd come to the Chaco to help people who'd escaped communism to practice their Christian beliefs. And here they were, coercing their own people to join Hitler's Nazi regime. This was exactly the sort of thing Miss Ana had said was happening in Argentina. He would write to her. But then he stopped himself. That heathen woman would almost certainly resort to violence, which would just make matters worse.

John was almost running. When he reached his hut, a boy with a broken arm was waiting with his parents in the hospital yard. Nazi sympathizers, no doubt. Why did they come at all hours, as if he was not a human? And why should he help these people at all, these lovers of the Reich? The boy shifted his arm and moaned. John collected himself. After all, the young boy was not at fault. He redoubled his commitment to remain uninvolved in the political upheaval. Was this naïve, given MCC's interest in fighting Nazism and promoting nonresistance in the colony? But there was no other way to stay true to his pacifist beliefs.

And yet, could he just stand by while a man like Fritz Kliewer and his followers commanded that the colony must divide itself into only two groups—the German and the anti-German group? Kliewer's group called itself "Der Bund der *Mennoniten*"—Mennonites of the Bund. A wry smile played on John's lips as he set the young boy's broken arm. Maybe he should organize a group called "Mennonites of Paraguay."

After setting the patient's arm, John trudged slowly home. The night was dark, with only the tiniest sliver of a moon. He'd been here only several months and already felt defeated and lonely. His thoughts turned to the young Mennonite nurse in Kansas. Had she received his letter?

John tried to sleep but tossed and turned under his mosquito netting. He really could use someone like Miss Regier here with him. He could speak with her about what was going on. He needed to find a way to get through to these people.

John could sympathize with the Völkische Bund about Germany having had tough breaks in the past. He also believed that if Germany took the wealth of both Russia and western Europe, it would be the greatest nation that ever was. But how could these people consider themselves Mennonites and want to enforce membership in a warring faction? Their ancestors had fled from nation to nation for centuries to avoid such enforcement.

John decided to speak with Herr Legiehn, the *Oberschulze* (mayor) of the Fernheim colony. Surely, he could do something to help.

The following day, he walked to the Oberschulze's home. Legiehn, a thin man with a pronounced forehead, wearing round dark-rimmed glasses, let John in and nodded to one of the wooden chairs.

John began without preamble. "It's absurd for a group like the Bund to tell others that they will lose the right to call themselves Germans if they don't join the Nazis. Obviously, no one has any choice but to stay here in Paraguay. Hitlerism is a deadly cancerous growth."

Legiehn sat quietly, eyeing the dirt floor. "I seek public peace," he finally said. "I will do what I can, but they are more powerful than I." The Oberschulze cleared his throat and continued. "John, I must speak to you about something else. You may not know that we have an *Ordnung* here in the colony requiring young men to marry by the time they reach twenty-one. It is our way of preventing illicit behavior among our young people. You stand out as a glaring exception, and it's making some people very uncomfortable."

"I will marry when I choose to marry," John said, wishing he felt as certain as he sounded.

Late October and already there was no escaping the merciless heat of the Chaco. John's face was wet with sweat, and his shirt stuck to his back. He was waiting for a horse and buggy that would take him to remote Mennonite villages to screen for trachoma. It had been almost three months since he wrote the letter to Clara, and he'd heard nothing back. Had she not received the letter? Was she choosing not to respond? Had he written something inappropriate?

Almost without thinking, he reached for his pen:

> I have not received an answer from you but while I'm waiting to be taken out to one of the villages, I thought I might write another letter.
>
> There is quite a struggle between two groups here.

He described the heightened tensions in detail, not knowing how Miss Regier would feel about all of this. His shoulders began to relax as he wrote. He ended the letter just as his horse and buggy pulled up:

> I read some time ago in The Mennonite Herald that a Regier girl got married and that her cousin Clara Regier played the wedding march. Do you play the piano?

It was only a few weeks before Christmas. The heat was oppressive, the persistent north wind had driven sandy dust into every pore of his body, and John's mood was dark. He'd just heard that Japan had declared war on the U.S. In general, he learned very little about the war these days and he asked even less. He wanted no part of it.

He stared at the notepad on the table in front of him. How would he finally convince these people that their many ailments were not due to the harsh conditions of the Chaco? The recent typhoid epidemic was not due to the environment, but to their lack of precautions. And the nutritional deficiencies resulted from their starchy diet, rather than the climatic conditions. The colonists didn't realize how fortunate they were to be living here. Sure, the climate was bothersome, but it had little to do with their health issues.

Through the window, he saw Schwester Maria approach, a bundle of envelopes in her hand. "The mail has come, Herr Dokta," she said, her gaze again lingering on him longer than he wished. It made him uncomfortable, but he said nothing.

John hoped he didn't seem too eager as he grabbed the airmail envelope on top with the return address Newton, Kansas. He waited until his nurse left and then ripped it open. A grin slowly formed, and he was temporarily transported into a brighter world as he read Clara's cheery reports about life as a nurse in training.

John immediately wrote a letter back to Clara, now realizing it could take at least three months for her to receive it. He wrote that his trunk had finally arrived and had suffered so much damage that he could hardly read the medical books he'd bought with his savings while on a $10 per month residency salary.

It's difficult, but there is important work for me to do here.

Christmas of 1941 brought John little joy. It did bring heat, dust, and patients with needs that often surpassed his knowledge of how to deal with them. On December 28, shortly after dinner, a patient was brought in with a ruptured appendix. John operated immediately, the typical tension rising in his shoulders. He shook his head when he found the appendix gangrenous and the infection beginning to spread throughout the abdomen.

Against all odds, the surgery was a success. For the first time in months, there was a spring to John's steps as he headed home. Despite the stifling heat that persisted even after dark, John began to whistle the tune to Bing Crosby's "I've Got a Pocketful of Dreams." He sat at his rickety table, the kerosene lamp casting shadows across the room, and picked up his pen.

Dearest Clara. I have a special purpose in mind for this letter. I never like to act innocent about things that are obvious. Especially at my age of 30 years (not complaining about being old, understand, because you're never older than you feel) it must be obvious to you what interest I have in our correspondence. Since we are so far separated from each other and have had personal contact only to a limited extent, we must reserve some decisions till later as a matter of justice to you as well as to me.

John wrote that he expected to leave the Chaco by the end of July, and that they would have plenty of time to get to know each other.

So you see, we need no final answer but just an understanding. If the idea of marriage is not in your program at all, maybe you'd be kind enough to tell me so. If you prefer not to answer the question, that is your privilege too.

He enclosed a small photo of himself.

Christmas 1941 in the U.S. was like no other anyone remembered. With the country's recent entry into the war, it was a time of upheaval and uncertainty. Clara read that all single registered nurses between the ages of twenty-one and forty were asked to enroll in the Army and Navy Nurse Reserve Corps for immediate active duty. She prayed that her Mennonite-based conscientious objector status would protect her from serving in the war. At the same time, she felt drawn to help in ways that were consistent with her beliefs. Her nightly prayer, kneeling beside her bed, was that the Lord might lead her to where He wanted her to serve.

Franklin Pauls returned home from Kentucky for the Christmas holiday, and he still seemed to think she was his girl. Clara decided that the relationship with him had dragged on long enough. They met three days after Christmas in the hospital cafeteria.

"I'm sorry, Franklin, but you must know that I will never consider re-baptism. It's over." Clara knew she was closing a door that would never again be opened. Her heart belonged to God, and she was committed to whatever form of service God had in store for her.

Despite her commitment to godly service, Clara felt despondent during the final days of 1941. Looking forward to the new year led to lingering doubts about the direction of her life. And sadness for her country, which was now officially engaged in an ugly world war.

So it was without much enthusiasm that Clara received John's letter on the last day of the year. She noticed that he'd written it back in October. She began to read with indifference. But her eyes grew wide when she got to the part about the Nazi activities among the Mennonites in Paraguay. She found it hard to believe that people calling themselves Mennonites would be involved in such sinfulness.

After John's lengthy descriptions of the conflicts in the Chaco, the letter unexpectedly shifted, and he wrote that he'd read about a Clara Regier playing the piano at her cousin's wedding. What an odd and abrupt way of expressing himself. And the man couldn't spell. But he seemed like a God-fearing man going through a difficult time. Maybe she could provide some comfort. She would write back. She'd share her newly found passion for surgical nursing, and about her re-commitment to serve the Lord in whatever way He led.

In the next few months, Clara threw herself into nursing with renewed vigor, finally freed from the burden of worrying about Franklin, and increasingly clear about her purpose in life. In January and February, her resolve wavered slightly when she was assigned to work on the Obstetrics floor. She was twenty-seven, after all, and this was a painful reminder of what she was giving up. But as the gray winter months passed, and the dazzling dogwood and wild plum trees on the hospital grounds began to show their colors, Clara again felt at peace, if not happy.

One early evening in April, as she left the hospital, exhausted after a ten-hour shift, a classmate ran toward her waving an envelope. "It's from Paraguay."

Clara frowned. It had been nearly four months since she'd heard from Dr. John. And frankly, she was just fine with that. Her life was full without that distraction.

She walked along the path and sat down on a wooden bench beside a bright patch of bluebells that seemed to nod at her as she slit open the envelope.

Her eyes fell on the bold script:

> I have a special purpose in mind for this letter. I never like to act innocent about things that are obvious.

Heat began seeping into Clara's face and she looked around to make sure no one was watching her. She swallowed hard and re-read the words. This important doctor from a far-away land was proposing to her? A small photo slipped from the envelope and onto the ground. She picked it up and studied the intense eyes staring back at her. She threw the letter and photo into her lap. Why did she always have to be so susceptible? And for that matter, who did this man think she was? The sort of girl who would jump at his advances? Without even knowing him? She had to put a halt to this. But she wasn't sure how. If she wrote him another letter, it might just lead him on.

A week later, Clara had not yet done anything about the vexing question of what to do regarding the disconcerting letter. Assigned to geriatric duty, she was walking slowly alongside a man with a walker, helping him navigate the hallway, when she heard Dr. Herb's loud voice. "Miss Regier. I must speak with you."

Clara felt the familiar throbbing in her chest when she heard the doctor's voice. She wished she could disappear behind her patient. But soon the doctor stood in front of them. "I'm on my way to Paraguay next week to help my brother with surgeries. I assume you'll want to send a letter along with me. Have you two decided to tie the knot yet?"

Her cheeks burned. She looked from her patient to Dr. Herb and back to her patient. "Excuse me, doctor, I need to get Mr. Snyder back to his room," she said, guiding her patient away from Dr. Herb.

"If you want to send a letter with me, have it in my message box by Monday," he said.

After her shift ended, Clara skipped supper and went directly to her room to compose the letter that she now knew she must write. The two brothers were in cahoots, and this had gone too far. But by the time she sat down at her desk, some of her outrage waned. She thought about John's words:

We need no final answer but just an understanding.

Maybe he wasn't just a fresh guy who needed to be put in his place. After all, he was a God-fearing missionary doctor. As she began to write, the words that formed on the page were about needing to get to know him better, rather than anger about his presumptuousness.

The next morning, after depositing the letter in Dr. Herb's message box, Clara wondered if she had done the right thing. Was she leading him on, when she knew there was probably no future for them as a couple? And besides, she still wasn't sure about John's motivations. He seemed so much like Dr. Herb, loud and overbearing. Were they both making fun of her? Just because they were doctors and she was only a nurse in training was no reason for them to humiliate her. During her lunch break, Clara returned to the box to retrieve the letter.

It was gone.

FOUR

The first half of 1942 had been an economic disaster for the Chaco colonies. A terrible drought, severe sandstorms, and a heat wave up to 120° F destroyed most of the crops. There was no feed for the horses and calves had to go into the bush with cows, which meant no milk for the people. No wheat for flour, no chicken feed, so no eggs. Worst of all, no fruit was growing, which led to increasing illnesses from lack of Vitamin C, numbness and tingling from lack of Vitamin B, constipation, gastritis, and headaches.

The critical conditions might have brought the warring factions closer together, but they did not. In fact, political tensions increased. The hardships and near-famine stirred Hitler's supporters to even greater fervor, especially among the youth. When news of mass murders of Jews at Auschwitz began to come in, Bund members easily dismissed this as false propaganda for the opposition. Even the colony Oberschulze was now an open supporter of the Bund.

John was more than a little discouraged. He wondered, as he had numerous times in the past months, what Miss Ana would think of all of this. He felt too ashamed to write to her, ashamed of his people, even ashamed of himself, about how self-righteously he had flaunted the virtues of Mennonite pacifism in his shipboard conversations with her.

Despite John's frustration with the Bund movement, he understood how much these people needed his medical services. In April, at John's request, MCC flew his brother Herb to Paraguay for a month to perform surgeries that were beyond John's capabilities alone.

The best part was that Herb brought letters from the U.S., including one from Clara. But the tone of her letter was non-committal, even slightly standoffish, saying she needed to know him better before writing about intimate things.

John felt Herb's eyes on him as he read the letter.

"What's the matter?"

"It's nothing," John said. Why did he always feel so inadequate around his brother?

"That Miss Regier of yours has been mighty cool toward me recently," Herb said. "Did I say something to offend her?"

"What have you said to her?"

"Ah, come on, John, you know me. I'm sometimes more direct than people can take," Herb said, grinning.

John left the room and stomped around the hospital grounds. So that's what happened. He needed to get this straightened out. He would write to Clara, assuring her that he was nothing like his brother. And he would send the letter back with Herb, so she'd get it quickly.

The Bethel College nursing program had originated in 1908 under the direction of Sister Frieda Kaufman, the Deaconess Mother in charge of the hospital. A deaconess was a woman serving Christ and His church, who was free from all other duties and desires so that she could devote her time and effort to the service of the Lord in ministering to suffering humanity. The deaconess program began with the stated purpose of providing young women with a new avenue of Christian service.

When Clara entered her training program in 1940, her instruction included nursing class work, studies in the Bible, and the history of the

deaconess movement, as well as practical nursing. Most of her classmates planned to finish their nursing degrees and then get married and
start families. Given Clara's advanced age and seeming lack of suitors,
the Deaconess Mother had something else in mind for her.

"It's clear that you love to serve, Clara. And your devotion to your
patients is unparalleled. Please consider becoming a deaconess," Sister
Frieda said, approaching her after a Saturday evening prayer meeting.

"I have committed my life to serving the Lord," Clara said. "The
deaconess path may well be what I'm called to follow."

A few weeks later, at the end of May, Dr. Herb returned from Paraguay.
The Paraguay connection had become a favorite subject for gossip
among the student nurses. They teased Clara about Dr. Herb singling
her out, and they pestered her about news of Dr. John. Sister Frieda,
who wore a permanent frown, scowled even more deeply when she
overheard the rumors.

Clara tore open the letter Dr. Herb had brought north. She skimmed
the newsy part, and then stopped when she read:

> I find that we agree much more than I had expected, and
> I believe you would feel the same way about it. I say this
> because you know Herb and might judge me by him.
> Although Herb and I have many similarities, we differ widely
> on ideas of religion, politics, and fundamentals of life.

Something about this preposterous man was beginning to intrigue
her. How did he know that she had concerns about him resembling
Dr. Herb? She would at least continue writing to him. What harm
could come of that? She wouldn't mention the fact that she was being
groomed to become a deaconess.

Clara wrote to John, describing her home on a farm east of Newton,
just a half hour's drive from Goessel, where she knew the Schmidt
brothers had grown up. Despite the geographic proximity, she under-

stood that their backgrounds were worlds apart. She was from the uptown High-German Mennonites who had emigrated from Prussia about the time John's clan emigrated from Russia. Plautdietsch Mennonites from Russia were considered less sophisticated than her Prussian High-German people. But he was a doctor. He had that going for him. And she knew the Schmidts belonged to the GC Mennonite church.

Then she waited. And waited. No response.

John had begun to think that maybe Paraguay could be his place in life, especially if the Allies won the war. He had envisioned Clara as an essential part of that picture. Now he doubted that she would agree to come back here with him. Herb had left Paraguay for the States two months ago. In John's impatience, he forgot that it took at least three months for letters to travel and wondered why he'd received no word from Clara. By now, he'd sent three letters, asking her hand in marriage, and inquiring if she'd agree to live in Paraguay. He had to know. So in another letter, dated July 26, he wrote:

It has been two months since I've heard from you. Maybe you feel unable to see through all the stuff I've written to you. It is not my nature to mislead girls. I'm not exactly a youngster and have made acquaintances with many girls but have never come to propose or come anywhere near to what I've said to you. So you see I realize the sincerity one should use in all moves.

In the months that followed, John threw himself into his work with even greater intensity, trying to shake his anxiety about not hearing from Clara. MCC had found no doctor to replace him, so his planned departure time in July came and went with no clarity about when he might leave.

In addition to his medical work, John started an agricultural program that experimented with crops that could withstand the extreme climatic conditions. And he oversaw the construction of a better dirt road between the Km. 145 railway station and the colony. One evening, at the end of a long day of felling trees and digging up stumps, John's fellow workers picked up their axes, spades, and other implements to load them onto the two horse-drawn wagons. John was struggling with a *palo santo* tree, which is one of the hardest and heaviest woods in the world. A ripping sound broke the stillness of the Chaco twilight as a palo santo branch fell as if aiming at him. John threw his axe as he jumped, but it was too late. The branch struck him on the forehead, knocking him to the ground.

As John slowly regained consciousness, his hand moved toward the gaping wound on the right side of his forehead. Shakily he got up and with help staggered toward one of the wagons, climbed up and sat with his head resting in his arms. With every jolt, the searing pain increased, and blood began pooling on the wagon bed. But it wasn't until John felt watery fluid draining from his ears that he was gripped by fear, knowing he risked blood clotting in the brain and/or herniated brain tissue.

Finally, the wagon stopped in front of his hospital. John walked slowly, holding his head in his hands, and lay down on one of the beds. In response to calls from the men, Schwester Maria soon arrived. She bent over him and then drew back, her hands trembling.

"Cerebrospinal fluid was running out," John told his nurse. "I think it's stopped now. I need you to sew up my head." She began cleaning the wound, and then stopped. "Herr Dokta," she cried, "I… I…" She shook her head.

"Well," said John. "If you can't do it, I'll have to. Can you at least get me a mirror?" Gritting his teeth, he swabbed the raw area with iodine. Picking up the curved needle, he threaded it with a steady hand. Stitch by painful stitch, he closed the red gash. After the stitches were in, he again swabbed the area with iodine and pasted a bandage over it. Schwester Maria stared at him, tears welling up in her eyes.

He waved her away. "I need to rest."

Clara thought about John as she tended to her patients, making up imaginary conversations with him. Although numerous months had passed since she received the last letter from him, which Dr. Herb had brought from Paraguay, John felt like a daily presence in her life. *What would you do about this patient's condition, Dr. John? Yes, that's also what I would recommend.*

And she thought about him late at night when she secretly entered the make-believe world of her romance novels, which she'd again succumbed to. She'd always felt guilty about her love of these trashy stories where men and women held hands and even kissed each other and had confessed this clandestine activity to no one. Now, when she visualized on the pages a man who resembled the little black-and-white photo of John, a torturous combination of pleasure and guilt ripped through her. Sometimes her body even twitched in embarrassing ways.

By the time Clara finally received John's letter (written July 26), he was as real to her as though she'd known him for a long time.

It is not my nature to mislead girls... I have never come anywhere near to proposing or to what I've said to you.

Clara held the letter against her chest. She would speak to Sister Frieda. And she would let John know what she looked for in a companion.

By the end of October, the scar on John's forehead was just a jagged dark line. Finally, the long-awaited letter from Clara arrived.

The letter I got from you today was of July 26. I hadn't really thought about marriage. But I will surely consider this indirect proposal... I must, however, give you an idea of the things I look for in a companion for life.

She went on to write that he needed to be a devout Christian, he needed to live a clean and vice-free life, and he needed to be mission-minded. Service in Paraguay together would not be out of the question. At the end of the letter, John found the words he'd been waiting for.

> I feel as you do, John, that now you should come back. I hope it is not only my selfish wish, but the Lord's will.

John put the letter in his pocket and headed out for a walk. It was a warm, sunny day. He knew he must leave Paraguay, but was this unusually lovely weather inviting him to return someday?

Outside of the village, John veered off the path, making his way through the thorny underbrush he'd explored numerous times before. He'd seen fossilized shells in the sand, remnants of a prehistoric sea, exotic butterflies, and a bounty of birds. Today, he saw vultures and parrots, wild pigeons, and even a small woodpecker with a bright red head. Around him flew hundreds of white butterflies, whirling like snowflakes against the blue sky. A flock of brilliant green parrots streaked overhead.

"I will return," he said aloud to no one, as he made his way back to the village to begin preparing for his departure.

In 1942, the Atlantic Ocean was heavily patrolled by German U-boats, so John took a train across the continent to sail north on the Pacific. On November 7, he boarded the freight ship *Copiapó*, headed north along the coast, then east through the Panama Canal, then to Havana, Cuba, and into New Orleans. His tourist-class cabin accommodated four men, with a single washbowl in the corner of the small stateroom.

John spent the days at sea reading, arguing with fellow passengers about the war, or doing just about anything that would keep his mind from turning inward. Underneath all the busyness, he sensed an anxiety he couldn't name and was afraid to explore.

On the twelfth day at sea, just before arriving in Panama, John dropped heavily onto his mattress. What would happen when he got home? Would he be drafted? Would he find a job? Would things work out with Clara? Would he be going back to Paraguay? Would Clara agree to come with him?

FIVE

On December 2, Clara received a telegram from New Orleans, letting her know John's ship had docked. He asked her to meet him on Friday, December 4, at the train depot in Kansas City, where she was completing part of her nurse's training at Mercy Hospital.

On Friday, Clara made arrangements to leave her shift early and rushed home to get ready. During her day off last Saturday, she'd sewn herself a new dress. It was dark blue with a white collar and white buttons down the front. The A-line skirt came down just to her knees.

She'd padded the shoulders like she'd seen in a magazine. But now when she put on the dress and looked in the mirror, she wasn't sure about the effect. It seemed a bit boxy. And then there was her hair. It had been pinned under a starched nurse's cap at work, so it looked flat and unattractive. She spent the better part of an hour pinning it up into soft rolls that framed her face.

Union Station was less than a mile from Mercy Hospital, but Clara had arranged to borrow her supervisor's car, given that a winter storm was blowing in, and John's train was not scheduled to arrive until 10:00 p.m. She arrived at the station at 9:30. Rowdy soldiers and sailors pushed their way through the Grand Hall of Union Station.

Clara sat at the edge of a wooden bench, clutching her purse, watching the commotion around her. Numerous times she reached into her purse and pulled out the small photograph of John. Would she recognize him? Would he even know who she was? She felt short of breath and wasn't sure whether it was from excitement or anxiety.

Clara checked her watch again. 11:03 p.m. The train was supposed to have arrived an hour ago. For the third time, she made her way to the washroom, just to make sure her hair still looked good. She stared into the cracked mirror. What if he didn't like how she looked? Was her dress stylish enough? Her blue eyes gazed back at her, sparkling with anticipation—or was it fear? She patted her curls and said out loud to her image, "Tonight is the night. He's finally coming home."

Clara returned to her bench. And waited. At last, his train pulled into the station. She stared at each person stepping off and rushing past her. She strained to see the men's faces, thinking she might be remembering John all wrong. Of all the people passing her, no one looked like the little photo she had of him.

She was about to leave when a thin, unshaven bum approached her with a wooden cane, wearing a long black coat and a black hat, and carrying two jaguar pelts under his arm.

The man stopped in front of her. "Are you Clara Regier?"

What followed was not what either of them had intended.

John reached to embrace her, mumbling an apology about how he looked. Clara smelled his sweat, shuddered, and pulled back. His gaucho-style pants were filthy. Under his tattered coat, his wrinkled shirt was untucked. John muttered, "I've been standing in a crowded military train for days."

They faced each other awkwardly.

Clara's eyes were on the floor. How could he be the same person who wrote devoted, sophisticated letters? Now he seemed ordinary, a filthy traveler. She glanced up and then looked down again.

John frowned. He wasn't about to beg for her affections. Coldly he said, "Shall we go?"

John walked briskly toward the exit. She followed him out of the depot and pointed to the car parked on Pershing Road.

As John loaded his bag into her car, Clara asked, "You had a long trip?" and immediately felt foolish for saying the obvious. "Where should I drop you?"

John gave her an address.

"You must be tired," she mumbled.

"I suppose so." John got in the car and stared straight ahead.

Was he acting rude just because he was tired?

Clara tried make sense of what was happening. She'd so anticipated meeting him. The man of her dreams.

John said nothing until they reached his destination. He stepped out of the car. "Thanks for the lift."

She wanted to say something to change what was happening but only mumbled, "Goodnight." Back in her dorm room, she threw herself onto her bed and sobbed.

The next morning, Clara sent a notice to the hospital that she was sick, and spent the day in bed. Between bouts of weeping, she knelt on the floor beside her bed. "Dear God. Please help me in my hour of need. I feel so much darkness all around me, and I don't know what to do."

She awoke the following day with a throbbing headache but pulled herself out of bed. She would do whatever it took to get back to the hospital with her dear patients. Surely that would bring her world back into some kind of order.

Clara spent the day carrying out her duties as though sleepwalking. The work did little to lighten the weight she felt in her chest, or to suppress the tears that seemed constantly on the verge of spilling out.

When she returned to her room that evening, there was a letter on her bedside table. Clara sucked in her breath when she saw the familiar loopy handwriting.

I just arrived at my brother Herb's about 10 p.m. I hope you will excuse me if I seem to act and write so frankly. I feel I made a flop of things at the train station.

He went on to apologize for looking like a bum. Clara dropped the letter into her lap. The room spun around her. She closed her eyes to find a place of calm, and then continued to read.

When I wrote from Paraguay that I loved you, I truly meant it. But I wonder now if I am not what you wanted— and if that's the case, dear Clara, please know that you can tell me, and I'll go away.

There he was. On paper. The man she'd fallen in love with. Clara pressed the sheet of paper against her chest. She immediately sat down to write:

When we parted, I was ever so sorry that we hadn't had another chance to talk together. I know things weren't right, and I felt that you were disappointed. How I wanted to talk to you! I am so glad you wrote so friendly and will try to answer the same way.

What should she say? She shuddered when she recalled him reaching for her at the station. He seemed so vulgar. She did want the man who wrote those letters. Clara pinched her eyes shut for a moment before continuing to write.

First, your appearance on our meeting didn't make any difference. I hope I can see deeper than that.

Second, my seeming reserve was not as intentional as it must've appeared. No, I wasn't disappointed, only I had you in mind somewhat differently, as I had gathered you from your letters.

Should she let him know that she'd never been kissed? That this was all new for her? Would he think she was naïve? She must tell the truth and ask forgiveness for disappointing him.

They exchanged a few more letters in the following weeks, with no mention of the difficult homecoming. It was as though their loving courtship-by-mail had never been interrupted.

Clara's term at Mercy Hospital in Kansas City ended just before Christmas, so she was home in Newton for the holidays. John was still in Newton, staying with his brother Herb. They agreed to attend her church together on Sunday the 27th. They met in the foyer of the First Mennonite Church. Clara noticed how dapper John looked in a dark double-breasted suit and black hat, but she again felt immediate discomfort in his presence.

They sat in the pew with more than the socially appropriate distance between them. She glanced at him, but he stared straight ahead. Why was he so quiet? He must be having second thoughts as well.

The pastor announced the opening hymn, *Großer Gott, Wir Loben Dich* (Holy God, We Praise Thy Name). They stood to sing. When the music rose to a crescendo at *Wie du warst vor aller Zeit, so bleibst du in Ewigkeit,* Clara stopped singing and looked at the man by her side, her eyes wide. John's head was thrown back, his eyes closed, and his resonant tenor voice rang clear and true. In that moment, she knew this was the man she could love for the rest of her life.

That night John wrote in his diary:

> During church today, I looked at Clara and realized I have what I once considered an impossibility—I have the best gal in the world—there is no other as good in any way.

During his time in Paraguay, John had received papers from the U.S. draft board that classified him as 4-E (LS), a conscientious objector available for limited civilian work of national importance. But a week ago he'd gotten a letter from them re-classifying him as 1-A-O, a conscientious objector eligible for military service in a noncombatant role. He immediately wrote a letter stating that he was willing to do anything the government wanted him to do, but that he refused to belong to a military organization. He'd heard nothing back.

The only way to handle this was to drive to the local draft board in McPherson and let them know how serious this was. He'd sit in jail before he joined the military in any capacity.

John drove to McPherson in a snowstorm that blanketed the fields and gusted across the road. He was at the front door of the government building before it opened.

"What is your business?" A young clerk looked up from a stack of papers when John entered the front lobby.

"I'm John Schmidt and I'm here to tell you I refuse to serve in the military," John said.

"One moment, please." The clerk turned to ring a bell.

A uniformed officer entered through a side door. "What seems to be the problem?"

"I'm more than willing to give my service and even my life to relieve suffering. But I will not join your military organization," John said, wishing he felt as authoritative as his voice sounded.

He gave the officer the personal data to locate his draft registration card.

"It looks like we've already accommodated your conscientious objector status," the officer said, returning the file and closing the drawer.

John took a step toward him. "Put me in jail if you must, but I will not serve in your military."

"That is your decision." The officer straightened his back, turned, and left the room. John frowned at the clerk as he walked out, wondering how he would tell Clara about this.

★

Three days later, on the last day of the year, John and Clara met at Newton's Athletic Park for a walk.

"May I take you to lunch to ring in the new year?" he asked.

Clara tucked her hand under John's right arm. "I would love that." This would be their special year.

They walked by the Wheat Memorial, an eleven-foot limestone statue of a bearded Mennonite wheat farmer standing erect, hat in hand, as though praying.

John stopped in front of the statue and read the inscription aloud: "Commemorating entry into Kansas from Russia of Turkey Red Hard Wheat by Mennonites 1874."

"I've not seen this," he said.

"It was just recently erected by the Junior Chamber of Commerce," Clara said.

John removed his hat and stood solemnly in front of the statue. "Those were my people, Clara," he said. "If it weren't for them, I'd probably be living in desperate poverty in the Chaco of Paraguay."

Clara looked puzzled. She knew about the Russian Mennonites coming to Kansas, but she was unaware of their relationship to the Paraguayan Mennonites. John told her his favorite stories about his Low-German grandparents fleeing Russia and coming to Kansas in 1874, after Alexander II reneged on promises that they were exempt from military service. If they had not escaped when they did, they would likely have been among the Russian Mennonites who decades later, in 1929, finally broke away from persecution in Stalinist Russia to settle in the Chaco of Paraguay, or, worse yet, the ones who'd been sent to Siberia.

"Why wouldn't they also have come to North America?" Clara asked.

"By then U.S. immigration laws prevented anyone with diseases to enter the country. Many of them had trachoma and other ailments. Paraguay was seemingly the only country that welcomed them."

John continued to stand, hat in hand, staring almost reverently at the statue. "I'll willingly go to jail to uphold the beliefs of my people," he muttered under his breath.

Clara stepped back to better observe John's serious demeanor and his fervent facial expression. She'd grown up among Prussian

High-German Mennonites who came to Kansas about the same time as John's people. She identified with her clan. But nothing like this. She'd never seen such a fierce sense of belonging.

John turned toward her and grinned. "How about that lunch?"

They walked to a café near the park and ducked into a booth. The place had shiny red and green Christmas decorations hanging from the lights and across the walls. Bing Crosby's "White Christmas" played on a tinny radio. Clara felt the touch of John's hand on her arm and blushed.

They ordered burgers. When the food arrived, Clara paused, waiting for John to lead them in prayer. He seemed oblivious, pouring ketchup on his burger, and bringing it to his mouth.

"Anything wrong?" John asked, chewing on the first mouthful.

"No. No, of course not," she said quickly. John didn't pray before meals?

The following Wednesday, John received another letter from the draft board confirming his 1-A-O classification and requesting him to report to the draft board in McPherson the next day.

The roads were covered with dirty packed snow, and John's car swerved as he turned onto Route 56 and made his way into McPherson. He strode into the front lobby of the government building. Before the door closed behind him, he demanded to see the officer.

"Put. Me. In. Jail. Now. I will not serve in your military." John's normal staccato enunciation was even more rapid-fire than usual.

The same officer he'd seen the last time stood in the open side doorway. Ignoring John, he bent down toward the clerk. "Revise Schmidt's classification to 4-E." His lips turned down as he faced John. "I hope the draft board finds that you're needed for service in China," he growled. "That's where the likes of you belong."

John picked up his revised registration card and headed for the door, resisting the urge to grin. These people obviously had no idea where he'd spent the past two years.

Clara was worried about the whole draft business. John had told her that New Mexico was on the list of areas with a shortage of doctors, therefore qualifying as a place of service for a doctor with his new draft classification. She was more anxious than John as they awaited an answer from his query to the University of New Mexico. At least it wasn't China.

The response came quickly. By early January, John was packed and ready to leave for Albuquerque.

Clara held onto John's arm as they made their way through high snowdrifts piled up around the Newton train depot. She pulled her scarf tighter around her face, blinking back tears.

"The position I'm filling is really very good, and I'll rank as one of the faculty members. Isn't that swell? I think you'd like Albuquerque if we lived there someday, except for the fact that it's not a Mennonite community. There's lots of hospitals so you can get a job there when you graduate in August."

Clara had been around John for only a little over a week, but she already knew he was a man of few words. She suspected that his chatter today meant he was as nervous as she about another separation so soon after they'd gotten together in person.

Before John boarded the train, Clara received his kiss and returned it for the first time. It was wild and a bit dangerous.

SIX

During the next four months, John and Clara's letter-writing resumed, except this time their letters traveled for only a few days rather than numerous months. The two lovers wrote multiple letters every week.

On a warm spring day in early April, Clara took a break from her patient rounds and wandered out onto the hospital grounds. She walked along the path and sat down on a wooden bench. Almost exactly a year ago, she'd sat on this same bench, feeling annoyed and susceptible when she read John's indirect proposal. So much had happened since then. Clara closed her eyes and allowed the sun to bathe her face.

She loved John. But she had become increasingly concerned about their differences. When she'd asked him a while back about not praying before eating, he wrote:

> I didn't want to make too much of a show in public places. Just know that when I have a home of my own, I'll always be man enough to pray before every meal regardless of who is dining at our table.

And today she received a response to the question she'd finally had the courage to ask him—whether he'd lived a vice-free life.

I've done things like dancing, drinking, and smoking.

He added that he thought these vices weren't sinful in themselves—only when they became enslaving habits. But still.

Clara buried her face in her hands. John had done all those sinful things, and he didn't even feel guilty. How could this be the man God intended for her? And what could she do about it now? She'd kissed him. And she'd told everyone about him, even her parents. What was she going to do?

Later that same day, John returned to his rented room and saw a light blue airmail envelope on his bedtable. He slit open the thin paper.

Anastasia.

The letter was dated October 14 and had been forwarded from Paraguay.

Ana began by apologizing for not writing sooner, explaining that she'd been in hiding in the hills north of Buenos Aires.

Argentina keeps a so-called neutral stance in the war, but Castillo's power base has a strong, very well-organized pro-Nazi element. The German embassy manipulated this support by financing and supporting a pro-Nazi manifesto, allegedly signed by a million Argentines, and presented to Castillo.

She went on to describe the revolutionary group she was a part of, alluding to clandestine and dangerous activities to counter the Nazis, without specifying what, exactly, her group was doing.

And how are things in the Chaco, Dr. John? As you anticipated? I have often thought about your courageous spirit, and trust that all is well with you.

John frowned. Courageous spirit? The most courageous thing he was doing was handing out aspirin. He had to find something worthwhile to do. He always thought he'd return to Paraguay. A month ago, he contacted Orie Miller at MCC, asking if there was a need for his services. Orie said they'd found a Dr. Gaede to take over the medical work in the Chaco, which had been without medical care since John left in November. But just this week, Orie wrote that Dr. Gaede was stalling. Would John consider going back? John had hesitated, but now he knew what he must do.

He sat down to write to Clara that a letter from someone named Anastasia, whom he'd met on his way to South America, had jolted him out of his wasted existence in Albuquerque.

He described Ana as someone:

> ...fighting hard to make the world a better place. I don't agree with many of her methods, but she goes after what she believes. Me, on the other hand, what am I doing?

A few days later, Clara was alone in her room at the end of her shift when she read John's letter. She dropped it into her lap. Dancing, drinking, smoking, and now this Anastasia? Who was she? And what did she mean to John?

Clara continued to read:

> I think you and I would do more in Paraguay than we could any place in the world. It is no easy job. I imagine the Nazi sympathies run as high as ever. And medical supplies will be hard to get. But at least we'd be doing something worthwhile.

The letter went on to say that he'd given Orie two conditions before agreeing to go to Paraguay. The first was that John needed a hernia operation. The second condition was that a dentist would go along. John said it was unbearable to see so many people going without proper dental care.

If they have no one else by July or August, we could begin to make all the preparations to be ready to go in September or October, OK?

Clara stared at the question at the end of the letter. This was all happening too fast. His dizzying pace was terrifying. But she also felt something else. Was it a thrill?

She looked at the flood of light pouring through her window from a nearly full moon. She ached to be with John. He was an honest man, or he would not have shared what he did about his past. He seemed to be a man who thought and acted not to fulfill others' expectations, but according to his own strong sense of right and wrong. Surely, he would be someone she could trust and minister beside.

Clara wrote:

We agree on our present view of these things, and after all, that is what counts. I have realized since I've been in Kansas City what a sheltered life I really had. Really John, the sinful behaviors I saw there almost made me sick. You have finished with all that, and your ideals are very high as compared to many of those I've met.

Had he really finished with all that? He was a godly man, right? She shuddered and ended the letter with:

Yes John, I hope that if you ever go back to Paraguay, it will be "We" and not "You." I was just thinking. Wouldn't it be something to start a nursing school? To be joint managers of the hospital?

Clara had encouraged John to petition for a release from the university in Albuquerque, since he felt increasingly useless there. He wrote that he'd try to fill in as needed in practices around Newton until her graduation in August if the draft board would allow it.

On a crisp spring day in late April, Clara drove to the depot in Newton to meet John's train. She walked toward one of the outdoor benches, her steps feeling as light as the breeze teasing her skirt. A young couple walked by, holding hands. Clara watched them until they disappeared around a bend. There was a dull ache in her chest. Her image of John's Anastasia drifted through her mind, as it had ever since he wrote about her. Long slim legs, shiny hair, maybe even painted lips. She shook her head to dislodge the picture. She must have faith in John.

Clara walked toward the tracks as the train rumbled into the station. She spotted John almost immediately. He swung out of the train and glanced up and down the platform. Then he saw her and held eye contact as he strode through the crowd. Clara held out both arms, and he clasped her to his chest.

John could hardly wait until they finally finished lunch with Clara's folks. He rose from the table. "Thank you, Mrs. Regier, for the lunch." And then, turning to Clara, "Would you take a walk with me?"

The two of them walked along the gravel road east of the farm. John kept fingering the little box in his pocket.

"Clara—"

Before he could continue, Clara blurted, "Who is Anastasia and what does she mean to you?"

John began to laugh, but when he saw the serious look on Clara's face, he stopped, pulled his hand from his pocket, and took both of her hands in his.

"Anastasia is someone who puts me to shame because I'm not doing what she is to serve those in need and make the world a better place." When Clara didn't look convinced, he added, "She's not one of us. She's not even a Christian."

Clara just stood there, saying nothing. What did he need to do to convince her that she, Clara, was the only one he would ever love?

John pulled the box from his pocket. "Do...do you feel ready to wear a diamond for me?"

Clara's eyes grew wide. "A diamond?"

John slipped the ring on her finger, pleased with himself that it fit perfectly. "God will bless our union and we will be of service together," he said. "If you'll have me."

"I do," she whispered.

That evening they had an informal engagement dinner at Clara's house with both sets of parents. Most of the conversation revolved around the couple's plans to travel to Paraguay. John's parents didn't seem particularly concerned. Clara's father remained mostly silent, while her mother complained that there would be no one to help if she got sick.

After dinner, Clara and John wandered out onto the porch. It was a warm night with just a slight breeze.

"I'm sorry about my mother's constant complaining. She's had nerve troubles since I was very young," Clara said. "I often took care of the family when she was sick." When John didn't respond, she added, "I'm afraid I don't come from a very perfect family."

"Clara, I doubt there is such a thing as a perfect family. My father beat me regularly until my bottom was bloodied if I didn't keep pushing myself to do more on the farm. I'm sure I deserved it, but mine was not exactly a happy family."

Just then John's parents came outside, ready to leave.

"Give me a moment," John said to them. He turned to Clara. "Could we say our nighttime prayers together before I leave?"

Clara nodded and they went inside and up the stairs together, to her room. Clara knelt beside her bed. When John continued to stand, she looked up.

"I say my prayers in no particular way," he said. "Kneeling by the bed is a new experience for me. I'm willing to do it, but I don't want it to have any special significance. To me it's the sincerity of thought that counts, which I can feel sitting up, standing, or kneeling."

Clara had never considered the possibility of praying before bedtime in any other way.

The following day, they had lunch at the home of John's brother, Herb, and his wife, Mariam. Mariam was nice if a bit uppity. Their house was fancier than any Clara had ever seen.

She still felt uneasy around the brash head surgeon of her hospital. But fortunately, John's favorite brother, Raymond, ten years younger than he, was also there. It was easy to be around this quieter, gentler Schmidt brother, who'd been crippled since childhood from polio.

At some point during lunch, the conversation turned to the war. Herb mentioned the "heroic" activities of Herman, one of their brothers, who served as an Air Force pilot. Raymond stared down at his food.

"He should be ashamed of himself, and I know Raymond agrees," John shouted, throwing down his napkin. Raymond said nothing, and Mariam shrank back in her chair. "Fighting heroically in a war is not what we Mennonites do. That's not how we were raised."

There was silence around the table. Mariam rose and began clearing the dishes. John pushed his chair back and escorted Clara to the door. As they drove away, Clara stared into her lap and said quietly, "You didn't have to scream, John."

John was silent for a while. "I'm not sorry for anything I expressed but I wish I hadn't been so noisy about it. I'll have to depend on you, Clara, to quiet me down when I get too noisy because that just isn't right. It makes it look like I'm trying to show off my convictions."

Clara didn't know what to say, so she said nothing.

Mid-May, John had his hernia repaired at Bethel Hospital. Clara had been assigned to work on the floor he was on, so she was with him when he came out of anesthesia. She visited him off the record several times during the day as well as every night in civilian clothes. In the morning, after singing with the nurses following breakfast in their dining room, she came by for a morning kiss. When not even his blanket could cover up how his penis reacted, Clara blushed and turned away.

John reached for her. "No, Clara, come back. I believe we should have some understanding of things related to sex before we get together. I have a book I'd like us to read together."

"Can it wait, John?" Clara glanced at the open door.

"OK, but we don't have much more time," John said, grinning.

Clara graduated on August 20 with nine other nurses. Her wedding to John took place five days later at the First Mennonite Church in Newton.

On the evening of the 24th, Clara was in the church basement finishing preparations for the rehearsal dinner when she heard a clatter on the stairs. Raymond, who would be John's best man the next day, hobbled over on his crutches.

"The work you and John are going to do in Paraguay...well, I think it's really important. I just want you to know that when I finish my medical degree, I want to come down to join you."

"What a lovely wedding present, Raymond," Clara said, hugging him.

Herb and Mariam invited the newlyweds to stay at their house on their wedding night. Clara flushed deeply when Dr. Herb showed them to their room.

"Mariam bought a little something for you," he said, grinning and pointing to the frilly pink lingerie on their bed.

John and Clara sat next to each other on the bed, still wearing their wedding clothes. John reached over and fumbled with the buttons of her white gown. Clara felt herself stiffen.

"I'm sorry, John. I'm your wife now, I know. But..." Her voice trailed off. She was staring into her lap.

John said nothing. He stood and began to remove his clothes.

"Can we please turn out the light?" she asked in a thin voice.

In the dark, Clara slowly removed her gown, folded it, and placed it on the dresser. She took off her stockings but decided to keep on her slip. She slid into bed and under the covers.

They didn't speak. John reached for Clara. She held her breath but didn't resist when she felt a sharp pain. When it was over, Clara lay perfectly still, confused.

"I'm sorry," John said. "We'll learn to do this right."

Still perplexed, Clara lay wide awake for hours beside her sleeping husband, wondering about what lay ahead.

HONEYMOON

1943-1946

"Love does not consist of gazing at each other, but in looking outward together in the same direction."

– Antoine de Saint-Exupery

SEVEN

The day after their wedding, Clara and John left by train to New Orleans. From there they flew to Buenos Aires, and then proceeded by riverboat to Asunción. With them came a dentist, George Klassen, and his wife, whom MCC had recruited to work in the Chaco. Klassen was older than John and a lot more Americanized. His wife, Helen, was a non-Mennonite, which bothered Clara, but John said it was irrelevant as long as George took care of dental needs in the Chaco.

Almost everywhere John and Clara traveled on their way to Paraguay, people gave priority to soldiers and sailors, so it took them over two months to get to Asunción. The newlyweds didn't mind. There was much to discover about each other.

"I brought along the book I told you about that I thought we might read together," John said as they were preparing for bed a few days into their trip. "It's called *Sane Sex Life and Sane Sex Living*."

John began to read aloud about "the engorged penis that deeply penetrates the female's vaginal passage. Mutual back-and-forth and in-and-out movements then further enlarge and excite the sexual organs," exploding into what is called an orgasm in scientific language.

"And here are some specific instructions." He grinned and added, "Mostly for me." The man should come between her spread legs with his body above her, sustaining himself on his elbows and knees, to keep his weight off her.

"Why is that so important?" Clara asked in a thin voice.

"Ah wait. Here's why," John said. "Because I need to give you full and complete freedom to move your hips as you choose, and as a successful climax demands that you should."

Clara blushed. She felt shy about her body, and she wasn't used to the way her new husband talked about sex so freely and openly. It just didn't seem like the Christian thing to do.

John read from another of the chapters, titled *Coitus Reservatus*. "In this act, the lovers simply drift, petting each other, chatting with each other, visiting, loving, caressing...the hands wander idly over the body...and the organs be slipped together easily... and then let them stay so, fully together, but do not go on...just lie still and enjoy the embrace."

"Can we try it?" he said hoarsely.

Clara pulled back, confused. Like all good Mennonites, she'd been taught to never acknowledge her sexuality explicitly and certainly to not talk, read, or write about it. Sex was meant for procreation, not pleasure. She knew well the message so often conveyed from the pulpit: "Our body is identified with the flesh. It is a major source of temptation, and it inevitably leads to sin."

"Please be patient with me. I'm just not as sure as you about all of this," she mumbled, trying to avoid his piercing gaze.

John abruptly closed the book and rolled over to his side of the bed.

"John, please..." She touched his shoulder.

"We'll figure it out together," he said with uncharacteristic tenderness.

In mid-October, they arrived in Buenos Aires, where they waited for a riverboat that would take them to Asunción. They'd been traveling almost two months. Clara looked exhausted, but John told his new wife that the worst was yet to come.

He felt it was best for her to not get pregnant on the trip to avoid the risk of miscarriage. He'd suggested a contraceptive before they started the trip, but Clara had responded that she would *never* do such an ungodly thing. John was perplexed by Clara's strong beliefs about the use of contraceptives. He thought they were okay for married people. But he agreed that they could manage by avoiding sex during her fertile period.

During the past few days, he'd been thinking of the approaching fertility period.

"Do you think we might be ready for the possibility of pregnancy?" he asked one night, as they prepared for bed.

Clara was pulling a flannel nightgown over her head. "Can we risk it?"

With a plea during evening prayers for guidance and direction, they proceeded. As he had many times before, John spent immediately on coming together. It was so annoying. He hoped Clara would not think he was selfish and uncaring. He turned toward his wife and together they lovingly and patiently explored each other's bodies.

On October 30, Clara's 29th birthday, they began the boat journey up the Paraguay River. Swarms of huge mosquitos were thick on their faces, arms, legs, and ankles. Clara wore a pair of John's pajamas under her slacks and stuffed a newspaper between her two pairs of socks, but the mosquitos still found their way up her legs. They continued by narrow gauge railway to Km. 145, and then by oxcart through the Menno colony, finally arriving in Filadelfia on November 9.

With some trepidation, Clara stepped into the broken-down shack, the Dokta *Haus*, which was to be their first home. She took in the mud floor, the two single beds made from roughly hewn lumber with straw-filled sacks for mattresses, a wardrobe, and a small table with two chairs. Against the wall hung a can with a nail in the bottom, which when pushed up, released water into a washbasin underneath. Even on her father's humble farm in Kansas, she had never seen anything this primitive.

"My back hurts." Clara wiped perspiration from her forehead. "I need to lie down."

"We can't," John said gruffly, pointing to the open doorway. "Don't you see that there's work to do?"

She walked to the door and looked out. They'd just arrived, and already the horse-drawn wagons were lining up with patients coming to see the doctor. Since Schwester Maria left when John did, the hospital had shut down, and the colony had been without medical care for the entire nine months John was gone.

"John, we've just traveled by train and plane, then by boat, then by train again and then by buggy. I don't even know what month it is. I stink. I'm exhausted. My back aches. And I feel nauseous. I need to lie down." She dropped heavily onto the bed and felt the coarse straw poking up out of the sacks.

"I have no other nurse," he said, pulling her up off the bed. "*Moak die wajch!*"

As she followed John out of their house, Clara wondered if she should have told him that she'd missed her period. She mouthed the Bible verse from the book of Ephesians that she knew so well: "*Wives, be subject to your own husbands, as to the Lord.*" When she saw the people gathered under the trees waiting for the doctor, she was reminded of the Bible stories of Jesus as he walked from village to village and sick people were brought to him.

A few days later, there was a clap at the front gate. Clara awakened from a deep sleep, pushed herself off the bed, grabbed her flashlight and stumbled to the door. The moon cast long shadows in the yard.

"Yes?" Clara hoped it wasn't a serious medical case, since John had ridden out to the southern region of the Chaco to see if anyone in that remote area needed medical care.

A woman stood at her doorway, supporting a frail girl by her side. "Frau Dokta, my niece has no more insulin. We need your help."

Clara pulled on a robe and led them to the clinic. "Have the child lie down. How old is she?"

"This is Neti Voth. She's eighteen. She has diabetes. I've given her insulin, but we have no more."

Neti began to convulse. "Please try to soothe her. I'll see what we have." Clara searched the cabinets and found just a few bottles of expired insulin. She injected the serum and waited. Neti went into shock.

"Stay with her. I'll go to the Neufeld house down the road, and we'll send a radio message to Asunción." Clara tied her robe more tightly around her and walked out.

After the radio contact and a few phone calls within the city, word came back that a small plane would bring insulin later that day. Since there was no place for a plane to land, the plan was to spread sheets on the ground, and the insulin would be dropped onto the sheets.

Neighbors spread the sheets on the ground in the agreed-to spot. Clara sat by Neti's side. At 10:00 a.m., she thought she heard a plane, but it must have been her imagination. By now, Neti was unconscious. Clara held her limp hand and prayed she would hold on. After a few more hours, she heard it. The plane flew low over the spot, and a makeshift parachute floated gently down and landed near the sheets with the medication that saved Neti's life.

Their workload continued to increase during the next month, as people throughout the region got word that the doctor was back. John had convinced Horst, his schoolteacher-turned-anesthetist, to return to assist with surgeries. But Clara was his only nurse.

One night after they were in bed, a horse-drawn buggy rolled up to their house and they heard loud clapping at their door.

"Herr Dokta." A man's shrill voice pierced the silence. "My wife is dying."

John pulled on his clothes and headed for the door. "C'mon, Clara."

Clara lay for just another moment on the lumpy bed, her body resisting what she needed to do. Tears slipped from under her eyelids and made their way slowly down her cheeks. She brushed them away and pushed herself up.

John had alerted Horst and by the time Clara reached the room used for surgeries, they were cutting the clothes from the woman's body and washing her belly.

"It's a ruptured appendix," he shouted. "Clara, get over here and help me with my gloves. Bring those instruments and move the lamp closer. Horst, we need to start right now!"

Clara tried to rush, but her nausea intensified with every movement.

"No, not those!" John threw the instruments she handed him onto the hard-packed mud floor and crossed the room to get what he needed. "I thought you were a trained nurse," he hollered.

Clara noticed that Horst kept his eyes down as he always did when John yelled at her.

Two hours later, the three of them carried the patient to an adjoining room and placed her on a bed. The surgery was successful. But the tension between John and Clara had escalated to seething orders from him and silent acquiescence from her.

As soon as Horst left the room, Clara burst into tears. "I can't do anything right. And it's so embarrassing when you yell at me in front of others. And I'm so tired and I'm—" She stopped. This was not the time to tell him.

John ripped off his surgical gloves. "At least you can't go home crying to your mother." He pressed his lips together. Why did he say that? He didn't want to sound so uncaring. But they nearly lost that patient. He strode out of the room.

Throughout the following day, Clara sat on a hard chair by the patient's bed, checking her vital signs every hour. Did John's angry outbursts mean that he was in love with Anastasia? Why else was he so brusque and impatient?

That night when they prayed aloud together, Clara ended with, "And bless our baby that will soon make us a real family—"

Not waiting for her "Amen," John whispered, "Clara, really?"

"I'm sure of it," Clara said, taking his hands and placing them on her belly.

John leaned down and gently kissed her. "You're carrying my baby," he murmured.

Patients continued to come, many needing interning and surgery. By early December, it became clear to Clara, still in the first trimester of her pregnancy, that even with a maid to help at home, she couldn't keep up with all the nursing needs.

"We need to start a nurses' training school," she said to John one morning after their devotions. "It's just too much. I can't do it all."

"We have no books, your nurses' training was in English, not German, and there's no one here with more than a grade school education," John said.

Clara stared into her coffee cup, and then continued as though she hadn't heard him. "I think we should plan to include all of the classes that I took in my training. Since we have no books, we'll just have to re-create them."

John was right, of course. But could they let that stop them? She had to find a way. Late into each night, she sat at their little table in the dim light of a kerosene lamp, writing down what she remembered from her training back home. Clara read her notes to John before going to bed, even though he continued to remind her that it was a hopeless task to translate her training into something people here would understand.

"The first class needs to be on Nursing Procedures," Clara suggested one night, beginning to outline the content of the class on the notepad in front of her. "They need to learn about safety procedures, infection control and patient care skills like bathing, dressing, and feeding patients, as well as making beds. We should also cover steps in checking vital signs."

"You want to spend an entire class teaching them to make a bed?" John asked. "I can't wait that long to get medical support around here."

"OK, then let's start with what they need to know to assist you?" Clara's voice rose to form a question. She had learned that if there was a way to make something his idea, John would usually get on board.

In the end, they designed the content for seventeen classes they would teach together.

Their first volunteers to take the classes were seven girls from the poor Mennonite farming communities around Filadelfia. Clara had been worried about teaching principles of nursing under the existing conditions—rough beds, straw sack mattresses, no running water, no electricity, and dirt floors. But then she remembered that the girls didn't know any other conditions.

Three of the girls could neither read nor write. The others had barely completed sixth grade. Only the ones who'd spent relatively more time in grade school were fluent in High German. The less schooled spoke mostly Plautdietsch.

One of the girls who volunteered for the class was Neti Voth. "I owe you my life. I want to learn to be a nurse to help save other lives," Neti said. "I taught myself to read. I can do this."

They began the classes in mid-December. Three evenings a week, after a full day of patients, they each lectured in their native languages, John in Plautdietsch, and Clara in High German. But they weren't sure the girls understood any of it.

After one of John's lectures on Human Anatomy, he and Clara squatted on their front stoop, eating slices of watermelon. They were taking a short break before working on next week's class material. The setting sun was a bright ball of fire on the horizon. Flies buzzed around them, drawn to the sweetness of the juice dripping from their hands. Clara watched John swat at them.

"I can't get through to those gals. They just sit there looking all dazed," John said, leaning against the adobe wall of their house.

Clara stared at the ground. This nursing school experiment wasn't working. She should have listened to John in the first place.

Then she had an idea. She walked down the road to where the nursing students shared a single room. Clara clapped at the gate.

When Neti appeared at the door, Clara said, "You're just the one I want to speak with. Let's take a walk."

Clara explained how important it was for the girls to learn what she and John were trying to teach them. "I know a lecture on Human Anatomy doesn't seem important to you, but it is."

"It's not that," Neti said softly. "We all know that these subjects matter. It's just that—"

"What?" Clara stopped and turned toward the young girl.

"It's just that Dr. Schmidt is…well, we're afraid of him. He's so brusque."

Clara smiled. "The doctor does seem gruff at times, but he means well. He wants you to learn this material and become good nurses. Can you talk to the other girls? Will you help us succeed together?"

Neti nodded. They walked a ways in silence and then she said, "What if we actually began caring for patients—supervised, of course—and learned the principles that way? Maybe that way it would make more sense to us?"

John tried to stay out of ongoing controversial meetings in the colony regarding the establishment of a new school. But the American dentist, George Klassen, attended them regularly, and seemed increasingly agitated. On a still, muggy night in mid-December, Klassen and his wife came to visit John and Clara to talk about what was going on. The four of them sat on low footstools under a palo santo tree in the hospital yard.

"The school that Fritz Kliewer and his wife, Margarete, founded in support of Hitler's Bund is losing widespread support now that the military outlook for Germany is less favorable," the dentist said. He went on to describe the level of bickering among the planners, especially regarding the appointment of a head teacher for the school. It finally looked like most of the colonists would not accept Fritz and Margarete to be their children's teachers anymore. People had lost confidence in them because it seemed like they'd only given in to Mennonite principles because the war was beginning to turn against them.

Klassen sighed. "But Oberschulze Legiehn is still fighting to keep them as head schoolteachers, for reasons I can't figure out. And Konrad Wolf is still stirring up trouble."

"Kliewer has lots of power over the Oberschulze," John said. He told them about his conversation with Legiehn back in 1941, when John had asked him to stop Kliewer's constant threats that if people didn't join the Bund, they would be left behind when the rest of them returned to Germany. Legiehn had responded that he would do what he could. But within days, Kliewer and his wife were back in full swing, with more students and more power than ever.

John kicked at a clump of dirt. "I always assumed it was because Legiehn saw Kliewer as his ticket back to Germany. I have no idea what Konrad Wolf is up to, but I intend to find out."

John watched Clara pull herself up off the footstool. He took in the fullness of her breasts. She was carrying his baby. If it was a son, they would name him John, just like he'd been named after his father, John. He reached out to give her a hand.

EIGHT

The sun had not yet risen when Konrad Wolf trudged slowly into his hut after milking their one cow. He stood for a moment in the doorway, watching his wife, Angelika, heavy with their third child, her blond braids wound around her head, setting tin plates on the small table in their one-room shack. Raising the corners of her long black apron, she shooed away the chickens scratching at the dirt under the table.

He looked around the room, taking in the mud brick walls, the wood stove in the center, and the straw-filled mattress on the ground in the corner of the room, on which he and Angelika slept with their two small children. How could things have become so desperate? He had some acreage, and he'd tried to grow cotton and peanuts, but during the past year, pests and drought had destroyed his crops. Fortunately, Fritz Kliewer had given him a class to teach at the school, or he'd be begging for food for his family. Konrad looked at his wife with a wave of shame.

As was so often the case in the early morning before his day began, Konrad remembered his opulent family home where he was born in the Omsk region of Russia. His father, Kornelius Wolf, had been a wealthy estate owner. And although his mother birthed nine children, she was always a lady. Her maids did all the housework. Konrad closed his eyes, remembering the smoothness of his mother's silk blouses against his cheek.

The inevitable next memory was his mother screaming, as bandits arrived late one night and hauled away his father. Konrad was only nine, but he knew who they were. Everybody knew that the Communists resented the wealthy Mennonite settlers. As the eldest child Konrad helped his mother and siblings escape their village secretly just a few weeks later, leaving behind all but the bare minimum they needed for survival. In October of 1929, they joined hundreds of other Mennonite families who were camped around Moscow in a panicked effort to escape communism and get back to their *Heimatland*, Germany.

Konrad's memory was fuzzy regarding how they finally got to Bremerhaven, and from there boarded a ship to Buenos Aires, and then slowly and with many delays, made their way to Paraguay. He did remember his mother's words as their wagon first clattered into the scrubby wasteland called the Chaco. "Konrad, *nü sand wi tüs*—now we're home."

Never. Not this desert. He'd learned in school that it was the Germans who'd arranged their rescue from the Russian Bolsheviks. It was the Germans who'd given them safe passage to Paraguay, and soon the Germans would welcome them back. He was sure that one day very soon his Angelika would have beautiful silk blouses. One day, her hollowed-out cheeks would again be plump and rosy. Like when he met her four years ago, when she was just sixteen.

Slowly, Konrad walked over to the wooden shelf against the wall and placed the pail of milk next to a basket of eggs. His shoulders slumped; his head bowed.

"Wot ess?" Angelika asked.

Konrad fingered the thick scar running down the left side of his face. "Dr. Schmidt is accusing Kliewer of being a troublemaker. He thinks Germany is evil, and he continues to insist that we escaped persecution in Russia because of the help of MCC in North America. And now he and his MCC are meddling in our affairs, trying to keep us from returning to our Heimatland."

He stopped. He mustn't worry his wife. She already had dark circles under her eyes. And her back was stooped even though she was only twenty.

"Come, Angelika, it will all be all right," he said, pulling her toward him.

But when Konrad walked toward the schoolhouse later that morning, his thoughts returned to the North American troublemakers. Sure, the National Socialistic motto was prominently displayed in the colony hall: "Gemeinnutz vor Eigennutz." But Schmidt couldn't seem to understand that in the colony, this meant working together. Being united was the only hope for survival in this hell hole.

Why did the Americans keep using the term Nazism, which by now was clearly tainted? It was the hateful term they used when referring to Hitler's most heinous crimes. To lump terms like "German," "*Heimat,*" and "*Vaterland*" together with "Nazism" was a gross misunderstanding of what these terms meant to his people in the colony. The Americans had no idea how hurtful such use of "Nazism" was. Probably, they never would.

Ten days before Christmas, John decided to attend one of the Bund meetings to see for himself what was going on. It was after 7:00 at night, but the oppressive heat of the day hadn't broken. The north wind had created a howling dust storm. John entered the meeting hall and looked around. Hitler's portrait was no longer on the wall, but otherwise not much had changed from the Bund meetings of a few years ago. The same thirty or so men on opposing sides.

Two men seated at a table in the front of the room were completing a presentation about the need to establish a new school and a new leadership team for the colony. "Times have changed, and we need to change with them," they said, standing up.

John recognized one of them as Jasch Neufeld, the young man Dr. Klassen was training to become his dental assistant. John remembered that Oberschulze Legiehn had been opposed to Jasch becoming an assistant to the American dentist. At first, he hadn't understood why, but eventually it came out that Jasch had blatantly countered Legiehn and Kliewer back in 1941, refusing to sign up with the Bund. Naturally, Legiehn would be concerned about Jasch connecting with the Americans.

A man strode to the front of the room. A number of men seated toward the front chanted, "Konrad *weiß, was wir brauchen.* Konrad. Konrad." John stared at the scar running from the left side of the man's forehead down across his cheek. Clearly, Wolf was no longer simply a Kliewer follower, as he had been a few years ago. He now took control of the room. Wolf stood tall and punched the air with his fist. The room fell silent as he scolded the opposition for scheming behind Oberschulze Legiehn's back, warning them that further betrayals would lead to serious repercussions.

"Fritz Kliewer is the only person in this colony who has the proper training to lead our school," Wolf shouted.

John rose from his seat. "Fritz Kliewer is a troublemaker," he said. All eyes turned to him in the back of the room.

John continued. "He has done nothing but cause unrest in this colony since he returned from Germany with all of the Nazi propaganda in 1939. You all escaped persecution in Russia because of the help of MCC in North America, and MCC will not tolerate Nazi support. It's time to take a strong stand against it."

John turned and left the hall. Very little had changed. Fritz and Margarete Kliewer were still clamoring for power, and they now had a spokesperson, who seemingly had become quite influential in the colony. What did Wolf hope to gain from the conflicts that continued to brew? John marched along the dusty path to their hut.

Was he being too passive about all this nasty Nazi business? He thought about his shipboard assertions to Miss Ana regarding how senseless it was to use force to counter evil in the world. Was there a point when force became necessary? He must write to Orie Miller.

When John arrived home, he immediately began the letter to MCC. He wrote that Nazi flames still burned hot in the Chaco, and that Kliewer remained at the center of the heat.

"Ana would have done this a long time ago," he muttered under his breath, too absorbed to notice that Clara stood nearby, watching him.

It was a week before Christmas. Clara was homesick and lonely. And recently, she'd again begun seeing in her mind the image of the long-legged, painted-lipped beauty that had haunted her before she and John were married. Who was this Ana whose name seemed to always come up whenever John was most distressed?

Clara had no one to turn to for support. She knew she no longer belonged with the single girls. Besides, she didn't like the way they ogled John when they didn't think she was watching. And she just didn't feel at home with the married women in the colony. She'd tried speaking their Plautdietsch, and they ridiculed her. Worse, they seemed so bitter about needing to make a living in this desert. Even Mrs. Legiehn, who'd graciously given Clara a suitcase full of baby clothes, spoke about very little other than her hard life. It bothered Clara that the women—and for that matter, their husbands too—seemed so focused on surviving in this foreign and hostile environment, and that most of them showed little interest in bringing the message of Jesus to the indigenous tribes that surrounded them. Their self-absorption was selfish and un-Christian.

After checking on a maternity patient who was not yet dilated, Clara walked alone through the hospital yard and onto the dusty trail that was the main street through the village of Filadelfia. A strong north wind blew sand around in thick swirls. She kept her head down, shielding her eyes with both hands. Was this the life she'd dedicated herself to the day she was baptized? At the very least, she should get a Sunday school going.

Clara returned from her walk and approached John, who as usual, sat at the table making notes. She tried to sound authoritative. "We need to start a Sunday Bible class."

John looked up and frowned. "Clara, we don't have time for that. As it is, we aren't getting all our medical work done. We're not taking on anything else. Period."

"Nothing about our work is spreading the love of Christ to those around us." She brushed away the tears that welled up in her eyes.

"Why do you always think crying is the way to win an argument, Clara? Why can't we sensibly discuss things?" John's voice was harsh.

Clara left the hut and hurried to the hospital room to check on her patient. Why didn't he understand how important it was to find a way to serve the Lord? Or was this his way of pushing her away?

John felt discouraged. "I get it that you want us to make the nursing course material more applied," he said. "But how do we control the quality of care?"

It was the day after their argument about a Sunday Bible class, which they still had not resolved. During their evening devotions the night before, she'd apologized for crying so often, and they had kissed and made up, as she liked to say. John felt awful that he'd been so gruff with Clara. It just wasn't the Christian way. But what was he supposed to do when she cried about every little thing? He stopped himself. Why was it so hard for him to just show her a little tenderness? To show her the love he really felt for her.

Now he and Clara were once again at their little table, throwing out much of the nursing curriculum they'd originally written, and trying to figure out another way to present the most important material.

They didn't have to wait long for the opportunity to arise. Two days later, near midnight, a wagon clattered onto the hospital yard.

John awakened even before there was a clap outside. He opened the door, and there stood Fritz Kliewer, hat in hand, his shoulders slumped.

"It's Margarete," Kliewer whispered hoarsely. "She's had a high fever for days, she's been vomiting, and she's too weak to even stand on her own. I don't know what to do."

They carried Kliewer's wife into the hospital room and laid her on the examining table.

"Let's take a look," John said.

Margarete's chest was covered with a skin rash and dotted with rose-colored spots.

"Typhoid," John muttered under his breath.

Kliewer's small frame seemed to shrink even farther into the dark corner of the room. "Please save my wife," he whispered.

John remembered the hateful stares of Kliewer and his followers less than a week ago, when he stood up during their meeting to denounce Nazi activism. He shook his head and said, "We'll do what we can."

They began a treatment of antibiotics, but the fever persisted. Margarete became weaker with each passing day.

Since typhoid was a very contagious disease, this seemed the perfect time to introduce isolation techniques to their young nurses-in-training, who knew nothing about such things.

"I have no time to lecture them on the role of pathogenic microbes in human illness. Or about disease pathology or immunology. We just need to get them to be bug-conscious and fast," John said.

Within an hour of listening to Clara's lecture, the girls were squirming in their seats, saying they felt typhoid bugs crawling all over their bodies. And when the lecture ended, they lined up at the washbasin to scrub their hands with disinfectant solution until they were sore. John figured they'd never forget the basics of isolation techniques.

Margarete Kliewer died on Christmas Eve. Fritz Kliewer sat by her bed, holding his dead wife's hand. When John offered to pray with him, Kliewer turned away from him and abruptly rose to leave the room, his dark eyes sinking even deeper into their sockets.

It was almost by accident that Clara finally found her longed-for opportunity for Christian service. During the week between Christmas and New Year, word reached the hospital that a baby from the nearby *Lengua* indigenous tribe was very ill. John was out vaccinating children in the surrounding Mennonite villages, so Clara walked the half kilometer to the Lengua settlement by herself, ignoring the warnings of the colonists that these primitive people captured defenseless white women and children and kept their scalps as trophies.

Loud noises greeted her. Men were chanting, women crying, children screeching, and dogs barking. Three men were bent over a naked child, sucking on her skin. Clara had often seen these brown-skinned people, and almost nightly she and John heard their chanting—for the spirit's benefit, they were told. The medicine men's main treatment was to suck the evil spirit out of a sick person's body.

Clara began to speak in a soft voice in High German, knowing they understood nothing she said. "You wander in deep darkness. But still, Christ died for you also, that you might have peace." She approached the child. The medicine men slowly backed away.

"May I?" She placed a hand on the child's hot forehead.

"She needs to see the doctor…"

The High German word for doctor is like the Plautdietsch word Dokta. A young woman at the front of the circle seemed to understand. She spoke rapidly in their clipped language, gesturing toward the hospital in Filadelfia. The woman came forward, wrapped the baby in a large cloth and held her for a moment before handing the child to Clara.

"Thank you, Lord, for bringing me tonight to these dear people. I am here to show them the way to your truth."

The young mother accompanied Clara to the hospital. When John returned, he treated the child for pneumonia. Gradually she grew stronger, and a week later was able to return home. The child's mother took both of Clara's hands, brought them to her chest and bowed her head. In that moment, Clara knew she was called to minister to these people. To let them know that it was the good Lord who looked after them, kept them safe, and healed them.

Every Sunday after that, despite John's protests, Clara walked to the Lengua village to tell them Bible stories, bringing with her someone who translated her German into Plautdietsch. She was finally fulfilling her promise to God on the day of her baptism.

In January 1944, U.S. Ambassador Frost gave the Paraguayan Foreign Minister a list of "German Nazi sympathizers residing in Paraguay who presented the most pressing examples of individuals who should be expelled or deported from Paraguay." Fritz Kliewer was number four on that list.

A few months after the list appeared, Oberschulze Legiehn traveled to Asunción for the stated purpose of creating a more binding legal statute for the Fernheim colony and its Kooperative. While he was away, copies of an anonymous letter spread through the colony, accusing Legiehn in partnership with Kliewer of trying to create a dictatorship in Fernheim that would "give the Oberschulze even more power than Hitler has."

Clara had heard John grumbling about the latest unrest, but she tried to stay out of it. One late afternoon about a week after the letter appeared, she was at the Kooperative to purchase a few food items when she ran into Helen, dentist Klassen's wife. Clara had never felt comfortable around this non-Mennonite woman, but tried to be polite whenever they met.

Helen stood close to Clara and whispered into her ear. "Clara, George has been telling me about the latest uprising among colony leaders. Have you and John heard about it?"

"I don't really know what you're referring to," Clara said, pulling away from Helen, and tapping on a watermelon to judge its ripeness.

Helen again came close. "They're holding many special meetings. They're angry with us Americans, and they're sure we instigated the letter. Some think George made his assistant Jasch write and distribute it. They resent us meddling in their internal affairs."

"Us?" Clara asked, raising an eyebrow. She knew John was upset about the continued Nazi leanings of the colony leadership, and that he'd spoken up about it at several Bund meetings. He had also been in touch with MCC about all of this. But John would never go behind someone's back with such a mean-spirited letter.

"John is outspoken about his beliefs, but he's not devious behind people's backs. That is just not his way," she said. She added, "Sorry Helen, I really need to get back to the hospital. It was good to see you."

A few days later, on the morning of March 11, Legiehn resigned from his post as Oberschulze, stating that he was doing so "under the pressure of circumstances."

John received the notice but had been too busy with patients all day to attend to the matter. At the end of the day, he sat at their table, the anonymous letter and Legiehn's resignation in front of him. Clara had cleared off the bowls from their supper of rice with warm milk. She poured hot water from a kettle on the wood stove into a bucket and began washing the dishes.

"Who's behind this? I agree that Legiehn lacks strong leadership skills, but this…" He waved the letter in front of him. "This is just going to provide more fuel for the conflicts that sparked a long time ago."

Clara turned from the wash basin, drying her hands with her apron. Should she tell John? Would he fly into a rage?

"John, I've heard rumors that colony leaders think we Americans were involved, but—"

"Why haven't you told me this? I know Kliewer's been avoiding me since Margarete's death. He probably thinks I killed his wife. And he also probably suspects me of adding his name to the list of Nazi sympathizers. I need to go see Kliewer to straighten things out."

"That's exactly why I didn't want to tell you," Clara said. "I'm afraid, John," she added under her breath, as he stormed out into the night.

NINE

On May 30, 1934, a man in a white silk suit and a bright pink tie swaggered into the U.S. Senate Chamber and delivered a fiery speech denouncing Standard Oil for provoking the Chaco War that began in 1932 between Paraguay and Bolivia. Senator Huey Long, a flamboyant and outspoken left-leaning populist, ended his speech with, "The imperialistic principles of the Standard Oil Company have become mightier than the solemn treaties and pronouncements of the United States government." Long called Standard Oil a "promoter of revolutions in Central America, South America and Mexico," which had "bought" the Bolivian government and started the war because Paraguay was unwilling to grant them oil concessions.

Long's speech made him a hero in Paraguay, even though there's little hard evidence to support the theory that oil companies had anything to do with causing the war or with helping one side or the other. In fact, quite a different story emerges from journalistic coverage of the dispute.

Historians agree that the Chaco War was the bloodiest military conflict fought in South America during the 20th century, between two of its poorest landlocked countries. Over 80,000 soldiers succumbed to bullets, thirst, malaria, and other diseases, as well as thousands more wounded or taken prisoners. They also agree that oil was a key factor in the outbreak of the war. Bolivia was desperate to increase its oil production to supply its rising urban consumption and its mining industry and, at the same time, to find an outlet to export the surplus via the Paraguay River to the Atlantic Ocean. The Chaco region was a gateway to the river, and it was thought to be rich in oil.

Both Bolivia and Paraguay had long considered the largely uninhabited and barren Chaco territory their own. When the Paraguayan government allowed the Mennonite immigrant colonists to settle in the region in the late 1920s and early 1930s, this action bolstered Paraguay's claim to the region, provoking Bolivia's military response in 1932.

Initially, the Mennonites may have been unaware of being pawns in this rivalry between the two countries. But after the Chaco War erupted, their involvement was intentional and significant. Bolivia enjoyed overwhelming advantages over Paraguay at the start of the war. It was three times as populated, had an army well-trained by a German general, and had obtained a large supply of arms through loans from American banks. But in the end, Paraguay prevailed, in large part because its supply lines were shorter, with Mennonite agricultural products in place to support the military efforts. Barter was especially common between the Mennonites and the malnourished soldiers. The latter sold military arms in exchange for watermelon, beans, peanuts, and other produce. Paraguay controlled most of the disputed zone by war's end. (Ironically, no commercial amounts of oil or gas were discovered in the part of the Chaco awarded to Paraguay until seventy-seven years after the war.)

When the war ended, the soldiers left behind their broken-down Mauser-type rifles, which they referred to as *mosquetones*. Mennonites in the colony had the mechanical skills to repair them.

And during the moonlit night of March 11, 1944, they had the motivation to use them against each other.

★

When John arrived at Kliewer's place, Klassen was already there. The two men stood facing each other on the front stoop and didn't see John approaching.

"You and your Nazi followers are responsible for this mess." Klassen's voice was harsh.

John came closer and saw two men with firearms on either side of Kliewer.

He heard Klassen continue. "Either you will leave the Fernheim colony or else Dr. Schmidt and I will leave. I've requested that soldiers be brought from the military post at Isla Poi for our protection."

The two men with firearms raised their rifles. Even in the waning light of dusk, John saw the deep red scar on the left side of Konrad Wolf's face.

"What's going on here?" John demanded, placing himself between Klassen and Kliewer with his bodyguards. "We will do no such thing, George. And you must call off the military. Such a foolish move makes us no better than them."

John turned to Kliewer. "You may not be responsible for this latest uprising, Fritz. But you have been planting seeds of unrest for a long time. Get your men to put down their firearms."

No one responded.

"C'mon, George. Leave this alone," John said, turning away.

A few hours later, as John and Clara stood at the doorway of the hospital, a small group of men marched through the dusty main street of Filadelfia.

"They're armed, John," Clara whispered, pulling back into the shadow of the room.

"And look who's leading the pack," John muttered, staring at Wolf. "They're on a warpath to punish whoever's responsible for the letter that led to Legiehn's resignation. Let's go home, Clara. We're staying out of this."

★

Later that evening, Clara readied herself for night and lay down on one of the beds. That's when she felt it.

"John, our baby's moving. Quick. Come. Feel this."

John knelt beside the bed, his hands on her swollen belly. When he felt the tiny quivers, he buried his face in her lap and clasped his arms around her.

Clara smiled. A full moon cast light across the narrow bed as John and Clara embraced each other with eager tenderness.

A sharp tap on the open window frame interrupted them. "Herr Dokta."

John rose from the bed. Through the open window, by the light of the moon, he saw Jasch Neufeld, dentist Klassen's assistant, his face bloodied.

"Herr Dokta, the devil is running loose!"

George Klassen's fists pounded on the small wooden table in front of him. John glanced around the packed meeting hall. Over two hundred men. More than he'd ever seen at a colony meeting.

Klassen glared at Kliewer and Legiehn, who sat at the front of the room. "You two could have raised one finger Saturday night and the mob would've gone home. This is all your fault. You call yourselves Mennonites? Do you not even care about our Christian pacifist way of life?" He paused. "I will do no more dental work in this colony until you both leave and order is restored."

It was Monday afternoon. Yesterday, John had spent most of the day stitching up and bandaging the wounds of the dozen or so men who'd been beaten up. At least no one was killed. John turned his attention back to the room. Klassen was clearly losing perspective. Against John's wishes, he'd even called in the Paraguayan military to maintain order. Early in the evening a truck with four soldiers had arrived to see what was going on. "I need to protect my wife," Klassen had said, when John confronted him.

Several church pastors had called the meeting this afternoon. They began by issuing a statement condemning Saturday night's disturbances. "We do not wish to take sides," they said. "Let us resume in peace."

That's when Klassen strode to the front of the meeting hall and began shouting.

There was a commotion in the back of the room, as Konrad Wolf made his way through the crowd to the front. "*You* talk to us about Christian pacifism?" he sneered as Klassen backed toward his seat. "*You* Americans, who have no right to interfere in our affairs. *You* are ordering our Oberschulze to leave the colony? *You* call us anti-pacifist, and *you* order the army to come into our midst?" There was a rumble of approval in the room.

Before Wolf could continue, John pushed himself up out of his chair, and from where he stood in the back of the room, said, "Let's all calm down here. I don't think Dr. Klassen means to say that any one person is at fault here. I don't believe that either Fritz Kliewer or Oberschulze Legiehn planned the unfortunate events of Saturday night. But Fritz, your teachings have created an atmosphere that allows and encourages the use of force. And that is not our way."

"What do you know of our way, *Amerikona*?" Wolf spat out the last word. His scar was pulsing a deep red.

Pastor Schellenberg rose and held up his right arm. He quoted the Bible verse, "*The Lord will fight for you, and you have only to be still.* We will form an arbitration committee to investigate this matter. Now let us pray."

The meeting was adjourned.

That night John wrote a long letter to Orie Miller at MCC, detailing the events of the prior two days. He noted his disapproval of George Klassen calling in the military. *It makes us as bad as them*, he wrote. He ended the letter with:

I'm quite certain that if Kliewer tries to stay in the colony, the Paraguayan government will forcibly remove him. Years of cultivating a Nazi political culture has made room psychologically for an outbreak of violence at a time when the colony government broke down.

Clara was already asleep when John blew out the lamp and dropped onto his bed. But sleep evaded him. How low could everyone sink? Were there no limits to what mankind was capable of?

During the following week, Clara watched John become increasingly despondent. He tended to his patients and taught his nursing classes. But it was as though the energy had been sucked out of him.

"John, please talk to me," she said one evening as she cleared away their supper dishes. John sat slumped at the table. "What's going on?"

The arbitration committee had not yet released its findings about the events of the night of March 11. Legiehn and Kliewer had not left the colony. Outwardly, nothing had changed. But there was a wariness in people's eyes, especially toward the Americans. Clara noticed that even their patients, who came to request the doctor's help, regarded him with suspicion.

A few days later, needing to understand what lay underneath all of this, Clara finally decided to visit Mrs. Legiehn, the Oberschulze's wife. She waited until the worst heat of the day had passed. Her pregnancy was beginning to weigh her down, and the dusty heat of the past week had been draining. Carefully, she made her way along the rutted dirt path to the Oberschulze's home.

Mrs. Legiehn raised her eyebrows when she saw Clara at her door.

Uncharacteristically, Clara started right in without even a greeting. "What's going on? What happened at that meeting last Monday? Something is eating at John, and I don't know what it is. I'm worried."

Mrs. Legiehn stood at the open door and remained silent. Finally, between pinched lips, she muttered, "Frau Schmidt, you come to me, believing I will betray my husband? Go home and leave us alone."

Clara backed away. Was this the same woman who had so graciously welcomed her when she and John arrived in the Chaco less than a year ago? The same woman who'd given her a suitcase of baby clothes. What was happening?

John refused to attend the next colony meeting, in which the arbitration committee released its findings. He read portions of the report the next morning:

> The attackers were armed with clubs, whips, and guns. At the demand of the ones beaten, the attackers are deprived of their voting rights and office holding for one year. Attackers who are too young to vote are sentenced to one month of labor for the colony.

From the perspective of the colony leadership, it had simply been a series of interpersonal quarrels. The matter was closed.

A few days later, around noon on March 21, John left the hospital after a busy Tuesday morning clinic. His head was down. He was deep in thought. He needed to figure out how to deal with the persistent vitamin-deficiency diseases that came with the lengthy drought they'd had.

He looked up when a horse-drawn buggy, carrying five men, clattered past him on the main road running through Filadelfia. The two men in front wore Paraguayan military uniforms. John frowned. What now?

One of the men in the back of the buggy, raised an arm and yelled, "Stop. That's Dr. Schmidt. We must speak with him."

John learned that they were a Paraguayan military delegation accompanied by three representatives from the U.S. embassy in Asunción. They brought an extradition order for both Kliewer and Legiehn.

"What's going on here? On whose authority do you come?" John asked.

The men looked puzzled. One of the embassy representatives said, "Dr. George Klassen submitted a request on behalf of the U.S. Mennonite Central Committee that these men be removed from the colony. Surely you were consulted?"

John's eyes narrowed. Fighting non-pacifist acts with equally non-pacifist military intervention was not a Christian solution to the problem. He agreed that the two Nazi activists should leave the colony.

He had said so many times. He also knew that a military intervention was not the way to go. But it was too late for his opinion to matter. Things were out of his control. He said nothing.

When the delegation left the next morning, and Kliewer and Legiehn made no move to leave, John didn't intervene. And when a U.S. embassy representative returned a month later, only to find that the two agitators were still there, John again did not get involved. Summons were served on the two men, ordering them to leave no later than the following day.

Kliewer and Legiehn left the Fernheim colony on April 22, 1944, and escaped to the eastern part of Paraguay.

TEN

During the next few months, the Fernheim colony declined into a stagnant and depressed condition. A persistent drought continued into early winter, rendering the parched fields of no use, even for the historically hearty cotton and peanut crops. Calves were dying, and the cows dried up. While the women kept their families alive on whatever dried rations were left over from the prior winter, the men sat on their verandas, grumbling about their unbearable lives in this uninhabitable place.

The high school was closed. Young people roamed the back roads, picked fights with each other, and were caught looting unguarded food products. Nearly all men and boys carried firearms—for their own protection, they said. The new colony administration was inexperienced and paralyzed in the face of the desperate conditions.

Illnesses became rampant. New cases of typhoid and malaria emerged, and John feared an epidemic of diphtheria among the children. He and Clara began giving diphtheria vaccinations to all children aged six months to a year, and typhoid vaccinations to children aged one to five. Their seven student nurses rotated duties each week, two in the kitchen and laundry, three on daytime patient care, and one on night duty and in the pharmacy.

It was not unusual for fifty to 100 patients a day to come to the hospital for medical care. Their carts, pulled by horses, mules, or oxen, lined up along the dirt road in front of the hospital. When it was their turn to see the doctor, the patients filed in, heads down. It was rare for them to look the doctor in the eye. And when John finished treating them, they left quickly with hardly a word.

At the end of a long day in early July, John wiped the sweat from his brow and crossed the yard toward their hut. His head was aching, as it was prone to these days. What illness had he picked up? He had no one to turn to for answers. He heard a cart rumble onto the yard, carrying a man with symptoms of acute appendicitis.

"Clara, we're not done," he called.

Clara's belly had become so large she could barely walk. She shuffled to the hospital, where John was already prepping the patient. When they opened his abdomen, it was full of pus. The tip of the appendix was attached to an abscess that had burst.

"I've never removed an appendix backwards before," John muttered, as he tied off and inverted the stump first, and then worked on the tip.

When the patient stabilized, John went outside to confer with the man who'd brought him. The man sat on a wooden bench, his hat in his hands.

"The patient needs to stay for a while, but he'll be fine," John said.

The man barely nodded and rose to leave, staring at the ground.

John squeezed his eyes shut against the searing pain shooting across his forehead. His lips flattened into a thin line. "You—" he began. The man was already walking away from the hospital toward his cart. There was no point in yelling after him.

John had heard the rumors. Colony members desperately needed his medical care, while at the same time blaming him and dentist Klassen for intervening in their concerns and bringing in foreign governments to manage their affairs. He'd tried to argue that he was not the one who called in the military or the U.S. embassy. But in their minds, he was the face of MCC, and MCC was the enemy.

John clenched his hands as he walked home.

"Clara, why are we even—?" John stopped. Clara lay sprawled across the bed, moaning with every contraction.

Their first son was born the following morning.

"Well done, Clara," John said, gently placing the baby on her chest. "John Russell is a healthy boy."

"Let's call him Sonny," Clara said.

The Travel Air six-seat utility aircraft slowly approached the wide-open peanut field just outside the village of Filadelfia. Dark swirls of dust clouded the sky as it landed, bumped along the ground, and skidded to a stop. John shielded his eyes against the onslaught of gritty sand. This was quite a sight, the first airplane to ever land in the Chaco.

Orie Miller emerged from the plane. Through the kindness of the U.S. air mission to Paraguay, he'd flown directly from Asunción to Filadelfia, taking less than three hours for a trip which usually took weeks. Despite the historic event, only John and dentist Klassen were there to meet the plane. They were not surprised that no colony members had chosen to come, resentful as they were about the intrusions from the North.

For two days, John gave Orie tours of the hospital and the many other areas of construction he'd overseen in the last three years. He was proud to point out the improved high hospital beds, brick rather than mud hospital floors, a better-equipped nursery, an improved charting system with the addition of daily progress and medication notations, and a new laundry room. He showed Orie his filing system of the history and physical examinations for each patient. More than 3,700 names, some patients with more than twenty visits, were on file. There were building additions: a large 80-by-19-foot clinic building which housed a larger and improved office, pharmacy, laboratory, dental offices, and a building added to the nurses' home which served as a dining room.

"These improvements were all made possible by the generous gifts from our churches back home, and especially from MCC," John said, waiting for some acknowledgement from Orie about how well he had put the monies to use.

John also showed Orie the many accomplishments he'd overseen in agriculture, roadbuilding, and industry, including the new equipment for processing oil and lumber.

"Raising cattle needs to be the focus of these colonies," John said. "They still have it in their heads that they're wheat farmers. That just won't work here like it did for them in Russia. I'm trying to convince ranchers to breed a leaner kind of livestock that can withstand the heat and drought of the Chaco."

Orie seemed impressed with all the progress. But he said very little.

Finally, on the third day of his visit, Orie requested a colony meeting. People came, but it was clear they would rather not be there. The men sat, hats in their hands, staring at the floor.

Orie stood in front of the meeting hall. "I know that recent events have caused you to distrust MCC. But you must remember that all the medical and dental services you depend on, the road building, the agricultural experiments and technical assistance in so many other areas, all of which have helped you medically, socially and economically—none of this would have been possible without the generosity of your neighbors to the North."

The men fidgeted.

Orie continued. "A grave concern I wish to raise is the fact that your boys and men, including even preachers, are carrying sidearms. You must understand the complete inconsistency of asking for the *Privilegium* (exemption from military service) from the Paraguayan government on the claim that you are nonresistant when your actions belie that claim. As the MCC representative, I'm here to tell you that we will not appear before the Paraguayan government to appeal for special privileges for you, unless your actions indicate unmistakably that you are nonresistant because of your religious convictions."

The men passed dark looks at each other around the room. John observed them from the sidelines and realized that nothing had changed. MCC was still the enemy.

But in the months that followed, it was MCC that again helped the colony to its feet. The agency gave highest priority to the training of new leaders and teachers, choosing only those who took a definite stand for Christianity and against the Völkische Bund.

During the following year, John and Clara continued to teach the student nurses and care for the ill. In addition, John spent many hours each week on agricultural projects, roadbuilding, and industry development. Sometimes he was gone for days, checking out different and more drought-resistant crops or more robust cattle in the outer regions of the Chaco desert, where occasional ranchers somehow made a living. Clara dreaded those times alone.

Their future was highly uncertain. After the deaths of Roosevelt on April 12, Hitler on April 28, and Mussolini on April 30, peace was declared on the European continent on May 12, 1945. As the war in the Pacific continued, John suggested that it might be wise to get established in the U.S. before all the war workers returned home.

For Clara, that wasn't the only reason it was time to leave. Patients continued to show up for medical care. Some even seemed to appreciate it. But mostly, she and John were treated as adversaries.

The latest blow came in June. Back in December, Clara had requested that their church letters from the U.S. be sent to the Fernheim colony, with the intention of joining the colony church *Gemeinde*. Maybe if they were members of the church, they'd begin to feel like they were part of the community. Their church letters were returned by the Gemeinde with no stated reason. What was the point of trying to be part of a community that rejected them?

It was a cool, drizzly evening in late June of 1945. Clara had gone to bed early, leaving dirty dishes in the sink for her maid in the morning. Her period was two weeks overdue, and during the last few days she'd felt a familiar fullness and nausea. She sighed and turned onto her side. She and John had been trying to time their intercourse so she wouldn't get pregnant. It would just be too much right now.

Besides the problems in the colony, there was trouble at home. Clara wasn't sure they could handle another child at this time. Little Sonny had just begun taking unassisted steps. But his temper and strong will were also developing, and John's reactions to the child's temper tantrums frightened Clara. Yesterday Sonny was in his highchair, and John was coaxing him to take another bite of mandioca.

"C'mon." John jammed the spoon into the baby's mouth.

Sonny grabbed the spoon and threw it across the room. Clara froze when she saw John smack the child across his little arms.

She didn't want to blame her husband. He suffered from the hostility of colony members, and even the ill will he felt from his student nurses. But there was something else. Clara had noticed the symptoms for some time. John was losing weight and he was sometimes bent over in pain when he believed no one was watching. Several times she'd awakened to the sound of his retching in the middle of the night. She'd asked him about it, and he'd say, "*Ach, dot ess nuscht*—it's nothing."

Clara placed her hands on her belly. It would just be too much.

Three months later, on Sunday, September 9, Clara and John attended church, as usual. John pulled her along to sit next to him at the back of the church, instead of the customary women on the right, men on the left. She wasn't sure why. She wished everyone wasn't eyeing them like they were heathens. She glanced at John and saw that his chin was thrust forward. Slowly, she inched her hand toward him and touched his elbow. That's when she felt the first small tremors in her belly. Clara forced a smile. They would have to get through this.

That afternoon, John developed another migraine headache, the third in just one week. He lay curled in a fetal position on his bed. "Clara, put blankets over the windows. The light is excruciating. And can you shut up that child?"

Clara rushed around, trying to do what John requested. What was happening to their world? What was going on with John? What would she do if he died?

John interrupted her thoughts when he suddenly rose and ran toward a basin to throw up. Sonny threw himself on the ground, screaming. Clara stood in the middle of their hut, eyes on the dirt floor. Under her breath, she mumbled the verse from Isaiah, "*Fear not, for I am with you; be not dismayed, for I am your God.*" In that moment, God seemed far away.

A few weeks later, after returning home at the end of a grueling day at the hospital, John grabbed Clara's arm. "I want to talk to you about an idea I have." He began pacing around the room. "Orie wrote in his last letter that leprosy is rampant here in Paraguay, between 6,000 and 10,000 cases. We've been trying to think of a way these Mennonite colonies can thank Paraguay for allowing them to settle here. How better to do this than by undertaking a project to care for lepers, the neediest in their midst?"

"What are you saying, John? We don't know anything about leprosy. You've never even seen a leper," Clara said.

"I plan to change that."

In the early morning of October 9, John set off to visit Paraguay's only leper colony, in Sapucai. From Asunción, he traveled another three and a half hours by train and continued on horseback the remaining twelve kilometers. When he emerged from a thick forest, he saw a cluster of yellow buildings. Everything seemed clean and orderly. Maybe conditions weren't as bad as he'd been told.

He introduced himself to a nurse, who showed him around. He soon found that conditions were far worse than he ever could have imagined. Many of the patients were blind, some had legs and feet so swollen that their whole foot made little impression at the end of their leg. Many had face lesions with purulent discharge along the corner of their mouths. Most had deformities of their fingers or no fingers at all.

The worst of it was the seeming lack of care these people were getting. The living quarters were filthy. The patients lay on the mud floor amidst their belongings, which were piled up in dirty heaps around them. The grimy kitchen was buzzing with flies, and oversized rats darted into dark corners when they entered the room. Bulky sacks of *galletas* (small hard rolls) were stacked up in the middle of the kitchen floor.

By the time John's tour of the leper colony ended, he had a plan.

When John returned from Sapucai, his health seemed improved, and his energy returned. He and Clara were busier than ever with their medical work and the classwork with their student nurses. They had plans to graduate the girls in December, and there was much to accomplish before then. At the end of long days with patients and students, John sat at their table late into each night. He scribbled notes about his plans for the treatment of lepers in Paraguay and wrote long letters to Orie Miller at MCC.

> This is the project we need to help the Mennonites focus on gratitude for their lives here, rather than pining about their lost Heimatland. And this can be a place for our Mennonite youth to volunteer their time, so they learn to serve others and not be so self-centered.

Orie responded with enthusiasm, indicating that he'd contacted the American Leprosy Mission (ALM) in New York. ALM's general secretary, Dr. Eugene Kellersberger, had led leprosy work in Africa for over twenty-five years and said he would support the envisioned project.

John sent Orie his thoughts about building a leprosy compound, not as an isolated colony, but as a settlement where several hundred patients could live together and be taken care of. He organized an ad hoc committee of colony members who seemed supportive of the proposed Christian service project. One of the first tasks was to search for an appropriate location. The Paraguayan government, supportive of the project, offered a 20,000-hectare tract of land near Concepción, not far from the Fernheim Colony. It met two of the main requirements. It was isolated, and yet still close enough to the Mennonite colonies to make the service program manageable.

Shortly before Christmas, John finished all his nursing classwork and prepared to leave for Concepción with several other committee members to check out the leper colony site. He loaded a sack of provisions onto the horse-drawn buggy. Clara stood at the doorway of their hut, one-and-a-half year old Sonny on her hip, his left leg resting on her swollen belly.

"John…"

"This is no time for crying," John said, putting his arm around her shoulders. "This is important work, and I'll be back soon." He jumped up onto the wagon and was soon out of sight in a cloud of dust.

Clara stood in the doorway, her eyes on the road where the buggy had disappeared. She wanted to support John's idea about leprosy service, but she just wasn't sure it was what they should be doing right now. She would lay their trials at her Lord's feet.

Sonny fussed most of the night. Around 2:00, she took his temperature. 102. She bathed him in cool water and coaxed him to drink. But the fever persisted.

Clara's back ached and her legs were throbbing. She paced back and forth from one side of the room to the other, holding her wailing son close. She remembered that the prior Sunday service had focused on the temptations of Jesus. The great temptation in her life was hanging too much on John and Sonny. She placed her son on the mattress, upon which he immediately began to scream even louder. Clara knelt by her bed and prayed aloud, "I surrender them anew to you God, who have given them to me. If Sonny doesn't grow up to be a Christian, dear Lord, please take him now."

By the time John returned home, Sonny's fever had broken, but the child was fussy and listless. Clara rushed out to meet her husband.

"John, our baby has been so—" John's body was propped up against a sack in the back of the buggy. He held his head in his hands. "What's wrong? What happened to you?"

The man at the reins jumped down from the buggy to help the doctor. "He's had a migraine headache for the past twenty-four hours, Frau Dokta," the man said, guiding John into the house. John stumbled toward the bed and dropped into it, groaning.

Clara rushed around the room, hanging blankets over the windows.

"Bring me a bucket. Now," John rasped, his hand over his mouth.

When he finished vomiting, he lay back on the bed and closed his eyes. Believing he was falling asleep, Clara picked up their son and began to leave the room.

"Wait. I must tell you. I...we have a bigger problem than my headaches. I have blood in my stool. And look at my vomit...see how red it is. I have a bleeding ulcer, Clara."

Clara set the screaming baby on the floor and stood in the middle of the room, staring at John. This couldn't be happening.

John stayed in bed Sunday and Monday, the 23rd and 24th. Every time he rose, he reached for the bucket, alternately for vomiting and diarrhea. Sonny was not yet well, and on Monday he relapsed with a rising fever. Clara cleaned out John's bucket, fed him warm liquids and cared for the baby, all the while praying, "I cannot carry this burden alone, dear Lord."

On Christmas day, John felt strong enough to sit up in bed. Clara had finished recording the nurses' final oral exams. Graduation was two days away.

All seven of the girls graduated. They stood, proud and tall, to recite the medical oath. "*Ich verspreche bei Gott, dem Allmaechtigen und Alwissenden das ich nach bestem wissen und Vermoegen* ... I vow to God, the Almighty and All-knowing, that I will to the best of my knowledge and ability..." Never mind that the home-printed and home-decorated roll of paper stating what they had accomplished meant nothing outside of the Chaco of Paraguay. Clara noticed that even John, hunched over in a chair in the front row, was grinning as the girls rose to receive them.

In the following months, John spent much of the time in bed and barely tolerated any nourishment other than warm milk. When Clara delivered their daughter, Elisabeth, on February 24, John sat beside her bed, instructing a few of the new nurses on how to manage the birth.

Clara's physical recovery time after the birth was unavoidably short. In addition to caring for John and the two children, she had to manage the hospital and seven nurses. The week after her delivery, she admitted three patients, one of them a young boy with a rattlesnake bite. His arm and hand were stiff, swollen, and red almost to his shoulder. She was tempted to ask John about the treatment, but she was afraid to disturb him. She started the boy on penicillin and was relieved that he survived it and healed.

That night, after putting the children to bed and feeding John his warm milk, Clara sat at the edge of his bed. "We can't go on like this, John. We have to tell MCC that we need to go home."

"I know how hard it's been," John said, putting a hand on her knee. "I feel so useless. The leper project is dead. And now this."

John had learned during his visit before Christmas to the area near Concepción that the land envisioned for the proposed leper colony was occupied by ninety-two squatter families who had prior claims to parts of it. Government officials had offered to have the military evict them, but that was an unacceptable way to begin a thank-you project for the Paraguayan people. Things were at a standstill with no alternate plan.

He added, "I'm worried sick about what will happen to you and the children if I die. I've written Orie asking for our release from this work as soon as they can find another doctor."

They didn't immediately hear back from Orie. When they did, Orie's letter proposed that MCC would arrange for them to get a good vacation, before again returning to the work in the Chaco. You must be tired.

Not tired. Done, **John wrote back.** You must find a replacement.

Finally, in early September, MCC found another doctor. On September 9, 1946, John and Clara left the Chaco with their two children, not knowing what the future held.

EMPTY YEARS

1947-1951

"It was a perfect circle, complete in
itself - and empty in the middle."
– Laurence Shames

ELEVEN

By early 1947, John's health had improved. He joined a small medical practice, and the family settled into a Mennonite community in Freeman, South Dakota. Throughout the brutal winter months, John left the house by 8:00 a.m. and didn't return until suppertime. Sometimes, he made house calls at night, leaving Clara alone with the children.

Clara reminded herself that her job now was to be a mother and homemaker. She wanted to be grateful for her two healthy children and the third on the way. But she found it hard to get up in the mornings. Piles of laundry and dirty dishes cluttered their cramped home. She just didn't have any energy to get to them. And the children did nothing but fuss.

In April, their third child, Wesley, was born. In the following months, Clara fell deeper into a dull sense of hopelessness. "I need some help, John. I just can't do all of this by myself," she said one night after the children were in bed. "Look at all of those vegetables that need to be canned, and the wash that needs to get done. My varicose veins are killing me. My back hurts. I just can't…"

John put his arms around her and gently said, "We can get someone to help out."

Clara looked up and saw the severe line of John's lips. This was hard on him, too. He was still not well, although the bleeding ulcer had calmed since they returned to the States. She should complain less. But John was never around, she was lonely, and she wasn't used to all this housework. If only she could serve her Lord and get some help in the home.

John worried about Clara. She had withdrawn into a world he didn't understand, and he felt ill equipped to help her. Their rented place was far too small for the five of them. And they didn't have many friends. Worst of all, he felt useless, treating common colds, setting broken bones, and delivering babies.

John kept telling himself that he should focus on building a decent life in the States for Clara and their growing family. But in the evenings after work, he pored over any news he could find about Paraguay. Orie Miller had written, informing him that the proposed leper colony venture remained in limbo. In fact, in early March of 1947, a civil war broke out in Paraguay between the Liberals and the Colorado party of President Morínigo. By August, Morínigo won back control, but by then the government had lost interest in the leper project. There wasn't anything for them in Paraguay.

By Christmas, John had another plan that would surely please Clara. "There's an opening in a small medical practice in Mt. Lake. We know the church and the community there from our fundraising back in 1943. We should make that our home."

They moved to Mt. Lake, Minnesota, in January, initially renting a small second-floor apartment.

On a balmy early summer afternoon, John and Clara stood in the lot of a car dealership. "Look at all those cars. I can't believe what's happening in this country," Clara said. "It seems like everyone has a car, a TV, a refrigerator, and people even own their own homes. Is this opulent life in line with our Christian principles of frugality?"

It was true. Life in America was arguably better than it had ever been. Within just a few years after WWII, almost two-thirds of American families achieved middle-class status, an amazing attainment given that fewer than half of Americans had any of these luxuries just thirty years ago.

"Are you sure we can afford a car?" Clara looked at John with veiled eyes, while wrestling with Wesley, less than a year old, who squirmed in her arms. The two toddlers tugged at her loose-fitting faded gray cotton smock, which was meant to conceal her belly already swollen with their fourth baby.

"We'll take this one," John said to the dealer, pointing to a cream-colored V8 Ford with sleek smooth external moldings and a decorative blue plastic hood ornament. The interior dash color was gold.

"That looks awfully fancy," Clara said, looking around for a place to sit with the children while John arranged to pay for the vehicle.

It wasn't just buying this car that worried her. It was the whole life they were living here. John was even talking about buying a house. It was all so disorienting, like there was a widening gap between herself and the person she thought she was supposed to be.

Six months later, John ran up the steps, taking them two at a time, to their upstairs apartment. Finally, he'd found a house they could buy. Surely, this would finally make Clara happy.

"I've found the perfect house for us," he said.

Clara looked up from the sofa, where she was feeding David, born just a month ago. One-year-old Wesley sat on the floor in the middle of the room, banging a spoon on a metal skillet and howling. The other two children were out of sight. John scooped Wesley into his arms and sat down next to Clara.

"It's a white house with blue shutters. It even has a white picket fence around the front yard. Downstairs there's a bedroom, a bathroom and a kitchen/living area." He looked at Clara, hoping this news might cheer her up. She didn't smile much anymore. "And there's a nice bedroom upstairs…" His voice trailed off when he saw her drawn face.

"John, we have four children. Are you planning on sticking them all into a single bedroom upstairs?"

Well, it's a lot more space than we now have. Out loud he said, "There's also an attic room that we can fix for the two older ones. C'mon, let's round up the children and take a look."

They bought the house and moved in the following month. John came home from his medical practice early enough in the long summer evenings to till the ground behind the house. He planted a vegetable garden and starters for plum, cherry, and apricot trees.

Clara said she wanted to can the produce from the garden. She talked about having rows of canned tomatoes, cabbage, carrots, beets and other vegetables and fruit, all perfectly lined up on the shelves John had built in their cellar. Most often, this canning never got done.

He'd hoped that the move to Mt. Lake would help. Clara's mother had suffered from "nerves" and had even undergone shock therapy a few times for severe depression. Was Clara going down the same path? And to make matters worse, the pain in John's stomach had returned, as well as the nausea and bloating. He tried not to talk about it, but Clara had mentioned his weight loss, so it was clearly adding to her worries.

In the months that followed, John lay awake night after night. As was often the case when feelings of anxiety and uselessness overwhelmed him, his thoughts wandered to Anastasia. He hadn't heard from her since she'd written about her clandestine activities in 1943. He'd read in the papers that Juan Perón was elected President of Argentina in 1946, and that his government had introduced numerous social programs that benefited the working class. Had Ana been part of the movement that got him elected?

John felt an almost irrational need to know what Ana was up to. Finally, in mid-July, he wrote her a letter, saying very little about himself, only inquiring about her political activities.

Ana's response came a few months later.

...I've aligned myself with Evita Perón ... we are building support to gain the right to vote for Argentine women...to alleviate poverty... we've created the Female Peronista Party, the first large female political party ... we are finally making real progress...

She ended the letter with: And what are you doing, Dr. John?

John frowned. He was about to have his fifth child, that's what he was doing.

And he was ill.

In October of 1950, John could finally no longer ignore his bleeding ulcer. He and Clara drove to Rochester, Minnesota, to the Mayo Clinic, leaving their four children with neighbors. Because she was a nurse, Clara watched from the gallery as four-fifths of John's stomach was removed.

Marlena, their fifth baby, was born the following April, adding more work and another mouth to feed. But her birth didn't fill the hollow space in Clara's American dream life. And she didn't think it was doing anything to calm John's increasing restlessness.

One rainy Saturday morning, John walked into the kitchen, holding a letter. "Clara, listen to this..."

MCC had identified a tract of land about fifty miles east of Asunción for a leper colony. The American Leprosy Mission (ALM) was on board for three-fifths of the operating costs of building and managing the proposed colony. But they had no medical director.

"God is giving us another chance to do something that actually matters," he said.

Clara stepped away from him. "But John, lepers are isolated and ostracized, and there's no cure for the disease." The words tumbled out of her. "How would we be able to help them?"

"We'll find a way if this is what the Lord wants us to do," John said.

Clara wiped the sweat dripping off her forehead and stared around the room at the half-packed boxes and crates. She closed her eyes and sank onto the sofa. Loud screams propelled her out of her seat and up the stairs to the children's bedroom.

"Sonny, stop picking on your sister." She sat on his bed and pulled her oldest son to her side, but before she could talk to him, she heard something crashing down the stairs. Had one of the children taken down the baby gate? She rushed to the top of the stairway and was relieved to see a box of toys rather than one of her babies lying at the bottom. Three-year-old Wesley grinned impishly and darted out of the way when she reached out to swat him. She turned just in time to see her two-year-old smearing poop from his diaper in circles on the wall. Before she could clean him up, the baby began wailing downstairs.

Clara tried to hold back the tears stinging her eyes. This was impossible. John had left almost a week ago to visit the leprosarium at Carville, Louisiana. It was the right thing for him to do. He needed to learn about that mysterious disease. And she'd agreed to finish packing at least the items they planned to take from their kitchen. But she wasn't making any progress. And she couldn't manage the children. The baby was fussier than usual, and the other children seemed to know that she had no energy to discipline them. How could she possibly get anything done?

"Your trials all point in the same direction. There's no longer any reason to keep these patients locked away," John said, studying the paperwork on the table in front of him, and then straightening up to face Sister Hilary, who sat across from him. The Catholic nun—with the big sailboat-like white hat worn by all the sisters at the Carville Hospital—did not look like someone who'd easily change her mind about anything.

John had spent the past five days making rounds with the staff, consulting with the doctors and speaking with many of the patients. Late into each night, he sat at the small desk in his room, reading about leprosy, and studying the results of clinical trials.

John learned that leprosy is a disease of the nerve pathways. The bacilli invade nerves close to the skin surface, shutting down the conduits for motor and sensory fibers, which then no longer carry messages of touch, temperature, and pain. Fingers and toes become shortened, and ears and noses become deformed as the cartilage breaks down and is absorbed into the body. And because of nerve damage, patients become vulnerable to injury, which leads to accidental damage, ulceration, and infection. Mucus around the eye may also be affected, often resulting in blindness.

John knew that Sister Hilary Ross, a Daughter of the Charity of St. Vincent de Paul and a noted Carville biochemist, had overseen the clinical trials of the sulfone drugs that had seemed so promising in the early 1940s. A major downside was that they required many painful injections. More recently, trials of the just-introduced Dapsone pills, pioneered by Dr. Cochrane, technical medical adviser to ALM, seemed even more promising. In fact, the drug appeared to be reversing some of the nerve damage, and even the skin lesions and inflammation of the throat and eyes. This was the long-awaited cure for this horrific disease. And Sister Hilary was considered an expert on the topic.

Sister Hilary sighed. "It's not that easy, Dr. Schmidt."

"But here's all the evidence we need." John pointed at the papers in front of them.

Sister Hillary was silent for a moment. "We've already gone over this. I agree that it should be possible for patients under treatment to remain with their families. I also agree that the treatment likely lessens the chances of contagion, although we can't say for sure."

"Then why…?" John threw up his hands.

"For one, there are indications that the bacilli may be developing Dapsone resistance." She hurried to continue before John could interrupt. "But that's not the most important reason. As a society, we are not ready for this, Dr. Schmidt. You've studied the medical charts. They tell only half the story."

John listened carefully as Sister Hillary explained the dreadful stigma associated with the disease. "When I first came to work here, people with leprosy were treated like criminals," she recalled. "They were held in jail, then transported to us in special trains with windows sealed and blinds pulled down. There was barbed wire around this hospital. When patients arrived, they lost their status as U.S. citizens. They could no longer vote. They suffered a double burden, the disease and the stigma. That doesn't go away because of a drug that may or may not be effective over time. If given the choice now, I can assure you that most of our residents would choose to stay at Carville."

"We have the opportunity to move out of the dark ages here," John muttered. But his voice had lost its insistence. He understood Sister Hillary's point that the stigma, secrecy, and shame were too deeply implanted in both the patients and society at large to be overcome without a long battle.

Clara sat on the sofa, giving Marlena her bottle. As usual, the older children were fighting with each other upstairs. She'd become almost immune to the screaming. She closed her eyes and dropped into a prayer, breathing in the Bible verse from the book of Matthew, *"Come to me, all who labor and are heavy laden, and I will give you rest."*

The front door opened. "John!" Clara's voice startled the baby, who began to cry. "I'm so relieved you're back," she said as he put down his suitcase and came to sit by her side.

"We have much to do," John said, placing an arm around her shoulders. "Look what just came." Clara handed John a telegram.

We hereby appoint Dr. John R. and Clara Schmidt to continuing service in Paraguay; Dr. Schmidt to serve as director of Paraguay MCC medical interests and as chairman member of South America area administrative and coordinating committee. Term allowance for a married couple is $55 per month, with an additional $5 per month for each child.

During the next few weeks, John and Clara packed their belongings and prepared to travel to various churches around the country to raise money for the leprosy work. They also made plans to drive to Akron, Pennsylvania, to spend some time with Orie at MCC headquarters, and from there to New York City, where ALM was headquartered.

Their travel papers and passports arrived in a single bundle. The planned departure date was August 21. They were scheduled to arrive in Buenos Aires in mid-September and dock there for several days before continuing to Asunción.

John stared at the tickets. Buenos Aires. Miss Ana. They could plan to meet. He could introduce her to his family. He wanted her to meet Clara. He wanted Ana to know about the important work he and Clara were heading off to do in Paraguay. He wanted Ana to know that he was finally living up to their shared principles.

He sat at the kitchen table and wrote to Ana, telling her about the stopover in Buenos Aires, and asking if she would meet them. He ended the letter with:

I am happy to finally have the chance to introduce you to my wife, Clara. I am so proud of her, and I know you, more than anyone else, will appreciate her dedication to justice and mercy for the poorest of the poor.

John addressed and sealed the aerogram and placed it on the counter to put in the next day's mail.

Clara parked the car in front of the MCC headquarters in Akron. It was 2:00 in the morning. John and the children were asleep. She rested her head on the side window and closed her eyes. But sleep eluded her.

Finally, Clara quietly slid out of the car. She walked along the empty dark streets, her thoughts racing and her chest pounding. Ever since seeing John's letter to Ana on the counter a week ago, she'd been tormented by the image of the long-legged, painted-lipped beauty imprinted in her brain. Why was this Ana so important to John? Clara wished she could talk to John about all of this. But he'd think she didn't trust him. She would have to place this at the feet of her Lord, as she had done since the first time John told her about Ana before they were married.

By the time Clara got back to the car, John and the children were awake. He looked worried and the little ones were restless.

"Where were you, Clara?"

His concern for her felt like warm salve. "Just walking, honey. Stretching my legs."

The meetings with Orie at MCC had to do mostly with setting budgets and finalizing logistical details. What John really looked forward to was the upcoming meeting in New York with the renowned leprosy expert Dr. Eugene Kellersberger, the general secretary of ALM.

"Is it possible for us to leave our five children with someone here in Akron, while Clara and I drive to New York for the ALM meeting?" John asked Orie the day before their planned departure for New York.

Orie looked surprised. "You want to leave even your two-month-old baby?"

"It's just not possible to accomplish what we must do with all of them underfoot."

Orie made arrangements with several families from his church for the care of the children, and John and Clara headed to New York. During the drive, John rehearsed what he would say to Dr. Kellersberger. After all, it was ALM's own technical medical adviser, Dr. Cochrane, who had pioneered the miracle drug Dapsone.

Best of all, John had conferred with his brother Raymond about the Dapsone drug. Because of his severe limp, Raymond had dropped out of medical school after two years and was pursuing a degree in pharmacology.

"Here at KU, we believe it's the miracle drug we've been waiting for," Raymond said. "In fact, tell your Dr. Kellersberger that I'm on board to come to Paraguay to work with you on finding a more humane treatment for leprosy patients. I just need another year to finish the program I'm in the middle of right now."

It was exactly what John needed to make his argument. With a bright pharmacologist validating the new miracle drug, ALM would surely agree that it was time to consider relinquishing the old colony model of leprosy treatment.

He and Clara arrived at the ALM headquarters on Fifth Avenue just after noon. It was a humid July day, but John hardly noticed the blanket of heat bearing down on the city.

"It's good to finally meet you in person. John. Clara." Kellersberger extended his hand.

After a few minutes of small talk, John launched into what was uppermost on his mind. He had anticipated numerous responses, and he'd thought about various persuasive counter arguments. What he did not expect was a closed door on the subject.

Kellersberger's terse statement was final. "We are sending you to Paraguay to build a leper colony, not to try out risky and untested new ideas."

MADNESS

1951-1956

"When life itself seems lunatic, who knows where madness lies? Perhaps to be too practical is madness. To surrender dreams—this may be madness. Too much sanity may be madness—and maddest of all: to see life as it is, and not as it should be!"

– Miguel de Cervantes Saavedra, *Don Quixote*

TWELVE

Orie Miller slowed his car and squinted at the genteel, quietly sophisticated structures facing a lush iron fence-enclosed park, searching for number 38 Gramercy Park. He had enjoyed the drive from Akron to New York City, especially the brilliant greens of the summer foliage. But he was also distracted. He'd met several times with Eugene Kellersberger, ALM's general secretary, in his Fifth Avenue office, to discuss the Paraguay leprosy project they were planning to jointly sponsor. But when he requested this meeting, Kellersberger asked him to come to his home. "It'll be more private," he'd said.

Orie wondered about the need for privacy but didn't resist. He had a lot on his mind that he needed to sort through with Kellersberger. John Schmidt was leaving for Paraguay in a few weeks. John had signed the contract with MCC, but he continued to question the wisdom of building a leper colony. Orie knew ALM's position on the matter, but he wanted to learn more about the reasons behind it. After all, Kellersberger was arguably the world's leading expert on the disease. He'd spent decades working with leprosy patients in the Congo and traveled to leprosaria around the world before taking on the role of ALM's general secretary.

Orie parked his car across from the wrought-iron gate leading into the private park and sat there for a moment before getting out. He took in the park's massive elms, flower-lined walks, and manicured grassy plots. John's voice kept ringing in his head: "Locking these people up like animals is not what Jesus would have done."

He made his way to Apartment 5G and knocked. "Thanks for agreeing to meet," he said when Kellersberger opened the door and led him inside.

Orie looked around the apartment, artistically decorated with an African motif. Animal flowerpots lined the sunny windowsills, a lampshade was a map of the world, and the shelves with neatly stacked books contained elephant-shaped bookends and candleholders. Why would someone working for a Christian service organization live in this much luxury?

"It's Julia Lake's touch," Kellersberger said, referring to his wife. "She always did love our Congo home. Please. Sit."

Orie took a seat. "There's just a lot I feel I need to learn about leprosy. As you know, John Schmidt has some ideas—"

"Nonsensical ideas!" Kellersberger interrupted. "There is simply no evidence to suggest that it's safe for leprosy patients to stay in their homes with their families. The only way we will ever eradicate the disease is to keep patients in strict isolation."

Orie opened his mouth to speak, but Kellersberger continued, "You know, Brother Orie, the spotlight of the medical world is focused on Brazil because they have found the sanest and most enlightened approach in the world to managing leprosy. I visited Brazil five years ago. Did you know that in the state of São Paulo alone, they had over seventy trained leprologists? I was told that 30,000 cases of leprosy were under control in Brazil, the patients living in colonies they referred to as 'Havens of Refuge.'"

"But I've heard that—"

Again, Kellersberger interrupted him. "I met a missionary lady while I was in Brazil, a Mrs. Eunice Weaver. She was especially instrumental in finding humane care for the children of leprosy patients. She has organized some twenty-five *preventorios*, where more than 2,500 children of infected parents are being reared. Those Brazilians have really figured this out."

Orie shifted in his chair. He wasn't used to being cut off like this. But this was not his area of expertise, and he wished to learn. He found an opening in the conversation to ask a few more questions. After a while, Julia entered the room with a tray of tea and small cakes. Their conversation drifted to the Kellersbergers' mission work in the Congo.

Before leaving, Orie said, "I think you need to reiterate your concerns to Dr. Schmidt. He can sometimes be a very stubborn man."

"Oh, he'll follow our model, or he will lose our funding," Kellersberger said. "Thank you for coming, Orie. Please give our best to Mrs. Miller."

On August 21, 1951, Clara and John boarded the *SS Brazil* with their five children, ranging in age from just four months to seven years. The seven of them were crammed into two small tourist class cabins, John with the three boys in one, and Clara with the two girls, including the baby, in another. Each cabin was equipped with a small rusty sink off in one corner. Laundry facilities were available only for first class passengers.

"This cabin smells like a toilet," Clara said a week into the trip, while washing dirty diapers with the limited soap she could find. "And it'll only get worse. The children all have diarrhea. I can't possibly keep up with all the dirty diapers and underwear in this little sink. And there's no place to hang it all."

John was leaning against the doorway. "You can hang some of it in the boys' cabin."

Clara was grateful for the gentleness in his voice. But she was concerned about the children. They still had weeks to go in these horrid conditions. And then, after they got there, what were they bringing them into?

Clara also worried about the children's physical safety on the ship. She had made cardboard signs with each child's name to hang around the necks of the four older children. She thought it might help get them back if they were lost. But by the end of the first week, the signs were gone, and the children were out of sight—despite persistent diarrhea—exploring the ship. Every morning when she rose and dressed her little ones, Clara breathed a prayer for their protection.

Most days, with the baby tucked away in a portable buggy, John and Clara sat for hours at a time, poring over the books and papers about leprosy they'd brought with them. One of the books was *Miracle at Carville*, an autobiography of a New Orleans debutante who, at nineteen, was diagnosed with the dreaded disease and in 1937 arrived at Carville, the leprosarium in Louisiana. The story described her battles to preserve her dignity and faith. It ended with a plea to not call these people lepers, but rather patients with Hansen's disease.

John put the book down. "The worst part of this disease is actually not the medical ailment. It's the stigma associated with it," he said. "I will no longer allow myself or anyone around me to call them lepers. They are people like you and me with human dignity who happen to suffer from an illness called leprosy."

The *SS Brazil* arrived in Buenos Aires on September 13. John had told Clara about the plan to meet Ana at the port. When Clara looked at herself in the little cracked mirror before disembarking, she noticed the gray streaks in her hair, and the lines beginning to form around her eyes. She tried to push some curls into place, but her hair fell flat. Clara frowned into the mirror.

She stayed a short distance back with the children and watched John move toward the tall woman leaning against the back wall of the custom's hall. As she came closer, Clara noticed that the green of the woman's tailored dress exactly matched her eyes.

Clara turned back to discipline David, who had thrown himself on the ground, screaming. In that moment, she saw herself and her family as the tall woman must be seeing them: four dirty, restless children and a wailing baby in the arms of a tired mother with graying hair.

"Meet my family," John said, pushing the children ahead of him, and reaching for Ana's hand. "This is Clara."

Was that pride she heard in John's voice? Clara reached to shake Ana's hand, and then stepped back and eyed her husband. Yes. There was no mistaking the warmth and pride in his face when he introduced her to Ana. Clara let out a long breath and took a seat on a wooden bench nearby.

She watched John line up the children, instructing each of them to say hello to Miss Ana. There was that look again. John was proud of his family.

After the introductions and a bit of small talk about the trip, Ana's voice took on an urgent pitch. "We've made much progress, Dr. John. Just last month we held a mass rally of over two million people. The crowds demanded that Evita announce her candidacy as vice president…it was the largest public display of support in history for a female politician…all those things we talked about ten years ago are beginning to happen…"

Clara looked up from changing the baby's diaper on the bench. "John, can you help me? I need a clean diaper." She pointed to the bag.

John reached down to hand Clara the bag and then turned back toward Ana. "We too, are finally getting a chance to make a difference, a real difference." He told her about the proposed leprosy colony and his idea that maybe patients could be treated in their homes.

Two of the older children were screaming at one another, David was hanging onto Clara's skirt, bawling, and the baby was writhing in her arms. John was absorbed in talk. It was Ana who held up her hand and pointed to his family behind him.

John immediately turned to tend to the children. Clara glanced at Ana, who was eying her with an affectionate smile.

John and Clara and their five children continued their journey and arrived in Asunción after nearly a month of travel, grimy, bedraggled, and emaciated from almost constant diarrhea. When they disembarked, Clara looked out over the ancient city that lay in front of them, crowned by low-hanging dark clouds. "I hope we're doing the right thing," she whispered.

John put an arm around her shoulder and said, "We know we are exactly where we're supposed to be. And we give thanks to Thee, oh Lord, for Thy protection."

Frank Wiens, a short young man with wire-rimmed glasses, was the Mennonite delegate who was there to meet them and take them to their apartment. The city seemed unchanged from the last time Clara saw it five years ago. It spread out over gentle hills in a pattern of rectangular blocks, covered by a sea of red-tiled roofs. The streets were smooth worn cobblestones lined with paraíso trees. With Moorish architectural features brought from Spain in the 16th century, the houses stood hard and impenetrable, offering passers-by cold walls with high wooden doors at street level, and shuttered French doors opening onto balconies high above the street.

Clara had seen all of this before, but she now saw it through different eyes. This time, they were not just passing through the city on their way northwest to the Mennonite colonies. Here's where they would live while they planned and built the proposed leprosy colony eighty-one kilometers to the east of the city.

Wiens was about to turn onto a steep downhill side street, but abruptly stopped. Just a short block in front of them, Clara saw that the cross street below had become a flood, carrying dead branches, broken plastic bottles, tattered pieces of clothing, rotted produce and what looked like feces. A bus was stalled at the intersection in the deep murky water, and pedestrians were unable to cross the street, which had become a swollen stream. Wiens made a sharp turn away from the torrent.

"What is going on down there?" Clara asked, holding her nose against the stench.

"You'll get used to this now that you're going to live here," Frank said laughing. "Asunción still has no sewage disposal system. So, when it rains, the garbage gets carried through flooded streets toward the river."

Frank stopped the car in front of an imposing dark outer wall. "This is your new home."

MCC had provided the Schmidts with a maid to care for the children, which allowed John and Clara to spend numerous days a week on the site of the new venture, often spending the night in a makeshift hut. They began calling it *Km. 81*, because the entrance to the leprosy station was at the 81-kilometer marker on *Ruta Nr. 2*, the unpaved highway from Asunción that ran east through the property to the Brazilian border.

During the first weeks in Paraguay, John spent many hours meeting with various health officials. He and Clara also visited the Sapucai leper colony together, traveling several hours by train and then continuing on horseback the remaining twelve kilometers. A guide accompanied them as they toured the compound.

An old woman with a broken-down nose endlessly smoked small black cigars. Their guide said the smoke kept the warble flies away from what was left of her rotted nose. A crippled woman, whose legs were useless stumps, slid along the floor on her stomach, using her elbows to move herself. When Clara knelt in front of her, the woman cried out "*Ko'ápe ou jagua'i*" in Guaraní, the indigenous language most people of the campo spoke. "It means 'here comes the little dog,'" the guide said. Truly, these people were treated like animals.

John learned that the first experiments with the new Dapsone drug at Sapucai seemed to be successful, and they'd considered ambulatory (home-based) treatment. Dr. Federico Río, the director of Sapucai, agreed with John that patients might be treated at home if Dapsone continued to be effective. But he was concerned about the risks at this early stage of using the new drug.

Was Kellersberger right after all? Was a colony model still the best way to treat the disease? John hadn't heard from his brother Raymond in a while. What had he learned about the Dapsone drug since they last communicated? Surely there was something that could be done to improve the quality of life of these poor people. He would put off the decision of treatment methodology until after he gathered more information.

John had agreed to direct the Paraguay leprosy venture on two conditions: that it would be jointly supported financially by MCC and ALM, and most important, that the program would eventually be owned and managed by Mennonites in Paraguay as a thank-you project for allowing them to settle in the Chaco and not be required to serve in the Paraguayan army.

A few weeks after arriving in Paraguay, he and Clara traveled to the Mennonite colonies, holding special church meetings in which they presented the leprosy station at Km. 81 as an opportunity for service. The program they envisioned was predicated on utilizing labor provided by a stream of short-term volunteers from the Mennonites in the Chaco, like the voluntary service program initiated in Canada and the United States as an alternative to World War II conscription. For John, providing this opportunity for Mennonites to serve at Km. 81 as a way of thanking Paraguay for welcoming them was as important as treating patients with leprosy.

"This is a chance for the Mennonite young people of the colonies to learn about service," John said, over and over, standing in front of one church congregation after another.

The response was mostly silence. John knew that the idea of service was foreign to these people, who had focused almost entirely on their own survival ever since landing in the Chaco in the 1930s. He also knew there were concerns about sending their youth away from the safety of the Mennonite colony to live out among the heathens, and worse, heathens with a dreaded disease.

John remembered the heated exchanges he'd had with Orie when MCC had decided on the location east of Asunción for the leprosy colony. John wanted the new settlement to be closer to the Mennonite colonies, so that oversight of the volunteers would be easier. In his letter to Orie about the matter, he had written:

> The most important part of this project—having Mennonite young people serve—would be lost at the location near Asunción, because colony people would not send 18-year-old people there and I do not want to be responsible for them there. Unless every effort is made to have colony cooperation in this project and every effort made to get them involved, I am not interested in the work.

Orie had assured John that MCC would support him in getting the Mennonite colonies involved in the project. But he remained firm in the decision to locate the leprosy work east of Asunción.

Now John struggled to find ways to get the Mennonite colony leaders to pay any attention to his pleas for help. They seemed uninterested, and MCC, far away in North America, was not intervening.

Clara loved helping John plan and develop the design of the leprosy station. John had taken courses in engineering before studying medicine, so together they designed the station layout and then he personally drew all the building plans. On those evenings when they were both in Asunción and the children were in bed, they met in the kitchen, which also served as the living area. It was a large room with whitewashed walls, high ceilings and a red tile floor. Late into the night, they stood together bent over their table, staring down at John's drawing of the property at Km. 81, 1,148 hectares (around 2,835 acres), with two small streams crossing it.

"MCC wants this to become a self-sustaining colony," John said. "We'll plant fruit trees, and we'll have cattle and pigs and chickens…"

"And vegetable gardens. The soil looks so fertile," Clara added.

A few days earlier, they had traversed the property by horse and buggy to determine where the buildings should stand, where wells should be dug, where trees would be planted and where cattle could graze. Clara took notes as they rode through the fields and along the streams. There was so much they could do with this land.

A few broken-down shacks and a lean-to shed stood where someone had once lived at Km. 81. MCC had employed Johann Teichgraef and his family from the Fernheim colony to live on the property, mostly to prevent squatters from moving in. Teichgraef spoke not only German, but also Spanish and Guaraní, which was important for communicating with the Paraguayan hired workers. With their help, John and Clara had begun fixing the structures and securing the borders of the land with fencing.

Now they were focused on the construction of a clinic building and homes for those who would work on the station. In accordance with John's drawings and MCC's promised funds, they had ordered lime to set 50,000 bricks, 6,000 clay tiles for roofing and 10,000 Guaranies worth of construction steel.

When it was time to pick up the materials, the funds from MCC had not arrived, so they had to cancel the order. After reassurances that the monies were on their way, they again placed the order for the needed building materials. It was now December, two months after the agreed-to money was supposed to be there.

"Does MCC want this work done or not!" John yelled, after cancelling the order for the second time. "I'm writing them an ultimatum. We just can't go on like this."

He sat at the table and began to write.

We have been anxiously waiting for the $1,000 you promised to send us for the leprosy colony. Materials have been ordered several times and had to be called off because of lack of funds. We might as well call it quits.

Clara stood behind him, looking over his shoulder as he wrote.

"John, how about ending with *It puts us into a very unpleasant situation*, rather than *call it quits*," she said quietly.

John turned around to face her.

"What is it?" she asked.

"Your eyes have not looked as bright for years as they do tonight," he said, smiling. "This work is good for both of us."

Clara said nothing, but she understood. She was leaning into their work with an enthusiasm she hardly recognized. Sometimes she couldn't get to sleep at night, feeling guilty about not paying enough attention to their five children. But she was doing what God called her to do. He would care for the little ones.

After numerous false starts, John and Clara finally received the funds to buy the materials required to begin construction. John had consulted with engineers about water rights and was ready to dig wells. A wealthy Paraguayan rancher sold them 200 cows for 200 Guaranies per head, and 100 heifers and fifteen bulls for 160 and 600 per head, respectively. He even offered to brand them with a hot iron and transport them to Km. 81.

John began spending more and more time at the station, marking the boundaries of the construction sites, and specifying the layout and depth of the foundations. The work was finally moving forward. He could see it taking shape.

But they still had only the one salaried Teichgraef family living on the station. The volunteer program they envisioned for the Mennonite youth from the Chaco was not working. Not a single volunteer had come forward.

In the sweltering heat of mid-December, John and Clara left their children in Asunción with the maid, and once again made the arduous ten-day trip to the Mennonite colonies. John felt the familiar pressure that had been lodged in his chest for weeks. This might be his last chance. He simply had to convince the Mennonite colony leaders that the proposed voluntary service program was essential, not only to the leprosy project, but to the spiritual and social development of their youth.

They gave their first presentation in the very same church in Filadelfia that had denied Clara and John membership five years ago, since it was the largest meeting hall in the colony. Church leaders and congregants from all three Mennonite colonies had been invited to attend.

John stood at the front of the hall, staring at his watch every few minutes. They'd waited fifteen minutes and still only a handful of men sat near the back of the room.

"It's time to start," John finally said. He had to get through to these people. He needed to make them understand that a life without service to the needy was a wasted life. He drew on the Bible to make his points, making sure they understood that this was not a plea to help him. It was an appeal to do the Lord's work.

He ended his presentation with the words, "Someday this will be your project, your way of thanking Paraguay for giving you a home and the freedom to not serve in the military. You will own the project and your leaders will run it."

These last words created a small stir, and a large man in the back row stood up. "MCC will not run it? We will?"

There was no mistaking him. He'd lost some weight, but Konrad Wolf's large frame was still impressive. And the scar running down the left side of his face had not faded.

The men shifted uncomfortably in their seats.

"It was one of the conditions I stipulated before I took the job, Konrad," John said, looking directly at Wolf. "It will be yours."

Wolf looked around at the men seated near him. "Then we need to step up and do our part," he said. He turned back to John. "I will find your volunteers."

The hall was quiet. John's eyes were still on Wolf, but they had narrowed into a squint. What was he up to now? After the conflict back in 1944, that crazed Nazi activist had avoided him, so John had not been in direct contact with Wolf since then. Was this a trap? Or maybe a ploy to make fun of and ultimately destroy the leprosy project?

John said nothing further and took a seat.

THIRTEEN

Grasping his black leather medical bag in one hand and his hat in the other, John boarded the small Panair do Brasil aircraft. He hardly noticed the blanket of mid-January heat radiating from the tarmac. He'd spent weeks preparing for this trip. Finally, he was on his way to São Paulo.

"I will get to the bottom of why isolationist policies for treating leprosy are still firmly in place all over Brazil," John had told Clara. The Brazilian model was still considered an exemplar for the rest of the world, and leprologists traveled long distances to study and learn from Brazil.

As far back as 1945, the American Public Health Association had begun to advise against isolating people with leprosy. But even now, seven years later, scientists were still far from unanimous concerning the patient isolation policy. And many influential experts responsible for establishing and expanding the leprosaria were determined to keep their traditional policies and institutions in place. Were they just playing on public fear of leprosy to keep their establishments alive?

John deplaned in São Paulo and saw the director of the Departamento de Profilaxia da Lepra of the State of São Paulo, Dr. Lauro de

Souza Lima, striding out onto the tarmac. Elegantly groomed in a three-piece suit, buttoned down despite the sticky heat, his slicked-back dark hair set off intense eyes staring out from under bushy black eyebrows.

"Pleased to meet you." John grasped his hand.

"*O prazer é meu*," Souza said, leading the way to his car.

Souza was the director of the leprosy branch of the Brazilian Health Ministry and a member of the World Health Organization's Panel of Experts on Leprosy. What did the man really think about the exclusionary colony model, which he publicly championed? All medical decisions in Brazil were centralized, so anyone who opposed compulsory isolation of leprosy patients was removed from office. Medical students were trained according to this model, and only those young doctors were recruited who subscribed to the official isolationist standard. No wonder the model was so resistant to change.

They drove the eighty-eight kilometers to Pirapitingui, the largest leper colony in Brazil. John sat in the front passenger seat, conversing with Souza through an interpreter who sat in the back.

"There is no adequate evidence to depart from the policy of isolation," Souza said, jerking down the stick shift and merging into traffic. "Isolation of all infectious cases is the only way to break the chain of infection. Eventually it will lead to the eradication of the disease."

"Many cases are infectious years before they are diagnosed and isolated," John countered. But he saw from the fixed set of Souza's jaw that he might as well stop, at least for now. Why didn't these people understand? The fear of being locked up only made patients hide their condition exactly when they probably were both most contagious and most curable.

Souza gestured to what looked like a dilapidated small town. John stared at the broken-down storefronts and nearly empty fruit stands along the road. And this wouldn't be the worst of it. According to what he'd read about this place, patients from other colonies dreaded being transferred to Pirapitingui because of its horrid conditions.

They stopped in front of the administration building, a tall, cement prison-like structure.

"I understand you will be staying with us for several weeks," Souza said, leading John through a side door, down a hallway and into a small room. "I hope you will be comfortable here."

John dropped his bags on the rough brick floor. "It'll be fine," he said, barely glancing at the single bed and a small wooden table and chair. "I am ready to begin making rounds with you now if you have the time."

They drove around the extensive compound, home to over 2,500 patients. John marveled at how much it seemed like a much larger version of what he had seen in Carville, Louisiana, before leaving for Paraguay. The colony had a strict division of space with three separate zones: the healthy, the intermediate, and the sick sectors. The healthy zone contained the entrance, the power generator, water tanks, store-houses, garages, administration offices, management, and other services necessary for running the colony. It also included the houses of the director, the doctors, and the administrative staff. The intermediate zone, located between the healthy and sick neighborhoods, was used for checking in visitors. The fenced-off sick zone, comprising most of the colony, contained the hospital and clinic, the dormitories, a psychiatric ward, a prison, and a church, in addition to the land for cultivating crops and growing animals. It was rigorously separated from the healthy zone, with a 300-meter buffer and a gate preventing anyone but authorized personnel from crossing the dividing line.

They passed by brickyards, repair shops, factories, and agricultural fields. Souza explained that the goal was to make the colony as self-sufficient as possible. The activities kept the patients occupied and even provided a small profit for the colony.

John took notes on everything he saw as they toured the place. Occasionally, he inserted comments in capital letters: *TREATED LIKE CAGED ANIMALS* and *I'LL NEVER DO THIS*.

He noted that the São Paulo model was based on the trinity he'd read about: leper colony, dispensary, and prevention center. The colony was the most important, according to Souza, as it insulated the sick. The job of the dispensary was to search for and document new patients. The role of the preventorios was to provide shelter for the children born to leprosy patients, to separate them from their sick parents, and keep them under close observation.

John spent his first week in Pirapitingui making rounds, talking to medical staff and patients, and staying up late into each night, writing extensive notes. Maybe he could develop the colony ALM wanted, but with Raymond's help, focus much of his efforts on a dispensary, while providing humane conditions to reduce patients' fears of being imprisoned. John wasn't at all sure he liked the idea of a preventorio for the children. Surely there must be a way to not tear families apart like that.

A beat-up diesel pickup truck sputtered as it came over the hill into view. Clara jumped to her feet, nearly tripping on the long canvas apron tied around her waist. With her left wrist, she pushed aside a strand of hair that had escaped her kerchief.

A half-dozen Paraguayan men in torn filthy shirts stood in the bed of the truck, passing a bottle around, their fists pumping the air. Who were they? She dropped the trowel still dripping with adobe sludge from the last brick she was setting, and stood, staring. As they grew nearer, she could make out their shouts.

"*Lepra de satán...que mueran todos...guerra contra satán.*"

Could she run? Escape? Clara jerked her head around to take in the rubble of recently cleared land where she and John planned to build the clinic, the thatched-roofed lean-to stacked high with adobe bricks, the tarp on the ground behind her covered with plaster, and the partial wall to her left. There was nowhere to go.

The truck slowed as it approached Clara. The men thrust their fists at her, and their voices rose to a wild crescendo. "Lepra...que mueran... *trabajo* de satán..."

Following the driver's lead, a few of them jumped to the ground, grabbed rocks from the truck bed and moved toward Clara. She backed up, grasping her apron as though it might shield her from the angry, wild-looking men. Why was John traveling around in Brazil when she needed him? Clara's lips trembled. He wasn't due back for another month.

Without taking her eyes off the men, Clara sensed by her side the presence of Johann Teichgraef. "Johann," she said between clenched teeth, "who are these men and what do they want?"

"They're from Itacurubí, Frau Clara, just up the road from us, and they're saying that you will not live and that they'll destroy this hospital. They refuse to let you bring lepers into their neighborhood."

The men pulled more rocks off the truck bed. Teichgraef continued to translate, his voice getting thinner and tighter. "They're saying that they've brought these rocks to destroy you and your satanic work here at Km. 81."

Clara's chest muscles constricted. She wished she knew Spanish. Surely, she could explain the Lord's work. Explain that they were here to help.

Clara took a deep breath and slowly turned to Teichgraef. "Please ask them if they would like to have some coffee and Zwieback." She pointed to the angry men, who were still pulling rocks from the truck bed.

Teichgraef relayed the message. The men stopped shouting. They stared at Clara.

Slapping her hands against the sides of her apron to remove some of the mud, Clara walked toward the lean-to where she kept what little provisions she had. "Here, I have this thermos full of iced coffee and these are Zwieback that my maid baked yesterday. You probably don't know what Zwieback are..." In her nervousness she forgot that they didn't understand a word she was saying. "Um... Johann, please tell them I'd like to pray with them before we eat?"

The men didn't move, their dark eyes darting back and forth between their driver and Clara.

Clara clasped her trembling hands together. "Lord, we thank you for your love and protection. Bless this food, we pray, in Christ's name. Amen." She held out the bag of Zwieback and motioned for the men to come.

The driver said something to the men and one by one they dropped their rocks. They ate Zwieback and drank iced coffee with Clara and then quietly climbed back onto the truck and left.

★

After several weeks at the Pirapitingui colony, John felt dispirited and restless. Souza and his staff had been very helpful in showing him the various phases of the work. And although they provided many seemingly valid reasons for their model of care, they were completely unresponsive to, even uninterested in his concerns about the isolationist model.

John's conversations with the leprosy patients themselves only convinced him further that this could not be the right way to handle the disease. He learned that people were treated as criminals from the moment they were identified as having leprosy. One patient told John, "When the soldiers came to get me because they discovered that I was a leper, they handcuffed me and hauled me away with one soldier marching ahead of me and another behind." Another reported that he was carried by four strong men and held over a fire to "burn off the disease." No amount of screaming saved him from his torment. And unfortunately, the patients didn't seem much better off once they were brought to the colony and locked into the sick zone. Couldn't Souza and his staff see that this was completely inhumane?

One ward housed about thirty blind women, with four patients in charge. John walked into the ward during a mealtime and watched how the blind women with crippled hands and stubby fingers tried to feed themselves. Many of them had eyes that were balls of red meat and noses that were rotted away. John's lips pressed into a thin hard line.

Through his interpreter, he began to talk with a few of the blind patients, and before long they all crowded around him to listen. They asked questions and seemed very interested in the plan for leprosy work in Paraguay. When John turned to leave the ward, many of the women felt their way along a wall and came out to the porch to wave goodbye with their stubby hands. They wished him God's blessing in his work and expressed their thanks for having come to see them. Did no one ever spend time with or talk to these people?

★

John had arranged to spend ten days in Rio de Janeiro after his visit to Pirapitingui, to learn about the leprosy work there. Specifically, he wanted to speak with someone he'd read about, a Mrs. Eunice Weaver. In 1935, Eunice had persuaded Brazil's President Vargas to organize official aid for her work. She had traveled around the country, launching a campaign to construct twenty-five preventorios for the children of leprosy patients.

Mrs. Weaver had also represented Brazil in numerous international leprosy congresses and had just recently been awarded Brazil's National Order of Merit. She was internationally known as an "angel" and a "saint" for her work. Maybe she would be an ally for John's conception of a more compassionate model of treatment.

As his plane dipped and circled above Rio de Janeiro before landing, John thought about his first visit in 1941, when he and Orie had flown from here across the mountain ranges and rain forests of Brazil to Paraguay. He hadn't known what lay ahead. John stared through the small dirty window of the aircraft as it flew past the colossal statue of Christ the Redeemer. He grinned. Once again, he didn't know what was next. He loved that. He felt alive.

Mrs. Weaver was at the airport to meet John and take him to her office. She waved her hands when describing her belief that it was un-Christian to leave children in a leprous environment, knowing that it was impossible to remove all infectious cases for some time to come.

Her voice was soft. "Jesus commanded that we care for the children."

The woman had such a Christian spirit. She worked tirelessly to show the love of Christ toward leprosy patients and their families. John also considered her argument that if he were to build a preventorio at Km. 81, the children could eventually grow up to contribute to the mission work. Maybe this was the right thing to do, after all, for children of leprosy patients.

The following morning, Mrs. Weaver took him to tour one of the preventorios. What he witnessed there left such an indelible mark on him that he remembered it for the rest of his life. The building was broken down. Part of the roof caved in. The children were dirty, emaciated, and listless. They scurried off to the corners of the room when he and Mrs. Eunice approached them. Had they been abused?

In the car, driving back to her office after the tour, John was silent for a long time. Finally, he said, "I don't think I will build a preventorio in Paraguay. It cannot be right to keep children away from their families."

"It is more complicated than that, Dr. Schmidt," she said.

John returned to Asunción on March 1. Clara drove to the airport with Frank Wiens to meet him. She'd received only three letters from John during the seven weeks he was in Brazil, which was unusual. And the letters had been filled with anger about the conditions he witnessed. What would this mean for their work?

On the drive back to their apartment, Clara watched John's eyebrows pull together in a deep furrow when she told him about the men with the rocks from Itacurubí.

"They're afraid of a colony. And with good reason." John was nearly shouting.

He summarized what he had observed in São Paulo and Rio. "I return with a briefcase full of notes that lead to many more questions than answers. The great Brazilian model of leprosy treatment is steeped in old traditions and institutions that are unwilling to accept new possibilities. For now, it seems we must build a colony. But we must find a more humane way to make patients less afraid to come to us."

John's letter to MCC and ALM about his trip provided many details of his findings, and ended with:

I am more than ever of the mind that an isolation policy has serious disadvantages. It breaks up the family and leaves the dependents unprovided for. For now, I will abide by the rule of isolation of infectious cases, but I plan to modify the method so that the patient may be attracted to come forward earlier for treatment.

A letter from Ana lay unopened on his dresser when John returned from Brazil. Clara didn't mention it, so John, buried in their work, had been back a few days before he saw the letter. He ripped it open.

As always, Ana skipped any preamble. She described at great length the turn of events in Argentina since they'd seen each other last September. She was working more closely than ever with Evita Perón, who until recently had been spending as many as twenty to twenty-two hours a day on her foundation, championing the cause of the poor. John's neck muscles tightened when he read what came next:

Evita has been diagnosed with metastatic cervical cancer and may not have long to live. She has asked me to take over her work on behalf of labor rights. Her organization has secretly purchased thousands of automatic pistols and machine guns to arm workers of the trade unions against the injustices imposed by her husband and his military. Despite the appearance of supporting the poor, Perón and his administration have resorted to organized violence and dictatorial rule—anything to protect his political base. I was so certain we were on the same side, fighting for the descamisados.

Dr. John, I am learning that the fight for what's right is not as black and white as I thought.

Ana went on to describe her work with a small group of former Peronistas who now opposed Perón. They had begun secret military training in the northeastern provinces of Argentina. She acknowledged how risky it was, but felt she had no choice. It was her duty to continue Evita's important work.

Was Ana purposely putting her life in danger? Was there anything she wouldn't do for her cause? He could understand that. But why her sudden questioning of the clear line between right and wrong?

A week after John returned from Brazil, Herb arrived from the U.S. John had asked his brother to come help him with a project he had in mind to aid the economically destitute Chaco Mennonite colonies. He needed Herb's connections with monied people in the North.

John remembered the years he spent in the Chaco in the 1940s, when the collapse of the colonists' dream of returning to their Heimat-land, not to mention the droughts, pests, and plagues, left them so discouraged that they often saw no possible way forward. Today, they still wondered if they would survive.

John continued to believe that the best way to build a better future for the Chaco was to develop large cattle ranches. Because the land was scorched and barren, and farming attempts had been a failure, colonists were pessimistic about John's ideas regarding ranching. They also had limited money for investment. John had convinced Herb to come to Paraguay to develop a proposal for MCC and other potential investors in North America to capitalize the industrial development John envisioned.

"I've already talked to a number of businessmen in Kansas who are very interested in our plan to invest in the Chaco," Herb said. "All they need are the specifics for moving forward. And Orie believes this is a great way to get the colonists on their feet so that maybe they can eventually pay back the MCC loans from the early settlement years."

John nodded, jotting ideas in the margins of a notebook filled with numbers, graphs, and growth charts. He was pleased that Herb seemed completely on board with this project. In fact, in his original letter about this to Orie, John referred to his brother as a "Paraguay Consul-tant and Enthusiast."

John thought back to the warm spring day when he'd ridden his horse home after the last day of his German grade school. He was twelve and he had a plan for his life. He ran up to his father sitting with twenty-year-old Herb on a bench next to the barn, smoking those hateful cigarettes. Herb was teaching in a small high school in Plains, Kansas, and had come home for a few weeks during a school break.

"I just passed my final exam in Geography. *Dot's aules*," John announced. "No more school for me. I'll be your helper on the farm now, Pa."

John expected him to smile in agreement, but his father said nothing, just pulled hard on his cigarette and glanced over at Herb.

"You'll do no such thing," Herb said sternly. "You'll enroll in English high school."

John did as Herb said. And four years later, John followed Herb into pre-med and medical school at the University of Kansas. He wished he weren't always following in his brother's footsteps. And he wished he weren't always in his shadow. John had hoped that going to Paraguay might finally be something he could feel like he was doing on his own. Without Herb's constant opinions and assistance. But here he was again, asking for Herb's help.

John pulled his attention back to his notes. "That all sounds good. But we need to be careful," he said to his brother. "The South American Mennonites lack respect for MCC. There are many reasons for this, and some of them aren't MCC's fault. But we need to be careful to not push this too much as an MCC project."

The two brothers left the next morning to begin the long journey to the Chaco Mennonite colonies.

Clara felt a sharp pain in her abdomen and bent over the shovel. She and Mrs. Teichgraef were digging holes to plant tree saplings she'd bought that morning at the Pettirossi market in Asunción. It had been challenging to load the trees onto the pickup by herself, and the road out to Km. 81 had been muddy and slick from a recent rainstorm. But Clara was determined to get the trees into the ground before John returned from the Chaco. He would love them.

"Johann, come. Frau Clara is sick."

By the time Teichgraef reached them, Clara was on the ground vomiting, her hands clutching her belly.

"We need to get her to the hospital in Asunción. Now." Teichgraef reached down and half carried, half dragged Clara to the vehicle.

FOURTEEN

A fierce wind raged from the north, scooping up the loose topsoil and mounding it into billowing dark clouds. Their horse-drawn buggy rattled along the dirt main street running through Filadelfia.

"This is one of the Chaco's famous *Nord Sturme*," John said, holding a handkerchief over his mouth and nose.

Herb nodded, cradling his head in both hands.

The two brothers had just arrived in the Chaco and were on their way to Konrad Wolf's house. The stated purpose of this trip was to gather information about investment opportunities to improve the economic status of the Mennonite colonies. But John's uppermost concern was the lack of response from the colonists to his repeated calls for voluntary workers for Km. 81. They could talk about economic investments for the region, but the real reason he was here was to find out why the Mennonites were still not supporting the leprosy work.

John slowed the buggy. Through the heavy dust, he stared at the dilapidated hut with two lean-tos attached to either side of it. Things obviously were not going well for the Wolfs. An old woman appeared in the doorway.

"Bitte. *Kohmt nenn*," she said as the two men jumped from the wagon. That's when John recognized the woman. It was Angelika, Wolf's wife.

"Konrad is on his way," she said, inviting them in. "This wind…"

Wolf appeared at the door. "Goondach," he said, extending his hand.

After introducing Wolf to his brother, John immediately launched into why they had come. "There's much work at Km. 81 and we have no volunteer workers, Konrad. What do we need to do to get you people to understand that we have an obligation to serve Paraguay?"

Wolf was silent. Was he trying to think of excuses? Was he going to confess that he really was opposed to the whole idea of a leprosy project for the Mennonites, but that he was stringing John along for a while until he could declare the project a complete failure?

"We are barely surviving," Wolf began slowly. "What we get paid for cotton and other products does not nearly keep pace with the increases in living costs. And since there's no road, it's hard to get our products to Asunción. Many of us wonder whether we need to look for another place to live."

"What are you talking about?" John slapped his knee. "This is good land, even though you don't see that. It may not be farmland, but there are plenty of opportunities for development. That's one of the reasons Herb and I are here. You've never been grateful for what you've been given." Something about Wolf's self-conscious demeanor stopped John from continuing.

"The Oberschulze wants to meet with you," Wolf said. And then, almost under his breath, "We need help from the American MCC, or we will not survive."

John's eyes narrowed. How was it even possible that this man was asking for handouts from the very organization he'd fought so hard against only eight years ago? Grabbing his hat from under his chair, John rose to leave. "We need workers at the leprosy station, Konrad, or *it* will not survive."

★

Herb and John rode to the home of Jasch Neufeld—dentist Klassen's former assistant—where they were staying. Jasch's wife, Anni, waited for them at the door, the wind whipping her long skirt around her legs. She was waving a piece of paper.

"Herr Dokta. A radio message came into the Kooperative. From the Baptist Hospital in Asunción. Frau Dokta Clara had an emergency appendectomy last night."

"Wot? How is she?" How had this happened? Who was with her?

"The message was that Clara is doing well, and the children are being taken care of."

John sucked in his breath. Who had performed the surgery? Did they even know what they were doing? And who had sent the message? How could he really know that Clara was all right?

The wind had loosened a piece of the tin roof. It hammered against the frame above their heads.

"Kohmt nenn." Anni's voice could barely be heard above the howling storm. They ducked into the house and helped Anni pull the door shut. Herb and Anni wandered to the kitchen, but John remained in the entryway, his hat in his hands. What should he do? What if something happened to Clara while he was gone? He stared out the window. The storm was still worsening, and had now picked up large tree branches, tossing them around like toothpicks.

Clara would want him to stay until he finished what he and Herb came here to do. He was sure of it. John joined the other two in the kitchen. "I need to get word to Clara that we'll be back in two weeks," he said.

The windstorm continued for the next several days. When it finally abated, it left behind piles of rubbish and debris, and gritty sand that had seeped into every crevice.

During the next week, John and Herb met with numerous colony leaders, beginning with the Oberschulze of Fernheim. John attempted to convince him that real and lasting economic development would require cooperation among the colonies, instead of the current competition. John expressed his exasperation about each colony's desire for independence. Staying separate was simply not feasible if they wished to survive.

Getting the three colonies to cooperate would not be easy. Although the members of all three were Mennonites, they had come at different times, for different reasons, and with different backgrounds. The first to come was the ultraconservative Colony Menno, with Canadian national identity and passports; next came Colony Fernheim from the Soviet Ukraine; and the last to arrive were members of the Colony Neuland, born in Russia, but with German citizenship and experience with the Wehrmacht. None of the three had ever trusted the others.

As the Fernheim Oberschulze elaborated on reasons for the lack of cooperation among the colonies, John's thoughts returned to Clara. Was she getting enough rest? To remove her appendix, the surgeon had to cut through her external muscles as well as the innermost layer of the abdominal wall that kept her internal organs in place. If she became too active before the inner layer healed, she risked developing a hernia, or even worse.

The Oberschulze's final words jolted John back into the present. "John, all this talk about cooperation sounds good, but it won't happen." He rose to show them out.

Before they reached the door, John had an idea. "Why not put together a committee with representatives from all of the colonies to manage the recruitment of volunteers for the leprosy work? That will give them a sense of common purpose." *And hopefully, help you people get out of your own way.*

After a bit more conversation, the Oberschulze finally agreed with John, on the condition that they receive economic help from the North. Although there was not enough buy-in or time to establish a formal committee before John and Herb left the Chaco, an ad hoc lepra Komitee was envisioned with delegates from each of the colonies. To John's surprise, Konrad Wolf volunteered to be the head of this informal group.

The horse-drawn cart jostled across the rutted road, approaching Km. 145, en route back to Asunción. John was eager to return home to Clara, who was recovering from the appendectomy. He noticed that Herb had said very little during the entire time in the Chaco. It wasn't like him.

"What's going on?" John asked.

Herb stared straight ahead and said nothing for a moment. Finally, he shrugged. "I'm not really sure why I came. You've pretty much figured this whole thing out. And you know these people much better than I ever will."

John shifted uncomfortably on the wooden cart bench. Was there a note of envy in his brother's words? Ach! That was nonsense.

"Herb, I'm glad you came. I know you'll help us raise money in the North for investment in these projects."

After riding along in silence for a bit, Herb turned to John. "So, Raymond is still planning on coming out here to work with you at Km. 81?"

John grinned. "Najo. He says he told his fiancée that coming to Paraguay with him after the wedding was a condition for their marriage."

"Smart man," Herb mumbled under his breath.

John stared at Herb. There it was again. Envy? Or maybe even resentment that John and Raymond were going to have a life of service and grand adventure in Paraguay?

John had been back for a week when Frank Wiens came to him with news that protesters, led by several prominent personalities from the department of Itacurubí de la Cordillera, where Km. 81 was located, were complaining about a leper hospital being built right next door. In their protest documents, they referred to a decree of July 14, 1945, dictating that the area around Itacurubí would be developed as a tourist destination. A leper colony would drive out all tourism.

John pounded his fists on the table. "This is why I was so insistent that we get the decree updated and signed by the health minister back when we arrived in Paraguay last October."

He still had no written permission from the Health Ministry to build the leprosy hospital at Km. 81. In decree no. 9560, dated January 18, 1950, the Paraguayan government had granted permission to develop the leper project in the Concepción area. When that land proved unusable, MCC purchased the current site. John had met with the health minister requesting approval of the new location several times since arriving in Paraguay. The minister repeatedly said that the permission would extend to the new site at Km. 81, and there was no need to sign a new decree.

Now this.

"What do you suggest we do?" Wiens looked at John.

"We contact our lawyer to have him finally get the thing signed."

Wiens shook his head. "Our lawyer was ill all last week and I tried to make contact this morning and he is still down and can't be seen until Thursday. In the meantime, Itacurubí officials are threatening to go to the Health Ministry with their complaints."

"Then I'll go see the minister again myself. Now." John strode out of the room.

One night in late July, John sat in front of his short-wave radio, as he often did in the evening after everyone was in bed. This was his time to plan the next day's activities, and to catch up on international news. After a report of a series of unidentified flying objects spotted over Washington, D.C., an urgent voice interrupted with the breaking news that Evita Perón had died.

Ana. Where was she? How would this impact her life? John knew Eva Perón had been ill, but this seemed rather sudden. He turned to his desk and began writing to Ana, ending the letter with:

Despite your prior doubts about Perón, you must find some
comfort in the fact that he is there to continue her work to
support women's rights, the working class, and the poor.

John sealed the letter and headed for bed, his thoughts wandering
back to the heady days on the ship back in 1941, when he and Ana had
such lofty plans about what they were off to accomplish. What had he
achieved? The Chaco Mennonite colonies were still only just surviving.
And the leprosy project was barely hanging on. He felt the restlessness
in his joints that often presaged another sleepless night.

A month passed. The health minister had still not made himself available for a meeting with John. Construction at Km. 81 was nearly
stalled due to lack of labor and funds. John had written three letters to
MCC, first politely asking for and then demanding that they send the
monies that had been promised for the leprosy project.

I was called to direct this work with a $25,000 budget per
year. Since I started October 1, 1951, we have received only
$1,000. This $1,000 plus $500 I personally put into the
project is nearly gone in spite of the fact that we postpone
buying important items in order to save money.

When another month later, they still had received only a fraction of
the promised funds, John began sending telegrams to the MCC office
in Akron. In one of them he wrote:

Every telegram we must send to request money costs about
6 square meters of a wall of our building. Shall we leave
some holes as reminders of this evil?

John and Clara barely made it through the final months of 1952,
with minimal funding and rising tensions about the project in neighboring Itacurubí. More than once, John threatened to drive to Itacurubí
to take on the protesters face to face. But Clara reminded him that they

had no legal right to be at Km. 81. It was better to ignore the protests as long as possible.

To make matters worse, the lepra Komitee of the Mennonite colonies had communicated to John that since they still had received no help from the North, it was proving difficult to find young people who wished to expose themselves to a project involving the dreaded disease. Only a handful had come forward so far.

John had just sat in a meeting with Frank Wiens, outlining the few options they currently had. Maybe if they could at least convince MCC to step up to help the Mennonite colonies, it would be possible to get workers for Km. 81. But without funds for the project...

In early December, John heard back from Ana.

Things are not always as they seem, Dr. John, she began. Yes, Juan Perón had improved the situation for women and for the poor, but it was now clear that all of this was motivated by his desire to build a loyal constituency to protect his political base. Led by Evita, women became aware that they'd been rejected by a demagogue who would destroy their rights if it served his purposes. John sucked in his breath when he read the next paragraph:

> Cancer did not take Evita's life. Very few know this, but Juan Perón forced his wife to undergo a prefrontal lobotomy to suppress her growing opposition to his policies. It silenced her and almost certainly caused her death. But he will pay.

John looked up from the letter, stunned. Juan Perón had always appeared to be the beloved leader of the poor and the working class, as well as women. *Things are not always as they seem.* He sat back in his chair. MCC *seemed* interested in the leprosy work, but their support was not forthcoming. And what about the colony leaders? Did they even care? Were things there also not as they seemed? Did anyone support the work God had asked him and Clara to do? Were they wasting their time with people who seemed to have no confidence in them?

Clara came into the kitchen and put her arms around him. John tensed for a moment and then allowed himself to relax into her embrace. Together, they would figure this out. They had to. What would Ana think if they failed and left? And where would they go—back to their boring lives in Minnesota?

Clara only half-heartedly began Christmas preparations. She would have skipped the holiday altogether—other than honoring the birth of Christ, of course—were it not for the children. They seemed well enough adjusted, the older ones going to the German Goethe School in Asunción, and the younger ones cared for by their maid. But Clara worried that they might not be getting enough family life. She and John were so often gone, sometimes for days—even weeks—at a time. Every time she became too concerned about them, she dropped to her knees and lifted them up in prayer, pleading for God's blessing on each of her dear little ones. He would care for them, as long as she and John were doing God's work. The pain of separation was a sweet sacrifice for her Lord.

Another issue was getting in the way of Clara's enjoyment of the holiday. John was so preoccupied with what was happening with the leprosy work, he seemed hardly present, even when he was physically around. The other night, after they blew out the lamp and lay in bed, she'd reached over to touch him. "John…"

"I'm sorry. I can't." John said. But he held onto her hand.

Clara occasionally caught herself missing her home, her family, and her friends in Kansas. The work she and John were doing here was meaningful. But when she lay in bed before drifting off to sleep at night, her thoughts sometimes wandered to more normal and less intense times in her life. Times filled with laughter and even silliness. There was no possibility here for any of that. Sometimes she allowed herself to admit—only to herself—that she missed those times. And then she immediately felt guilty for having such feelings.

The day before Christmas, the much-awaited letter arrived from Orie. Clara watched John as he read portions of it aloud:

> Could you give us a clear statement of progress made in the leper project development? What items are underway, how far are they along, what would be a fair value of the cash investment in it to this point? How soon do you expect to be able to actually begin serving lepers and to what extent as far as numbers are concerned?

John sputtered as he paced around the kitchen. "What items? How far along? How dare they ask for a plan when they've failed to send most of the promised money? And how could I possibly have time to think about patients, when all my time is spent on construction, farming, raising money from our friends and family back home, and finding more workers?"

Clara was silent. She didn't know what to say, but she needed to come up with something. They just had to let go of some of their frustrations and focus on Christmas. They needed to spend some time with their children.

"I pulled some pine branches when I was out at the station yesterday," she said. "And I have a pole with holes drilled into it. Would you help me shape the branches into a make-shift Christmas tree? I'm sure the children would love to help as well."

John stopped pacing. Clara breathed in a prayer, asking her Lord to stand by them and give them a blessed Christmas.

On Christmas day, a telegram arrived from Kansas. John read the words aloud:

Raymond killed in car crash last night. Herb.

Raymond gone? John bent down and held his head in both hands. He hadn't realized until this moment how much he'd counted on things turning around when Raymond and his new wife finally came to Paraguay after their wedding, which was only two weeks away.

Eight-year-old Sonny, whom they now called John Russell, ran into the kitchen, cheeks red from the hot afternoon sun. "Wesley broke one of my new stilts—" He stopped, his dark eyes moving from one parent to the other.

"I'm sure we can fix it." Clara led her son out of the room.

God, why hast Thou forsaken me? What dost Thou ask of me? John continued to rock his head in his hands.

He was still sitting in the same hunched over position almost an hour later, when he heard Clara enter the room. John jerked his head up. "The Lord has given me a renewed vision of why we came here in the first place, Clara, and why Raymond wanted to join us. We simply can't give up now. I'm ready to respond to Orie."

They sat down at the table together. The letter began by asking that MCC give their entire leprosy program another airing. It ended with:

We enjoy our work here as we have never enjoyed anything before, despite the difficulties. We praise the Lord for this. Our desire is that we might all move forward while we still may. We might be cut off before we accomplish anything, but we would like to at least be found trying when the judgment day comes.

FIFTEEN

John and Clara collected enough money through their personal connections to continue with the construction of their home, as well as the station clinic. By the beginning of 1953, they even had a half-dozen volunteers from the Chaco to help with the farming and the construction. John figured they were pulling this off, despite all the odds.

A dedication service for Km. 81 was planned for January 17. John hoped it might soften the hearts of people whose time and money they needed to survive. About 120 planned to attend, mostly Mennonites from the Chaco or Asunción, and a few from the U.S. Konrad Wolf had said that members of the *GemeindeKomitee* (the committee now formalized to support Km. 81) from all the colonies were coming. Even Orie was flying in from the U.S. John had made sure that no government officials or Paraguayans from the local area were invited, given that he still did not have official permission to carry out the leprosy work.

The service was postponed due to rain and impassible roads, finally beginning at 1:00 p.m. the following day. Benches were positioned in neat rows on the soggy ground. Clara placed a little white doily on the speaker's table.

John stood off to the side and watched participants take their seats. Orie seemed to be in serious conversation with Konrad Wolf. What kind of trouble were they stirring up? He'd wondered why Orie was even here. To check up on them? He'd cornered Orie when he first arrived, asking about MCC's lack of support. Orie had been evasive, saying only, "These things take time, John."

John saw Clara gesturing at him to begin the service. He started with a prayer for God's guidance in this important work, and for the support they would need to carry it out. He then laid out the various plans for the station. He was only a few minutes into his presentation when a man's hand shot up.

"Do you have the required approval from the government to build the leprosy station?"

John did not hesitate. "We will receive the approvals. It's just a matter of time. This should not stop us."

Several members of the GemeindeKomitee spoke next about rules that should be put in place for the young people volunteering at Km. 81: no drinking, swearing, backbiting, dancing; no "dubious" social games; and no mixing with the Paraguayan neighbors.

Orie was the final speaker. He praised the work as the first occasion for Mennonites in South and North America to formally work together. John stared at Orie as he spoke.

Shortly after the dedication ceremony, John received a copy of the letter Orie wrote to ALM about his time at Km. 81. Orie wrote about being impressed with the construction so far, and with the interest and support of the Mennonite colonies. He said he was completely convinced that the project was in good hands, and that it must continue as planned.

John scratched his head. Were things ever as they seemed?

★

In April of that year, John and Clara moved out of their Asunción apartment and took their children to live at Km. 81. Their house was not nearly finished. The brick walls were up, but they had not yet been smeared with mud or whitewashed, and none of the doors and windows were in. But they had to vacate the apartment, so they took this as a sign that it was time for their family to live at the station.

They moved their boxes from one room to another, as each part of their house was worked on. Within the first month, they and their five little ones had slept in every room. The children didn't seem to mind. *They're like birds freed from their cage*, Clara wrote in her diary. Wesley, Elisabeth, and John Russell, now ranging in age from five to eight, attended a little one-room school of six students. A preacher from the Mennonite colonies had come to teach in the school. It seemed like things were finally settling into a routine.

By now, there were over a dozen voluntary workers on the station. John managed the young men. Everyone knew their roles. One was responsible for the farming and had various helpers with him. Others did the cattle work, the vegetable gardening, the beekeeping, caring for the chickens, the construction, and so forth. The only time off for the workers was an hour for siesta after lunch and evenings after Bible study and prayer meetings.

Clara had a maid at home to take care of the housework and the children. Her time was taken up managing the volunteer girls' work in the kitchen, sewing, and laundry. Even though they did not yet have any patients, Clara was especially grateful for Schwester Neti, who'd shown up unexpectedly a few weeks ago, suitcase in hand.

"You saved my life eleven years ago, Frau Dokta. I'm here to help you with your work," Neti said.

In addition to supervising the personnel, Clara kept the books in a loose-leaf notebook, where she tracked revenues and expenses, their own private money, and the money for the mission. To raise awareness of their work, Clara began putting out a quarterly newsletter, which she called *Im Dienste der Liebe* (*In the Service of Love*). The old mimeograph machine someone had donated often broke down. Sometimes the sheets wouldn't go through, especially the back side, which could still be moist. She had to put them in the oven to dry them out.

One evening, a few months after moving out to the station, John sat with his family around the blue formica-topped table on the veranda, eating their supper of leftover Borscht. They all wore their coats since the cold dampness of the winter was penetrating.

Clara began slumping down in her chair. John jumped up to grab her. He stared at the tile floor at her feet, where a large pool of blood was forming. Pulling her into his arms, he carried her to their bed, raised her feet, and stuffed rags between her legs. The bleeding didn't stop.

"What's wrong with Momma?" The children had followed John into the bedroom.

"Please go to your rooms. Elisabeth, take care of the little ones. I'm taking your mother to the hospital in Asunción." John carried Clara out to the car and laid her across the back seat.

The baby was very premature, perhaps a boy. They buried him on the south side of their house with little ceremony. There was so much work waiting for them.

During the remainder of 1953, the responsibilities of operating the leprosy station continued to increase, and it seemed that there was not enough time for John to do anything but manage what they had begun to call the "farm." During one of his visits, Frank Wiens mentioned that he'd heard rumors that John's medical certificate might not be recognized by the Paraguayan Health Ministry. John shrugged it off. After all, he'd practiced medicine in the Chaco for years and no one had complained. Besides, there was far too much work to be done to worry about the Health Ministry's latest whims.

One of MCC's requests had been that John and Clara grow a self-sustaining farm on the leprosy station that would eventually pay for itself when the colony was developed. John agreed. He saw the agricultural mission as part of God's plan and threw himself fully into the farm work. Sometimes he wondered when there would ever be time to begin the medical work. But he continued to manage the farm, never letting on that he was tired or discouraged.

There were now thirty people on the station, twenty of them volunteers from the Mennonite colonies, who came without pay for three to six months at a time. The land had to be plowed twice before gardens could be planted; a workshop was built; and bricks were burned. Portions of the land were prepared for later plantings of mandioca, corn, sorghum, and alfalfa. And John continued stocking the site with cattle.

The official word came in early 1954, in the form of a sealed legal document from the Health Ministry. Clara was at home when it was delivered by a uniformed officer. She invited the man in for coffee. They were sitting, silent, across from each other when John arrived.

John ripped open the envelope. He stared at the paper in his hand, and then without saying a word, he strode off the veranda, leaving Clara and the officer at the table with their coffee.

"I apologize for my husband," Clara said in broken Spanish. "He's very *preocupado*."

"Sí, señora," the man said, standing up.

After he left, Clara rushed outside to find John, who was pacing back and forth in the back yard.

"John, what is it?"

"Read it for yourself. It's in Spanish, but even I can understand what it says." John threw the document at her.

Su certificado médico no ha sido reconocido en el Paraguay. Para ejercitar la profesión médica en este país usted debe cumplir el requisito de rendir y aprobar los siguientes 33 exámenes médicos...

Clara sucked in her breath. "What will we do?"

"We'll keep doing what we're doing," John said. "I don't speak Spanish well enough to take those thirty-three exams, and even if I could, they would teach me nothing I don't already know about leprosy. This is simply unjustified harassment."

"It says here that you will go to prison if you keep practicing medicine without proper certification," Clara said in a shaky voice. Since Raymond's death, John had seemed more fixated than ever on continuing this work, no matter the consequences. It was scaring her.

"Then so be it." John grabbed the document from her, crushed it in his hand, and threw it to the ground.

A month later, John heard that Bill Snyder, MCC's assistant executive secretary—who lately seemed to be taking over many of Orie's duties—was scheduled to visit the Chaco colonies to learn about their economic situation firsthand. Evidently, he had also scheduled a meeting with Chris Graber, an elderly man who was standing in for Frank Wiens for one year as MCC's Paraguay representative. Graber was a trusted Mennonite leader in the U.S., having worked with Orie for decades at the Mennonite Board of Education.

John frowned. Why had he not been invited to the meeting with Snyder and Graber? What was this all about?

During Snyder's stay in Paraguay, he also visited the leprosy station. Clara and John were meeting with the voluntary workers under the Linden trees near the partially built kitchen and main dining/meeting hall when the Asunción MCC vehicle drove onto the grounds.

After exchanging pleasantries, John took Snyder on a tour of the station in his Jeep, especially pointing out the many agricultural developments MCC had requested, which were well underway. Over time, John had become increasingly convinced that the agricultural projects were a critical part of the mission at Km. 81.

"This year, we harvested about fifty kilos of strawberries, and we've had a hearty vegetable crop. We get forty liters of milk and several dozen eggs a day. This means we have a different diet than we did a few years ago. We even borrowed a combine from the agricultural experimental station (STICA) and harvested 1,400 kilos of corn and ground it into flour." John pointed to the mandioca field and the rows of banana trees. "And those are tung trees."

"What are tung trees?" Snyder asked.

John looked at Snyder, believing he was kidding. "Tung oil is made from pressed seeds from the nuts of those trees. We use the oil for finishing and protecting wood," he said. "It's especially good for—"

"Listen, John," Snyder interrupted him. "This is all fine. But I'm here on behalf of the MCC Executive Committee to let you know that getting the government's permission to practice medicine in Paraguay is of primary importance to us. It is essential that you acquire it."

So that's why he had come, and that's what the secret meetings with Graber were all about. John stopped the Jeep and turned toward Snyder, whose high forehead, under a prematurely receding hairline, was beaded with perspiration.

"Bill." John paused and shifted in his seat so he could look Snyder squarely in the eyes. "The responsibility of the Health Ministry of a country is to care for the sick. We are in a country where that's not happening. They're reacting out of their guilt. Never has the government actually attempted to stop us. In any case, we have a God-given command to care for the sick."

"But they're threatening to imprison you," Snyder said. "It'll cast a bad light on MCC."

John bit into his lower lip until it almost bled. "Look, if you're trying to tell me I need to back down on this and cave in to the government's threats, then I'm not your man. You'll have to get someone else."

"I…I didn't mean to say…I mean, you know, it was concerning. But I'm sure that in the end everything will be fine. Of course, you can be assured of our full support and cooperation."

They returned to the rest of the group, still gathered under the trees. During the remainder of the visit, nothing more was said about the government demands. John breathed easier than he had since Snyder showed up. What the future held was unclear, but at least he had MCC's support.

SIXTEEN

"**S**chmidt is a loose cannon. Completely reckless and irresponsible. By ignoring the government's mandate, he's putting in jeopardy everything MCC has done in Paraguay." Bill Snyder folded his arms across his chest. It had been a month since he'd returned from his Paraguay trip, but the MCC Executive Committee was only now convening. "My recommendation is that we cut off all funding and shut down the leper colony until John acquires the required credentials."

Orie was silent. John's behaviors were sometimes outlandish. But the man's intentions were honorable. In fact, Orie had never known anyone as principled as John when it came to doing God's work by helping the poor and the sick. But he'd seen it before: In the process of doing what he felt was "right," John sometimes destroyed important relationships. What should be done about this latest fiasco?

"What if we give him a bit more time? Maybe he and the government officials will work something out?" Orie looked around the conference table. The men's faces were grim. For them, there was no other option than to pull the MCC and ALM funding for Km. 81.

"I'll write the letter," Orie said, rising slowly and leaving the room. He hated what he had to do. Maybe it was time to retire.

Clara noticed that after Bill Snyder's visit, John seemed more preoccupied than ever. He spent many hours at his desk, poring over the various documents MCC initially had drawn up in proposing the leprosy colony at Km. 81.

Late one evening, she tapped him on the shoulder. "What are you looking for in those papers, John? It's time for bed. You need to get some rest."

"There has to be a way to continue this work," he said, tapping his pen against the desk. "All the Paraguayan government really wants from us are payoffs, which I'll refuse until my dying day."

Clara had heard all this before. Besides that, several of the most respected physicians in Asunción had repeatedly told them not to worry about government approval because in Paraguay it was not worth the paper it was written on. But still...

John looked up, and Clara saw the familiar glint in his eyes, which both encouraged and frightened her. He slammed his fists on the desk. "Sure, there's a chance the government will force us to leave. But better to be cut out knowing that we've tried to do the right thing, than to be a disgrace to our Lord by engaging in bribery."

Clara turned to prepare for bed. Of course, bribery was a sin if that's really what the government officials were after. But wasn't it also sinful to disregard government requirements and the instructions from MCC to comply with them? Despite the early February heatwave that didn't break even at night, Clara shivered under the bedsheet.

It was after 2:00 in the morning when she heard John approach the bedroom.

"John, you have to stop this—" Clara propped herself up on her elbow.

"I have a plan." John's voice was urgent. "I know what we can do. How we can continue to serve here."

Clara sat up.

The words tumbled out of him. "I've always thought of our program as reaching many people. I still think that's an important goal, but what about helping suffering patients, one by one? We need to get out there into rural areas to find and treat individual patients. Our work out in the backcountry won't be hindered by the Health Department. They won't even notice."

Clara was now fully awake. "But how can we get to areas where there aren't even roads? How will we know how to find them? And how would we even talk to them?"

"I've been thinking about some of those things, and I have a plan. But some of this we'll just have to learn as we get into it."

John described his idea of holding clinics in several towns in the area, but also riding out from there into the countryside to find patients in their homes. They would establish a clinic in Barrero Grande at Km. 72 where the asphalt road from Asunción ended, and another one in Coronel Oviedo (100 kilometers to the east) and Villarrica (fifty kilometers south of Coronel Oviedo). He'd met someone named Don Florencio Boggs looking for work, who spoke both Spanish and Guaraní.

"We'll ride out into the campo together," John said, blowing out the kerosene lamp.

Long after John was asleep, Clara lay wide awake, imagining the many dangers he would surely encounter in Paraguay's wild back country. Was this God's will or simply the iron will of her husband?

On a cloudy early Tuesday morning in mid-March, John and Don Florencio threw bags of provisions across their horses and began the trek from Coronel Oviedo into the countryside.

They stopped mid-afternoon to eat sandwiches they had packed, and to give their horses a break. Dark clouds began to form, and thunder rumbled from a distance.

They were still sixty kilometers away from the area where someone named Don Francisco Fernández lived. They had learned that he made his living by selling wood to Coronel Oviedo, and that he might agree to help them find patients in his area. At their rate of five kilometers an hour, they'd have to stop for the night somewhere midway.

They had planned to sleep under the stars, but since the rain was coming, they stopped in front of a dilapidated hut and clapped. Don Florencio explained who they were. A woman with no front teeth, wearing a tattered dress, invited them to come under her thatched roof. She had nothing to eat but generously shared her yerba tea. At night, she offered them her bed, which was a pile of sacks in one corner.

John lay on the sacks next to Florencio, listening to the thunderclaps and watching streaks of lightning flash across the sky. He pulled his raingear over his face to keep off the rain falling through the holes in the roof. He wished the folks at MCC and ALM, sitting in their fancy offices, could see the plight of these poor people. And the generosity.

It rained all night and into the next day. The lowlands were completely flooded, but the woman said they'd get through, with a bit of a detour that she described to them. John and Florencio set out in the rain. Other than getting soaked, the first three hours were uneventful.

They emerged from a patch of forest, and suddenly before them lay a sea of water. A narrow line of brushy trees protruded from the middle of the water, suggesting where the opposite bank of the lake normally lay. Florencio prodded his horse into the water ahead of John. When they reached the deepest water at the edge of the trees, Florencio's horse lost its footing, sprang into the air, and crashed back down. Florencio tried to dismount, but his foot was caught in the stirrups. John held his breath. If the horse continued to be restless, the worst could happen in this deep water. But the horse quieted down, and Florencio was able to release his foot.

"Let's try a path off to the side," John yelled out to his companion. Florencio walked cautiously in the waist-high water, pulling his horse along behind him. John followed, gently nudging his own horse forward. For a moment, Florencio lost his footing, but reached for a branch and was able to cross the torrent, his horse still behind him.

Then John watched in horror as—facing the steep bank on the other side—Florencio's horse got wedged against a tree trunk and fell back into the water. John dismounted, tied up his horse, and waded through the water to help Florencio. The water was deep enough that they could pull and push the horse around, but every time they got it halfway up the bank, the horse fell back. The animal seemed completely helpless. Finally, they both gave it a large shove, and the horse began to swim. John's horse had similar difficulties, but they eventually got to the other side of the lake and were able to move on through the muddy terrain.

They continued to ride in the rain. Was all this worth it for the possibility of just a few patients? John shook the water off his hat. This wasn't only for the few patients they might find. The point was to protect the entire surroundings against this disease by controlling it in the whole area. Besides, this was the command from his Lord. Jesus was his example, going out to find the one lost sheep.

John and Florencio arrived in the general area where they believed Don Francisco Fernández lived and stopped a few times to ask for directions before they found him. After a bit of conversation, Don Francisco agreed to put his wood storage shed at their disposal for medical consultations and for the two of them to sleep.

When asked if there were any people in the area with a skin malady, Don Francisco laughed and said, "Oh yes, we have *nambi tortillas* here."

John looked questioningly at his companion.

"It's half Guaraní and half Spanish for 'pancake ears,'" Florencio said.

Francisco told them where to find one of them named Santa Cruz, about a two-hour horseback ride away. "But be careful," Don Francisco said. "Señor Santa Cruz does not go to sleep without his revolver, and he knows how to use it."

John and Florencio found Santa Cruz's place at the end of a swampy camp hidden in a clump of forest. A man sat on the ground near the hut. There was no doubt that he had an advanced stage of leprosy, with large nodules on his face and deep bloody ulcers on both legs.

A woman emerged from the hut when John and Florencio rode onto the grounds. "Get away from here," she said, throwing a sack over the man's legs.

"Please tell them we are here to help," John said to his companion. "We're not here to haul him off to a colony."

Don Florencio explained why they were here; that this was a doctor who would take care of Santa Cruz's wounds and let him stay in his home. The couple continued to look at them suspiciously.

"Let's sit for a while, just talk with them," John said, squatting on the ground next to Santa Cruz. After a while, the couple began to relax, eventually allowing John to examine and care for the patient.

As they rode away, John smiled and patted his horse. Those two people found hope and courage today, two things more important than any medicine.

They spent the next several days riding out from Don Francisco's place, examining people who had come into contact with Santa Cruz, and asking others along the way if they knew anyone who was sick. On Saturday, they began their journey home, spending one more night sleeping under the stars, and arriving Sunday morning in Coronel Oviedo.

The six-day trip resulted in one new leprosy patient and the examination of twenty-one relatives and acquaintances. John wished he could do much more. But they had brought relief and hope to a suffering individual. This was what he was here to do.

Clara was on the veranda of their home when John returned. She saw the lightness in his step. Something deep inside her ached. She wished she didn't have tell him what she was about to say.

"This is how we can make a difference, Clara. You should have seen the look on their faces when they learned that I was there to help them, not lock them up," John said, grinning.

"John. Come inside. We've received a letter from Orie."

She watched as John read out loud:

When I visited Km. 81 for the inauguration last January 1953, the status of the development and the stated goals and planning seemed satisfactorily clear and mutually understood.

John looked up and shrugged, as though wondering why Clara was making a big deal out of it. He continued to read.

Now, over a year later, the Executive Committee does not
sense the same unanimous clarity, for which reasons our
Executive Committee felt (A) That we could not approach
the American Leprosy Missions for their 1954 committed
share of the costs and (B) we should not proceed with
further development of the leprosy project until this clarity
again evolves.

John pursed his lips. "Why doesn't he just write in plain language
'We no longer have any confidence in you or your work?'"

The remainder of the letter reiterated that, based on Bill Snyder's
recommendation, MCC and ALM were cutting off funding for the
leprosy work, and no further development should take place until an
agreement was reached with the Paraguayan government.

John stood in front of Clara, clasping the letter in his hands. His
silence said it all. This betrayal cut deeper than just the loss of funding,
although that was worrisome as well. How would they survive? Were
they supposed to just pack up and leave? But it was the vote of no
confidence that really hurt, especially after Snyder had assured them of
MCC's support. If only MCC and ALM could be made to understand
that John had found a way to treat leprosy patients completely apart
from the government's restrictions.

Clara had never felt more compassion for her man than in this
moment, witnessing his complete devastation. She wanted to offer
words of encouragement, but there were none. She watched John turn
and briskly walk toward the clinic construction site.

The next few days and nights were silent and tense in the Schmidt
home. The children seemed to sense that something terrible had
happened and stayed out of the way. John had still not spoken to
Clara about the letter. But she knew he was thinking of little else.
Sometimes, in the middle of the night, she heard him pacing back

and forth on the veranda. And his body was even more rigid than usual. When she reached out to him, he tensed and pulled back like a wounded animal.

"John, we need to talk about this," Clara finally said. The children had left the breakfast table, and their maid was clearing away the dishes.

"I've written a letter to Bill Snyder that I'd like you to type." John said, handing her two sheets of paper.

Clara's tears made it hard to focus her vision on the words she was typing:

> I was frank in telling you how I stood on the issue of government recognition, and you seemed to agree with me. When you were here, you assured us that everything was going fine. I find out months later that you were not frank, nor man enough to express your thoughts, but used underhanded, and in my way of looking at it, very un-Christian methods of shutting us down.

John ended the letter with:

> I don't ask for any apologies or statement about your sincerity. The relationship of our project to MCC after your visit to South America speaks louder than words.

Without telling John, Clara added a P.S. at the end of the letter:

> Today we are courageous despite the odds. With a heavy sense of responsibility, we are looking for patients out in the back woods. We understand your decision. It was the way it was done that almost shattered our faith. Clara.

Clara dreaded bringing up the conversation about sending John Russell and Elisabeth to the Chaco for their schooling, but they had to confront it. "We need to decide what we're going to do. John, please talk to me."

The little schoolroom on the station only offered studies to the third grade, so they were left with no option but to leave the station or place the older children in school elsewhere. A couple they knew from their time in the Chaco had agreed to keep the two children during the school year. But were they going ahead with that plan? Were they even continuing their work?

For the past week, John had sat at his desk, reading, making notes, and manipulating numbers. This morning, he told Clara he'd found a record of an MCC check for $725 from a few months ago that they had not yet collected from the MCC office in Asunción.

"We're going to keep doing our work," John said, looking up from his papers. "We'll cash the last MCC check, and we have enough donations from family and churches back home to continue as we are until the end of the year. By then, based on our service to leprosy patients, we'll have local officials on our side, if not the Health Ministry." Almost as an afterthought, he added, "So yes. We must take the children to the Chaco."

"It will be hard to let them go," Clara said. Just yesterday, she'd watched John Russell jump up onto his beloved horse and had marveled at how tall he was. The children were growing up so fast, and now she had to send two of them away. She prayed for strength.

John went on as though he hadn't heard her. "We can recruit more volunteer help while we're in the Chaco. I also want to meet with colony leaders about ideas I have to build a road from the colonies to Asunción."

It had been John's dream since his early years in the Chaco to build a road connecting the colonies, located about 250 miles northwest of Asunción, to the market trade center of the country. The products brought in from the Chaco currently came to market via a grueling haul by truck, rail, and river freighter, which was destructive to the goods and expensive for the Mennonites. The colonies were struggling economically. Without a road, no amount of relief and development efforts would do any good. He just needed to get it through their heads that the three colonies would have to work together to make this happen.

Leaving the younger children with their maid, John and Clara packed John Russell and Elisabeth into the Jeep and headed for the Chaco. On the way, John stopped by the MCC office in Asunción to pick up the last MCC check.

He entered the office, mumbled a greeting to Chris Graber, the interim Paraguay representative for MCC, and went directly to the safe in the back corner. There was no check.

John turned toward Graber. "Chris, there's supposed to be a check here for Km. 81. Do you know what happened to it?"

Graber pulled a notebook from the drawer and ran his fingers down one of the pages. "All I can tell you is that it's among the list of checks that we received here at the MCC office. Beyond that, I don't know. But I can check with Akron National Bank to see if all of the drafts have been returned."

John left the office, shaking his head. $725 couldn't have just slipped away accidentally. He remembered the secretive meetings between Graber and Snyder earlier in the year, leading up to Snyder's recommendation that the leprosy project be put on hold. As was so often the case, he thought back to Ana's words: *Things are not always as they seem.*

When they finally arrived in the Fernheim colony, John dropped Clara and the little ones at the children's new home and continued on to meet with Konrad Wolf. The small flow of volunteer workers to Km. 81 from the Chaco had completely stopped. He figured it was all part of Snyder's work. Maybe the whole debacle with MCC was giving the colonists an excuse to hide out and not show up to serve.

It took Wolf very little time to get to the point. "The people of the colonies are not willing to support an illegal operation that you are using to get rich by building a cattle ranch."

John was no longer surprised by this accusation. "Konrad, we must listen to Christ's commandments, rather than the commands of a corrupt government." He stopped, hearing the sharpness in his own voice. More quietly, he said, "We're grateful for the open hearts that have supported us so far. But we need young men for construction, planting, fence repair, brickmaking..."

Even as he spoke, John knew his words were futile. He left without mentioning his idea about building a road to Asunción. What was the point? The colonies would never cooperate with each other.

Clara was waiting for John at the door when he returned. "The children are playing in the back yard. I've already said goodbye... probably best to go while they're distracted," she said.

They drove down the dirt lane away from the house. In his rearview mirror, John saw Elisabeth running after the car, reaching out her arms, crying. He turned to Clara, who sat with folded hands and closed eyes.

"Stopping now would only make it harder for her," he said.

Clara nodded, tears spilling into her lap.

In May 1954, a Paraguayan coup led by Alfredo Stroessner resulted in the overthrow of the current government. The change brought in a new health minister, Dr. Enrique Arza. Initially, John was hopeful that Arza might support his medical work in the interior of Paraguay. He might even waive the government's ridiculous demands. But he soon learned that Arza was also a Colorado Party leader and had no time for dealings with a gringo doctor. He repeatedly sent John's requests to see him on to Dr. Ugarriza, his director of the Department of Lepra.

John met numerous times with Dr. Ugarriza, sharing their progress in locating new patients and treating them in their homes. In the past three months, he had examined thirty-eight leprosy cases. Last month alone, four new leprosy patients had come to ask for treatment in the consultation room in Coronel Oviedo, as word spread that it was safe to do so. Several had been sent by local doctors. Surely the director welcomed this kind of cooperation.

Dr. Ugarriza's responses puzzled John. On one hand, he acted as though John was a dangerous character. On the other hand, he asked what the total number of patients was at this time; he said he would see if he couldn't get biopsies done more cheaply; and that he would provide some data forms so John's patients would have uniform records. But bottom line, Ugarriza—like the prior administration—required that John have a certificate proving that he had taken specialized courses and had passed the exams.

John decided it was best to decline any help Ugarriza offered and to not divulge the total number of patients he was seeing. Better to duck back under the radar. After all, he was developing good relationships with several local doctors. Why ask for trouble when there was none?

SEVENTEEN

Orie Miller sat at one of the desks in what was referred to as MCC's Main House, its headquarters at 21 South 12th Street in Akron. It was a sunny, unusually warm day in May. Since it was Saturday, no one else was in the office. It felt a bit stuffy, so Orie rose to open the windows. As he looked across the lawn, he allowed himself to reminisce for a moment about the early days, when there was no Main House, just the little corner office in his own home a little over a mile away. Those years had been difficult, but also simpler in many ways. Orie sighed, pushed his black glasses further up his nose, and turned back to the papers on the desk.

In preparation for his upcoming trip to Paraguay, Orie had dug up all the correspondence he could find between Paraguay and MCC headquarters in Akron. Schmidt had been carrying on the work at Km. 81 for over a year without any funding from them. Orie trusted Graber and it was time to visit him to get to the bottom of what was going on down there. He knew there'd been an exchange of letters between Graber and Bill Snyder. But Orie had been too occupied with MCC work in Korea to pay much attention. He'd set aside this weekend to learn what he needed to know before traveling to Paraguay next month.

Orie had found a stack of letters dating from early 1954 to early 1955. He'd sorted the letters by date. The first letter in the pile, from Schmidt to Snyder, written on March 16, 1954, felt like a punch in Orie's gut, especially when he read the words:

> ... very un-Christian methods of shutting us down.

All correspondence from Paraguay seemed to stop after this exchange—until a half-dozen letters from Graber addressed to Snyder, all written between January and March of 1955—just a few months ago. Orie examined them one by one:

> Jan 8, 1955: It appears that the Schmidts do not keep close tabs on their monies. Mrs. Schmidt must do the bookkeeping and keep up with the rather free practices of her husband ... Maybe this experience of missing funds will impress upon John the need for a better system of accounting for his funds.

What experience? What missing funds? Orie scanned the next letter, from Graber to Snyder, written three weeks later.

> Jan 29, 1955: Have you ever thought of making the Km. 81 farm a Brook Lane for mental health services in Paraguay? It will definitely not be used for a leper colony.

What was the land at Km. 81 currently used for, if not for a leper colony? Maybe John really was shutting down the leper operation. But then again, the next letter seemed to suggest otherwise.

> Mar 17, 1955: John is getting some sizable gifts directly from friends and congregations in the states. He and Clara are very good at propaganda.

John and Clara were the only missionaries Orie had ever known who raised more money than they spent on the mission field. But what were they using the money for?

What came next troubled Orie the most.

> Dr. John cannot think or act in a continuing clear line. He jumps from one idea to another and from one approach to

another. I feel this is part of the reason he has not gotten
further in his government approval.

There are three programs going on at Km 81:

1. The leprosy program – which can be run with a much smaller budget.
2. The volunteer program for colony Mennonites - a luxury item and very expensive both in terms of money and energy.
3. The farm – which has nothing to do with either number one or number two except to provide some work for number two.

It suits John's personality to play between these programs
and thereby the whole issue is beclouded.

Orie smiled when he read Snyder's response to this letter:

You have a tough personnel problem, Brother Graber. I went
through similar experiences with John, and it is not easy.
But I made the mistake of thinking John was not essential
to the success of our work in Paraguay. Don't make the
same mistake.

The last letter from Graber referred back to the missing money
business, emphatically denying John's accusations that MCC had
spent the $725 meant for Km. 81 on other projects. Graber wrote:

Read this letter and then destroy it. I have already
destroyed the duplicate from our files here.

Why had Snyder not destroyed the letter, as Graber requested? And
why had Graber asked him to destroy it? The letter ended with:

I would certainly not recommend any enlargement of the
program under John's direction. But Orie and I will have to
go into all of this when he comes.

They certainly would.

On a trip into the back country in early May, John and Florencio rode into a deserted clearing that surrounded a small thatched-roof lean-to of about two square meters. In one corner, on a pile of filthy rags, lay a thin, scabby, drawn-together heap of misery, hardly recognizable as a person. When Florencio asked about her among the neighbors, they said "Oh that's Doña Ramona. Nobody goes near her."

John very slowly knelt next to the sick woman. His back had been giving him a lot of trouble lately, making it difficult for him to get to the ground. The woman appeared to be around the age of forty. Her arms and legs were covered with open wounds. Her face was one big crusty scab.

John looked around him, spotted a small pan and heated water on the embers from a fire in the middle of the hut. He tried to clean her bloody limbs but stopped when she let out a thin wail. There were too many raw wounds on her emaciated skeleton to do anything about cleaning them out here. He poured a bit of warm soup from a thermos he'd brought with him, and fed it to her, a few drops at a time. Her blistered lips opened just enough to take in the broth very slowly. Kneeling there beside Doña Ramona, John thought about the prayerful intention he set for himself every morning before starting the day: *We must give these patients the courage to live by showing them love without wanting anything in return.* He thought he glimpsed a life-force shining from the woman's sunken red eyes.

When John rose from the woman's side, he spotted a young boy standing at the edge of the clearing. They learned that he was Doña Ramona's twelve-year old son, who showed early signs of leprosy. He seemed bewildered and was mumbling something.

"They don't have any galletas left to eat," Florencio translated.

John and Florencio arranged to get Doña Ramona and her boy to the leprosy station on an ox-drawn cart. After a week of care and feeding, the oozing boils began to heal, and she became stronger. But that didn't last. She soon came down with another case of high fever and new boils.

Doña Ramona and her child were John and Clara's first patients-in-residence. The guesthouse they had begun to build for such cases was not nearly ready. But even in its unfinished state, it was a safe shelter for Km. 81's first two guests.

Orie emerged from the aircraft and breathed in the smoky air. He loved visiting Paraguay in the winter and made a mental note to avoid traveling south in the summer months, if possible, especially in January and February. But then again, he would probably not make many more of these trips.

Graber was waiting for Orie in the terminal building. They exchanged small talk while walking to the car.

"I am very sorry about your father's death, Brother Orie," Graber said. "I regret that I could not be there for his funeral. I always regarded your father as a lifelong friend."

"Thank you," Orie said, remembering how much his father had appreciated Graber's contributions to Mennonite higher education.

When they arrived at the MCC office, Orie dropped his bags in one of the guestrooms upstairs and then went back down to find Graber. "As you know, I'm mainly here to determine what should be done about the leper station," he said, taking a seat across from Graber.

Graber smoothed his tie and sat up straight. "It's an expensive setup and Schmidt is spending most of his time running the farm rather than healing lepers. He'd like to develop the farm into a full-blown dairy and cattle ranch. But what about our mission to the sick?"

"You may not know this, Chris, but I and the rest of the Executive Committee requested that John develop a farm, which we believed could someday be self-sustaining," Orie said, wondering why Graber seemed so on edge.

"It's a financial disaster. There have been missing funds. John and Clara keep their personal cash and MCC cash in the same drawer, even after I told them to get a better handle on the money situation. With your MCC shortage of funds for other necessary work, I feel you will have to put Km. 81 on a completely self-sustaining basis or close it out."

"Tell me about the missing funds," Orie said.

Graber explained that a check had gone missing, and he was sure it was due to John's sloppy money management. "John blamed us here in Asunción, saying we were responsible for the shortage, that we were careless with the money or used it for other MCC programs. But in the end, he offered to donate their piano and a microscope to MCC to make up for the lost money. To me, that proves that it was his mistake."

Orie raised his eyebrows but said nothing. Clearly, this man did not know Schmidt at all.

Graber continued, "I saw in the Executive Committee meeting minutes that Dr. Herbert, John's brother, is paying $200 per month support for John, with a $2,200 gift for the children. Is this an income tax deduction through MCC? These gifts help MCC carry the load, but they seem a bit excessive to me."

Orie stared at Graber through his thick glasses and frowned. Was Graber jealous of John's ability to raise money outside of MCC? "I see," he said.

Graber sank back into his chair. "I am merely reporting these things so that you can decide what should be done with Km. 81."

John and Clara had finished breakfast and were sitting with their children around the table on the veranda. Clara smiled. Even John Russell and Elisabeth were back home, after a year of schooling in the Chaco, resuming their studies at home via correspondence courses. It was hard to find the time to supervise their schoolwork, but she was grateful to have them home again.

Clara had read the morning devotions, and John was now praying, as he did every morning after breakfast. "I ask Thee to bestow wisdom on President Eisenhower, as he and the other leaders meet in Geneva." He continued his prayer for peace in the world, for the health of family members back home, for the poor and the sick, and for each of his children. Even with her eyes closed, Clara could sense that her youngsters were fidgeting, as they always did during John's long prayers. But it was teaching them to live a devout and prayerful life.

"And finally, dear Lord, we ask Thy blessing on the visit with Orie Miller. May Thy will be done in all our deliberations. Amen."

The children ran from the table, leaving John and Clara alone. "I'm afraid Snyder will have poisoned Orie against us again," John said. "And if MCC continues to cut off our funding, we'll have no choice but to call it quits."

Call it quits? They were treating almost seventy patients now. And the farm was flourishing. "Surely the progress we've made speaks for itself," Clara said.

"I just don't trust Snyder one bit. He'd turn all of this progress into wrongdoing if he could."

"That was a year ago," Clara said softly.

"How did you do it all?" Orie Miller had just arrived at Km. 81. John stood with him in front of the newly constructed dining/assembly room.

"Special funds from our home churches helped," John said. "And our Chaco Mennonites have been more and more supportive after seeing what we're doing here. We now have almost fifty people living on the station, about half of them short-term volunteers."

"Well, this all looks quite different than it did the last time I was here," Orie said.

That sounded hopeful. "Come. Let me give you a tour." John led Orie to his Jeep.

They drove past fields of corn, sorghum, and rice. John pointed out the trees he had recently planted: paraíso, mulberry, tangerine, orange, peach, lemon, grapefruit, and plums.

"We have cattle and chickens. And we now even have sixteen hogs," John said with a grin as they passed the livestock area.

"In our ambulatory service, we have some cases that are so wretched that they need help getting started on the right track. Also, in the past we had to send our acute leprosy cases home, because we had no place to keep them. Now we're building this guesthouse which will have three rooms big enough for two people in each room."

The 300-meter dirt road leading from the station's main compound to the leprosy guesthouse was lined with rows of newly planted Linden and eucalyptus trees. "I learned when I was in Brazil that these trees provide a protective barrier between the sick and the well zones of a leprosy colony," John said. When he saw Orie's quizzical look, he added, "Of course we don't have a colony here. This guest area is being built up like a small Paraguayan *chacra*, so patients can grow some of their own food. It has no resemblance to a colony or even a hospital."

"John, let me get to the point. We must decide about MCC and ALM's future involvement in this work. Are you still operating without government permission?"

"There's nothing new on that score." John frowned. So that was still their bottom line. He pulled up next to the guesthouse, stopped the car, and turned in his seat to face Orie. "As I said, we're not focused on building up a colony, so government officials are pretty much leaving us alone. We're treating nearly seventy leprosy patients now, but most live in their homes, out in the backcountry, somewhere in the 100-mile-long by forty-mile-wide area we cover." John got out of the vehicle. "I want you to meet someone."

John introduced Orie to Doña Ramona, who sat on the veranda of the guesthouse drinking *tereré* (a Paraguayan tea sipped through a metal straw) with Don Florencio. Her body was covered with scabs, but she flashed a toothless grin when the two men walked toward her. Don Florencio translated as Doña Ramona talked about her prior living conditions and her lifelong fear of being locked up. They described how they had found her and the boy.

John reminded Orie that leprosy patients still went to great lengths to never be found. "I firmly believe that the patients we're now treating will be good witnesses for our work," he said as they walked back and climbed into the Jeep. "They'll tell their countrymen about our concern for their wellbeing, and people will begin to trust us. My dream is that someday patients will come to us to look for treatment rather than hide when we come near them."

While they drove back to the main compound, John explained that Km. 81 also held a general medical clinic three days a week for anyone needing medical care in the surrounding community. The patient load was steadily increasing, and along with it, the trust of their neighbors.

During all of this, Orie said very little. John parked the Jeep in front of his home. Clara was on the veranda, placing a large pot of Borscht on the table, which was set for lunch.

"Where are your children?" Orie asked after greeting Clara.

"Our maid Aggie has them hoeing in the pineapple patch today," Clara said. "Welcome. Please, have a seat."

During lunch, John and Clara continued to describe to Orie all the progress that had been made on the station since he was last there. Km. 81 had grown into a cohesive Mennonite community, and they felt personally responsible for the spiritual and emotional development of the volunteer youth. In the evenings, when there was not a Bible study or prayer meeting, Clara gave them piano and typing lessons. Clara also talked about the Bible programs they held numerous times a week in the neighboring villages. They hoped to soon have a baptism service for new believers.

"We are getting more and more recognition," Clara said. "Our guest book has almost one hundred entries from visitors just in the past year." She described the quarterly magazine *Im Dienste der Liebe* they distributed as largely responsible for spreading awareness and raising support both in the Mennonite colonies of Paraguay and in the North.

Orie asked many questions but didn't offer any opinions. John couldn't make out what he was thinking. Would MCC really allow the lack of government permission to prevent them from carrying out the work that no one else was doing for these poor people?

EIGHTEEN

Before leaving Paraguay, Orie had told John and Clara that he needed to confer with the committee before deciding about MCC's future support. There was a time when he would have made such a decision on his own. But the MCC organization was bigger now, and he was nearing retirement. It was best to decide these things as a committee.

Orie scheduled a meeting. Snyder, Orie's right-hand man, and the person he'd chosen to succeed him as executive director when he retired, entered the room before the other committee members arrived. He put a stack of papers on the table and sat down across from Orie.

"I've read through your Paraguay report, Orie, and I am relieved to see that our initial investments in the leper project have not been in vain. It is quite remarkable what the Schmidts have pulled off this year without support from us or ALM. The question is, will ALM be willing to get back on board with the project?"

Orie's head jerked up. Had he heard Snyder correctly?

Under his breath, Snyder mumbled, "Clearly, I underestimated John…"

Before Orie could respond, the remaining committee members arrived, and the meeting began. Everyone had read Orie's report, and after a brief discussion, they unanimously voted to reinstate MCC's support of the leper project in Paraguay.

"Now we wait to hear from ALM," Orie said. "As you know, there's been a change in leadership. Dr. Kellersberger has retired, and Reverend Harold Henderson is the new general secretary. Although Henderson oversaw a leprosy home in Korea, he is not a physician and therefore may be more amenable to…" Orie paused and chuckled. "… to some of John Schmidt's outlandish ideas about treating people in their homes rather than building a colony."

Nearly two months after Orie's visit, John and Clara finally received a letter from him. Clara had just finished filing notes on the last patient of the morning, a child with severe malnutrition. She sat on a footstool in the shade of a Linden tree in front of the clinic building, peeling an orange, when one of the co-workers brought mail from Asunción.

The envelope contained two letters. Clara quickly scanned the first one, which indicated MCC's support for their work.

She called out, "John, it's good news."

By the time John emerged from the clinic, Clara had read the second letter, this one from ALM, restating their concerns. The main problem was John's heavy involvement in building up a farm when there were only two patients in residence. She handed him the letters.

"They continue to think of this as a colony," John said, throwing them on the ground.

"It's so great that MCC will support us. We just need to explain things to ALM. They continue to think as they do because they haven't heard from us directly about our progress. Let's write a long description of exactly what we're doing and how it's working."

That afternoon, she and John composed a report detailing their work. It began with:

From your correspondence, we gather you think of our establishment at Km. 81 as a leprosy colony. Our aim is to treat as many cases as possible by the ambulatory method, and to not have more than possibly 5% of the total number of cases treated, or less, if possible, who will need a period of internment at our quarters at Km. 81.

The report listed several disadvantages of an ambulatory treatment approach, including the intense labor and expense required to locate cases, and the inability to have mass meetings. Also, treating patients on an individual basis meant that there was no opportunity for evangelization or health education in large groups.

The advantages of ambulatory services included keeping patients with their families, reducing patients' fear of starting treatment, and fewer room and board expenses compared to a colony. And in the long run, ambulatory treatment would be more effective in lowering instances of the disease since patients would be more willing to seek treatment. The letter included statistics on Brazil's extensive system of leper colonies instituted in 1924. At that time, the occurrence of leprosy was .07% out of 1,000 with five million inhabitants. By the mid-1950s, it was 2.86% out of 1,000 with ten million inhabitants. Even Dr. Lauro Souza, the internationally known Brazilian leprologist, had admitted that the millions of dollars Brazil spent for colonies had not helped to cut down the frequency of leprosy in the country.

Clara read what they had put together and scratched her head. This was all good information. But it didn't give ALM a feel for what these poor people were going through. They needed to include some true stories.

Late into that night, Clara sat at her typewriter, creating detailed descriptions of Doña Ramona and her boy. She went on to note how important it was for John to see the home environment of the patients to help them live a healthier lifestyle, for example, by showing them where and how to dig toilet holes and plant gardens. She ended with:

When we lovingly help them in their homes, these people become friendly and more trusting instead of suspicious. So, despite the extra cost and work of ambulatory service, we think it is worth it. What could be closer to the service Jesus commanded in the story of the good Samaritan?

In October, John and Clara heard back from ALM:

We can hardly thank you enough for the admirable letter. We now understand, as we have not understood before, exactly your purpose with respect to ambulatory patients and the way the fixed institution will be an accessory to it and a "home base" for the workers.

ALM was back on board.

By that time, their leprosy cases had steadily increased, bringing the number of patients under treatment to well over a hundred. John found that most of them showed improvement after a few months, which increased the probability that some of these patients and their families would be healthy enough to come see him at the Saturday clinic for further treatment.

Being of the poorest of the poor and utterly deserted, these people continued to express surprise, even shock, that John and Clara had an interest in them. Though they were unable to pay for the services, they occasionally brought tokens of their gratitude. Just the other day, after John amputated a woman's disease-ridden leg, her husband offered him a pair of white rabbits, which were very rare in Paraguay. John brought them home to the delight of five-year-old Marlena.

Most patients, however, were not able to travel. So, John continued to visit them in their homes once a month, in addition to searching for new patients. Each trek into the backcountry took numerous days. Between those lengthy trips, running the general clinics three times a week (which Clara managed when he was out in the bush), and the leprosy clinic every Saturday, as well as taking care of the station personnel and farm, John was so stretched that some days he hardly had the strength to continue.

To recover some of his energy, and to escape the heat of midday, he and Clara began to lie down after lunch for a brief siesta. One afternoon, just moments after he dozed off, a loud crash and boisterous laughter awakened him. He pulled on his trousers and rushed out of the room just in time to see his four oldest children, now ranging in age from seven to eleven, giggling and fleeing into the woods that surrounded their house.

"They hid my bunnies," wailed Marlena, throwing herself on the floor of the veranda.

"Don't ever make noise like that again when we're trying to rest. Ever!"

When he returned to their room, Clara was sitting up in bed. "John, this is too much. We've talked about the fact that we need a second doctor here to do some of the work. You know it's just going to keep growing. And you're already doing so much more than you should. You're losing weight. And you look frazzled all the time."

"I'm sorry, Clara. I hate it when I yell like that, but those children sometimes…"

"Shh…" Clara pulled him down on the bed. For the next half hour, John forgot about the stress of the work.

MCC agreed that another doctor was needed, especially for the long trips into the interior. John knew of a Dr. Joachim Walter, whom he'd met during one of his meetings with health officials in Asunción. When he approached the doctor about joining him in the work at Km. 81, Walter agreed. John worried that Walter was not a Mennonite, not even a Christian as far as he could tell. And he smoked. But he was a leprologist well trained in Germany, and the needs were sufficiently great that John believed he could overlook the man's flaws.

The medical work on the station ramped up even more quickly in the coming months. At the leprosy consultations in their Saturday clinic, they were seeing up to a dozen patients. In the last three months of 1955, they treated nearly seventy leprosy patients at the station, and had examined twice that number of neighbors and relatives. Local doctors from the villages in the surrounding area were even beginning to send leprosy patients to Km. 81.

The patient guesthouse was complete, and was now full, housing six patients who were all progressing well. The idea was for them to be as independent as possible, with their own milk cows and vegetable gardens. They prepared their meals with additional food from the station kitchen. Clara and Schwester Neti visited them once or twice daily, depending on their needs.

Given that Dr. Walter now carried some of the medical load, John finally had more time to devote to developing the farm at Km. 81, as well as to seriously begin building up the cattle ranch that had long been discussed but never properly implemented. They had 3,000 acres, of which only a portion was used for the buildings and the farm. The rest was rolling pasture. Paraguayans were beginning to move onto the unused land as squatters. When Orie Miller was at Km. 81 back in 1953 for the inauguration ceremony, he'd suggested that it might make sense to fence the property and for mission people working at the station to invest their personal funds in raising cattle. Until now, John had not had time to devote to this. A cattle ranch was clearly a win-win endeavor, as it would eventually provide a source of income for himself and other station workers; and it would keep squatters off the land.

It was a hot sunny day in January. John sat up straight on his horse and began to whistle *When My Baby Smiles at Me*, a tune he hadn't thought of since he was young. He rode slowly through the property, devising plans for the fencing and the cattle operation. This task was the perfect complement to the demanding medical work. Just this morning, one of his long-term patients, Raul González, who'd been progressing well for two years, had come to the clinic, his body covered with oozy boils. Relapse was so common for these poor people.

It was good to focus on new growth. John figured that was why it felt so satisfying to plant trees, grow vegetables, and raise cattle. Besides, it would be shameful to not make the most of this fertile land. He rode along one of the two streams that ran through the property. These streams would provide plenty of year-round water for the cattle. He figured the 500 acres of MCC land across the Ruta could carry from 150 to 200 head of cattle, including bulls such as Hereford, Angus or Shorthorn, which they would eventually need to buy. But about fifty native cows and three bulls would be a good start.

He planned for about 500 acres of the 2500-acre track on the station side of the Ruta to be used for another fifty head of native cows with two Brown Swiss or Milking Shorthorn bulls. They'd keep the bulls in the corral and allow the cows in only during the breeding season.

Finished with his inventory and ranch planning for the day, John turned his horse toward home. He threw his shoulders back. The breeze on his face felt soft and easy.

In that moment on his horse, with his world feeling in right order, John realized he hadn't thought about Ana for many months. He wondered how she was, especially since he'd read that Juan Perón was ousted and had escaped to Paraguay in a fishing boat. John prodded his horse into a slow gallop. *I'm just too busy to think about Ana right now.*

At the beginning of 1956, the Paraguayan Health Ministry published new regulations for the ambulatory treatment of leprosy. They decreed that the work at Km. 81 had to be overseen by a Paraguayan doctor. The health minister Dr. Enrique Arza vowed to close down all activities if they were not in compliance by February 7.

John's first reaction to the new decree was the same as it had been two years ago: "If we must put government permits ahead of God's work, I'm not the man for this job."

But everyone around him, including Dr. Walter and even Clara, counseled him to abide by the new regulations.

"We can continue this work, John," Clara said. "They're not requiring you to get the credentials. All we have to do is hire a Paraguayan doctor as director of our medical work."

John sensed that maybe this time the threat was real. If he wanted this work to continue, he probably needed to do as they requested. The worst part of this was the use of mission funds to pay a Paraguayan doctor to supervise his work. Government business was often so corrupt. And he worried that with this step they were opening the door of the mission to people who had no understanding of God's work. This could someday lead to them successfully acting against what the mission was attempting to accomplish.

In the end, John realized he could not win this fight. Dr. Eduardo Rodríguez from the Health Ministry was given the responsibility to go to Km. 81 every Saturday to oversee and report on the work.

On February 20, 1956, according to resolution Nr. 24 of the Ministry of Health, Km. 81 received official permission for the lepra work as *Dispensario Menonita*.

UNSTOPPABLE

1956-1971

"The question isn't who is going to let me; it's who is going to stop me."

– Ayn Rand

NINETEEN

By May of 1956, John and Clara's agreed-upon five-year term had nearly come to an end, and they planned to leave for the States in a few months. John had sent numerous letters to MCC, asking if they were going to be invited to return to their work at Km. 81 after the upcoming furlough. Why did they not respond? Graber was pushing to have the leprosy project taken over by a recognized Paraguayan doctor. Didn't MCC understand that this would undermine the Mennonite values and contributions foundational to the work's very existence?

John drafted a long letter to MCC restating the importance of Km. 81 as a Mennonite thank-you project for Paraguay allowing the colonists to immigrate into the country.

The leprosy program was suspended years before we began the work, and it would make us feel bad to see the work fall back again, for it has become part of us. But we don't have any pleasure in pushing this so much. We don't want to beg.

This time, Snyder's response arrived within a few weeks, indicating MCC's desire for the Schmidts to return to Paraguay after a one-year furlough. He outlined an itinerary for their travels throughout North

America. MCC wanted them to show slides, report on, and raise money for the leprosy project. From Winnipeg, Manitoba, south as far as Oklahoma and Kansas; and from California east to New York, with many stops in between, it would be nearly a full year of traveling. John and Clara agreed to the itinerary and requested that their maid Aggie, who had Canadian citizenship, be hired to stay with the children in Kansas while they traveled.

Clara folded the last piece of clothing, placed it in the suitcase and knelt on the case to close it. She shivered against the damp cold air as she sat down on the bed. She'd been on the verge of tears all day. Was it about leaving their home for a year? Was it about the extra work of sorting and packing their things? Was it that she was entering menopause? Was she ready for this new barren life phase?

Their five children were growing up so fast. Clara thought about when they were little. Where had the time gone? There was a heaviness in her chest. What had she missed while devoting herself to God's work day after day as her children grew, especially the youngest three? First baby steps. First words. Marlena was even beginning to read *Hänsel und Gretel* by herself.

Clara sighed and rose to begin packing the next case. It wouldn't get any better once they got to the States, since she and John would be traveling almost non-stop throughout the year. She would once again be forced to leave her children. Pushing away the tears, she reminded herself that she was following the Lord's will. All would be well.

Early on June 27th, the Schmidt family left Km. 81. A few hours later, they were on a Braniff flight headed north. They'd made sure they left before John Russell turned twelve on July 7, when his ticket would have doubled in price. After stops in La Paz, Panama City, and Houston, they arrived in Wichita, Kansas, where a crowd of relatives had gathered to greet them.

Their temporary home in Newton, which Herb made available to them, was a small, flat-roofed two-bedroom house across the street from a shopping center Herb owned and managed as an investment. John wished they could have found other housing—anything rather than Herb's charity. But it was their best option. He closed off the front of the house's garage and turned it into the boys' room. The children loved playing in the large parking lot across the street. And Herb offered the older ones jobs, cleaning bathrooms in the shopping center for 25 cents a week.

They had been in Kansas for only ten days when John and Clara were scheduled to attend a conference in Minnesota. Clara's brother Edwin had loaned them a Ford sedan. And they'd arranged for the children to stay with various relatives during the two weeks they'd be gone. As they left the family farmyard where their nine-year-old Wesley was staying, Clara spotted him waving at them from the top of the silo, his legs hanging over the edge. She whispered a prayer.

On their way to the conference, John and Clara stopped in at the Mayo Clinic, where they'd made appointments for routine check-ups, gratis for medical missionaries.

"That can't be." Clara had seen a doctor and gone through a battery of tests the day before. Now she sat across from him in his office.

Her doctor checked his notes. "I would say the baby is due the last week of February."

"I've had lots of spotting for about a month. I was sure it was menopause."

The doctor looked up from his notes. "Spotting? You didn't tell me about this. That's not good." He shook his head. "I'm going to have to order that you discontinue all travel after you get back to Kansas.

No more trips until the baby is born. No need for bed rest, but no traveling."

Clara hardly flinched. "That's out of the question. My husband and I have a very full itinerary coming up. We'll be traveling around the U.S. and Canada for most of the year."

"Are you telling me that you would risk the life of your unborn child?" His eyes looked accusing.

Clara fidgeted in her chair. God would protect her baby if she was doing His work. "I'll talk to my husband about this," she finally said, heading for the door.

"Yes, I also want to speak to him," he said. "Please come see me again together."

Before returning to Kansas, John and Clara picked up their maid Aggie, who had taken a bus from Winnipeg, Canada, where she'd been visiting relatives. Aggie had agreed to help, even though it was illegal for her to earn wages in the U.S.

During the drive, John was adamant about Clara not traveling after they got home. Reporting on their work was clearly important to her, but they just couldn't compromise the pregnancy. Clara countered every argument he raised, chiding him for his lack of faith that God would look after them.

John saw Aggie fidgeting in the back seat. "It's God's will that you rest, Clara," she said.

The truth was, John wanted Clara by his side as much as she wanted to be there. She was such a good storyteller. And she had worked daily with their leprosy patients on the station. She knew them more intimately than he. That mattered a lot when it came to touching people's hearts so they would give donations for the work.

"I will do my best to share with people the amazing mission work you do, with never a complaint, caring for the patients, resolving arguments among the voluntary workers, giving typing and piano lessons to station workers, and conducting Bible classes in our neighboring towns." He looked over at her. "And I will miss you."

"Well, at least I'll have Aggie," Clara said.

In the coming weeks, while John sat at his small desk in the corner of their bedroom preparing his talks and sorting through slides, Clara tried to get the children ready to start school. Her intention had been to teach them a bit of English since they spoke mainly German. They resisted her efforts, so she gave it up. They'd pick it up quickly enough in school.

Before John left for Canada, she and the children went with him to numerous churches in the region surrounding their home in Newton. They lined the five children up on stage, from oldest to youngest, and had them sing German and Spanish songs, Clara accompanying them on her autoharp. Then they would show slides and give a report of their work. At the end, just before passing around the offering plate, the children were again expected to sing a few more songs. That's when Clara was most proud of her young ones, even though it was hard to get them to line up properly and sing. Marlena was especially difficult, often pushing and kicking. She didn't seem to care that they were helping raise money for the important work back home.

Eventually it was time for John to start his travels. On a humid morning in early August, Clara stood at the front door and watched her husband pull out of their driveway. She felt more alone than she had since she was a young girl on her father's farm. But there was something else underneath the loneliness, a feeling she couldn't name.

A few weeks later, just before supper, there was a knock on the door. An official-looking man asked if a Miss Agatha Braun lived there. When Aggie appeared at the doorway, he asked for her passport. The man copied some things from the passport and asked, "Are you working?"

Clara came up from behind. "She's just helping us out. We're missionaries—"

"I am working." Aggie's voice was flat.

The officer left, saying Miss Braun would be hearing from someone very soon.

That night, Clara knelt beside her bed and prayed for forgiveness. She had been willing to *almost* lie to keep her maid. What had come over her? But how would she manage the children without Aggie? And who had told the immigration department about Aggie's work here?

The official government letter arrived a week later, stating that Aggie was in violation of immigration laws and demanding her immediate deportation to Canada.

After Clara's brother Edwin picked Aggie up to take her to the airport a few days later, Clara sank down onto the sofa. Two of the children wrestled on the floor, screaming. She knew it was time to cook something for supper. And there was laundry to do. But she just sat there.

Clara somehow made it through the evening and the next few days. To John, she wrote:

> The responsibility of the children is such a big strain for me. They try, but you know how they are when you are not around. I am very thankful I am as well as I am. Otherwise, I just couldn't take everything. I do get very nervous at times.

Numerous relatives stopped over during the next several months to bring food, help with errands, or sit with the older children as they struggled with their English homework. Clara's bleeding had stopped entirely, so she didn't understand why she was not by John's side. But there was very little she could do about it.

John was home for a few weeks during the Christmas holiday, after very successful meetings that raised significant funds for their work. Clara loved the nice watch he brought her in appreciation for all she had to do and because she couldn't travel with him. When they were all together as a family, John read from the Bible and prayed with them. Clara reminded herself that they were still a very united family, and God was looking after them.

John left again mid-January to visit churches throughout the Midwest. The icy gray roads matched his mood. He worried about Clara. Before leaving, he'd sat down with John Russell and Elisabeth, and they solemnly promised to behave and take care of Momma. But this was all too much for Clara, and it would only get worse during the next six weeks or so until the baby came.

In between his many programs, sometimes more than one in a day, John wrote Clara letters of encouragement as often as he could. He'd scheduled a free week to be back in Newton at the end of February for the birth of their sixth child. He was there when the baby was born at 4:15 a.m. on Sunday, March 3, a healthy blond, blue-eyed girl. They named her Mary Lou.

After a few more months on the road, nearly a year after coming to the U.S., John packed up his family of eight to return to their work in Paraguay.

The MCC station wagon entered the Km. 81 grounds on the chilly evening of July 9, 1957. A group of station workers had gathered in the meeting hall to welcome them. Despite the warm embraces, Clara sensed that something was wrong. A kind of quiet desperation hung in the air.

Finally, Clara took Aggie aside. Aggie had returned from Canada a few weeks ago and would know what was going on. "Where are the rest of our workers, Aggie? And why does everyone seem so nervous?"

Clara's brow twisted into deep creases as she listened to Aggie describe that almost a third of the Mennonite workers had left during the past year. Many of the crops had died, livestock had dwindled, and morale at the station was at an all-time low. Aggie said she didn't know why.

Later that night, lying next to John, Clara conveyed what Aggie had told her.

"I'll get to the bottom of this." John's voice held the kind of edge that nearly always led to some sort of confrontation.

Clara sighed into her pillow. It was good to be home. But why couldn't there be at least one peaceful day?

"Why didn't you write to let us know that so many of our Mennonite workers were leaving the station?" John glared at Dr. Walter from across the desk in the clinic. "And why did they leave?"

Dr. Walter frowned and shrugged his shoulders. "They were volunteers. They must have had other plans."

"That's not what I heard." John spat out the words. "I've been told that the workers left Km. 81 because they believed it wasn't the Lord's work if you, a non-Christian, was leading it."

"I guess that's their right," Walter said.

This was the last straw. He needed to get Walter out of here. But first, he must focus on getting the work back on track.

"We're going to get things back in order here," John said. "And we'll start with the medical work. I see from the records that many of our patients in the backcountry have not been seen for months. You will resume the monthly trips to each of our outposts."

Walter rose and pulled a pack of cigarettes from his pocket as he walked out of the clinic.

"And you will not smoke on these premises." John's voice was harsh.

"These are not your premises." Walter cupped his hands around a cigarette and lit it.

John clenched his hands into fists and strode out of the clinic. He would write to Orie about Walter. His insubordinate behavior was not tolerable. He had to go.

During the next few months, John spent every waking hour trying to re-energize Km. 81, beginning with the medical program. He sat through numerous lengthy meetings in Asunción with members of the Health Ministry. Together, they devised and implemented a plan of mass screening for leprosy patients—especially children—throughout the Departamento de Caaguazú, a region of about 4,500 square miles that included the area around the Km. 81 station. They examined around 60,000 people, identifying over 150 leprosy patients.

Unfortunately, patients with advanced symptoms of the disease still were hard to find and did not show up voluntarily at Km. 81. But those who came with early symptoms had a decent chance of healing. The broad screening communicated to even those in outlying areas the possibility of ambulatory treatment, slowly reducing patients' lack of trust. And the joint project signaled in a way that had never happened before that the Health Ministry acknowledged the efficacy and legitimacy of the ambulatory leprosy program at Km. 81.

Boosting the agricultural projects at the station was more challenging. To halt Paraguayan squatters from encroaching on the mission property, John's first task was to repair the fencing and reinvest in cattle. Fortunately, a new group of volunteers had now arrived at the station, due to John's urgent requests. But they didn't seem to respond well to John's demands for more hours of labor and fewer tereré breaks. They didn't counter him directly, but their behaviors changed only when he was present. Did they really think he didn't notice that their lazy habits resumed as soon as he was gone?

Clara was happy to be back home. Yes, that's what it felt like, home. A young woman from the Mennonite colony had come to teach the younger children in German, while the older ones continued with correspondence courses in English. And Aggie again took over her role as cook, housekeeper, and the children's disciplinarian.

One morning in late October of 1957, a few months after their return, Clara squatted on the ground next to Aggie, who was plucking feathers from a chicken she had just butchered. "Aggie, what do you hear from the station workers? Are people happier now?"

Aggie stopped plucking for a moment and looked at Clara. She squinted as though trying to decide whether Clara really wanted to hear the answer. "Well, honestly, no, Clara." She began tugging at the feathers more forcefully. "You and John always talk a lot about how important it is to live simply, like our neighbors. But no matter how simply we live, people like you and me, who can travel to North America and back again, we raise a great deal of envy."

"Our workers are jealous?" That was the last thing Clara thought she would hear. She was used to hearing that her husband was too demanding, or that he hurt someone's feelings because he was so direct. But envy?

"That's not all, Clara. They resent the fact that you, and especially John, make such a big deal about not living above your neighbors, but your lifestyle isn't anything like theirs."

Clara slowly rose and walked away. This would be very hard for John. He felt so strongly about living a simple life and not standing out. When she or one of the children asked for an item of clothing or something else non-essential, John's response was always, "Just look at the people around us. If they can't afford to have that, what makes you think you deserve to have it?"

That night, as she and John were preparing for bed, Clara said, "John, I have something to tell you—something I found out about how our workers think about us."

John stopped what he was doing. When she shared what Aggie had told her, he sank onto the bed, his head in both hands. Clara wished she had a salve for her dear husband's latest wound. He wasn't well to begin with. The regular B12 injections he gave himself didn't seem to be stemming his severe anemia, and he continued to drop weight from an already thin frame. And now this.

TWENTY

Konrad Wolf's scar on the left side of his face throbbed as it always did when he was distraught. He wished he hadn't gotten himself so tangled up in the leprosy project at Km. 81. It was true that MCC had helped the colonies recover economically in the past few years, and Schmidt clearly had a lot to do with this.

But the man was intolerable. First, he thought he could carry on as a doctor even though he still had no credentials to do so in Paraguay. Konrad figured Schmidt had resolved that issue by bribing the health officials. And now he had been back in Paraguay only a few months and was already busy making himself rich by developing a cattle ranch on mission property. Was there anything the man wouldn't stoop to?

Konrad had written a long letter to Orie Miller. *You might as well call Km. 81 the Schmidt Ranch.* The whole cattle venture that Schmidt was so enthusiastic about had nothing to do with the mission work, and in fact, as far as Konrad could tell, it was a big distraction. A way for Schmidt to line his pockets, nothing else.

Now he stared down at Orie's response on the desk in front of him. Orie reminded him that they had had this conversation when they were at the station's inauguration ceremony back in 1953. It was not out of line for mission people working at the station to buy cattle as a means of investing their personal funds.

Konrad fingered the left side of his face. So why hadn't Schmidt told him about MCC's approval of his ranching activities when Konrad had confronted him about it at their last meeting? Was Schmidt as distrustful of him as he was of that American doctor with his crazy ideas about cattle ranches and road building?

They'd been back in Paraguay for six months when it finally seemed that John's dream of building a trans-Chaco road linking the colonies to Asunción would come true. For years, he'd worked to engage the Paraguayan government to provide workers and equipment; the U.S. government to furnish funds; MCC and the Mennonite colonies to train equipment operators; and ranchers along the route to offer fuel and repair facilities for the machinery.

Over the years, Konrad Wolf had been one of John's most vocal opponents. "The road project will never happen—there are too many moving parts to coordinate," Wolf said.

On a hot humid day in mid-March, John invited Wolf to meet him at the south end of the construction site. The two of them watched the heavy earth moving equipment at work. John couldn't wait to prove Wolf wrong. And to entice him to join him on another project he had in mind.

He pushed his hat back and grinned at Wolf. "At this rate, it'll take years. But our dream for the colonies is finally beginning to take shape."

"*Our* dream?" Wolf raised his eyebrows.

"Look, Konrad. We've had our differences. But we've always shared a desire for the Chaco colonies to thrive. Isn't it time we put aside our grudges?"

Wolf kicked around clods of dirt.

Undeterred, John continued. "I'd like to talk to you about managing a Chaco cattle ranch for me. Five years ago, I secured the investment dollars to purchase thirty square miles outside of the colony land…"

Why was Wolf staring at him like he was nuts? This was a great opportunity for them to jointly create something that would benefit them personally and be a model for the colony.

"I'll have to think about that," Wolf mumbled.

"I want your answer by next week," John said, turning to leave.

Clara and John had been back in Paraguay for nearly a year. Clara enjoyed the nursing work, but she most especially loved the regular Bible study and prayer meetings with the leprosy patients and with people in their neighboring towns. One of the churches in the North had donated a small pump organ, which folded up into a container the size of a large suitcase. She loaded it onto the station Jeep and took it to neighboring towns, delighting in teaching people how to sing *coritos* about Jesus.

Best of all, seven of their leprosy patients were ready to be baptized, including Doña Ramona, their very first guest at Km. 81. They had hired a missionary from the colonies, Johann Regehr, to provide religious leadership for these new Christians. Clara sewed white skirts, trousers, and shirts for their baptism.

On baptism Sunday, a solemn group of people from the station walked about one kilometer through marshy fields to a pond they referred to as *Paso Malo*. John carried Clara's fold-up organ. Reverend Regehr already stood in the waist-high muddy water when they arrived. Clara set up the organ in the tall weeds beside the pond, turned over a tree stump to sit on, and began pumping out the hymn *Tal Como Soy*. One by one, the white-clad patients walked into the water to receive their benediction. When it was Doña Ramona's turn, one of the other patients helped her cover the short distance into the water. As she hobbled slowly past Clara, Doña Ramona beamed a toothless smile, as though saying, "I have never been so happy." Clara's fingers missed a few beats before she recovered and continued to play.

Apprehension mixed with Clara's joy. There would surely be trouble from the churches in the Chaco about this baptism. The Mennonite church leaders had already sent angry letters to MCC about Reverend Regehr, who represented only one congregation's beliefs about the right way to baptize new church members. John had scoffed at this latest set of tensions, arguing that they should all want to spread God's word without letting petty differences get in the way.

Petty differences. Still pumping out the final hymn, Clara could hardly suppress a smile when she thought about Franklin and her refusal to get rebaptized by submersion. She hardly recognized the narrow-minded girl she'd been only fifteen years ago. But she was grateful, because in the end it had brought her here. To this work.

"Amen," Clara whispered as the reverend gently dipped Ramona's head under water.

Besides managing the books, caring for patients, running Bible classes and prayer meetings, giving piano and typing lessons, and putting out the quarterly newsletter, Clara's responsibilities included hosting the many guests who came to see the Mennonite leprosy compound. In the past year, there had been over fifty guests each month. People came from all over the world, from all walks of life, and for varied reasons. Some wished to contribute to the work, some wanted to show their opposition to a leper colony in the area, and some were merely curious.

Clara welcomed everyone with the same hospitality. Non-Christians gave her the opportunity to be a witness for her Lord. She loved introducing guests to the patients who lived on the station. People needed to know that these patients were dignified human beings with an illness, not dreadful monsters to be avoided. Visitors frequently shared a meal with the Schmidts, sometimes even staying overnight, sleeping in the children's beds.

One day, U.S. Ambassador Ploeser's wife and another dignitary from the Paraguayan embassy came to visit. Both were nice ladies and seemed very interested in the work. But their red nails and bright lipstick were so showy. Something about them stirred a faint memory of Anastasia Brighton. *I just prefer plainer people*, Clara thought.

On a humid afternoon in late 1958, just as Clara finished filing the charts from the day's clinic visits, an oxcart clattered up the hill onto the station and stopped in front of the clinic building. Clara rose to see who it was but stopped when she saw a man jump from the cart, yelling something in Guaraní. Clara watched as he roughly pulled a thin woman from the cart and then grabbed a small child—no, it wasn't a child. It was a little person who looked as wide as she was tall—and threw her onto the ground. The little one's face hit the dirt and she stayed there, not moving.

Clara rushed toward them, asking in broken Spanish what was going on. Before she reached them, the man had turned the cart around to leave. Clara approached the tall, thin woman, noticing how frail and old she looked. Her nose cartilage was not caved in as was often the case, but her eyes were swollen nearly shut, and her mouth was deformed from the collapse of her nearly toothless gums. Her hands were permanently clenched, with all the fingers bent in at the first and second knuckles.

"*Che memby michïva...* che memby michïva..." the woman wailed, waving her arms around her in a disoriented way that made it clear she was almost entirely blind and must be looking for the little person.

Clara gently touched her elbow, led her to the still motionless human heap on the ground, and said, "She's here."

"Che memby michïva..." The old woman buried her face in the little person's back.

"What is your name? And who is this on the ground?" Clara asked.

"I ... Josefina, and my little one, Amalia," she whispered, in broken Spanish. "Neighbors say we have curse...stay away forever."

"You are safe here," Clara said, gently rolling the little one over onto her back. Amalia appeared to be a woman in her fifties, with a large head and prominent forehead. Her chest was no more than ten inches from chin to waist, and her spine curved around so that her body was always in nearly a seated position. She didn't seem to measure much more than a few feet from the bottom of her flat round feet to the top of her head.

"Let's find you something to eat and a place to sleep," Clara said, helping Amalia sit up.

Amalia was only thirty inches tall, and almost equally wide. Her form of dwarfism was a genetic mutation called skeletal dysplasia, a condition of abnormal bone growth that causes disproportionate dwarfism, with a normal-sized head but with very short arms and legs and small hands and feet. Although dwarf characters are often thought of as mythological creatures in fairy tales and fantasy fiction, in Paraguay during the 1950s, dwarfs were regarded with disgust and revulsion. They were seen as a voodoo curse. Dwarfs with leprosy carried a double stigma.

Josefina and her little one lived in the hallway of the overcrowded leprosy guesthouse for a few months. When it became clear that the two of them would never have anywhere else to go, John and Clara raised money to build a small home for them near the other guesthouse.

In early 1959, John received an invitation to meet with the new health minister, Dr. Raúl Peña. Had Dr. Walter, whom John finally had convinced MCC to fire just a few months ago, stayed in Paraguay? Was he making trouble for them? There were now fifteen patients living at Km. 81, six in the original guesthouse and the remainder in small houses they had built nearby. John made sure everyone always referred to their lodging as guesthouses rather than a hospital, to keep people from thinking he was building a colony. Had Walter snitched on them?

"We are treating well over 500 leprosy patients by the ambulatory method," John began.

Dr. Peña waved his hands, saying he already knew all about the many patients who were being served. What he really wanted to talk about was how the ambulatory model worked. "It seems to me that this should be the preferred means of treating these patients. You have shown that many more can be helped than we have been able to manage with the colony model."

Peña continued to ask a barrage of questions about John's methods, suggesting he'd been thinking about this for some time. John swallowed hard and dug his thumbnail into his palm to focus himself on Peña's questions. Why was he so interested in their work?

Peña ended with, "We recently hired the doctor you fired a few months ago. Joachim Walter. He'll oversee the ambulatory work in your area and east to Coronel Oviedo. You will be reporting to Dr. Walter as the leading leprosy health officer there."

A clock on the wall made a clicking sound as it ticked off the seconds.

So that was what this was all about. Even though the workload was too much for one doctor, it had been a good riddance to let Walter go. Their relationship had only worsened over time. Now John would have to report to him as a representative of the government? And why did they suddenly not need a Paraguayan doctor to oversee the work?

John slapped his hat onto his head, nodded a curt goodbye, and left the room.

Clara sat in her rocker, staring through the high brick arch at the end of the veranda. The breeze gently stirred the orange blossom-laden branches of the Chivato trees in the yard. Beyond the trees were rows and rows of grapevines, and on the other side of the vines, papaya, orange, and tangerine trees dotted the hillside that sloped down toward a stream.

This was her home. This was where she belonged. Could they really leave it all behind? She looked down at the sheet of paper John had given her, which listed all the reasons he believed they should just give it up, go the States and live a normal life. He'd hardly slept at all last night, and this morning he handed her his list:

    *   Voluntary service men don't listen to me

    *   Health Department competition/ no government plan for eradicating leprosy

* Fights among the colony churches about proper
  Christian leadership at Km. 81
* Envy of our neighbors and coworkers about how well
  we live
* I'm not recognized as leprologist – Km. 81 listed
  under Dr. Rodríguez's name
* No one seems to know the source of my blood/anemia
  problem
* Children's education – are we willing to send them all
  off to school somewhere else?
* Leadership in the colonies never sending enough
  volunteers
* Load too heavy - over half my time is spent on
  non-medical issues

Clara felt a weight on her chest that was beginning to be all too familiar. It lifted when she was bathing and bandaging the wounds of her patients, or when she delivered a healthy baby at the clinic; it lifted when she sang coritos with and told Bible stories to people in the neighboring villages. But when confronted with the reality of their many challenges, she just wanted to cry.

She heard John's footsteps behind her. "What shall we do, John?"

"Our early furlough request should be on Orie's desk by now. Maybe they'll finally get it when we're gone that our work is worth something here. If not, maybe we're dispensable."

Clara wondered which "they" John referred to, but she didn't ask. He felt bombarded from all sides. It wasn't a good idea for her to try to sort out the specifics. Of all their challenges, Clara was most concerned about John's health. He'd been to numerous specialists in Asunción, and none of them had any idea why his anemia was not responding to the B12 shots or the iron he was taking. Of course, they didn't know that the iron he took was powder from old pieces of metal he ground up at the station workshop.

"Let's pray that the Lord helps us find a way," she said, turning back to stare through the arch at the rows of grapevines now almost disappearing into the dusk.

TWENTY-ONE

They'd been in Paraguay two and a half years, half of the normal mission term. But John had been clear when they returned in 1957 that he made no promises about how long they'd stay. MCC had denied his request for the contractually guaranteed raise in allowance after their sixth child was born, so as far as John was concerned, they no longer had a set contract. Besides, the challenges at the station sometimes seemed insurmountable.

He was somewhat surprised when only weeks after his request for an early furlough, Bill Snyder wrote back that MCC would find a replacement doctor to lead the work at Km. 81 for a period of two years, beginning in mid-1960. This would give John plenty of time to sort out his health problems, earn some money, and figure out their children's education. They would receive no support from MCC during those two years, and there was no expectation that they would return to Paraguay. If John's health improved, however, they were welcome to go back if they wished.

John didn't know what to think. Konrad Wolf had agreed to manage John's ranch in the Chaco, and now MCC had found a replacement doctor. They needed to get out of this place for a while, so all of this was good news. But Snyder hadn't even voiced any argument about the early furlough. Had MCC wanted him to leave all along?

Shortly after receiving Snyder's letter, John burst into their home office, where Clara was trying to balance the accounts. "Clara, I think this is the perfect time for us to plan the car trip to the North that I've always wanted to take. Now that the Pan-American Highway is almost complete, we can drive most of the way between here and Kansas. And we can stop to visit missionaries all along the way, raising awareness and money for the leprosy work here. And we can visit leprosy colonies en route to share how successful ambulatory forms of treatment can be. And we…"

Why was Clara looking at him like that? Like he was crazy or something. And why was she shaking her head?

John clenched his hands under the table. He'd asked Orie to come to Paraguay, and he'd called together a dozen church leaders, representing all three of the congregations in the colonies, to convene in Asunción. Formal spiritual work at Km. 81 had ceased because of the fights among them. John figured the only way to restart this important part of their mission was for MCC to manage it. But there would be a battle. That's why he needed Orie there.

"That baptism at Km. 81 was nothing but a power play." The leader of one of the three Mennonite congregations in the Chaco pounded his fist on the table.

Numerous voices spoke at once, and a few of the men pushed their chairs back from the table. A large man directly across from John stood up and towered over the group. "I don't know why I'm here. I've already said my piece."

Orie held up his hand. "I have given this much thought and even brought it to our Executive Committee in the North." John saw eyes begin to roll. Orie continued. "MCC as a body represents all Mennonite churches. We would like to propose that we hire a missionary who will report to us, rather than to any one of your churches."

"But then we'll lose all control," one of the men countered. "We know how much MCC likes to manage everything its own way."

John had remained silent. He now stood up, looking one by one at each man around the table. His voice was low. "This is not about control. This is about spreading God's word without letting your differences get in the way. And how dare you—"

Orie's calm voice interrupted him. "You will have control. We will choose a committee to work together with MCC and the director of the leper station for the purpose of managing the entire mission program."

John shuddered. He was relieved that MCC was willing to take on the spiritual work at the station. But another committee?

Clara loved Christmas celebrations at the station, and they had become a well-attended tradition over the years. Christmas of 1959 promised to be bigger than ever. With an acceptable and legitimate spiritual director in place, the news about Km. 81's celebration of the birth of Christ had spread far and wide.

People from the neighboring villages were invited to come to the station for a program at 6:00 on Thursday, Christmas Eve. John, Clara, and the rest of the personnel had spent the day setting up planks across sawhorses, covering them with white sheets, and piling them high with cookies, cakes, and fudge. Small gifts, such as combs, bars of soap, toothpaste, and such, donated from MCC, were placed in the center of one of the tables.

The guests started to arrive around 5:00. By the time the program began, there were over 600 people, seated around the tables and on the ground.

Clara rushed around, making sure everyone was comfortable and felt welcome. She brought a chair to an elderly woman who was clearly arthritic. "Señora, por favor." The old woman leaned over to kiss Clara on both cheeks.

It was time to bring her children forward with their skit. Clara had rehearsed it with them over and over, and she hoped they would get it right. They were acting out the manger scene without dialogue, since most of their guests didn't understand German. The oldest two children had grumbled a lot about playing the roles of Joseph and Mary. But the others seemed to enjoy dressing up as shepherds and wise men. Baby Jesus, of course, was Mary Lou, now two and a half years old.

"Now. It's time." She led the children to where she had cleared a space for the skit. She placed her baby into the makeshift manger and then walked off to the side, hoping the children would remember their parts. There was a little confusion and bickering about who should stand where. Through it all, Baby Jesus lay quietly in the manger, waiting for the rest of them to behave and do what Momma said.

The skit was a big hit. The minister delivered a brief sermon. Clara led everyone in singing a few Christmas songs, pumping the tunes out on her organ. Then iced coffee was served, and people were invited to eat. The program ended with her six children singing a few songs for the crowd in Spanish and German.

The next night they repeated the same program for the leprosy patients. Because it was still unknown how the disease spread, they tried to keep leprosy patients apart from others. In addition to their resident guests, over sixty patients came from the surrounding area. Clara welcomed each one with loving tenderness. She helped Doña Ramona to a seat near the front since her hearing had deteriorated. And she guided nearly blind Doña Josefina toward a chair. Amalia followed along behind them, using her arms to scoot forward on her bottom.

"Here, little one," Clara said. "Let's get you up higher so you can see." With the help of a few station workers, she gently lifted Amalia and placed her on a platform Clara had asked the carpenter to build for this purpose.

The children's skit began. Clara stepped to the side and looked at the crowd gathered around the manger scene. Several of the patients had amputated limbs. Others were covered with scabs or open wounds. Some of their hands were so crippled that they could only move their thumb when she grasped their hand in welcome. Many were blind but they laughed along with others when Mother Mary lifted Baby Jesus from the manger, and the patients saw that Jesus was a chubby little girl with curly blond hair.

"*Feliz Navidad,*" they said, as they accepted the treats and little gifts. "Gracias. Feliz Navidad." Clara watched as one of the patients held a bar of soap against his chest with both crippled hands, tears running down his cheeks.

During the first months of 1960, John spent most evenings late into the night plotting out their car trip to the States. He figured it would take about three months, given all the stops he envisioned along the way. He identified and contacted missionaries in the countries they would pass through. Most of them were non-Mennonite, but he also planned to visit the Mennonite colonies in Bolivia, British Honduras—which would have to be a side trip by plane—and Mexico. ALM had asked him to visit and report on four leprosy colonies in Bolivia, Ecuador, Panama, and Costa Rica. The most important thing was to use this whole trip to learn about other missions throughout South and Central America, and to spread the word about their ambulatory leprosy work in Paraguay.

John ordered a Volvo station wagon from Sweden, believing it would handle the rough terrain they were likely to encounter. On the side of the Volvo, in large black lettering, he painted the words *Lucha Antileprosa en el Paraguay.* And below that: *Misión Menonita.*

He asked Clara to sew a tent that could be attached to the side of the Volvo. When he specified the tent dimensions he had in mind, Clara shook her head and eyed him quizzically.

"That will barely hold three people. There are eight of us, John."

"The rest of us will sleep in the car when we're not staying with missionaries," he said. "It's as large as we can make the tent, given that it will only be supported on one side."

John was still anemic. He had continued to lose weight in the past year. And he had frequent diarrhea. But the thought of this trip made him feel young again. He'd dreamed of doing this since he first landed in Paraguay in 1941. Of course, it would have been a lot easier before he had a big family. But this would be a good adventure for the children as well.

During the day, there was no time for trip planning. Now that the work on the station had the government's grudging approval, it was growing at a rapid pace. There were twenty patients in their overfilled guesthouses, and Km. 81 served almost half of the total 1,200 reported cases of leprosy in the country. John continued to ride out several times a month to treat existing patients and to seek out new ones. There were still many unreported cases. He was sure of it.

Most validating for John was that the World Health Organization just this year had publicly recognized the effectiveness of the Km. 81 treatment methods. And after considerable turnover in the Paraguayan Health Ministry, the new minister, Dr. Torres, adopted their ambulatory system as the countrywide model. The troublesome Dr. Walter had left for Africa.

With all this growth on the medical front, the limitations of the rustic and rudimentary buildings on the station became increasingly evident. This had to be addressed before they left for the States. The growing number of workers, including the volunteer youth, the nurses, the cook, and a seminary student, all slept in thatched roof buildings with mud floors. Constant mosquitos and rats, and occasional poisonous snakes, shared their space.

Worse was the fact that John had only one clinic room where he examined both leprosy patients and all the general medical patients, and where he delivered babies and performed operations. One morning recently, on a general clinic day, one of his leprosy patients came in for a tooth extraction. A father had just arrived with two children suffering with hookworm, so John decided to take care of them first. By the time he called in the leprosy patient, six more people were waiting for general medical care. They looked askance at the leprosy patient who walked into the consultation room ahead of them. John couldn't blame them.

He had sent MCC a proposed building plan for a girl's dormitory, a leprosy consultation and supply room, and another guesthouse for new resident leprosy patients now living in the hallways and on verandas. He proposed that the whole building program would cost around $7,000. This did not include a Spanish grade school he planned to open for neighboring families, which was already in last year's budget. He ended the letter with:

> All these buildings will not cost more than one church building at home.

The more John told her about the upcoming trip, the greater were Clara's concerns that this would be too much to take on with their six children, now ranging in age from three to fifteen. Worst of all was John's health. His migraine headaches, which were more frequent than they'd been in a while, left him completely debilitated for hours at a time. And his anemia was still not responding to treatments.

It was a warm fall day in late April, only a month from their departure date. Clara was sorting through the children's clothes, selecting the bare minimum they would need for the trip. There wasn't much room in that little Volvo. In fact, she didn't know how they would all fit, along with their food stuff, clothing, and a tent.

Her boys were excited about driving through the Bolivian Andes, maybe getting lost along the way, even getting to the end of dead-end roads. Their imaginations went wild. Clara smiled. They were so much like their father. The riskier the undertaking, the better.

But her girls were another matter. Especially Marlena, who kept threatening that she wouldn't go if it meant being cramped for three months in that "stupid little car that doesn't even have back windows that roll down." Clara sighed. Not even John's harsh beatings helped that girl. Worse yet, it sometimes seemed that Marlena asked for them.

Clara looked up when John entered the room. "John, I've been thinking. Our girls aren't looking forward to this trip. Is there anything we can do to make it more fun for them?"

"Make it fun for them?" John's clipped laugh said it all. He wanted the trip to be about spreading the word about and raising support for their mission. But underneath all his mission-mindedness, this was a grand adventure for John and his boys. Clara swallowed and continued sorting the clothes.

A week before they were set to leave the station, John and Clara were at the MCC Home office in Asunción with Frank Wiens, who was back in his role as MCC director for Paraguay. They were finalizing the preparations for the transition of the leprosy work to a Dr. Hiebert, who would not arrive until two months after the Schmidts left. John and Clara had made a list of everything they thought the Hieberts needed to know:

> Feel free to use everything in our home; consider bringing medical supplies—a ten-pound bag of supplies should not be a problem in customs; a stethoscope is a must since John's scope from student days is in bad shape; there are many non-medical tasks, like keeping the peace and sustaining the interest of the station workers; stay in contact with neighbors, colony leaders, the Health Ministry and MCC; and finally, you will host many guests and you'll need to send out thank-you letters for gifts and donations.

"I hope this doesn't scare them off." Frank shifted in his seat. "John, Clara, I have received word about your funding request."

Frank said that although MCC understood the need for the additional buildings, they had no funds for the project. They had agreed as a committee that raising the money would be a good furlough project for John and Clara. In fact, given the added expense of the spiritual director, the funds for any kind of building, including the new school, were even less than expected.

John threw up his hands.

"I've tried to convince them." Frank handed John a stack of letters. "The answer is no."

John turned to Clara, and she nodded. "Clara and I have enough money from the personal donations of our family and friends to start the construction. I'm not leaving Paraguay without your assurance that this project will be a priority."

On May 23, the Volvo station wagon was loaded. They had packed most of their luggage in the rack on top of the car. The rest they stuffed into a makeshift wooden box in the back, which also served as a place for the younger children to sleep on. They'd said their goodbyes to the group of station workers and patients who surrounded the car. Doña Josefina waved at them, tears dripping from her shrunken cheeks.

At Itá Enramada, they crossed the Paraguay River on a barge and made their way into Argentina on a rough dirt road with no signage. Getting lost the first time was fun. Setting up the tent the first time was fun. Even eating the dried-pea soup, cooked on their small primus at the side of the road, was fun.

But the fun didn't last. By the time they reached the Bolivian border at Yacuiba on Saturday the 28th, the younger children were fussing. Everyone was tired and hungry. And the border patrols said they didn't have the right papers.

"They just want a bribe." John said between tight lips. Clara knew this meant that they weren't going anywhere for a while.

"It's cold and threatening to rain again," Clara said. "I don't think we can put up a tent."

"What are we supposed to do now?" Wesley asked. Fun and adventure had quickly turned into restlessness and boredom.

"We'll figure something out." Clara tried to smile. One of the customs officials had mentioned in passing that there were *evangélicos* in town. "Who wants to walk around with me to see if we can find some missionaries?"

She and her older daughters walked around mud puddles on a deeply rutted road, asking for evangélicos along the way. They were finally directed to a small adobe building next to what looked like a warehouse. Clara clapped at the gate and waited.

A white woman appeared at the door. "Yes?'

"My family…we're from Paraguay…we're missionaries…" Clara had been so preoccupied with finding missionaries who might help them, she forgot to rehearse what she would say. "We're looking for a roof to sleep under for the night," she blurted.

"Well, my goodness," the woman said.

Jane Wilson and her husband were United Evangelical missionaries from England, there to provide Christian service to local and foreign oil workers. Jane sent one of her children to get John with the car and the rest of the family. "My husband is in the church now, conducting an evening service," she said. "You can join in."

John pulled up. One by one, the rag-tag children piled out of the little Volvo. "Well, my goodness," Jane said again.

John and Clara joined the service, reporting on their work and showing slides. At the end, their six children lined up in front of the group and sang coritos in German and Spanish. After a quick bowl of soup, they settled onto the cold hard church benches to sleep, the two older boys sleeping in the Volvo to keep it from being stolen.

In the morning, the missionaries helped them with their papers at the border, and they were off again. Clara wrote in her diary: God is good. Someday she hoped to publish the story of this trip and God's gracious protection.

★

This was exactly how John had dreamed it would be. Either he and Clara knew of and had contacted missionaries along the way, or they hunted them down when they arrived in town. Each one provided an opportunity to share God's work. The mission workers nearly always greeted them enthusiastically, inviting them in as though they were comrades in arms.

By the beginning of June, they started climbing into the Andes. The Volvo was mostly in first gear. Numerous times along the way, the car sputtered to a halt, and Clara and the five oldest children had to push it until, with its reduced weight and running start, it reached sufficient speed to take off on its own, leaving them to trudge up the steep road behind it.

They reached Sucre on Sunday, June 5, election day in Bolivia. Road patrols were everywhere. Very slowly, they bounced along a road that was often no more than a winding oxcart path. John stared straight ahead, often checking the rearview mirror to see how the children were doing. They looked worried. At least they were quiet, for once.

Suddenly, a dozen or so men wearing Basque-style berets and tattered tunics over frayed trousers appeared in front of the car, a chain stretching across the road. The men crowded around the Volvo, yelling in Quechua, and waving sawed-off shotguns at them.

John stopped and opened the door, not really knowing what he was going to do. "Que quieren?" he asked.

The men pushed him roughly aside and walked around the car, waving their guns at Clara and the children, signaling for them to get out of the vehicle.

Just then, an open Jeep clattered up the hill behind them. Two uniformed soldiers were in the front seat. The guerillas stopped, turned, and ran up the road and off into the brush.

John wiped his forehead and noticed that his hands were shaking. "Gracias, muchas gracias," he said to the soldiers as he slid back behind the wheel.

John checked the rearview mirror as he started the car, and saw that Clara was crying. "Let's not make this a bigger deal than it was," he said tersely. He couldn't let on how scared he'd been.

During the next month, as they made their way through Peru, Ecuador and Columbia, John kept a tight rein on his emotions, and he did whatever it took to keep the children in line. These kids were more challenging than he'd anticipated, for sure.

On Sunday, July 17, they boarded a ship that took them through the Panama Canal. Clara was pleased to see that the children were fascinated with the locks, the lock gates, and the electric towing locomotives on cog tracks on either side. This was such a good educational experience for them. They'd been on the road for nearly two months, and it had not always been easy. Clara regularly had to take little white pills John gave her for her nerves. She wished she had more patience with her children. But at least she had John by her side. He was such a strict disciplinarian. He kept them mostly in line.

When they reached the border of Costa Rica at the end of July, Clara handed a customs officer their papers.

"*A donde van?*"

"We're passing through on our way to Nicaragua," John said from the driver's side.

The officer shook his head. "We have just finished our stretch of the Pan-American Highway. The roads are all covered with new gravel. But there are no bridges, señor," he said. "There are thirty-eight rivers you would need to cross. It is impossible for you to continue. The only thing you can do is go back to Panama City and take a ship to Nicaragua, skipping Costa Rica entirely."

Clara nodded. That would be a great idea.

"But that would mean going back for two days to where we came from. That's not an option," John said.

The officer explained that the only vehicles on the road were bulldozers and trucks.

"Well, then maybe bulldozers can pull us through the rivers." John said.

"We are in the rainy season, señor. The rivers are two or three meters deep. But maybe I can get an engineer for you to speak with."

Clara needed to put her foot down. This was crazy. "John, this is not a good idea."

John grinned. "You know, Clara, for me the greatest thrill of this journey will be over once all the questions are answered about how we'll get through what's next."

Was he forgetting that he was bringing his whole family into danger just because he and his boys loved the thrill? But there was no talking him out of this.

They managed to cross the deep rivers on rafts or with bulldozers pulling them in their Volvo, which floated and bobbed across the water. They met almost no other vehicles or people on that road in Costa Rica other than road workers, who all seemed happy to help them.

The Schmidts crossed the border at El Paso, Texas, one day short of three months from the day they started. Clara's diary entry a few days after they arrived in Kansas read:

On Sunday afternoon May 22, we left the station and arrived in Newton on Aug 24. 94½ days. 53 of these were on the road. 35½ were visiting missions, 2 days on a ship and 4 on a train. The distance directly is 15,500 km, but with our detours to visit missions, we drove 18,340 km. with no flat tire. We never got sick, even though we sometimes ate and drank questionable food. Amoeba is rampant in these countries. We praise the Lord that no one got this terrible parasite. We spent 5 nights in our tent, 3 nights under the stars, 5 nights in hotels, and the rest of the nights with missionaries.

It was a wonderful family experience!

TWENTY-TWO

Orie smiled and re-read the letter from Frank Wiens dated August 19, 1960, only three months after the Schmidts had left Paraguay. Frank wrote that Km. 81 was in dire financial straits, seemingly due to large supplemental contributions that had stopped after the Schmidts left for North America. In addition, he believed John and Clara supported numerous development projects out of their own personal allowance, which of course we can't expect the Hieberts to do. Frank ended with:

> The leprosy mission is completely out of money and in an embarrassing position.

Of course they were running out of money without the Schmidts. Didn't Frank know John and Clara well enough by now to understand that they had always raised a significant portion of the money needed to support Km. 81? He just prayed John would be well enough to resume the work at the end of their furlough.

Clara saw the *Herald Press* return address and quickly ripped open the envelope.

> 2/27/61. We are sorry to inform you that we cannot accept your manuscript for publication. It is a story of God's grace and blessing but...

She walked slowly from the mailbox back to the house, reading the rest of the rejection letter. Oh, how she had daydreamed about publishing a book that consolidated all her diary entries from their three-month trip coming north. And given the *Herald*'s focus on discipleship, mission, and spirituality, she had been so sure they would publish it. The royalties would have been eight percent, and she could have been a published book author.

They had been back in Kansas for six months. The children were all in school, often staying with various relatives around Newton, while she and John traveled across the country during the first few months back, to again report on the leprosy work and raise money. Clara worried about her children, especially the older ones, growing up in a world full of sinful appeals. Every night she prayed that they might resist Satan's temptations.

Back at the house, Clara sat down on the top porch step and dropped the rejection letter into her lap. While on the road, she and John had held church meetings almost every evening, and up to three times on a Sunday. It had been exhausting and her nerves were often frayed, but they had raised quite a lot of money for the important building projects at the leprosy station.

Now John was all set to work for six months at three different clinics in the Newton area to earn money for the family. Even then, they would be reporting in numerous churches at nights and on weekends.

Clara stared across the icy fields around their house and wondered how she would manage the children with John working more than full-time. She knew it was him she should worry about, not herself. He had frequent migraine headaches and still suffered from diarrhea. Their recent visit to the Mayo Clinic had provided no answers. Still, she would be the one needing to deal with their children—alone. The boys just seemed to do whatever they wanted, and her two older daughters didn't show her any respect. She rose from the step and sighed in a prayer for strength and grace to be a better mother.

After John's six-month stint to earn money for the family, he and Clara were on the road again in July 1961, traveling through Canada and the U.S. to raise funds for the station. They showed slides and told stories about their leprosy patients.

Their audiences seemed to especially love little Amalia, so Clara told long stories about her optimistic spirit and her generous personality, despite all her hardships. John spoke passionately about the need for a special clinic at the station devoted to treating only those with leprosy. They also shared their dreams for further extensions of their mission work to include a Spanish school for the illiterate poor children in the surrounding area, a library, a hookworm program, statistical research on leprosy treatment, and continued expansion of the territory they served. By the end of most reports, many people were in tears, and the offering plates were usually heaped high with bills.

Toward the end of the year, John sent MCC a letter, asking for a report on donations. He wanted to make sure he and Clara had raised enough money for his proposed building plans. When he heard nothing back, he asked more forcefully. He finally learned that their donations had been consolidated into the general MCC funds.

Not this again. It had happened numerous times before. It was probably not malice on their part. Naturally, MCC viewed all their many projects as worthy of funding. And the other mission work was important, for sure. But he and Clara were doing all this traveling and reporting to support Km. 81, not the many other worthwhile projects.

John wrote:

How did the money we raised in the past six months get put in the general MCC fund versus specifically for Km. 81? This has happened a hundred times and it's not acceptable.

His letter did not ask—it demanded a clear accounting from MCC of all the funds he and Clara had raised for Km. 81.

By July of 1962, it was time to say goodbye. Clara was relieved that MCC had asked them to return to Paraguay. But this meant leaving their three oldest children behind to continue their studies in the States. John's mother had agreed to take in Elisabeth; and Clara's brothers each took in one of the boys. In Paraguay, Frank Wiens and his wife agreed to have David and Marlena, aged thirteen and eleven, live with them so they could attend school in Asunción.

"I just keep wondering if we're doing the right thing by our children," she said to John about a week before they were scheduled to leave. They were weighing boxes of medical supplies and drugs they planned to take back to Paraguay with them.

"They'll be in good hands, Clara. This is not the time to start having second thoughts."

"But don't you ever worry that we aren't being good parents?" Clara persisted.

John placed a box of medications on the scales. "We are raising our children to love the Lord. That is the most important job God gave us as parents."

Clara wished she could be as sure as John.

Surrounded by their children and a large group of relatives at the airport in Wichita, John and Clara sang *God Be with You 'til We Meet Again*. The goodbyes were tearful. But by the time their plane circled for landing over the red-tiled roofs of Asunción, their focus was on the work that lay ahead.

TWENTY-THREE

It had been ten years since John had been in touch with Ana, so he was surprised when he received her letter shortly after their return to Paraguay. He was even more shocked by what she wrote. John knew that there had been a ban on Peronismo in Argentina since 1958. And he figured Ana would probably have taken up another cause by now. Or maybe finally settled down to marry and have a family. Instead, he learned that Ana was part of a clandestine group, secretly lobbying for Juan Perón's return to power. Really? John stopped reading and looked up, remembering Ana's disdain for the man shortly before Evita's death. What on earth would have her support him now?

He turned back to the letter. Ana had put together a small group of activists to meet with Paraguay's President Stroessner, who had publicly supported and provided exile for Perón back in 1955. She was traveling undercover to Paraguay? Had she lost her mind? Didn't she know that Stroessner was just as corrupt as she claimed Perón had been?

That evening after the rest of the family had gone to bed, John sat at his desk, the kerosene lamplight flickering across Ana's letter. There was no point in trying to dissuade her. That would be futile. He'd write to ask her to visit Km. 81 while she was in Paraguay. She would be thrilled to see how his and Clara's dream of improving the spiritual, social, and physical lives of people with leprosy was coming true.

John leaned back in his chair. It would be gratifying to show Ana what they had created in and around the station. He thought about all the progress they'd made. His clinic files showed more than 8,500 patients registered for general medical care. And he had treated nearly 600 patients with leprosy, mostly in their homes. A new drug regimen, rifampicin/isoprodian, had recently been introduced, but John didn't believe it was as effective as what he was currently using. He expected to see marked improvement in most of the leprosy patients he treated, even the severe cases, although they would likely never get off their meds.

It wasn't just the medications. John was convinced that the attitude of the patients influenced their chances for improvement. That's why he was so focused on their emotional and spiritual health. And general hygiene mattered a lot more than medical textbooks implied. Just this year, John had expanded Km. 81's outreach to help neighbors with sanitation and toilets; and to provide vegetable seeds and planting instructions. He and Clara wanted to heal lives, not simply the disease. That would be most important to Ana as well.

He was especially heartened by the change in attitude of the public toward Km. 81 and leprosy in general. Neighbors who knew of suspicious cases now often directed them to the station. The public was gradually gaining a better understanding and less fear of the disease. This probably gave John the most satisfaction, because only by reducing the social stigma would widespread healing of this disease ever be possible.

Yes, Ana would love what was happening at Km. 81. After so often feeling useless in the face of her bold activism, he could finally show her that he was making a difference in the world.

"Clara, do you remember Anastasia Brighton, the woman you briefly met during our stop-over in Buenos Aires back in 1951?"

Clara stopped folding the bandages she had just created by ripping an old bedsheet into long strips. "Yes, of course I do, John. Why do you ask?"

"She's in Asunción on a business trip, and I've invited her to come out to Km. 81 to see our work."

"Why is she in Paraguay?" Clara thought about the woman she'd met when they disembarked in Buenos Aires. On fire about what she felt called to do. So much like John. Of course Ana would be interested in what they had accomplished here on the station.

"She has some business with President Stroessner. It's all pretty hush-hush," John said.

By the time Ana arrived at the station a few days later, Clara had resolved to show her nothing but Christian kindness. She had prayed, asking forgiveness for the hard feelings she used to have toward the woman. Despite being a non-Christian, Ana probably understood their work better than most.

Together, she and John took Ana for a tour around the station, beginning with the leprosy guesthouses. John began explaining why it made sense to treat most leprosy patients in their homes. "It's high time we emerged from the dark ages—"

Ana raised a hand to stop him. They stood in front of Josefina's little house, where Amalia sat with her mother under a tree, drinking tereré. "And who is this?"

Clara introduced them. "Amalia is the main coordinator of our Bible schools in the area. And she has organized a ladies' sewing group to help women make and sell items to support their families." Clara went on describing Amalia's many contributions.

Ana knelt in front of Amalia and for a moment said nothing, just studying her face. "You and I are champions of women, Doña Amalia. I wish to support your work. I will stay in touch with you through Dr. John and Doña Clara."

Clara watched John's shoulders stiffen. Did he resent Ana's interest in Amalia's work with women? Did he think it was less important than the leprosy work?

John turned and began to walk away. "This is all good but let us show you how far we've come in building up this work," he said. "You must see the plans we have for a new clinic."

John led the way, pointing out various aspects of the lush farm, the animals, gardens, and new building sites. Ana remained mostly silent.

They stopped in front of the main kitchen where the volunteers were gathered for the noon meal. Ana spun around to face them. "You have created a village of meno-nitas." Her voice was so sharp that Clara stepped back as though she'd been struck. "I'm sure you're helping the lepers, but this..." She waved her arms.

"But—" John looked stunned.

Ana was not finished. "You're sharing no power with your neighbors, you live in European-style luxury while people in surrounding villages live in huts with dirt floors, and you arrogantly stick to your German language and traditions. Would it really surprise you if local communities came to confiscate all of this and bring you down?"

Now John was visibly agitated. "We are following God's will. This is the Lord's work."

"You must ask yourselves if your God supports this..." Ana seemed at a loss for words. She gestured at the surroundings. "...*esta supremacía blanca.*"

"We are using all that God has given us to help those who are less fortunate." John spat out the words. "I did not expect you to be critical of work that helps the poor and the marginalized."

"John, please don't misunderstand..." As though knowing that her words were falling on deaf ears, Ana turned the conversation to the state of medical science regarding leprosy.

In addition to her regular duties, Clara ran numerous Bible schools in the neighboring villages. She often found that the children were starving, both physically and spiritually. Amalia had become the lead person in bringing together large groups. Initially, the children came because they were curious about this strange little creature. She smiled at them when they poked at her, and she laughed with them when they sniggered at her. Before long, the children came to love Amalia. They told their friends about her. And many more came. Amalia became a phenomenon. Visitors from all over Paraguay—and some from the U.S.—came to see the little one and her good work with the children in her region.

At one of the Bible school gatherings, Amalia sat on the ground in the shade of a tree, surrounded by nearly a hundred youngsters. She recounted Bible stories in Guaraní, taught the children coritos, and told them how much Jesus loved each one.

Clara sat at her pump organ and marveled at the scene in front of her. She saw Jesus in the face of her dear friend.

After the stories and singing, Amalia distributed galletas and oranges. She then scooted over to where Clara sat. "Doña Clara, I need to speak with you."

"Yes?"

Amalia stared at the ground. "I…I need to ask you about something," she finally stammered.

Clara rose from her chair, sat down on the ground next to Amalia and grasped her round, misshapen hand. "What is it?"

"Don Nicasio, he has asked…he wants…"

"That's wonderful!" Clara exclaimed. She'd heard the rumors. Nicasio Ayala was another of their leprosy patients in the guesthouse. "You will marry him?"

"I don't know. I don't know if I'm…" Amalia's voice trailed off.

Clara understood. "Amalia, you are a woman, and you can be with a man just like any other woman." When she saw Amalia's lips almost form into a smile, she continued. "You might want to experiment with different positions, you know, so that you can both be comfortable." Clara knew that Amalia was experiencing increasing pain caused by her abnormal bone alignment and from nerve compression in her spinal cord.

"I don't know anything about all of that," Amalia said, again turning her gaze to the ground.

"Talk to Don Nicasio. Together you will figure it out. I'm very happy for you both," Clara said, reaching across to hug her.

★

Nicasio Ayala and Amalia were married a few months later in a double wedding with Adela and Oscar Ciani, two other leprosy patients at Km. 81. Clara played her organ. Amalia had never looked so radiant. She wore a dark blue dress with a white border around the collar, three white buttons down her short chest, and a double border of white around the bottom of the skirt that came down to her feet. She sat up as straight as she could in a brand-new wooden wheelchair, which had just been built with funds donated by one of the Mennonite churches in the Chaco. Nicasio wore a dark suit and an open-collar white shirt, with a small white handkerchief in the breast pocket.

Clara was especially pleased that they were moving into their own hut, which Nicasio built on a small plot of land she and John had acquired for them four kilometers from the leprosy station.

Shortly after the wedding, she visited their home to bring a quilt she had made as her wedding gift to them. She noted the small bed, very low to the ground. *So Amalia can scoot herself up onto it without anyone's help.*

In her windowless kitchen, Amalia sat in front of a low wood stove, with rough shelving at ninety degree angles from her on both sides. From her seated position in the middle of the tiny room, she could reach the stove and the shelves on either side. The shelves, lined with newspapers, held her kitchen utensils: several rusty tin containers, a bottle of oil and a few tin plates and cups.

"I've never had such a beautiful kitchen, built exactly to my size, Doña Clara," she said, smiling.

John whistled as he strode from the leprosy guesthouses toward the clinic. This was a big deal. The general secretary of ALM, Dr. Oliver Hasselblad, who had taken Reverend Henderson's place in 1959, had never visited Km. 81. John and Clara had just received word that he and his wife Norma were coming to Paraguay at the end of August 1963, on their way to the Eighth International Congress of Leprology to be held in Rio de Janeiro on September 20. The plan was for the Hasselblads to spend a few days at the leprosy station and then drive with John and Clara to the conference. John had looked forward to this conference for a long time because it offered the opportunity to meet with other experts in the field, and to learn if there were any new treatment methods. And being there with Dr. Hasselblad was a bonus.

John thought about the early days with ALM, and the fights he'd had with Kellersberger, who could think of nothing but a leper colony. Kellersberger never did concede that an ambulatory approach made sense. But ALM was now fully onboard with John's method. They were even implementing it in other locations around the world. John was eager to show Hasselblad firsthand what they were doing at Km. 81.

Around noon, on Saturday, August 31, Frank Wiens brought the distinguished guests to the station. The air was hot and humid, and thunder rolled across the dark sky.

"I thought August was your winter?" Hasselblad laughed as he got out of the car.

"In Paraguay, we can have hot days year-round," John said. "It's good to have you here, Oliver. Norma. We'll put your bags in the children's room, where you'll sleep. Now please, we're about to sit down to eat. Join us." John motioned to Clara to add three plates at the table.

"I didn't imagine this would all look so lush," Hasselblad said, gazing out across the rows of mulberry, peach, and loquat trees that surrounded the Schmidt house.

Clara served steaming bowls of Borscht and passed around freshly baked Zwieback. When Norma commented on how delicious the meal was and how could she possibly have time to bake with all that seemed to be happening at Km. 81, Clara smiled. "Thank you, but I didn't prepare this meal. We have a maid." Aggie had left a few years back. Their maids now were volunteer workers from the Chaco.

During the meal, John shifted the conversation to what had been most especially on his mind since the prior Wednesday. *Voice of America* on his short-wave radio announced that over 200,000 people, mostly blacks, had marched in Washington D.C., advocating for civil and economic rights. In the past three days, John had prayed very specifically for them and for their cause. Surely, skin color should not determine people's rights. He wanted to learn more about the specific issues from his North American visitors.

"I've been listening to the news from Washington. What is your take on the situation?'

The discussion turned to the rapidly expanding Civil Rights Movement. There were, in fact, demonstrations and marches of protestors across the United States. The march on Washington was just one important part of a much larger movement.

John listened carefully to what his U.S. colleagues had to say. He was surprised by their general disinterest in the movement. No matter how one looked at it, from a Christian perspective or even just from a humanistic point of view, it simply made no sense that some people were seen as inferior to others, whether that was because of a disease they happened to have contracted or because of their skin color.

During the next few days, John took Hasselblad with him on his rounds to see patients in the guesthouses. He explained that it was most important to give these people a sense of dignity and hope, and to teach them clean and healthy living behaviors. When patients returned to their communities, they would know how and where to dig their outhouses and wells, and they would understand how to tend a garden. "We're treating them for a healthier lifestyle, not just the riddance of a disease," John said.

On the general clinic day, Hasselblad observed the large group of poverty-stricken, sick, and undernourished people sitting on the ground under the Linden trees near the clinic, patiently waiting to be seen. John went about his work as usual but was keenly aware of Hasselblad's eyes on everything he did. Encouraged that his visitor seemed pleased with what he saw, John consulted Hasselblad on several recalcitrant cases. What a wonderful opportunity to have a respected colleague to consult with about especially challenging medical issues.

★

On Tuesday September 3, the Schmidts and Hasselblads began their journey to Rio in the Km. 81 station wagon. Their first stop around noon was Coronel Oviedo, where several dozen leprosy patients waited for a consultation. The two doctors conferred with each other, especially regarding one of the more acute patients, whose neighbors had carried him in on a plank of boards tied together with strips of leather. The man was covered with open wounds, and he was doubled over coughing. It turned out he had tuberculosis in addition to leprosy. John explained that these diseases often coexisted, which was why he wanted to build a facility for treating TB at Km. 81.

It was almost evening by the time they reached the border, where a ferry took them across the Paraná River into Brazil. They stayed in a small hotel in Foz do Iguazú.

"Today we have a ten-hour drive to Curitiba," John said, knocking on his visitors' door before 6:00 a.m. They filled their thermoses with coffee and were off. The car bounced along on rutted dirt roads, passing small transport trucks with colorful paintings on the sideboards. Mrs. Hasselblad, who had said very little during the drive, mostly waving an ornate fan in front of her face, blurted, "Brazilians are so creative."

John met Clara's eyes in the rear-view mirror and saw that she, too, was trying not to laugh.

Suddenly, there was a loud clanging noise. John stopped on the side of the road to inspect the car. The rear axle was leaking. "We'll have to flag someone down to take me to the next town to see if I can find a mechanic who can tow the car and change what looks like a bad axle bearing."

"And what do *we* do?" Mrs. Hasselblad asked, waving her fan vigorously.

"We wait—there, under those trees. It could take many hours," Clara said.

"I'll go with you into town after you get back here with the tow truck," Hasselblad said to John. "There are some things I've been wanting to discuss with you. This will give us the time."

While John was busy hitching a ride into the next village, finding a mechanic, and arranging to have their vehicle towed, he wondered what "things" Hasselblad wanted to discuss. Maybe he had ideas about additional sources of funding for the TB work? John was eager to hear what he had to say.

Finally, their car was with the mechanic, who said the work on it would take at least four hours. John pointed to a bench in the corner. "What's on your mind?"

"You're doing fine work at Km. 81," Hasselblad began. "But…"

The "but" took John by surprise. He stared at his guest.

"John, there is so much more we could be doing for these patients. Teaching them how to build toilets is all very nice. But what we should be focused on are repeated mass examinations, as well as beginning more modern treatments like physiotherapy and plastic surgery so that they can lead a more normal life."

John sat up straighter and pulled his hat down. "Oliver—"

"Treating tuberculosis is simply a distraction. Let's get focused on doing a better job with leprosy patients. We at ALM are not interested in getting into TB."

TWENTY-FOUR

Oliver Hasselblad was fifty-four, only two years older than John Schmidt, but he felt much too old for the Schmidt style of travel. After getting the axle repaired, Schmidt insisted on continuing, even though it was already late afternoon. They had driven well into the evening and had finally stopped at a cheap hovel for the night. Norma slept very little after several large rats scurried from the bed when she pulled down the sheets.

Driving from Km. 81 to Rio would have been challenging enough without the many stops Schmidt insisted on making en route. Hasselblad didn't understand why it was so important to him that they visit all these places, like the Plautdietsch Mennonite colony of Witmarsum seventy kilometers west of Curitiba. The man seemed obsessed with making connections with everyone he knew along the way, showing slides and reporting on their work at Km. 81. Hasselblad wished he and Norma had flown to Brazil on their own.

They were still a full day's drive from Rio. The women were attempting small talk in the back seat. Norma's fan was on high speed. Schmidt's lips were pressed together, his eyes focused on the road. Hasselblad thought about the conversation they'd had while the axle was being repaired. If one could call it a conversation. He'd never dealt with anyone so stubborn and so combatively self-assured.

He turned to face him. "John, about the mass examinations—"

"I tried to explain to you why that doesn't make any sense in Paraguay at this time. Better control and treatment from now on must come from the patients' voluntary efforts. Repeated mass examinations are as useless as boxing shadows. But one can only know this by being on the ground in our context."

Hasselblad decided to ignore the insulting insinuation that he wasn't capable of making decisions for the Paraguayan context. But he wasn't about to let Schmidt have the ultimate say about the treatment protocol at the leprosy station, given how much money ALM was contributing to its maintenance and growth.

On a hot summer day at the end of 1963, Clara was filing the last charts from the day's clinic when she heard a clap at the door. On the clinic veranda stood a bedraggled and skinny man, holding a skeletal child in his arms. He coughed in long deep spasms.

The man's name was Don Duré. He had tuberculosis and had come for medications. While Clara prepared his meds, John told him he would try to secure a bed for him at the TB sanitorium in Asunción. Duré stared at him blankly, took his medicines and left. Clara eyed John standing at the clinic doorway watching the man slowly trudge over the hill and out of sight. She knew what John was thinking. So many of their patients had tuberculosis, especially those with leprosy. And most of the time, she and John were unsuccessful in finding a place for them in the sanitorium. She wished they could do so much more for them.

The following week, they managed to find a bed in the sanatorium for Don Duré and headed out to look for him. After numerous stops to ask for directions, they came upon a lean-to made of twigs and branches, with no walls and a partially caved-in thatched roof. The sick man, constantly coughing, was sitting on the ground with the baby in his arms. Around him were three other small children, scantily clothed in tattered rags, barefoot, their hair matted.

Through a neighbor who spoke some Spanish and Guaraní, Clara conversed with the man. She learned that the baby's mother, seven months pregnant, was away hoeing in someone else's mandioca field to earn a bit of mandioca for her family to eat. The man said he didn't think he could go to the sanatorium for treatment. How could his woman continue to work and take care of the children?

Clara turned to John. "We'll take the baby and care for it." It was a statement rather than a question. "The child is sick. His huge belly is full of worms. We'll nurse him back to health."

The boy's name was Cresencio. They learned that he was almost two, even though he couldn't sit up by himself. He was all head and tummy, his thin little arms and legs dangling from his body. The child didn't even have the strength to cry when Clara took him from his father.

When they got back to the station, Clara watched Marlena—home from Asunción for summer vacation—hover over the child like it was her own baby. She sighed. Maybe caring for someone else would straighten her out. No matter how hard John whipped that girl, she continued to defy him, which only led to more beatings. Sometimes, Clara stood outside the bedroom door, listening to Marlena's screams, wondering if John was being too hard on her.

For the next few months, Marlena hardly left Cresencio's side. When it was time to return him to his parents, she begged to keep him. In the end, his parents didn't want him back, and when his sister Josefina was born, they asked John and Clara to take her as well. "Chris" and "Josie" became the newest members of their family.

The work at Km. 81 continued to expand rapidly during the next few years. John provided treatments for hookworm and delivered smallpox vaccinations. Despite ALM's protestations, he initiated a TB program and had already treated several dozen cases. He lived here, he knew what was needed, and there was no way he would let ALM leaders sitting in their posh New York offices control what was being done to meet people's needs in Paraguay.

On the non-medical side, John organized programs to help their neighbors with sanitation and toilets. He distributed vegetable seeds and personally rode around the countryside to educate people about soil and plant care. He helped Clara raise support for a literacy campaign, and together they created a library.

At night, John often lay awake. The more he and Clara reached out to help the people in their surrounding area, the more inadequate their efforts seemed. So much more was needed. On one of his latest rounds to vaccinate young children, he became aware of the educational and medical needs of mothers with infants. Far too many newborn babies were dying. They desperately needed help. Didn't Christ instruct them to help the poor, crippled, lame, and blind? How could they turn their backs when so much was needed?

One night before going to bed he said, "Clara, too many infants are dying. We need to start a healthy baby clinic. We could hold one every Wednesday. We'll examine the babies, give them vaccinations, and educate the mothers about infant care. But if we do this, much of it will fall on your shoulders."

Clara walked around the bed and put her arms around his waist. "That's a wonderful idea. We can send them home with cans of powdered milk."

They spread the word. And on their first healthy baby Wednesday, John and Clara examined and vaccinated over sixty infants. Every week, the numbers grew.

The leprosy work, too, was expanding in rewarding ways. There were now around thirty patients in the leprosy guesthouses. They mostly took care of themselves and each other. Clara visited them every morning, and Schwester Neti every late afternoon to pray with them, clean and rebandage wounds, and to help them with their everyday chores and concerns.

By now they had declared 150 of their leprosy patients free of the disease. John wanted his patients not only to be free of leprosy, but also to work again and be fully integrated into society. For example, even though cured of the disease, many patients were left with deformed limbs. To respond to this need, John introduced a physiotherapy program to help patients regain at least limited use of their hands and feet.

But to live anything close to a normal life, these people needed a place to call home. Why was it so hard for donors to step up to help with this? He had traveled with Clara to each of the Mennonite colonies in the past few months, showing slides and raising awareness of the needs. When they showed slides of bloody stumps and oozing wounds, people donated generously. But when they asked for support in finding and purchasing plots of land to rehabilitate the recovering patients, no one seemed to care.

He and Clara had just returned home from the Chaco after the latest round of slide shows and requests for support. "Clara, we have some money of our own put aside. And I know where we can buy a good-sized plot of land to resettle some of our patients. Are you OK with us using our own funds to buy land for them?"

"Of course, I am, John. I'm especially happy for Oscar and Adela. They are so ready to be in their own home."

In that moment, noticing Clara's lack of any hesitation and seeing her eager smile, John was reminded again why God had chosen this remarkable woman to be his partner in life. "Given how shorthanded we are, I'll probably need to go out there myself to help clear the land and start building. But it's the right thing to do."

By mid-1965, Clara saw that Schwester Neti's diabetes was taking its toll. She was nearly blind and had become bedridden, so she could no longer tend to her patients. Day after day, she lay in bed ripping up old bedsheets, donated from the colonies in the Chaco, and rolling them into strips for bandages.

Every night after supper, the leprosy patients from the guesthouses who could walk came to Neti's window to sing coritos for her. Clara joined them whenever she could. When they finished, they called to her through her window, "Dios te bendiga, querida Doña Neti."

Clara especially looked forward to Sunday afternoons when she and Amalia met at Neti's bedside for devotions and prayer. Amalia's health, too, was declining. She coughed a lot and had trouble breathing. It wasn't surprising that her reduced thoracic size and lung growth would lead to pulmonary insufficiency. Was it finally too much for her body to manage?

In the months that followed, Amalia suffered from increased shortness of breath. She could no longer sing, but she could still tell Bible stories. And she always smiled with a friendly word when the children showed her their drawings.

When Clara arrived with her pump organ for Bible school on Sunday, June 26, Amalia was not sitting in her spot under the tree in her yard. The large circle of children sat in unusual silence, their questioning eyes on Doña Clara.

Clara entered the hut. Amalia lay on her side on the low bed, her breath coming out in raspy wheezes. She put her hand on the little one's broad forehead. "You have a fever, Amalia."

"I think I must have the flu, Doña Clara." Her voice was a whisper.

Clara filled Amalia's tin cup with fresh water and placed a wet cloth on her forehead. "I'll come back to check on you tomorrow," she said.

Amalia died of lung failure during the night.

Clara handed the rough piece of fabric to Schwester Neti, who lay propped up on pillows. In response to Neti's raised eyebrows, she said "From Nicasio."

Neti brought the handkerchief to her nose and inhaled the smoky smell. "She's really gone?"

Clara took Neti's hands in hers. "She died during the night. Nicasio said it was peaceful. He thought Amalia would want you to have her handkerchief as a reminder that a piece of her will always be with you."

Neti held the piece of cloth to her eyes. "She was a true and loyal friend."

Clara sat quietly next to Neti's bed.

Neti turned to her. "You know, Amalia used to say she was looking for a husband for me. She said being married was such a blessing in her life. She felt guilty about having such a good life, when I did not."

Clara smiled. A crippled dwarf with leprosy, feeling guilty about living a better life than Neti. What an example of Christian love.

Schwester Neti Voth died in a diabetic coma the following week, a small piece of cloth clasped in her hands. Her body was placed in the ground next to Amalia in the small station cemetery.

"What's going on?" John rose from his desk. It was after 9:00 at night, and two of the station volunteers had clapped at the gate.

"Herr Dokta, there is a problem. We have found a gun. You must come."

John followed the young women with his flashlight into the moonless night. On the way, they told him they'd heard loud squawking from the chicken coop next to their dormitory. When they investigated, they found a burlap bag that was moving along the ground. Three chickens were in the bag. A gun was propped up against a nearby tree.

"See, there's the gun." One of the women pointed.

By now, numerous other station personnel had gathered at the scene. They all stared at the doctor.

"Who knows how to unload a gun?" John bent down to release the chickens and put them back into their pen.

The next day, John drove to Itacurubí with the gun to notify the police. They collected the information and promised to find out who had bought the gun. John doubted he'd ever hear from them again.

Three days later, the police arrived at the station with the gun's owner. "We've brought him to you so you can press charges," the officer said.

John noticed how emaciated the young thief was. How tattered his clothes. And the look of panic on his face. "Officer, you can do as you wish. But I will not press charges. I am not this man's judge. Only the Lord God can be a judge of our deeds." This poor man needed compassion just as much as their leprosy patients.

Within a few months, the chicken thief became a member of the church at Km. 81 and worked part-time as a volunteer, helping John sort medications at the clinic.

A few months after Amalia's death, Clara began raising money to build a church in her honor. She created an Amalia Fund, and people from the Mennonite colonies and even from North America began sending donations.

The local neighbors, mostly mothers of Amalia's Bible school children, enthusiastically pitched in. On a warm Sunday afternoon, nearly a hundred of them gathered under Amalia's tree. They sang coritos and passed around a bucket, raising money for their pe michïva's church. At the end of the meeting, one of the women stood up and asked for silence.

"Señor Diós…" She prayed for Amalia, thanking the Lord for bringing the little one into their lives. She asked for God's blessing on all the money they had been able to raise for her church.

Clara stood off to the side. They had asked to do this on their own, so she had not been involved. They were so excited to be raising money for this important building project.

The woman's prayer ended with a resounding Amén. She brought the bucket over to Clara and almost reverently placed it in her hands.

When Clara returned home and counted the money, she found they had raised almost 300 Guaranies (a little over $2, which even at that time in Paraguay did not go far). "God bless these gifts of pure love," she whispered.

The neighbor women wanted to continue raising money, so Clara met a large group of them on Thursday afternoons for the sewing circle Amalia had organized in Nicasio's yard under the trees. They began each meeting with a prayer of thanksgiving for all Amalia had done for them. Each time they finished sewing a few small items, like handkerchiefs, they had a sale. But because they and their neighbors were all poor, they earned only pennies at a time.

Clara had an idea. Why not wait until they had sewn many items and have a grand sale, inviting people from the larger surrounding area to attend? And as a special bonus, Clara informed them that an Amalia admirer in Argentina had pledged to donate twice the amount they raised at the sale. The women were thrilled, and within several months, they had sewn a large number of pieces, even quilts and rugs made with patches and rags that had been donated from the Mennonite colonies.

Since they held a special evening prayer meeting one Sunday a month in Boquerón, Clara proposed to the women that they present the items for sale after that meeting, along with a short program of singing and reciting Bible verses. She had her doubts about whether this would work. First, these women knew nothing about putting together a program. Second, it was winter, which was an especially hard time of year when people had even less money than usual. But trusting that the Lord would guide them, she moved forward with the plan.

With Clara's help, the women put together a simple program of songs and verses. On the day of the big sale, they displayed the numerous sewn items in Amalia and Nicasio's yard. The place looked festive. Nicasio had raked the ground and whitewashed the tree trunks. But even after all of the preparations, would the ladies from her sewing circle show up, or would they be shy and even a bit ashamed in the end, and not come?

Nearly all of the women came. And many others they had invited from throughout the area came to hear the program. Everything except one blanket was sold. After subtracting the costs, the women raised about 5,000 Guaranies (almost $40) for the Amalia Fund. Including the anonymous pledge from Argentina, they raised 15,000 Guaranies.

John strode into the MCC Home in Asunción. He'd recently received word that Frank Wiens was leaving, and that Orie was asking John to step in as interim MCC director for Paraguay. John had numerous concerns about this. For starters, he had no spare time, and he was not physically in Asunción to manage operations, especially matters having to do with the Chaco colonies.

Perhaps most concerning to John was the fact that this was a challenging moment for Mennonites in Paraguay. Orie had made it very clear that it was time for MCC to begin pulling out of the country, and for colony leaders to take over responsibility for their future. This was not a problem. In fact, it was long overdue. John had noticed that some of the colony leaders, especially from Fernheim, kept receiving donations from Germany and North America, even though they had become relatively wealthy. Things needed to change. But John wasn't at all sure he was the man to lead the change. And he was concerned that the people he depended on for their contributions to the work at the leprosy station would be among the greatest resistors of the transition to local leadership.

"Hello, John." Frank was packing boxes in his office.

"Let's get right to the point here," John said. "The colony administrators are indifferent, they keep almost no records, and they don't know how to manage themselves, much less other MCC ventures in Paraguay, like Km. 81. For the past few years, MCC has expressed a desire for them to take over more responsibility. So far nothing has happened."

"So, what do you propose?" Frank sat down and gestured for John to sit across from him.

"My thought has been from the beginning that if we want the Mennonite colony leaders to take over responsibility for themselves and for the future of social and medical services in Paraguay, we shouldn't expect them to continue in our footsteps. I can tell you from personal experience that they've only tolerated MCC influence because they've become comfortable depending on our financial support. We might say we stand ready to counsel them, but otherwise we need to just let them figure out how to do things their way."

"But what if they're incapable of working together?" Frank looked unconvinced.

"Until now they haven't needed to," John said. "When their survival depends on it, they'll figure it out."

TWENTY-FIVE

John slowed his horse and stared across what used to be useless thorny brush and was now grassland that extended as far as he could see. He'd come out to meet Konrad Wolf to review the progress on his ranch. Wolf rode up beside him, wiping his forehead with the back of his hand.

"You've done a good job, Konrad," John said.

It had been twelve years since John secured funds from U.S. investors to purchase the thirty square miles outside of the colony for the ranch, and seven years since Wolf agreed to manage it for him. He and Wolf had often clashed about how to develop the ranch, like where and how to clear the brush to plant grassland and dig the water holes. But it was now a thriving enterprise with several thousand head of cattle.

They bred Holstein and Pardo Suizo cattle for dairy production. And they raised Brahma cattle for meat, crossbreeding them with Angus and Hereford to get the desired levels of marbling. The whole Chaco region had excellent conditions for intensive cattle production. Frequent droughts were worrisome, but they'd dug numerous watering holes where water could accumulate during the rainy season.

Their largest customer was a German company Liebig, a producer of corned beef and a thick, dark, syrupy beef extract paste sold in glass bottles and tins. Liebig had opened a large plant in Paraguay back in 1924. By the mid-1960s, the plant was buying and shipping frozen beef in addition to the original products.

"John, we've had our differences. But I've been thinking a lot about what you've done for us here in the colony." Wolf paused. "You were wrong about Fritz Kliewer, but—"

"Stop right there," John interrupted.

Wolf raised his hand. "What I'm trying to say is that you have been wrong about some things in the past, but you were right about the economic possibilities of this region. And without the trans-Chaco road, none of what we're accomplishing would have been possible."

Why did he have to bring Kliewer into this? Why dig up old history? The Kliewer chapter seemed to never end.

He turned in his saddle to face Wolf. "You know that MCC wants to turn over the responsibility for Km. 81 to the colonies?"

"I heard such a rumor," Wolf said. "But I can't imagine that all of the church groups will ever work together."

"They'll have to find a way," John said.

In early August of 1967, Clara was busy preparing for a grand celebration to inaugurate the new clinic, a small hospital for acute TB and leprosy patients, and a new guesthouse for residential leprosy patients. They expected well over a hundred people to come for the event, including Dr. Hasselblad. They had invited neighboring Paraguayans, doctors and pharmacists from Asunción, and many Mennonites from the colonies. They even sent an invitation to President Stroessner, although they didn't expect he would come.

Unfortunately, the clinic was not yet complete. The windows had been set the week before, but the floor tiles had not yet been laid. And their workers were too busy with other tasks to help complete the work.

Clara finished applying varnish to the last window frame and walked over to where John was shimmying the doorframe into place. "The celebration is only a few days away. And this dirt floor doesn't look very inaugural." She frowned. "I know we have clinic all day tomorrow, but what if we just lay the floor tiles ourselves tonight?"

That night, by the flickering light of a small kerosene lamp hanging from a hook on the wall, John and Clara were down on their hands and knees. John stopped occasionally to stretch. With each tile she placed, Clara breathed a prayer for her husband. He was having a lot of trouble with his neck, pain radiating from the right side of his head, sometimes all the way down his leg. Was it arthritis? Kidney trouble? Something worse?

When they finished setting the last tile, the sun was just beginning to rise.

On the day of the big event, cars began to roll in by mid-morning. Clara welcomed everyone with hot coffee and Zwieback. John invited their visitors to roam around the station. They had placed tables and benches under the trees by their house. A Paraguayan couple had made a pork rib asado, chipa guazú and mandioca for the noon meal.

They had asked Hasselblad to lead the afternoon program of thanks for and dedication of the new buildings. Clara sat on a bench next to John near the front of the crowd. Her thoughts wandered back to another inauguration, fourteen years ago, in January of 1953. It was hard to compare what Km. 81 looked like then and now. Back then, there had been only a few shacks and several partially constructed buildings. Today, there were twenty-three buildings on the station. Clara smiled and grasped John's hand. He turned to her and grinned. Thanks be to God. This was a blessed day.

Hasselblad rose. He cleared his throat, and after a few words of welcome went on to deliver his message. "In the first place, so far as I am aware, Dr. Schmidt was the first to establish a leprosy control program based on domiciliary treatment of the patient. This was a courageous and pioneering venture. No one had tried it before. Today domiciliary treatment has become the basis of leprosy control work throughout the world."

Clara felt John's hand tighten around hers.

Hasselblad continued. "The second element is equally important. Leprosy work must be an integral part of the health services offered to any community where the disease is endemic. For centuries, leprosy has been looked upon as a disease apart, out of the mainstream of medicine. Dr. Schmidt and his coworkers have accepted the responsibility for the treatment of patients in the community, regardless of the cause of their disease. Here, we have leprosy treated with the same care, using the same facilities, and applying the same skills offered to patients with other diseases. Today, it is accepted that until and unless leprosy work is fully integrated into the public health services of each country, there is no hope of eliminating the disease. Here at Km. 81, it has been proven that this method actually works."

Loud applause broke out from the audience.

Hasselblad held up his hand. "But that is all about the past. We must now turn to the future. From the more than sixty years of experience of the World Health Organization and the American Leprosy Missions, it is evident that Km. 81 is no longer keeping up with the latest leprosy treatment methodologies."

The celebratory mood shifted to somber silence. Clara glanced sideways at John, who had pulled his hand away from her. His mouth had flattened into a thin, tight line.

When the inauguration ceremony ended mid-afternoon, John rose before the other attendees began to leave, and walked briskly toward the patient guesthouses. He hadn't paid attention to the details Hasselblad shared about all the ways that Km. 81...no, all the ways that *he* had fallen behind the times. He'd heard them all before. The man was still yapping on about mass examinations and plastic surgery.

Ten years ago, it was about building a colony, until ALM finally woke up to the truth. Or at least he thought they had. Today it was plastic surgery and examination of contacts. Those swanky New Yorkers just didn't have their feet on the ground. What was different about today was that this time Hasselblad had publicly humiliated him.

John's heartbeat pounded in his chest when he heard Clara and Hasselblad approaching.

"John, these are issues we've talked about before," Hasselblad said when they caught up with him.

"Right," John muttered. "Sorry, I have a few patients to see."

As he walked away, leaving the two of them standing together on the path, John overheard Clara saying, "I'm so sorry, but please understand that..."

John continued toward the leprosy guesthouses. The patients greeted him with their usual smiles and eagerly reached out their crippled hands to grasp his. Here's where he belonged. This was why he was here.

"Let's take a look at your arm," John said, carefully removing the bandages from Luís, their most recent guest, a young man with advanced symptoms. "This is looking much better. Are you remembering to apply hot compresses every day?"

"Yesterday Doña Clara showed me how to do it with one hand." Luís's right arm was a bloody stump that ended just above his elbow.

"Very good," John said.

He moved on to check in with the married couple, Oscar and Adela. Both were in remission. "I spoke with the agricultural minister just this week, and he confirmed, Oscar, that he is finding you a job near Caaguazú. And I'm still working at getting a plot of land there for you to build your own home," John said. "We're close."

Their smiles renewed John's conviction that he was doing the right thing. Oscar was brought to Km. 81 in 1961, on his deathbed with sepsis due to infections all over his body, kidney failure, and advanced-stage leprosy. By the time Adela, a pretty, young lady with ulcers all over her arms and on the bottoms of her feet, came to the station a year later, Oscar was able to sit up and feed himself. They both responded well to treatments, and before long, they fell in love and were married in the double ceremony with Amalia and Nicasio Ayala.

For the past six years, the couple had worked as coordinators for the patients in the guesthouses. But John knew that Oscar had completed agricultural school before he became ill. For months, John had tried to contact someone in the Agricultural Ministry who would help. Finally, last week, after many trips, he was able to speak with the minister himself, who was moved in hearing Oscar's story and remembered him from when they were both in school together. He promised to find him a job.

After checking in on a few more patients, John headed home. His heart had stopped pounding. It was more important to be a compassionate Christian than to comply with Hasselblad's demands. And no amount of fancy plastic surgery would help these people as much as giving them a little assistance in establishing normal lives with a home and a job. Fortunately, when Hasselblad returned to his luxurious offices in New York, the man would forget about Paraguay, and the real work here would continue.

The letter John had sent to Ana a few weeks ago was returned, unopened, *Devolver al Remitente* scrawled across the envelope. He'd wondered when he sent it if the letter would get to her. This confirmed his fears that she was once again at the forefront of dangerous and risky activities.

Ana had told them when she was in Paraguay that she was joining the *Montoneros*, a leftist guerilla group of Juan Perón supporters. He'd recently read that the Montoneros were launching attacks against the military-appointed president who was supported by the U.S. and by corrupt multinational corporations. The Montoneros publicly denounced the government for masquerading as a democracy, while operating as a fascist regime with no concern for human rights. Apparently, the guerilla attacks sought to force the government to give up their pretenses and to operate openly as a fascist entity, expecting that the Argentine people would then mobilize to support the guerrilla cause.

The Peronismo movement had been banned since Perón's exile. What did Ana think she and the rest of the Montoneros could accomplish, other than get themselves killed?

Clara was relieved that their work at Km. 81 continued to expand, despite Hasselblad's assertions that they weren't keeping up with the latest developments for leprosy treatment. John had said all along that it was nothing but a power play, and that things would be just like normal once Hasselblad was back in his comfortable New York office. It had been over six months since the inauguration. Thankfully, it seemed that John was right.

The Paraguayan Health Ministry had recently enlarged John and Clara's geographic area of responsibility for leprosy patients to the north and east, including the entire department of Caaguazú. It required them to travel twice as far for their patients. For years, John had ridden on horseback, seeking out individual patients and treating them in their homes. In the process, he'd often formed close personal relationships with them, while helping to improve their day-to-day lives. Now, to serve their expanded area of responsibility, John and Clara began running clinics every other week, driving out the first and third Tuesday of each month to existing hospitals in the various areas. So now, most patients came to their clinics for treatments.

They saw many more patients this way, but Clara worried that by not going to patients' homes, they were not giving them the personalized care they deserved. She made sure to always bring along a large collection of care packages to every clinic. These included vegetable seeds and illustrated diagrams with instructions for how to plant and manage a garden, and how to properly dig toilets and wells. They also contained personal items such as towels, blankets, and food stuff like powdered milk.

It was the first Tuesday clinic in March. Clara and John were up and had their car loaded before sunrise. Leprosy patients from the station often rode along with them on these clinic days, to return to or visit their homes. On this day, Oscar and Adela waited for them in front of the guesthouse with the few bags that held all their belongings. They were on their way to their new home, not yet built, on a plot of land John had acquired near Caaguazú.

"Adela, Oscar, please get in. This is an exciting day." Clara opened the car door for them.

The Schmidts first stopped in Coronel Oviedo, where they saw an unusually large number of patients with various skin disorders. After a snack, they drove on to Caaguazú, where there was again a long line of patients waiting for them. After caring for them, they finally moved on to the new settlement where Oscar and Adela were going to live.

They drove to a small clearing. In the center, stood a lean-to with a broken-down thatched roof and no walls. "Welcome to your home, dear ones," Clara said, embracing Oscar and Adela. "I would like to offer a prayer for your new place."

The four of them stood in a small circle, arms around each other, while Clara lifted up their new lives to God's grace and protection.

After sharing a quick meal from the food box with Oscar and Adela, John and Clara drove on to an outlying area called Tobatí, a small community nearly forty kilometers from the Ruta. It was a new settlement of Paraguayan families, along with a small group of Amish and German Mennonites who'd recently moved to the area from the Chaco.

On rainy days, the winding dirt road to Tobatí was nearly impassable slick red mud with deep ruts left by logging trucks and tractors. On this evening in March, the roads were dry, but it was dark by the time John and Clara turned off the Ruta. They slowly made their way around bumpy detours to get past ruts that were too deep to maneuver.

They came around a corner, and John stomped on the brakes. In front of them, barely visible in the darkness, was a bridge that had collapsed. Someone had placed two uneven planks across the river.

"John, we can't cross that," Clara cried out.

John got out of the car to survey the situation. By the way he pulled down his hat as he marched back toward the car, Clara knew they were continuing.

"You need to walk ahead with a flashlight. I'll steer the car onto the planks behind you," he said.

It was after midnight by the time they reached the home of the family who had agreed to have them stay for the night.

She and John had only recently learned of the desperate need for medical services in this remote area of east Paraguay, so they had added Tobatí to their bimonthly clinic route. On Wednesday, they saw numerous patients, most of them suffering general medical conditions, but a few also with leprosy. It was rewarding to provide services in a community that otherwise had no medical care. After seeing the last patient, they drove the long 200 kilometers back to Km. 81. It was well into the night when they returned home, tired but energized.

On their clinic days, both at the station and in the remote areas, Clara loved working beside John as his nurse. She remembered the early days in the Chaco when she'd frequently broken down in tears because of his gruff manner. John was still often impatient and short-tempered, but underneath his crusty shell was the most loving and caring man she'd ever met. They had learned to work well as a team.

With one exception. Since the early years on the station, John had insisted on offering birth control to leprosy patients. Clara had prayed ardently about this issue, and she had tearfully argued with John that this was not the Lord's wish. It couldn't be. If sexual intercourse was all about lust without intending procreation, how could that possibly be what God wanted? John had firmly stood his ground, arguing that too little was known about how leprosy spread, and he didn't want to risk a bunch of children contracting the disease just because he was too cowardly to prevent their birth.

Over time, Clara had come to accept that they were doing the right thing for their leprosy patients. But recently, John had begun to talk about the need for contraceptives among their Paraguayan neighbors who were not leprous. Just the other night, they'd had another one of their many arguments about the matter.

Clara worried that John's views were based entirely on practical circumstances, rather than Biblical teaching. "It's not God's will that we alter His plan for sexual intercourse," she said, knowing even as she blurted it out that it would make no difference. She could tell when he'd made up his mind.

"Clara, I'm not sure we know God's will about this, and it's selfish of us to allow our personal opinions to get in the way of helping these women. They are the ones who do most of the work in the gardens and fields. And many of them already have way more children than they can clothe and feed. The World Church Service has supplied us with the intra-uterine devices. It would be completely irresponsible of us to not make them available to these women. We just can't let the men know that we're doing this."

"I will never agree with you on this," Clara said quietly.

TWENTY-SIX

Bill Snyder sat across the desk from Dr. Hasselblad in the ALM office at 297 Park Avenue. He ran a hand across his forehead and stared around him. He'd been here before, but each time he was struck by how different this was from his office space in Akron. Was all this luxury really necessary? Was this the best way to spend money by an organization responsible for the care of leprosy patients around the world?

He brought his attention back to what Hasselblad was saying. "Since your letter of November 29, 1967, to Schmidt, asking him to respond to ALM's concerns about his many distractions from leprosy work, there has been no response. And it's been eight months." Hasselblad waved his hands in the air. "Distractions like farming, ranching, buying land and building homes for patients, digging toilets…the man seems incapable of focusing on what we're paying for—the treatment of leprosy."

Bill opened his mouth to speak, but Hasselblad continued. "I am inclined to believe that his position in Paraguay has become even more rigid and the opportunities for moving ahead less encouraging."

It was not posed as a question, but rather a matter of fact. This was not good. The leprosy work depended on ALM's financial support. Bill cleared his throat. "I have written Dr. Schmidt again, calling his attention to the information you need and encouraging him to make every effort to keep alive our meaningful relationship with ALM. I feel confident you will be hearing from him very soon."

Hasselblad pushed back from his desk. "Beginning January 1, 1969, we will need to come to a clear agreement regarding the work at Km. 81 and ALM's support. I am sure you understand our position in this matter. We are prepared to drop our involvement in this project if Schmidt does not cooperate."

It seemed like a signal that the meeting had ended. "We at MCC know that Km. 81 needs the financial support that ALM has provided, but even more than that, we value your broader vision of the work. This is especially true now that the responsibility for Km. 81 is transferring from MCC to a committee of Mennonite colony leaders."

"Oh, yes, about that," Hasselblad said, bringing his slender fingers to his forehead as though remembering another significant problem. "They keep sending their reports to us in German. Is it really too much to ask for reports written in English?"

Again, before Bill could answer, Hasselblad continued. "I know Schmidt is asking for a furlough. He seems to think ALM will support him in attending the Ninth International Leprosy Congress in London in September, on his way back to Paraguay."

"Yes, we believe it's a good idea for John and Clara to take some time off from the work. The whole move to colony leadership will not be an easy transition for them."

"Just so you know, ALM will not support Schmidt's attendance at the Congress. It is far too advanced and technical for him in any case."

Hasselblad rose, and Bill understood that this time the meeting really was over. Clearly, ALM had the ultimate expertise in the world about the treatment of leprosy. He just wished John wasn't so stubborn about doing things his way.

★

"I can't believe it has been twenty-five years." Clara moved over to John's side of the bed and put her arms around him.

"You're the best decision I ever made," John said, hugging her back.

Clara laughed. "You used to say that it was God who brought us together, not you."

"Well, I think I had something to do with it." He pulled away. "We have a lot of work before our guests show up. For one thing, our Saturday clinic doesn't go away just because we're celebrating our Silver Anniversary."

It was a crisp sunny Saturday in August. Wesley and Marlena rode out from Asunción on his motorcycle to help prepare for the celebration. The two of them whitewashed the trunks of trees in the yard to the west of their home. And they set up enough chairs and boards across sawhorses to seat eighty people for a meal.

Around noon, people began arriving on foot as well as in oxcarts and cars. They came from Asunción and the neighboring villages, and from as far away as the Chaco in the west and Tobatí in the east. Over 250 people were served beef, pork, and sausage asado, mandioca, cabbage salad, Zwieback, and lemonade, topped off with cake and coffee. While eighty at a time ate their meal, others milled around, listening to Marlena play her harp and Mary Lou recite poems Clara had composed about their courtship by mail and their wedding day.

After everyone had eaten, people assembled around the Schmidt veranda for a program of songs and more recitations.

John Russell was the emcee. "And now we'll hear a few words from the couple we're here to celebrate."

Clara rose and walked with John to the top steps of the veranda. "I didn't think marriage was in my future. In fact, I was chosen to become a deaconess. But then John came into my life. I can't imagine what he saw in me—"

John interrupted her. "It was really quite simple. I needed a nurse to help me in my work." Loud booing from their kids on the side of the veranda stopped him. John grinned and grabbed Clara's hand. "I am grateful for the years God has given us, and I pray we might have twenty-five more."

In the evening, they showed slides against a large white hanging sheet: Baby John Russell ("Sonny") surrounded by the first group of nursing students in the Chaco—young Neti Voth beaming into the camera; a construction site during the early years of Km. 81, their children in various precarious positions on the piles of rubble; their five oldest children pushing the Volvo up the mountains in Bolivia. The slides depicted their life as a family, and John's commentary connected each family photos with important moments in the development of their work in the Chaco and their mission at Km. 81.

Clara swallowed against a lump in her throat as the slides of her children flicked against the sheet. Over the years, she had entrusted the lives of her little ones to the Lord. But recently, that trust was shaken. Several of their children had lost their way and were living an un-Christian life. *Nothing is impossible with God*, she reminded herself.

The following day, Sunday, August 25, which was their actual anniversary day, they prepared the same meal for the leprosy patients living in the guesthouses, as well as other patients who came from the surrounding area, along with their families and friends. During the program, the patients shared heartfelt words of gratitude and affection toward the doctor and Doña Clara.

Clara was able to hold back the tears stinging her eyes, until Doña Ramona stood up to speak. "It's only because of you that I am alive today. I thank God for you every day."

Clara blinked a few times and looked at their guests, standing and seated on chairs and on the ground around the veranda. Yesterday's celebration had been larger. And yesterday's guests had worn more festive clothing. But this moment, surrounded by the love and gratitude of these dear people was the high point of all the celebrations. Clara smiled. Of course, it was. That's why they had planned it for their real anniversary date.

★

On December 15, 1968, John and Clara left for a six-month furlough to the U.S. John's brother Herb agreed to take over the work at Km. 81 for part of their absence. And the colony leaders had identified another physician named Franz Duerksen to fill in during the rest of the time. Dr. Duerksen was the son of a prominent minister from the Mennonite colonies, and had obtained his medical training in Argentina.

Most of John and Clara's children had returned to and were living and working in Paraguay by now. They had only their three youngest along, whom they left with relatives in Kansas, giving John and Clara ample time to again travel around the U.S., raising money for their work back home.

John was disappointed that the European trip at the end of their furlough did not materialize. The ALM treasurer sent him some flimsy excuse that the trip via London to New York and back to Paraguay would cost $1,400, when it actually would cost only $818. To work on the front lines of the attack on leprosy with a salary that was next to nothing was not a big deal. But such a cold and impersonal attitude from ALM was insulting.

Before leaving to return to Paraguay, John met with Herb, who said he wanted to report on his time at Km. 81. John drove up to the modern A-frame home Herb had recently built and was reminded of how different their lives were.

Herb met him at the door, his stinky tobacco pipe in his right hand.

"I appreciate you stepping in to cover the work for part of the time that we've been gone," John said.

"Yes, I want to talk to you about that." Herb gestured for John to sit on the sofa across from him. He pulled on his pipe and slowly let out small puffs of smoke. "The way I see it, Km. 81 should be seeing two to three times as many leprosy patients and hold a lot fewer prayer meetings."

"That's what you have to say to me?" John knew Herb didn't share his passion for Christian service, but he didn't think his brother was against it. *Why do I always seem to hold Herb in such high regard, when I find so much of what he stands for unconscionable?*

★

Konrad Wolf sat back, his hands behind his head, and stared out of his office window. This all sounded like big trouble. He wasn't at all sure his committee could handle it. In front of him were three letters: from MCC, ALM, and Dr. Franz Duerksen. He'd received the MCC letter a week ago. It officially transferred MCC's responsibilities in Paraguay to his newly formed GemeindeKomitee, which consisted of representatives from all the Mennonite colonies. That was no surprise. They'd been expecting it. The other two letters were more worrisome.

The letter from Hasselblad copied MCC and Franz Duerksen, but not Schmidt. That immediately signaled trouble. The letter itself was more like a report, a numbered list of things that needed to happen at Km. 81 if ALM was to continue to support it.

1. Grounds built according to protocol – buildings torn down and new construction with consultation of ALM

2. All farming operations discontinued

3. GemeindeKomitee to provide an experienced manager to keep accurate statistics on profit and loss and determine if the station's cattle operations should cease

4. Fewer voluntary service workers

5. Leprosy control based on sound public health principles of mass examination

6. Expanded physical therapy and introduction of plastic surgery

7. On the Caaguazú settlement of leprosy patients that has been financed privately by Schmidt, the project will not be expanded beyond the present plans

The letter went on to say that Dr. Duerksen, who was currently serving at Km. 81 during part of Dr. Schmidt's absence, had expressed an interest in returning to the station to begin a program of plastic surgery. In September, ALM would finance a year of training for Duerksen at the All-Africa Leprosy and Rehabilitation Training Center (ALERT) in Addis Ababa, Ethiopia.

Hasselblad's letter ended with ALM's full endorsement of Dr. Duerksen:

He is a skilled and highly trained surgeon whose work
will yield rich dividends for the cause of leprosy sufferers
throughout Paraguay and South America. ALM will
increase its support if this kind of program is developed
with adequate personnel to carry it through.

Finally, Konrad re-read Duerksen's letter, addressed to MCC and ALM.

There is much work, and one worker on the team is as
important as another: The physiotherapist, the cobbler,
the surgeon, and the doctor who leads and holds all these
together.

We are personally interested in the surgical work here and
may return after a year of study to be a cog in the wheel.

These were major changes that would impact the Schmidts both personally and professionally. Why wasn't Schmidt copied on any of this correspondence? Sure, he had been domineering and sometimes out of control, but this was a stab in the back he did not deserve.

Clara and John returned to Paraguay on July 30, 1969, re-energized and full of ideas for further expanding their work. John drew up building plans to enlarge the cobbler facilities at Km. 81. He sent the plans and his justifications for the expansion to MCC.

After a long delay, the response from MCC was that 1) all requests needed to now be directed to the GemeindeKomitee instead of MCC, and 2) ALM needed to be consulted on all new building projects. Since Dr. Hasselblad was on an extended visit to Nigeria and would not return to the U.S. before traveling to Paraguay for an upcoming visit, it would be best for John to discuss these plans with Hasselblad in person.

"What does he mean, I can't send my requests to MCC?" John flung the letter down on the desk. "I know the GemeindeKomitee is in charge, but I'm part of MCC, so of course MCC is where I'll go with these plans for important areas of expansion."

"Does he really say that you can't approach MCC at all?" Clara asked.

John threw the letter at her. "Here. Read it for yourself. Maybe we just need to raise the funds ourselves to construct the new cobbler building I designed."

Later that evening, John wrote a column for the Km. 81 quarterly newsletter *Im Dienste der Liebe* titled To Be Alone and Not Alone.

For us, now that we're back in the work at Km. 81, it's again important that we belong to a group of people and to a work. We have no reason to believe that we're alone.

The wonderful feeling of not being alone makes our contact with the leprosy patients even more important. Being alone is something that is a reality for most of them. We especially feel compassion for them when we acknowledge that they are not at fault for getting the disease and therefore being alone. What can we do to make these patients feel less alone? I am interested in us treating the patients as people, not just treating their disease. We must always put ourselves in their place.

He ended with:

My dear reader, think about what it means to be alone. Are you grateful? Let's work together for these patients who are alone in so many ways.

★

In late November of 1969, a doctor from the Hospital Bautista sent word that Marlena, who was studying in Asunción, was in the hospital, pregnant, with gonorrhea, and an abdominal tumor. They rushed to her side and learned that their recalcitrant daughter had had an affair with a much older married man.

Clara's reaction was to cry. But John was furious. How could she? He and Clara had enough problems on their plate, and now this?

During the next few weeks, Marlena was at home to heal from the gonorrhea and gain strength for the upcoming surgery to remove the tumor. She stayed mostly in her room, not joining them for meals and not helping with any household chores.

Finally, John had enough. "Get yourself out of that bed right now, Marlena. If you don't want to eat, that's fine, but you're going to make yourself useful around here." His voice held a bitter edge.

"I'm not getting up," Marlena muttered.

He grabbed her arm and pulled her off the bed, dragging her behind him, out onto the veranda.

"Let go of me," Marlena screamed.

Clara came out of the kitchen, her face drawn. "John..."

Still gripping Marlena's arm, John's voice exploded in a sharp staccato. "There. Are. Plenty. Of. Other. Children. To. Love. I. Don't. Need. You. I. Want. You. Out. Of. My. Life." His nostrils spread wide and taut.

The weight of Paraguay's late afternoon humid stifling November heat fell heavily on the three of them standing in an awkward semicircle on the open veranda.

No one said another word. In fact, as was the case regarding many other painful experiences within the family, nothing further was ever said about this incident. In the end, Marlena was not pregnant, and the tumor was benign. But a new wariness now seemed to cloud her eyes.

★

During the next year, Clara watched John throw himself into their work with renewed vigor, spending long days seeing patients and managing farm operations, and then staying up late in the evenings drawing more building plans. But all was not well. She often heard him pacing back and forth on the veranda in the middle of the night. Correspondence from both MCC and ALM had stopped almost completely, and the colony GemeindeKomitee seemed to still be figuring things out, since they'd heard very little from them as well. Clara knew they had reason to believe they were more and more alone in this work. In fact, she was pretty sure that's what had prompted John to write the newsletter column To Be Alone and Not Alone when they returned from their furlough almost a year ago.

Clara had tried numerous times to talk with John about all of this. But he invariably turned the conversation to the work at hand. They had secured and privately funded five additional plots of land for leprosy patient settlements in the Caaguazú area near Oscar and Adela. The work on these settlements, in addition to their regular duties, meant they were even busier than usual.

John had just returned from several days in Caaguazú, helping the patients build their homes. It was past midnight, but Clara was still up. She'd received word that there was to be an important meeting in Asunción in just a week, on August 10. Representatives from ALM and MCC in the North, as well as from the GemeindeKomitee in the Chaco, were going to be present. Dr. Duerksen was also going to attend. John and Clara's presence was requested.

John looked exhausted and his overalls were filthy. He sat at the table on the veranda and took the cup of tea Clara offered. "We made some good progress on the buildings. But I'm worried about their children. Clara, these children have never seen a book, and yet some of them seem to have gotten through fourth or fifth grade. How is that even possible with no books? We need to ask the GemeindeKomitee to help us get school supplies for these children."

Clara smiled sadly. "John, I'm concerned about how MCC and ALM will react when they hear about the new settlements."

"I've chopped and sawed and hammered for days, and I just drove for almost five hours to get home tonight. I'm too tired to care what those

North Americans think they know about our people here in Paraguay. The integration of our patients with others in the surrounding area promises to be the single biggest breakthrough in helping them find their place in society. Besides—"

"John. Please stop. We need to talk. I received word from Asunción about a meeting…"

TWENTY-SEVEN

John and Clara arrived late to the meeting because they had stopped on the way to drop off a patient at the sanatorium in Asunción. Clara entered the room behind John and took in the severe faces of the men seated around the table. Hasselblad sat at the head, to his right were Bill Snyder and Edgar Stoesz, the MCC representatives. Across from them sat Dr. Duerksen and three members of the Gemeinde-Komitee, including Konrad Wolf, whose eyes were on the floor.

Hasselblad was speaking. "As I said, I agreed to come to Paraguay for this meeting on the express condition that we discuss freely all aspects of the leprosy work and that we raise all questions in an open and frank way."

Clara watched John's jaw tighten as he listened to the men around the table report their vision for the future of the leprosy station, never once asking his opinions. Regular examinations of all household contacts; a two-doctor program with Dr. Duerksen joining as plastic surgeon; no more settlements for leprosy patients; and no more agricultural activities. Then they presented the new organizational chart, outlining lines of authority and responsibility.

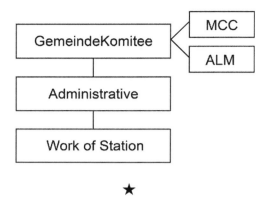

★

Konrad Wolf turned off the Ruta at the Km. 81 marker. He'd been at the leprosy station many times, but never under these conditions. This was the most distasteful task he'd ever been asked to do since heading up the GemeindeKomitee. Konrad was driving MCC's Paraguay representative, Edgar Stoesz, to the station. They came to manage what would almost certainly be a volatile situation when Dr. Duerksen arrived at Km. 81 with his family later that day.

To smooth the transition in leadership, ALM had requested a one-year overlap between the Duerksens arriving and the Schmidts leaving the station. But Schmidt had argued for an early furlough, so ALM asked for a minimum of an eight-week overlap of the two doctors. Schmidt had plans to travel to the U.S. and from there to Vietnam for some months of medical service before returning to Paraguay in July of the following year. No one seemed to know exactly what would happen upon their return. Some people speculated that they would resume their twenty years of leadership at Km. 81. Others believed they were retiring in the Tobatí area of east Paraguay; or alternatively, that they were going to establish a new leprosy clinic in that area. Some even said the Schmidts and Duerksens would work together to expand the leprosy program at Km. 81.

Konrad maneuvered the car slowly around the muddy ruts caused by last night's rainstorm. "With all of our planning, we still have not determined who's going to be the boss at Km. 81 if and when Schmidt returns next year."

"That's the million-dollar question, isn't it?" Stoesz shifted in his seat. "I think the more pressing issue right now is whether Schmidt will even allow Duerksen to enter the station grounds today."

They drove up the hill and around the curved road to the Schmidt house. "OK, let's face the fire," Stoesz said, leading the way onto the veranda.

"Hello," Wolf called out, clapping at the entrance.

There was no response, so the two men walked to the station's main kitchen and meeting hall, where the workers were just finishing their noon meal.

"Schmidts? They left this morning," one of the workers said. "We had a big going-away ceremony for them last night."

Konrad turned to Stoesz. "I guess we don't have to worry about a nasty confrontation, at least not today."

Hours before Wolf and Stoesz arrived at the station, Clara and John had loaded their car with the last of their belongings and headed out. Clara stared out the car window as the red-tiled roof of the home she and John had built and raised their children in slipped out of sight. It was Thursday, November 18, 1971, the last day she would ever call this beautiful spot her home. Almost exactly twenty years ago, she and John had arrived in Paraguay, bringing with them only a dream of what this place could become. She pinched back tears as they drove past the main station kitchen, where a large group of their workers had assembled and were singing, *Gott Mit Euch, Bis Wir Uns Wiedersehn.*

Clara took in John's tight grip of the steering wheel. She reached over and placed a hand on his knee. She had never seen him suffer as he had in the past few months. Some nights he slept hardly at all. And during their daily devotions after breakfast, his prayers spilled out of him. "Lord, grant us Thy peace as we continue to serve Thee in the best way we know how."

Clara wished she could do something to ease John's distress. They had talked for many hours about their decision to leave Km. 81. Both agreed that plastic surgery was probably something that needed to be added to the mix of services for their patients. But many of the other ALM stipulations simply made no sense in their Paraguayan context. Worst of all, John's opinions didn't seem to matter anymore to ALM or even MCC.

They drove in silence past the station buildings, down the hill, across the clattering bridge and to the Ruta. When he reached the highway, John turned left, heading east toward Tobatí. Clara watched the buildings of Itacurubí pass by, remembering the men from there who'd come to Km. 81 to throw rocks at her and destroy their property when they were just beginning to develop the station. God had watched over them then. He would do so again. Clara sighed. If only the people who made the recent decisions about Km. 81 could have followed a more Christian approach, John wouldn't have felt completely betrayed; so betrayed that in the end, he didn't have it in him to stay and face those who conspired against him.

Clara's mind turned to their future. They would stay in Tobatí for six days, before flying to the States to spend a month with relatives. In early January, they planned to travel to Vietnam for a four-month tour of service. The American Medical Association had accepted John under its Voluntary Physicians for Vietnam program. After making sure that the program was not connected with the Army in any way, John had signed up to help train lay workers in the care and treatment of leprosy patients, and Clara would join him as his assistant.

Clara wanted to continue to fulfill her lifelong commitment to the Lord's service. But she felt a little uneasy about their plans for what they would do when they returned to Paraguay. She remembered the moment several months ago, when their ideas about moving to Tobatí had come together, while sitting in front of the fireplace in their living room with Marlena and her new husband.

After a year in the U.S., Marlena had returned to Paraguay in June with her fiancé, Steve Fiol. They were married with a small informal ceremony in their home at Km. 81. Clara prayed that this marriage would mean that her lost child, who'd given them so much grief, was finally finding her way.

On a cold, rainy evening in early July, the four of them sat around the living room fireplace. John threw a log into the fire. "We're wondering what your plans are now that you're married. Will you be heading back to the U.S.?"

"We haven't yet bought our return tickets. We aren't sure how long we'll stay," Marlena said. "Why do you ask?"

John cleared his throat. "We have something we'd like to discuss with you."

He described the most recent decisions about Km. 81 and its leadership. "It seems I'm an MCC worker who can no longer contact MCC directly. Everything needs to go through a cumbersome committee. But that's not the worst of it. ALM has all sorts of high-falutin' ideas about the control and treatment of leprosy that are nonsense in the Paraguayan context."

Clara patted John's arm. "John, we talked about the fact that plastic surgery is—"

John threw up his hands and rattled off the statistics he'd gone over in his head for months. Around thirty percent of leprosy patients in Paraguay had severe foot trouble like ulcers, bone infections, and paralysis; fifteen percent had severe hand lesions (nearly one hundred percent had small sores and scars on the hands); thirty percent needed dental care; ninety percent had hookworm; ten percent had other complications from leprosy; and many had concurrent diseases of heart, lungs, kidneys, or liver.

He ended with, "Only about three to five percent can actually benefit from plastic surgery."

Clara leaned forward. "So, the reason—"

Again, John interrupted her. "What you need to know," he said, turning to Steve and Marlena, "is that ALM's idea that we can control leprosy in Paraguay through mass examinations of contacts is based on ignorance and complete disregard of the facts here in Paraguay." He went on to explain that only about five percent of his new patients came from direct contacts. Almost none of them knew anyone else with the disease or had any idea where it came from. "I'm sure it's unusual in the rest of the world, but patients actually come to us because they know we will take care of them and not lock them up."

Marlena looked confused. "What are you saying?"

"Well, I've drawn up these plans." John reached for a notebook on the shelf beside his chair. "Mom and I are taking some time off to serve in Vietnam. When we return to Paraguay next year, we want to establish a new home in Tobatí. Here are the drawings for the house. We just don't know who will build it—"

"It's God's will," Clara said quietly when she saw the shocked look on Marlena's face.

After further conversation about their travel and house-building plans, John blurted, "We're wondering if you'd consider staying in Paraguay to oversee the construction of our new home and take care of Chris and Josie."

Clara wished they'd prepared Marlena for this moment.

Now, as she and John headed east toward Tobatí, Clara smiled through her tears. It was hard to leave their home of twenty years. Even harder was the way this whole thing had been handled. But the Lord had blessed them. After considering the idea for a few days, Marlena and Steve had agreed to build their new house and to care for their two youngest children while they were in Vietnam. And when they returned, maybe their medical services in Tobatí could someday even be an offshoot of the work at Km. 81.

Before leaving, Clara had published a statement in the station newsletter *Im Dienste der Liebe*, planting the seed about coordinating with Km. 81.

We want to share with you plans that we've had for some time. God willing, we want to take on a service in Vietnam for four months. We see this trip as an unearned opportunity. We plan to return at the end of June 1972 to our beloved workplace here in Paraguay. While we are away,

Dr. Franz and our dear personnel will continue the work here. Upon our return, we will confer with him and the GemeindeKomitee about how we will continue with the work.

Clara did not mention the anger or the pain.

RISING AGAIN

1971-1983

"I'm a little wounded, but I am not slain; I will lay me down to bleed a while. Then I'll rise and fight again."

– John Dryden

TWENTY-EIGHT

Bill Snyder sat at his desk and re-read the letter he'd just received from Schmidt. The return address was somewhere in Vietnam. He was writing to inquire about the status of their relationship with MCC when he and Clara returned to Paraguay. He laid out their plans to work in the Tobatí area, offering leprosy clinics and general medical services for that underdeveloped region. He indicated a desire to acquire more settlements for leprosy patients to build their homes.

> How much help for leprosy work can we draw from the GemeindeKomitee through the Km. 81 budget?

Schmidt had some nerve. Snyder picked up the phone and dialed Hasselblad's number.

After a few niceties, he got right to the point. "We have a problem." He explained that John and Clara Schmidt were returning to Paraguay in July and described their plans.

"Did you know about this before the Schmidts left Paraguay last year?" Hasselblad responded harshly.

"There were rumors," Snyder said. "But we made it clear to John that under no circumstances was he allowed to expand the settlements for his leprosy patients, nor was he allowed to initiate facilities and services that duplicate what's being done at Km. 81."

There was a pause before Hasselblad said, "We will not support a program that is parallel to Km. 81 or weakens that effort. I guess your Paraguayan committee has some work to do."

Clara turned onto her back and pushed her blanket aside. Despite the Valium (which she referred to as her "helper"), she couldn't get to sleep. She pulled on her robe and shuffled to the living room. They'd been back in Tobatí a few months, after a perilous tour of service in war-torn Vietnam. Despite exposure to great danger, God had protected them. And now they'd come back to the beautiful house Steve and Marlena had built for them. She and John had so much to be thankful for. Why did it all feel so heavy?

Since arriving in Tobatí, they'd become deeply involved in the church and the booming new community, primarily dependent on logging operations and soybean production. The community included Amish, Mexican Mennonites, and Mennonites who'd moved to Tobatí from the Chaco colonies. Many Paraguayans and Brazilians were also moving in and buying land in the area.

Clara and John had developed a clinic in a run-down shack to serve the various diverse groups surrounding Tobatí who were without medical care. They had already registered thirty patients. Just the other day, they discovered an area thirty-five kilometers away, Santa Ana, where they began vaccinations. More than a hundred children in the first three grades were crammed into a four-room schoolhouse the community had built on their own initiative. Clara distributed used books she had acquired, and John helped them organize a local committee to supervise toilet building for each family—not really a building—just a hole that always had to be at least a meter deep and far enough away from their water source.

It was everything they had planned. Clara stared out the large picture window into the darkness. Why was there no joy in it? Some mornings she couldn't even get out of bed.

She heard John approach from behind. "John, I just feel like crying."

"I don't see what there is to cry about," John said. He went to the kitchen and poured himself a glass of water.

Clara knew John was suffering as well. In the months since they'd been back in Paraguay, twenty pounds had dropped from his already bony frame. He seemed to be crumbling under the weight of some unbearable burden. Clara had a good idea what it was, but John refused to talk about it. He had seemed depressed ever since returning from Vietnam. But last week, his despondency deepened markedly.

Konrad Wolf had come out to see them, bringing their small stipend from MCC, which supplemented their income from their Chaco cattle ranch and the few patients who had money to pay for John's medical services. Wolf delivered the news that MCC did not approve of their plans to build a hospital in Tobatí, and expressly forbade them to build new settlements for leprosy patients.

John had gotten all worked up. "The new hospital is not an MCC project. Clara and I are funding it personally and with private donations, along with possible support from the local EMC church community here, who've asked me to plan and supervise the construction."

Surprisingly, Wolf smiled and expressed his opinion that a hospital in this area was needed. The GemeindeKomitee saw no problem in such an undertaking.

Before Wolf left, John threw the envelope with the MCC stipend down in front of him. "We don't need MCC's support."

Clara had watched in silence as John cut his ties to the organization that had been a major part of his life since graduating from medical school. During the past week, she'd prayed that the desperate needs in the Tobatí area would once again reawaken John's spirit of service and adventure.

★

During the next few years, the Paraguayan government encouraged and supported people to settle in developing areas like Tobatí, and many more Paraguayans and Brazilians moved into the region. It was an increasingly desirable place to live because of the hydroelectric plant near them on the Paraguay–Brazil border. Over three hundred Brazilian families had already moved into the area, and more were buying land every day.

If the Mennonites and Amish who had settled there wanted to maintain their land and their customs in Tobatí, they would have to organize and develop the area themselves. John ran a campaign to raise money to purchase additional acreage and he helped draw up a plan for a new Mennonite colony named Tres Palmas with a central town named Lucero. Lucero meant "bright star." John hoped their presence in this area might be a bright star of hope for those in need.

One afternoon after seeing over forty patients in his small clinic, John visited Janzen, one of the leaders of the Tres Palmas community.

"We have so many new settlers with medical needs," he told Janzen. "My clinic can't handle them all. We need to get more active about raising money to build a new hospital."

"John, our little community has no money. I'm sure there are needs, but I don't see how we can do this."

"Let's not assume we can't do this until we know we can't." John grabbed his hat and rose to leave. "Where there is faith, God provides."

John stomped back home. Why didn't these people get it? It wasn't only because of medical needs that it was important to build the new hospital. It was essential that the Mennonites contribute to the area if they wished to continue to be accepted. John worried about the revolutionary spirit in the surrounding countries, especially Argentina. He'd read that by 1973, Argentina's economy had fallen apart and the still-popular Peronista party gained the support they needed for Perón's return from exile. Perón was welcomed back to Argentina with wild enthusiasm, but the excitement was short-lived. With terrorism on the rise, Perón began imprisoning people without trial. John wondered if Ana had once again turned against Perón as she had toward the end of Evita's life. He hadn't heard from her in quite a while.

The poverty and human rights violations that motivated the revolutionary spirit in Argentina were also present in Paraguay. President Stroessner had broken up several attempts at insurgency. Eventually his regime would end. There were rumors that he and his close friends had deposited great wealth in Switzerland. There was probably no need to panic, but there was every reason to believe Paraguay was headed for an insurrection. Building a hospital to serve the poor and the needy in this area was not only the right thing to do. It was a good way to protect themselves by providing value for the region in case of a revolution.

In November of 1974, Wesley graduated from medical school in Asunción. And the following year, the GemeindeKomitee asked Wesley to take over the medical responsibilities at Km. 81 for three years while Dr. Duerksen continued his studies in Canada.

Clara and John were invited to come to Km. 81 with Wesley and his wife, Esther, for dinner as a farewell to Dr. Duerksen and a welcome for the young Dr. Schmidt. A lump formed in Clara's throat when she walked onto the veranda of the house that she and John had built together so many years ago. The bougainvillea at the entrance looked the same. Beyond the archway, the grapevines sloping down to the creek also looked as they used to. How could things seem so unchanged and so normal when everything was so different?

The six of them sat around the table on the veranda, talking mostly about medical issues at the station.

"You're not saying much," Mrs. Duerksen said, turning to Clara.

Clara smiled. "Oh, I'm just enjoying the conversation, and I'm so happy that Wesley will be continuing the work here." What else could she say? She was struggling to reconcile the pride in her son and the personal loss of the work that had meant so much.

In 1976, John and Clara were once again invited to come to Km. 81, this time for the station's twenty-fifth anniversary celebration. Over 300 guests from all over Paraguay, Brazil, Canada, and the United States gathered for a two-hour program, which included some of the over 500 workers who had served there during the past twenty-five years.

John watched Wesley, who was sitting in the front row, as one dignitary after another praised the work at the station. John thought about another celebration here, only nine years ago, when Hasselblad announced that Km. 81 was no longer keeping up with the latest leprosy treatments. That had been the beginning of the end of his time at the station.

He saw Wesley turn around to look at him, grinning. In that moment, John experienced a surge of pride for a son who was so capably taking over the work he and Clara had begun twenty-five years ago. John felt no rancor, but also no gratification, when Roger Ackley, then president of ALM, presented a plaque to the chair of the GemeindeKomitee, recognizing the outstanding leprosy work at Km. 81 and expressing readiness for further cooperation.

Less than a year after the twenty-fifth anniversary celebration at Km. 81, John and Clara received a letter notifying them of Orie Miller's death. John remembered the day he first met Orie in June of 1941, before they boarded the *SS Argentina* to travel to Paraguay together. Over the years, Orie had shared John's dream for the Chaco colonies and for Km. 81. Often, Orie had stood by John's side when no one else had.

They had accomplished much together. And now Orie was gone. Were he and Clara doing anything worthwhile anymore? John had raised a lot of money to buy land in the Tobatí area, but no one seemed to want to step up to help him develop a colony.

John's lips formed into a slow sad smile when he listened to Clara reading Orie's obituary in the *Lancaster New Era* newspaper. It ended with:

> A Bible, the Mennonite Yearbook, and a world map, the three musts which Orie Miller always carried in his briefcase, formed the framework within which he lived his life.

"That could be you they wrote about, John," Clara said softly.

TWENTY-NINE

I t was a week before Christmas. Clara stared at mounds of dirty snow piled up against their building. They'd been back in the States since September to get John checked out at the Mayo Clinic. For years, he'd had fainting spells, but recently they'd become so frequent he could no longer blame them on low blood pressure. Lately, his mouth and tongue were beginning to feel numb, and he had some hearing loss in his right ear. Not to mention the frequent headaches.

The previous week, the doctors at Mayo Clinic had ordered brain scans, and now they awaited the latest results. Clara shook her head. She and John just didn't belong in the U.S. anymore. The other day, she'd gone to see a dentist about an abscessed tooth. After suggesting an expensive procedure Clara objected to, he became very rude, saying her teeth were "horse shit." She shuddered, remembering.

Just then, John burst through the door. "Clara, please sit down."

So it was that bad. She sat at the edge of the tattered sofa in their rented room. Silently, she prayed, "Lord, give me strength."

"God has been good to us. I have a brain tumor."

Clara's eyes grew wide, and her mouth dropped open. Did John really see this as God being good to them? She waited for him to say more.

"The surgeon at Mayo Clinic has made an appointment for the surgery on December 28," John added matter-of-factly. "We need to leave for Rochester on Christmas day."

Clara sat next to John at the Christmas Eve service in the Alexanderwohl Church in Goessel, Kansas, wishing she could shake off her sadness. When his strong tenor voice soared above those around them, singing "It Came Upon the Midnight Clear," Clara bent over her lap. She remembered hearing John singing a hymn in church just after returning from his first trip to Paraguay. Reaching over to grasp his hand, she recalled that his true, clear voice had given her the assurance to say yes.

They arrived in Rochester around noon on the 27th. After checking John into the hospital, Clara found lodging in a rooming house called The Elms for $4.50 per night. Before unpacking her bags, she walked to Woolworth's to buy John a pair of pajamas, since he owned none and he had a roommate. She walked both ways, even though the temperature was well below zero. The bus charged 75 cents each way!

By 9:00 the next day, John was in the OR. Clara waited. And prayed. Finally, at 5:30, the surgeon informed her that the tumor was extensive, but appeared to be benign. Although it was fully removed, unfortunately John's facial nerves were cut, leaving him with paralysis on the right side of his face. This would require another surgery to repair.

John's second surgery was postponed several times due to weight loss, low blood pressure, and repeated fainting spells. Finally, on January 7, John said, "Let's get it over with." For six and a half hours, three surgeons transplanted a part of his hypoglossal nerve from under his tongue to repair the severed facial nerve.

Clara stood up when the surgeon entered the waiting room. "You can go see him now. But I must tell you that he is suffering from some mental confusion."

As she approached John's bed, Clara saw that he was writhing from side to side, trying to loosen his arms from restraints on his wrists. "Vietnam...there's the hand...in Vietnam...decide whether I should live..."

"John, it's OK. John." Clara rushed to his side.

Empty eyes stared at her. "Vietnam...deciding now whether I die."

During the next few days, John regained mental clarity, but he suffered several severe migraine headaches, he could not sit up without fainting, and he continued to lose weight. The days passed as a blur of prayer and worry. Clara took a "helper" almost every night, and still lay awake much of the time. She had never felt so alone.

On January 20th, Clara ordered a television to be brought to John's room for the Inaugural Day event. When she arrived in his room, he was holding his head in his hands, moaning. She called off the television delivery, but the nurse brought it anyway.

John continued to groan, but when Jimmy Carter spoke the words "...and what doth the Lord require of Thee, but to do justly, and to love mercy, and to walk humbly with Thy God," John smiled his first now lopsided smile since the surgery.

On January 29, over a month after checking into the hospital, John was allowed to leave. Clara watched him slumped over in the wheelchair, saran wrap taped over his right eye to keep it from drying out, with the right side of his mouth sagging, and thought, "He went in as a vibrant young fellow and he's leaving as a tired old man."

They returned to a mess in Tobatí. During the months they were gone, most of the fruit trees John had planted near their house had died and weeds had taken over the yard. The house was infested with ants. There were wasp nests in the washing machine. And the well had gone dry.

A single nurse, Leni, had run the Lucero clinic in John's absence. Conditions were more primitive than even those of the first years in the Chaco. Leni used a wood-fired oven for sterilization and there was almost no charting or record-keeping. She countered John's suggestions with bristled resistance.

"This place is about right for me now," John mumbled under his breath as he tried to clean out the gas diaphragm of their range, which wasn't functioning properly.

What troubled John most wasn't the broken-down property, not even the crude medical facility. The other night on the news, he'd heard that in Argentina the mothers and grandmothers of the disappeared, referred to as Madres de la Plaza, were gathering in the Plaza de Mayo, demanding word about their missing children and grandchildren. The movement was gaining popularity, leading to increased tensions.

John frowned, remembering Ana's letter from over a year ago. He'd wanted to speak with Clara about it, but during his medical crises, he'd put it aside, deciding it was the wrong time. He hadn't even remembered what he'd done with the letter. But just the other day, he'd found it tucked into the pages of a medical journal.

The first part of her letter shared disturbing news. She wrote that after Perón's death in 1974, political activism was forbidden. By 1976, the junta brought the government under military control. Thousands of suspected dissidents were abducted from their homes, blindfolded, and taken to detention centers to most likely never be seen again. Once the prisoners were too broken to be useful as laborers, they were often drugged, loaded onto an aircraft, and thrown out, still alive, into the Atlantic Ocean so there would be no dead bodies as evidence.

That news was bad enough, and John feared for Ana's life. But after describing the situation in Argentina, the tone of her letter changed and became more personal. Ana wrote the words now etched in John's brain, words he wished he had never seen:

> It's only a matter of time before I, too, am detained and abducted. I have lost my fight—I must let it go. I doubt that I shall ever see you again, Dr. John. So, I feel obliged to tell you something I thought I would never divulge. I love you. I have loved you since the night we met on the SS Argentina.
>
> My love for you will see me through the long, dark years I undoubtedly will face. Be well, dear Dr. John.

John put down his wrench and the grease-soaked rags he was using to clean the stove and pulled himself up off the floor. That just wasn't at all how he thought about their relationship, and he didn't know how to respond. One thing was clear. He must talk to Clara about it.

Clara tried to hide her smile. "John, honey, why does this surprise you?" He looked more awkward and uncomfortable than she'd ever seen him. And contrite, like he was guilty of something, which of course he wasn't.

Her man, so strong—even bull-headed out in the world—was completely naïve when it came to women. Of course Ana loved him. So had other women along the way. Clara remembered the way the young nurses-in-training in the Chaco had gawked at John with open longing—despite their fear of him—when they didn't think anyone was watching. It used to bother her. But after all these years, she no longer minded. In fact, she secretly took pleasure in his lack of awareness of his effect on women.

But Ana was different. This was not an infatuation. It was as though she and John were mirrors for each other. Ana understood John's inner demons that propelled him to always do more and never be satisfied, because she and John were oddly similar in this regard. Clara had seen that familiar glint in Ana's eyes when she visited them at Km. 81 and spoke about her work. And she recognized in both a similar commitment to fight to their death for their beliefs.

Clara wrapped her arms around John. "She is a strong and honest woman. We will pray for her."

During the next five years, John and Clara continued to devote time and money toward developing the new Tres Palmas colony. Now in his seventies, John still believed that a thriving hospital was essential for this growing area. It was a way for the Mennonites to provide needed services as a thank you to Paraguay, just as they had at the leprosy station.

He attempted to bring the medical services up to minimal standards. But every time he intervened, Leni's resentment increased. Maybe there was no point in pushing any further the idea of a new hospital. Everyone agreed that it was needed. The people here appreciated all the hospital-project money John and Clara had donated themselves and raised from North American donors. But much more funding was needed. And no one else seemed willing to step up to make it happen.

On a blisteringly hot afternoon in late March of 1980, John sat at his desk, pen in hand. At the Fernheim colony's recent fiftieth anniversary celebration, the Oberschulze had publicly recognized John and Clara's contributions in the early years. He'd asked John to write a column in the colony's *Menno Blatt*.

John heard Clara enter the room. "So far all I've written is the title," he said, turning to her. "What We Were and What We Will Be."

Clara smiled sadly.

"What's the matter?" he asked.

"Your title feels like it's more about us than about the colony, John. We know what we were, but what does the Lord have in store for our future?"

John understood what she meant. He felt useless despite the numerous commendations and recognitions he and Clara had received in the past several years for their various areas of service.

The headlines of a recent *Mennonite Weekly Review* article read:

Dr. Oliver Hasselblad, world leprosy expert until recently president of the American Leprosy Mission, credits Km. 81 with pioneering home treatment.

And soon thereafter, the same publication ran another article:

John Bertsche, Mennonite Medical Association president, is pictured reading the citation of "distinguished achievement" to Dr. John R Schmidt and wife Clara who have served with Paraguayan Mennonites at different intervals since 1941.

Anything he and Clara had done was the work of the Lord, not for personal recognition. But a slow crooked smile formed when John thought about one recent breakthrough. He was copied on a communication between MCC and the GemeindeKomitee that read:

Recommendation: That MCC donate the 888-hectare property at Km. 81 to the GemeindeKomitee of the Mennonite churches of Paraguay for use as a large cattle ranch, as the soil is too rocky and poor for agriculture. Recommendation is to raise cattle and use the income for Km. 81 medical programs.

No one attributed the "new" plan for a cattle ranch to what John had argued from the beginning was the right model for the leprosy station. No matter. At least they were finally doing the only thing that made any sense.

John's thoughts turned back to the present. The real question that mattered was what he and Clara were doing now. Not much of anything. And it was embarrassing to be out in public. His facial nerves hadn't come back. He hated the pity in people's eyes. It was time to give it up.

RESTLESSNESS

1983-1993

"My soul is impatient with itself, as with a bothersome child; its restlessness keeps growing and is forever the same. Everything interests me, but nothing holds me."

– Fernando Pessoa

THIRTY

When word came in 1983 that the home for the aged in Goessel needed a part-time doctor, Clara prayed this was the ministry the Lord was giving them for their retiring years. John seemed ready to slow down. Clara hoped he would feel less self-conscious about his facial paralysis among the elderly in the home.

They bought the house in Goessel that John's mother had built many years ago. It was small and compact, with a yard that had space for a vegetable garden and even room for some fruit trees, as well as gooseberries, rhubarb, and strawberry plants. They acquired an old car with 200,000 miles on it for almost nothing. And the second- and third-hand furniture they obtained was just as comfortable as anything new would have been.

Clara helped John set up his own private medical office in an annex of the Bethesda Home for the Aged. Their income of around $15,000 qualified them for Social Security and Medicare. This wage, plus money from their investments in Paraguay, was more than enough for them to live on. They were blessed to be able to support numerous missions they believed in, as they had done before. By the end of the year, they had donated $7,500 to various organizations, the largest piece of it going to MCC. All was as it should be.

Gradually, they settled into their semi-retired life in Goessel. John spent only a few hours each day at the office, leaving plenty of time for gardening, watching basketball games on their small television, and visiting with Mary Lou and her family, who lived nearby. Everyone they knew thought it was the perfect retirement situation.

At first, John also believed they'd discovered an ideal place to spend their last years. But over time, a gnawing grew inside of him, a longing to be part of something more worthwhile. He stayed in close touch with the Tres Palmas colony leaders. The settlement continued to survive, but barely. Many families were moving out due to the lack of economic sustainability, and there were no indications that the situation would improve. As John went about his mostly meaningless days, his thoughts increasingly turned to the dilapidated little clinic, the underserved population around it, and the lost opportunity to make something of the Tres Palmas colony.

On a snowy day in mid-January, nearly five years after coming to Goessel, John trudged home after a few hours at the office. Clara was in the kitchen preparing their supper. "Clara, I know I've said this many times, but I'm feeling it more urgently. We should try to get back to Tres Palmas. I can't get it out of my head that we can help that place survive."

When Clara didn't immediately respond, he added, "And I've been thinking. Let's redo that car trip in reverse, from Kansas to Paraguay, just the two of us. What d'you think?"

Why was Clara staring at him like that?

It didn't surprise Clara that John wanted to get back to Tres Palmas. It was a failed project that he still felt passionate about. She wasn't opposed, really. But this crazy idea of his for the two of them to drive to Paraguay? Did he even get it that he was seventy-seven years old, and she was seventy-four? But then again, if it brought back the fire in his eyes, it would all be worth it.

Clara watched John from across their cramped hotel room in Oaxaca, Mexico, as he threw the cardboard box into the garbage can beside the sagging bed. Papers spilled out onto the rough tile floor, and one envelope flew across the room and landed near her feet. It read, *Requisitos para viajar a Nicaragua: Documentos para Turistas.*

"This is the worst disappointment of my entire life." John slumped onto the bed and held his face in both hands.

Clara said nothing. They had made it as far as Oaxaca before it was finally clear that the van could go no further. It was unfortunate, yes, but the worst disappointment of his life? She thought about the nightmare their trip had become during the past few weeks, and quietly breathed in a prayer of gratitude that it was finally over.

A few months ago, they had bought an old VW van. They replaced the engine, and John had fixed it up with a little stove, a fridge, and a mat to sleep on. By May (1989), they were all set, and began their drive south from Kansas to Paraguay. John was excited about revisiting many of the contacts they had made during their three-month 1960 family trip north in their Volvo. They drove long hours each day and at night parked with permission in strangers' yards, by the side of busy roads, in restaurant parking lots, malls, and truck stops, finding bathrooms wherever they could.

After less than a week on the road, their old van began to give them trouble. Poor electrical connections and loose hoses occasionally caused the motor to shut down abruptly. Three times it stopped so suddenly that the two of them had to get out and push the vehicle off the busy highway. Clara shuddered, remembering one of the times she was starting to push the van, when it began rolling backward so fast that an open door knocked her to the ground before John could climb in and slam on the brakes.

After crossing the border, they learned that gasoline in Mexico didn't work with their van's fuel injection system. So, John re-entered the United States illegally to buy a new carburetor, leaving Clara with a friendly family they met when the car broke down. After John returned with the carburetor, he hitchhiked into three different Mexican villages before locating a tow truck and a mechanic. After several additional costly maintenance stops along the way, they passed through Mexico City and reached Oaxaca, where they learned that the vehicle was finally beyond repair. Since they couldn't sell the van, they'd given it to the Red Cross and had purchased plane tickets to Asunción.

Clara looked across the hotel room at John, who still sat hunched over on the edge of the bed. What was at the root of his suffering? After all these years together, parts of her man remained an enigma to her. For reasons Clara couldn't understand, John's bent-over figure recalled words from Ana's last letter back in 1976: I have lost my fight—I must let it go. Of course. That was it. This trip had represented John's last-ditch effort to not let go, to prevail one more time over a seemingly insurmountable force. And now defeat was staring him in the face.

"I'll go out and get us something to eat," Clara said quietly, moving toward the door. She wanted to comfort John, but his well of anguish was too deep for her to soothe. At least for now.

John and Clara returned to a changed Paraguay. After nearly thirty-five years of political stability in the country, President Alfredo Stroessner had been ousted in a bloody coup in February of 1989, just a few months before their arrival. He was ordered out of the country by the second-in-command of the army, General Rodríguez. *The Voice of America* was still John's preferred source of world news. He crouched in front of the radio for hours in John Russell's house in Fernheim, where they were staying, his good ear pressed in to hear the news.

The newscaster reported on the numerous similarities between Stroessner and Argentina's Juan Perón. Like Perón, Stroessner had kept his country in a constant state of siege, regularly torturing and killing political opponents. Membership in his Colorado Party had been a prerequisite for job promotion, free medical care, and other services. Both leaders modified the constitution to legitimize their re-elections. On the positive side, both promoted projects that developed their country's infrastructure, such as the improvement of highways and the development of schools in rural areas. Once again, things were not as simple as many people on both sides wanted to believe.

The reporter also asserted that, like Perón, Stroessner had maintained mostly good relations with the United States. So, while over 5,000 people led by Domingo Laino, one of Paraguay's best-known human rights advocates, gathered in downtown Asunción to cheer the ouster of Stroessner, the U.S. State Department issued a statement saying it was improbable that General Rodríguez would be a force for democracy, given that he had been implicated numerous times by U.S. and international drug organizations as a kingpin of the drug trade in Paraguay.

John had suspected for years that such a coup would happen. Stroessner had been a staunch supporter of the Mennonites in Paraguay. Now their future was uncertain. John worried that the current relative prosperity of the colonists in the Chaco would jeopardize their relationship with their impoverished Paraguayan neighbors. He feared the Mennonites had not done enough to give back for the privileges of settling in Paraguay, governing their own colonies, and being exempted from mandatory military service. That was one of the reasons he'd fought so hard to build a hospital to benefit people surrounding the Tres Palmas colony.

Tres Palmas. John could still taste the bitterness of the latest rejection. They'd gone to Tres Palmas immediately after arriving in Paraguay. Things looked just about as they had five years ago. There was much work to do. But when John approached the head nurse, Leni, about his plans to expand the clinic, she made it clear that she did not welcome his help.

It was the last straw. They decided to sell their Tres Palmas house to the family who'd been renting it. They priced it at ten payments based on the fluctuating cost of 649.35 kg. meat, 2,066 liters of milk, 1,893.9 kg. peanuts and 853 kg. cotton.

Now John and Clara were staying with John Russell and his family in Fernheim. Mary Lou and her husband, Rusty, had moved to and were working in the Chaco. They seemed to think their parents should retire in Fernheim. John no longer cared one way or the other. He spent much of his time listening to the news on a shortwave radio and brooding over the state of the world.

A few weeks later, on a cold drizzly afternoon in mid-July (1989), Mary Lou opened the door of their tiny bedroom in John Russell's house. John was slumped in front of the radio, wrapped in a gray wool blanket, listening to Jim Dobson's "Focus on the Family" program. Dobson's guest was a young man speaking about his relationship with his parents during a challenging time in his life. He was saying that it made all the difference in the world that his father stood behind him and believed in him.

Mary Lou rushed toward John when she saw tears streaming down his face. She'd never seen her father weep. She turned off the radio.

"Dad, what is it?"

John began openly sobbing, clutching the blanket to his chest. Between deep spasms he cried out, "...not worthy...I don't deserve..."

Mary Lou tried to hug him, but he threw her off, continuing to cry out mostly incoherently. His eyes were enflamed, and his face flushed. He bent over in his chair and feverishly called out the names of each of his children with more agonizing cries of "I don't deserve..."

"Dad, you're so special. We're so proud of you."

Still weeping, John sputtered, "I'm so ordinary... I don't deserve... you children...I..." More desperate sobbing.

Mary Lou drew in her breath, placed her hands on his shoulders and whispered, "We forgive you, Dad. All of us know you were doing what you thought was best. We love you very much."

John continued to clutch the blanket, his cries gradually subsiding to low moans. Finally, pointing to the radio, he muttered, "Mom always says she doesn't like to listen to this kind of program because it makes her feel terrible about how we failed you children."

Mary Lou just stood there, holding onto his shoulders, hardly believing any of this could be real.

After his emotional crisis, John never spoke of it. He shut down as if his life no longer mattered. What happened to the fire in his eyes? It led Clara her to wonder if Ana, too, had given up her fight. Or maybe she had died.

One day when John was slouched in front of the radio, as usual, Clara interrupted the reporter describing revolutions sweeping through the Eastern Bloc in Europe. "What do you know about Ana?"

"Huh?" John looked up, deep lines cutting furrows down the middle of his forehead.

"Anastasia. Did she survive the war in Argentina?"

John shut off the radio and turned to face Clara. "I don't know. The Dirty War ended six years ago. I've heard that democratic elections and civilian rule under someone named Alfonsín have brought a return to justice and retribution for victims of the war."

"Well, let's find out what Ana is doing." Clara flipped through their tattered black address book. "If she's still alive, she's probably at her old address in Buenos Aires—here it is, 2961 Manuel Obarrio. I'm sure she's found renewed strength to fight for what she believes in."

Clara pretended to ignore John's peculiar look.

Hot wind raged from the north, pulling up large swirls of dust around her. Clara covered her mouth with a handkerchief and picked up her pace. This place was so familiar, even though much had changed since she and John had lived here in Filadelfia during the 1940s. The hospital they'd founded and the nursing program they'd started were thriving, but how many people even remembered them for that work these many decades later? The dirt road running through Filadelfia was now lined with tin-roofed brick houses, rather than the low adobe struc- tures with thatched roofs she remembered. And now there were even electric lines. But the familiar aroma of smoke mixed with the scent of palo santo trees still permeated the air, and the Kooperative stood out, much as it always had, as the epicenter of the colony.

Clara approached the hospital, now a much larger and fancier brick building than the little two-room shack that had served as their clinic and hospital in the 1940s. She stopped, remembering the long line of horse-drawn carts waiting to see the doctor when they first arrived.

It would be perfect for them to live on the Old Folks Home premises in Filadelfia. It seemed like a good way to spend their final years, close to where they began their married life. A few weeks ago, they submitted a formal letter to the Oberschulze, requesting permis- sion to buy a home in Filadelfia, since the colony system technically only allowed colony members to be homeowners. No official word had come back, but there were rumors that their request would be denied.

John's reaction had been to throw up his hands. "We're still the enemy!" But Clara couldn't just leave it at that. She had to get to the bottom of what was going on. And she figured Konrad Wolf would know.

She clapped in front of the Wolf home, taking in the white picket fence and the picturesque garden surrounding an attractive brick house with an air-conditioning unit protruding from one of the windows. My, how things had changed.

"N'dach, Frau Dokta." Wolf removed his hat and extended a hand.

He was mostly bald now, and his once bulky frame was thinner and somewhat bent over. Only the scar running from the left side of his forehead down across his cheek looked unchanged.

"I'm here to find out—"

"I know why you're here, Frau Clara. I wish I could help. I really do. I'm no longer part of the leadership committee, so I have no say."

"But why—"

Again, Wolf interrupted. "The colony leaders do not divulge their reasoning. But the answer is no. I'm sorry."

Wolf looked genuinely regretful. But something deep inside Clara's chest ached. Why weren't the colony leaders at least Christian enough to tell them the truth up front?

The following week, John and Clara received Ana's response to their letter. John read it out loud.

> Dear Dr. John and Clara, it was wonderful to hear from you... I spent five years in a detention center with extreme methods of torture...such brutality, such waste.

"She was released six years ago," John muttered under his breath, continuing to read:

> I have had many dark hours and days and months and years to reflect on our conversations about the best way to bring about justice in this unjust world of ours. I am beginning to doubt that my approach is the best means to bring about change.

Clara put her arms around his waist. "I didn't think Ana would ever have any doubts..."

John had a faraway look in his eyes. "Clara, I think we should take the offer from the Menno Colony. What do you think?"

"It is good to feel wanted, even if it isn't where we thought we would live," Clara murmured.

When their plan to settle in Fernheim hadn't worked out, they'd put out feelers in the other two Mennonite colonies in the Chaco. Menno Colony offered them the opportunity to build a house on the grounds of their Old Folks Home and to work part-time caring for its residents.

John wasn't sure why Menno would want an old, impaired guy like himself. But he didn't really have any other good options.

At the end of July, John took over the part-time medical position at the Old Folks Home. The Menno leadership offered him 600,000 Guaranies per month (the equivalent of about $500). John told them that was way too much and accepted only a portion of it. He drew the design for a small but bright and airy home that was built according to his specs, down to a shuffleboard deck alongside the house.

"It's our dream house," Clara said, putting dishes into the new cupboards. "We'll be so happy here, John."

Surprisingly, it felt true. John's patients seemed genuinely grateful for his care, and the community accepted them as one of their own. Clara kept busy providing physical and occupational therapy as well as massages. The church, the Menno Colony Kooperative, and the hospital were all within easy walking distance. And they had lots of fruit, especially as much papaya as John wanted. Papaya was his favorite fruit.

In September, John wrote in a letter to his sister Wilma:

After the great disappointment of the trip and the negative response from Tres Palmas, we tried only Fernheim as a place to live. Once we came to Menno Colony it was so very different. We just have a welcome spirit here from everyone.

John and Clara grew to love their life in Menno. The work was just enough to keep them feeling useful without being overly taxing. They developed friendships within the community. The church welcomed them into the congregation. And as a bonus, they enjoyed spending time with many of their children and grandchildren who'd settled in the Chaco.

RAISING THE STAKES

1993-1995

"Nothing can withstand the power of the
human will if it is willing to stake its very
existence to the extent of its purpose."
– Benjamin Disraeli

THIRTY-ONE

Clara sat in a rocker on their spacious veranda. She looked up from her stitching to watch a hummingbird flit onto the feeder hanging from the rafter above her, and then dart out of sight. She breathed in the post-rain Chaco air smelling of wet earth. The storm that had passed through the area that afternoon had lifted the humid heat and cleared the dust, and now the air sparkled. It was February 1993, and Clara whispered a prayer of gratitude as she had so often during the past four years since they moved to their semi-retirement home in Menno. It was a wonderful place to grow old and eventually retire.

Clara spotted John coming up the walkway toward her. She smiled, again feeling thankful for the way things had turned out. John seemed happier than he'd been since his brain surgery. She thanked her Lord every day for guiding them to this peaceful place.

"We just received a letter from Norbert Thiessen, the new Oberschulze of Tres Palmas," John said, sitting down on a chair next to Clara and ripping open the envelope.

"Why would we be hearing from him?" Clara asked.

John scanned the letter. "It seems he would like us to visit Tres Palmas. He thinks there might be work for us there."

Clara laughed. "Well, fortunately, we already have exactly the work God wants us to do in this place we love."

John seemed thoughtful, staring at the letter.

"John, you're not thinking..." Clara's voice trailed off.

John looked up with a lopsided grin. "No, of course not. But there's no harm in taking a look at what's going on there. We haven't been in Tres Palmas for years. Maybe they've finally managed to develop that little colony into something viable."

Several commitments kept them from leaving immediately. But by early April, John had fixed up their old vehicle and readied it for the long trip to east Paraguay. Despite having to dodge deep ruts all along the trans-Chaco road, he couldn't help but feel almost giddy about the fact that there was now a continuous road between the colonies and Asunción.

It took seven hours (versus the ten days it used to take) to reach Asunción and another hour to get to Km. 81, where they planned to stay for the night. John turned left off the Ruta onto the winding road leading to the station and felt a rush of emotion he couldn't name.

He reached for Clara's hand. "It'll always feel like home here, won't it?"

"Yes, it will. But I'm grateful for the lovely home we've made for ourselves in Menno. The Lord has been so good to us."

After another eight-hour drive the next day, John and Clara finally pulled into the town of Lucero in Tres Palmas. John clenched his fingers around the steering wheel, his head swiveling from one side to the other. What had happened to this place? Why were there so many boarded-up buildings? And the clinic looked like it wasn't even being used.

"John..." Clara began and then closed her mouth.

John clenched his jaw. He said nothing.

Oberschulze Thiessen met them as they drove into his yard. "N'dach," he said. "I'm happy that you've come."

John wasted no words. "What has happened here?"

Thiessen invited them into his home and proceeded to explain that the few investors who put money into the development of Tres Palmas had pulled out. The head nurse, Leni, had left, leaving only one part-time nurse unable to carry the load. The clinic and the whole colony project were in danger of completely shutting down.

John listened without saying anything. He thought about the reasons he'd been so adamant about forming the Tres Palmas colony back in the early 1970s. Only a colony structure would allow Mennonites living in this area to maintain their language and their culture. And only a thriving Christian clinic, serving not only the Mennonites, but also the large regional populations of Paraguayans and Brazilians, would keep the local Mennonites from eventual persecution. That had been his reasoning twenty years ago. It was even more important today, given the recent governmental upheavals.

Finally, John said, "Why didn't you tell us what was going on here?" His voice was tight.

Thiessen stared at the floor. "I wanted you to see for yourself."

That night, Clara lay completely still next to John. She felt his tense body next to her. "John, talk to me."

"We must come back to Tres Palmas. We have no choice. If we don't, the whole project will close, leaving this entire area without medical care."

Clara closed her eyes, seeing the rose garden in their yard in Menno. She saw her beloved hummingbirds flitting around. The shuffleboard deck. The papaya trees behind the house. The friends who had become so dear. And the people who were counting on them for care at the Menno Old Folks Home.

"I thought we had found the perfect spot to grow old and retire..." Even as Clara said this, she knew that God was calling them once again to a new area of service. She could not be the one to turn her back on the Lord's will.

Within days, they were back in Menno. When John announced that he was leaving, people were shocked and openly expressed their disappointment and concern. But John and Clara packed the belongings they could fit into their car, and a week later were on their way east to their next calling. Once more they were trusting the Lord to guide them through the seemingly insurmountable challenges ahead.

Before they left, Clara urged John to write to Ana, letting her know of the next chapter of their service adventures. "She would want to know," Clara said. "I know you've been wanting her to find something to believe in again. This will help her."

It was true. John didn't understand and was disappointed in Ana's lack of activism since her release after the Dirty War. They'd corresponded a few times, and Ana's biggest news seemed to be about organizing opportunities for women in the workplace.

President Alfonsín had implemented democratic reforms, as he promised, drastically cutting the military budget. But economic challenges had forced him to resign, ushering in Carlos Menem in 1989. A hopeful Argentina referred to Menem's politics as the *Nuevo Peronismo*. But within weeks, the true right-wing President Menem emerged, and by 1993, he had reversed Alfonsín's policies and had pardoned members of the military junta involved in the Dirty War atrocities.

Was Ana still doing nothing but her work with women? Had she shut off her passionate sense of justice for the poor and underserved?

John wrote in the letter to Ana:

Your president promised what he has not delivered. He has done nothing for the poor. On top of that, he has been involved in arms smuggling and he's a flamboyant, no-good womanizer. You cannot just stand by doing nothing.

It had rained all day and was still drizzling, so the winding road from the Ruta to Lucero was slick with clay-red mud. At dusk, it was difficult to see oncoming vehicles, which were mostly logging trucks, especially as they came around the many tight curves in the road. John gripped the steering wheel with both hands and kept a steady foot on the gas to avoid sliding into the deep ruts on both sides of the road. Despite his best efforts, the car skidded, the tires spun, and abruptly they were stalled in the sticky mud.

"Clara, here's the flashlight. You need to get out and walk up the road around the next bend to alert anyone coming, or we'll get hit," John said. "I'll see if there's anything I can do to get us out of this ditch."

Through the mud-streaked windshield, John watched Clara stagger away in almost ankle-deep muck. No wonder they couldn't keep a nurse or doctor in this place. Given the frequent rains in this part of the country, it was often nearly impossible to get in or out of there.

John tried rolling the car back and forth. In the darkness without a flashlight, he clomped through the mud to collect rocks and pieces of wood to place around the tires. All to no avail.

It was well past 10:00 when a logging truck approached from behind. Two men in coveralls jumped from the cab of the truck. They exchanged a quick greeting and then attached chains to both vehicles and slowly pulled the car out of the muddy rut.

After a few more near mishaps, John and Clara drove onto the clinic yard in Lucero just before midnight. The car's headlights flashed across the figure of a man, stumbling toward the door, blood dripping onto the ground. A woman emerged from the clinic. It was Annemarie, the nurse who'd barely held things together after head nurse Leni left.

"Looks like someone needs our help." John stepped stiffly out of the car and grabbed his black bag from the back seat.

The man said he'd struggled for several painful hours to get to the clinic. He claimed to have been attacked with a machete and was suffering from deep cuts on both arms.

"Annemarie, Clara, let's get some boiling water," John said. "I need to stitch up these cuts before he loses more blood. We've almost lost him."

A little over an hour later, the man's wounds were stitched up and dressed, and he was resting on a mat on the clinic floor. John dropped his instruments into a washbasin and looked at Clara, who was wrapping a blanket around their patient. "This is why we're here," he said.

There was a loud clap outside their door. Clara groaned as she pulled her aching body off the low hard bed. It was still dark outside. She found her glasses and stared at her watch. It was only 4:30 in the morning. Who could that be? She tapped John's shoulder.

"Wot ess?" John sounded bewildered. "Where are we?"

"John, we're in Lucero. We've slept for only a few hours, and someone's at our door."

After caring for their patient the night before, John and Clara had left him with Annemarie and had gone to the shack in the clinic yard they'd been told would serve as their temporary home. They'd both dropped into bed without even removing their clothes.

Clara fumbled to push her hair into place and opened the door.

"The word has already spread that you are here. There are five patients waiting to see the doctor," Annemarie said, and turned to go back to the clinic.

Clara looked around the shabby little room they would be calling home until they built a new house. In one corner was a basin with a pitcher. In the opposite corner was a bucket she and John had used as their commode before dropping into bed. Next to their bed was a small wooden table that leaned to one side on the uneven dirt floor and two wobbly chairs. Clara shook her head. This was even more primitive than their first home in Filadelfia in 1943.

She walked over to the basin to wash her face. The pitcher was empty.

"I'll get us some water," she said.

John sat at the edge of the bed, rubbing the sides of his head with both hands. "Najo…"

Clara grabbed the dirty bucket in one hand and the empty water pitcher in the other and headed out. Apparently, they shared an outhouse with several other homes since it was quite a distance away. It was a good thing they had a bucket in their room. There was no way she'd make it to a toilet this far away. Clara emptied the bucket and then walked another stretch to what appeared to be a community well. She rinsed the bucket and filled the pitcher.

For a moment, she stood and looked around, breathing in the heavy scent of moist earth. The place looked deserted. Tangled vines and tall weeds had taken over the area where there were traces of a path and garden plot. When she and John lived in the house Marlena and Steve had built them up the hill a few kilometers away from here in the 1970s, they had such big dreams for this new colony. How very sad.

On her way back to their shack, she passed a small broken-down structure with no roof. The door was ajar. Clara saw a bucket hanging from one of the walls. So, this was their shower.

By the time Clara returned to their place, John was at the clinic. She quickly washed her face and hands and prepared to join him. When she entered the clinic, Clara saw Annemarie, hands on her hips, explaining something to John. She caught the last part of it. "She's not progressing as she should. We need to get her to a hospital."

Clara noticed the thin set of John's lips. "What's this about?" she asked.

Neither of them responded. John turned and strode out of the clinic. Clara watched Annemarie prepare the patient for the trip as though the case was closed. "Annemarie?"

In an exasperated tone of voice, Annemarie explained that, despite John's protests, the pregnant woman needed to be hospitalized. She should be taken to Coronel Oviedo, the nearest town with a hospital and doctors, 135 kilometers away. Under her breath she added, "It's good someone around here knows what needs to be done."

★

In the weeks ahead, when not seeing patients, John drew the plans for their new house, which they would build across the road from the clinic. He figured that in their efforts to recruit a permanent doctor, the house could be used as an inducement. By the end of June, the foundation was laid, and John found a carpenter to put up the frame. It wasn't anything like the big house on the hill they lived in when they first moved out to east Paraguay. But it would be comfortable, and it would have plumbing.

John sat back in the rickety chair next to their bed, remembering the vow he'd made to himself just last night. It had been a chilly, rainy evening. John happened to look out the window and saw Clara crossing the yard to the shower hut, wearing a raincoat and boots, and carrying a flashlight and a bucket of warm water. She rarely complained. But he would make sure she eventually had a proper shower and toilet.

Just then Clara walked into the room. "The carpenter says it's time for us to decide where we want the shelves in the kitchen. This is so exciting."

John handed her the kitchen design he'd been working on. "How's this?"

Clara sat down beside him. "Oh, I love this. It feels like we're newly-weds again, planning our new home."

A clap at the door and the arrival of a patient with a gunshot wound to the head interrupted their newlywed dreaming. That night, they both took a "helper" to get to sleep.

Clara found that she easily fit into the work at the clinic. She often managed the delivery cases by herself, even when they came in the middle of the night, and she oversaw all the patient files. But she felt lonely.

"We've been here for over a month, and we still haven't had a letter from anyone. I feel shut off from the rest of the world. It seems like our only contact is with mosquitoes, snakes, lizards and now the latest— sandflies…" Clara's voice trailed off.

A few weeks ago, they had both begun itching all over their bodies, and didn't know the source. John had suggested washing their feet with gas in case they were picking up sandflies. Sure enough, they soon discovered that their bodies were covered with sandfly bites. In addition to ongoing discomfort, the most serious concern was leishmaniasis, a parasitic disease contracted from a bite of an infected sandfly.

"I wish that was the worst part about being here," John said.

They were preparing for bed. It had been a long day, beginning at 2:00 a.m., when John was called to the clinic to see a patient with an acute appendix. It was immediately clear that the man needed emergency surgery, so Annemarie's husband had taken him to the hospital in Coronel Oviedo. A few hours later, a woman arrived. John diagnosed a tubal pregnancy, which again required that the patient be transported to a hospital with a surgeon.

Clara knew how hard it was for John to send cases away for surgeries he'd performed many times. They often talked about it. John was not accredited in Paraguay, and at age eighty-three, if something went wrong, people would blame it on his age.

"I feel so useless." John dropped onto their hard bed.

There was no point in reminding him that if he were not here, the hospital would be closed, leaving an area with nearly 40,000 people without any healthcare services. And what was left of the Tres Palmas Mennonite colony would also soon disappear. Knowing all of this wouldn't alleviate John's torment about doing what he felt was half a job.

Clara lay down next to him, feeling his wakeful restlessness. She silently breathed an extra prayer that the Lord might show them His way.

They'd barely fallen asleep when there was a clap in the yard. Clara stumbled to the door.

"The doctor is needed." Annemarie turned back to the clinic.

Clara saw that John had not even stirred. She tapped him on the shoulder. Still no response.

"John, there's a patient at the clinic." She shook him. "John."

"Wot ess?" John mumbled, finally pushing himself up from the bed.

Clara watched him stumble trying to get his pants on, finally sitting on the bed for a while, and then lying back down.

"Is it the dizziness again?" Clara put her hand on John's forehead.

During the past several weeks, John had suffered from dizziness that was sometimes completely debilitating. On one occasion he had even requested a short rest before seeing a patient. He'd gone into a rage when he later discovered that Annemarie had immediately sent the patient to Coronel Oviedo.

John sat up. "Ach, dot ess nuscht," he said, standing up on wobbly legs and making his way unsteadily to the door. Clara rushed along beside him.

The patient had a cut across his forehead from a tire blowout accident, requiring ten stitches. By the time they returned to their shack, John was steady on his feet again.

THIRTY-TWO

John sat across from Norbert Thiessen in the Oberschulze's office, which was just a nook in the corner of his small living room. He and Clara had been in Tres Palmas for nearly a year. The new house that was to be used as enticement to bring in a permanent doctor was finished. Not only was there still no word about hiring a doctor to replace John, but the very survival of the colony continued to be in jeopardy. What John had just heard was deeply troubling and he needed to confront Thiessen about it.

"You said it was serious, John. Wot ess looss?" Thiessen leaned back in his chair.

"Why don't we talk about the real reason the dairy business failed." John watched Thiessen fidget. He wondered if the man would ever have told him the truth, had John not heard it elsewhere and come to confront him about it.

Since its inception in the 1970s, Tres Palmas had lacked needed investments in land, infrastructure like roads and bridges, as well as viable industries. In the beginning, John and Clara had donated significant personal money and had raised funds in North America, especially for the Lucero hospital. When they left in 1983, they were discouraged by the overall lack of support for the project.

The colony had barely survived during the past decade. Now, in 1994, it faced a crucial juncture. Paraguayans, Brazilians, and Mennonites were again moving into the area, which was now receiving affordable electric current from the Itaipú hydroelectric plant on the Paraguay–Brazil border. Logging operations, soybean production, and dairy farming were all potentially viable economic ventures. But sufficient funding was still lacking.

When he and Clara arrived nearly a year ago, John had been more determined than ever that Tres Palmas needed to survive, not only for the sake of its members, but to maintain peaceful relations with the Paraguayan government. Mennonites simply could not take their privileges in this country for granted. The services of the Lucero hospital and the Christian witness of colony members were essential ways for the Mennonites to give back.

John had encouraged Thiessen to set up operations to produce cheese and yogurt, using local dairy sources. At the time, John personally donated $1,000 and promised to invest more after the sale of their Menno house. The dairy business failed, presumably because of insufficient milk. But John recently heard another story.

When Thiessen remained silent, John blurted out, "You used my money to pay your colony debts, rather than investing it as we had agreed."

Thiessen stared at his lap.

John continued. "Look, Norbert, I know how desperate things are. And I know you're doing your best. But we must have an understanding here. Clara and I have sold our house in Menno, and we are prepared to donate half of it for much-needed road and bridge construction here. But the question is, are we in this together?"

Thiessen looked up, his eyes growing wide.

John didn't wait for him to respond. "We want a significant portion of the rest of the money from the house sale to go toward building a decent hospital here. I've already drawn up the plans. No wonder we can't attract a full-time physician. The facility is pathetic. Did you know that the other day we had to tear off parts of the roof over the fireplace in the hospital to clean up termites that have been in there for years and were starting to make holes in the ceiling?"

"John, I…I'm…" Thiessen stopped and shook his head.

"Let's leave the past in the past. But going forward, I want a clear accounting of the use of funds." John rose to leave and then turned back. "We've only gotten started, Norbert. I'm selling my land out here and am planning to donate half of the proceeds to starting up soybean production. I think that should do really well in this climate." He headed for the door. "And I've submitted a grant request to the Showalter Foundation for $10,000 for the Lucero hospital project."

Clara was pleased to see John's growing enthusiasm about the colony's development. It helped counteract his feelings of uselessness as a physician. But she feared he was pushing himself too hard one more time. Just this morning, after being up most of the night treating a man with boils all over his body, John complained about numbness and tingling in his legs. But instead of lying down, he insisted on finishing a column he was writing for the Chaco colony's publication *Menno Blatt*, titled "The Pioneers of the Chaco." He lauded the Chaco Mennonites for their support of Km. 81 in the early days of developing the leprosy station. He ended the column with:

> We now need that kind of support for Tres Palmas. I think Tres Palmas can be for the Mennonites as meaningful as Km. 81.

As she proofread the column for him, which she always did because he was a terrible speller, Clara marveled at John's tenacity. She knew his recent sense of purpose seemed partly fueled by his disappointment that Ana had lost her passion for justice. Based on her last letter, Ana had rejoined the famed mothers of Argentina's *Desaparecidos*, but other than that was doing nothing to actively protest Menem's corrupt regime.

Clara finished proofing the column and looked across the room at John, now sprawled on the bed, his clothes still on, sound asleep, his open mouth sagging to the right. The Lord had called them to do this work until a suitable doctor could be found. But for how long? It wasn't just John's dizziness that worried her, or even his increased drooling. She'd had frequent bouts of diarrhea and abdominal pain recently, and last night her urine was bloody with clumps of pus. John started her on antibiotics and checked her blood pressure, which registered 150/90. Clara had been surprised by John's concern. Should she tell him that this was the range it had been in for quite some time? Were these all signals that it was time for them to slow down?

In early November, a woman came to the clinic with a retained placenta. She had traveled for hours on the back of a pickup truck after not delivering the placenta when she gave birth. Now, nearly eight hours later, her uterus was so contracted that John couldn't remove it manually. Annemarie had to take the patient to Coronel Oviedo.

That night, John wrote in a letter to Marlena:

> This work is so mixed up. Sometimes, I feel I can help a patient, and find out they've been sent home without my permission. Other times they come, and I can't help them. All in all, I think it is high time we stop. We paid for the house we live in and never got a penny for salary. Kinda hard for them to get rid of us if they wanted to, not so? We plan to leave in the middle of December, whether they've found another doctor or not.

Just a week after John wrote that letter, they learned that a Dr. Reyes, a young physician with a wife and two children, was interested in the job at the Lucero hospital. Reyes planned to visit Tres Palmas as soon as the roads became passable after a week of hard rains.

John put the finishing touches on his building plans for the hospital extension. He was pleased with the design, especially the area he'd specified for surgeries. And between the money he and Clara had donated and the funds they'd raised in the North and from the Chaco colonies, there now were sufficient resources to build the new hospital addition. Finally, Tres Palmas would have a proper hospital and someone who could perform emergency surgeries, rather than having to send people away.

On a hot and humid Saturday, December 3, Dr. Reyes and his wife arrived in Tres Palmas. John showed them the clinic, the house that would be their home, and his drawings for an expanded hospital. It wasn't until after Reyes signed the contract that John realized he'd been holding his breath as though his life depended on this man taking the job. In some crazy way, he supposed his life did depend on it.

Now that this chapter was closing, John was eager to focus on their plans to get back to their little house in Goessel, Kansas. He and Clara planned to give away all their South American possessions other than a few small bags of clothing. This felt enormously freeing. But John noticed that Clara was having a harder time letting go.

"Do you remember when we bought this table, John, in Mt. Lake, before we were called to start the leprosy work?" Clara ran her hands over the chipped, blue formica tabletop, thinking about the many guests who had eaten with them around this table on the veranda of their home at Km. 81.

"Pretty silly that we shipped a table to Paraguay," John said. Seeing tears well up in Clara's eyes, he came over and put his arms around her. "It'll be OK, hon."

EXODOS

2001

"The reasonable man adapts himself to the world: the unreasonable one persists in trying to adapt the world to himself. Therefore, all progress depends on the unreasonable man."

–George Bernard Shaw

THIRTY-THREE

May 11, 2001. They were on their way to the leprosy station, Wesley at the wheel. Clara sat in the back seat next to John. It was strange to be back in Paraguay after living in Goessel for the past six years. At the same time, it felt oddly familiar to see Wesley incessantly honking the horn and weaving around cars, buses, motorcycles, and ox-drawn carts.

They turned left at the Km. 81 marker onto the narrow dirt road leading to the station. It curved up a gently sloping hill, deep ruts still making it easier to maneuver on foot than by car. Clara turned to John, hoping that the familiar scene might jog his memory and bring him out of his inaccessible shell. He sat with his knees tucked together and his head down, hands folded in his lap, a bit of spittle running down the right side of his chin. Clara reached over and placed a hand on his.

They had come to celebrate Km. 81's fiftieth anniversary. It was to be a huge affair, widely publicized, with over 700 friends, colleagues, dignitaries, and government officials in attendance from all over the world. All eight of their children were there for the event. Clara had prayed that John would come back to his old self just long enough to witness and enjoy the many acknowledgements of his contributions over the years.

Just a few weeks ago, John had suffered a series of small strokes. Although he seemed to understand the purpose of the event at Km. 81, he appeared uninterested in it. He knew who Clara and each one of his children were, but he could barely speak and had turned inward, a blank look on his face, as though ensuring that no accolades during this event would penetrate his shell.

They passed over a small bridge that crossed what used to be the stream that fed the pond they called Paso Malo, where they had baptized their converted leprosy patients. The stream had long since dried up and the bridge boards were loose. The car clattered across it and made its way up the hill. On the left were rows of blossoming orange trees and mulberry bushes exploding with purple bounty. Clara remembered when John had brought the mulberry seeds from Kansas, carrying them in his coat pocket during the entire trip. She clasped her fingers around his.

Konrad Wolf stood at the entrance of the large auditorium that the station workers had prepared for the anniversary program. Because of his involvement over the years in the leprosy work, the leaders of the Mennonite colonies had asked him to give a formal presentation on behalf of the Paraguay Mennonites.

Konrad watched two men approach the building and recognized them as Dr. Franz Duerksen, the physician MCC and ALM had hired to take over the leprosy work in 1971, and Edgar Stoesz, now chair of the ALM board. Konrad thought about the day in mid-November of 1971, when he had driven Stoesz to the station, believing that there would be a standoff and that Schmidt would refuse to leave Km. 81. Konrad shook his head, remembering their surprise when they learned that the Schmidts were already gone.

He wished he could undo some of the deep pain that the bungled leadership transition at Km. 81 had caused for the Schmidts. They'd had their differences early on, but over time, Konrad had come to respect and admire Schmidt's refusal to ever compromise his integrity. Konrad hoped he would do him justice in his talk today.

"N'dach." Konrad reached to shake Dr. Duerksen's hand. "This is turning out to be quite a large affair."

"We're celebrating quite a large accomplishment," Duerksen said. "Many of us contributed, but John and Clara were the pioneers who started all of it. Without them, none of this would exist."

Konrad spotted Norbert Thiessen, the former Oberschulze from Tres Palmas, walking toward them. "I haven't seen you for a long time, Norbert. How are things in Tres Palmas?"

"They've never been better. We have a thriving hospital, a first-rate school, and our colony is finally sustaining itself economically. We have the Schmidts to thank for that," Thiessen said. "I can't wait to tell John that his dream has come true. Tres Palmas has become what he always believed it could be. Where are the Schmidts? I haven't seen them."

"They just arrived," Konrad said. "But John's not well. He's had a stroke."

"I'm very sorry to hear that," Thiessen said.

"Today, Schmidt will not need to speak to us about the right thing to do. Today, we are finally here to speak for him," Konrad said, the scar across the side of his face pulsing.

Clara looked around her. Preparations for this grand event clearly had been going on for a very long time. Km. 81 looked like a resort, with freshly whitewashed buildings, manicured lawns and bushes, and bright-colored flowers. Brazilian *Portulacas*, with their tube-like leaves, sent large flamboyant flowers shooting from the ends of sprawling stems. *Pentas*, called starflowers in the U.S., showed off their hairy foliage and bunches of star-shaped flowers in bright tones of lavender, red, white, and pink. Cockscombs were blooming everywhere. The softly textured bushes were bursting with flowers in shades of purple, yellow, orange, and pink.

"I hardly recognize this place," Clara said, feeling John's weight as he stumbled along beside her, holding onto her arm for support.

"*Dot ess veschwenderisch*," John said, mouthing the words emphatically, even if with some difficulty.

"I agree that it's a bit wasteful, but it sure is pretty," Clara said. She pressed his arm close to her side. Had she heard a shade of resentment in his words? Was John offended that this place, *his* leprosy station, scarcely resembled what they had built? He had practically singlehandedly planted the trees, planned the construction of the buildings, and organized the station grounds fifty years ago. The trees were still here. The buildings still stood. But the place looked nothing like it had when they lived here.

They walked past the grape arbor, now covered with thick vines. Clara remembered the day she and John had found the perfect spot for the arbor, at the heart of the station. A sad smile formed when she thought about their kiss, standing at that very spot.

The formal program began. Konrad stood at the back of the auditorium, checking his notes. Dr. Carlos Wiens, the current medical director at Km. 81, opened with a prayer, and then various prominent officials gave speeches. Km. 81 was touted as a revolutionary beam of light, bringing healing and compassion to what had once been a dark world of shame and stigma. Edgar Stoesz presented a plaque that celebrated the fifty-year partnership between Km. 81 and ALM.

"And now Konrad Wolf will say a few words," the emcee announced.

Before stepping onto the podium, Konrad stopped in front of the Schmidts, who were seated in the front row. He bent down and placed a hand on each of the old man's shoulders.

"John."

Schmidt's eyes focused on his for just a moment before the light went out again. It was the absolution Konrad needed from this man whom he'd so despised in the early days in the Chaco; whom he'd deeply hurt by his own, MCC's and ALM's mismanagement of the transition at Km. 81; and who was the most uncompromisingly principled person he'd ever met.

"Liebe Geschwister," Konrad began. "I met John Schmidt in 1941." He turned to Clara and smiled. "Even before he married you, Frau Dokta. It was a dark time in the history of the Mennonites in Paraguay…" He described the early years in the Chaco. The Bund. The droughts. The lack of roads. The locusts. The desperation and poverty.

"Schmidt had a dream of what was possible for the Mennonites in the Chaco. He and Frau Dokta personally gave everything they had, and today, their dream has come true."

Konrad looked down and was silent for a moment. "For John Schmidt, it was always about what was best for the Mennonites in Paraguay. This place, this extraordinary place of healing for the outcasts with leprosy, this too, was a gift for the Mennonites. 'We must give back' was his motto. 'This station is a place for us to give back.' And Tres Palmas is no different. It is a thriving colony, largely because of the pioneering efforts of the Schmidts. But there again, the work flowed from John Schmidt's motto: 'We must give back.'"

Konrad ended his talk on a personal note. "Many of us found John Schmidt insufferable. I certainly did." Konrad glanced at John, but there was no sign of response or recognition. "I wonder if great and revolutionary changes can only happen with his kind of stubborn persistence, driven by a deep love of God and a fierce desire to make the world a better place. I leave you all with this Bible verse from Micah 6:8. Frau Clara has told me that it is John Schmidt's favorite Bible passage, and it offers a challenge for all of us: '*And what does the Lord require of you? To act justly and to love mercy and to walk humbly with your God.*'"

It was time for John to address the crowd. Clara had written the script for him, and John Russell was to accompany his father to the podium and read it for him. Clara watched as her "Sonny" stood and turned toward his father to offer his arm for support. She remembered the horrific fights John had with his firstborn child when their tempers flared. Now John clung to his son's arm as a small child might who is just learning to walk. Everyone watched in silence as, very slowly, they made their way together onto the stage.

"Our father welcomes you and thanks you for being here. He wishes he could speak to you, but it is difficult for him at this time."

John looked bewildered.

When Clara joined them on the stage, she gave a cheery speech about how important this work had been to them. Then she called their children to stand. She asked each one to remain standing until she had introduced all of them. She smiled when all eight of her children broke into applause. Despite their many failings as parents, God had blessed them with a loving family.

Clara looked out across the audience before stepping off the stage. Her eyes fell on a stooped white-haired woman standing at the back of the hall. Something about her looked familiar. Then, even from this distance, Clara recognized the piercing green eyes.

When the program ended, Clara spotted Ana coming toward them.

"Dr. John and Doña Clara, I am so happy to be part of honoring you and your many contributions." Ana held her arms out to both of them. "And I am sorry to hear of Dr. John's failing health," she murmured to Clara.

"He cannot express it, but I know he's happy you are here," Clara said.

"Can we walk together, Doña Clara?"

Clara left John in John Russell's care. The two women walked away from the crowd.

Ana, more stooped than Clara, rested a hand on Clara's arm for support. "Would you take me to the house you built for Josefina and Amalia?"

They walked in silence. When they reached the little house that had once belonged to the dwarf and her mother, Ana said, "She was radiant."

Clara raised her eyebrows, and Ana continued. "Amalia. The dwarf. Her face was so radiant when I met her here in front of this house. In the few moments we spent together, she taught me something I pondered all those years I was tortured and imprisoned." Ana wrapped her arms around her body, and Clara noticed how frail she was.

"Service from a place of loving joy is more uplifting than service from a place of angry righteousness." Ana's voice was muted, and she spoke the words like a mantra. "That is what Amalia's glowing face taught me. And finally, I grasped the truth of it..."

Clara stared at the ground. What was she supposed to say?

Ana continued. "I'm an old woman now. I spent too much of my life consumed with anger. I now know how depleting it was for me to believe I was worthless if I didn't push myself to save the world. And Dr. John...well, I came here because I wanted to tell him..."

Clara looked up. "What led you to believe you had to save the world?"

Ana didn't hesitate. "When I was a child, my parents held me to unrealistic standards that I was never able to meet. I learned that I was no good unless I achieved the unattainable. I believe your John and I shared this. But I don't know what his demons were that drove him to keep striving to do the impossible."

"It's simple. God drove him to do the work," Clara said.

It was true. And yet...from the deep recesses of Clara's mind, a memory trace began to surface of John's words the night of their engagement, something about his father beating him regularly if he didn't keep pushing himself.

"Thank you for coming, Ana," Clara said. "I wish John could have..." Her voice faded into the sound of approaching voices. "I guess we should rejoin the celebration."

EPILOGUE

My parents, John and Clara, stayed in Paraguay after the Km. 81 event because Dad was too weak to travel back to the States. He was a shadow of the man he once had been. His body, which had always been slender and strong, was now feeble. His dark eyes had lost their penetrating sharpness.

John Russell, now part of the Fernheim Colony leadership, made special arrangements to allow our parents to move into the Old Folks Home in Fernheim, just a few short blocks from the small hut in the Chaco they first called home.

In early November of 2003, my father suffered a massive stroke. He died a week later, on November 7. My mother continued to live in the home until she died seven years later.

INVITATION TO READERS

Thank you, dear reader, for joining us in celebrating the life and work of John and Clara Schmidt. Their powerful legacy lives on in the three regions of Paraguay where they built communities and established hospitals. We asked two of their sons and a grandson to share glimpses into the Chaco colonies, Km. 81, and Tres Palmas in 2021. You will find these updates in the following pages.

We invite you to visit CalledASaga.com to see photos, original documents, book club questions, and references to all source materials used to write this story. It is an interactive site that features comments and reactions to the book from other readers. Please share your own reflections and/or experiences regarding the Schmidts and their work in the space provided on the site.

If this story touched you, you might also enjoy Marlena Fiol's memoir, *Nothing Bad Between Us: A Mennonite Missionary's Daughter Finds Healing in Her Brokenness*, a very different version of John and Clara's story, as told through the eyes of their daughter. Read an excerpt of that memoir at the end of this book.

Finally, we'd love for you to post a rating and review of this book on Amazon and Goodreads.

UPDATES 2021

Chaco Update

Dr. Wesley Schmidt – son of John and Clara
If you ask any Paraguayan about the Chaco, they will mention two important events: 1) the Chaco war waged with Bolivia 1932–1935, and 2) the Mennonites settling in middle of this region. The Chaco includes almost sixty percent of the country's geography and only four percent of its population. Most Paraguayans would concede that the presence of the immigrants in this "green hell" transformed it into a prosperous axis in the western part of the country.

Communication
In the 1950s and 1960s, Dad headed up the recruitment of engineers and construction workers, and coordinated financial assistance to build the trans-Chaco road, providing a vital 300-mile connection from the colonies to the markets in Asunción. This road has since been paved, and now the government is turning it into a four-lane highway projected to connect the colonies to neighboring Argentina, Bolivia, and Brazil.

Communication in the Chaco has also been revolutionized with a modern fiberoptic internet that connects the colonies to Asunción and the world. Telephone towers in the area make phone connections possible throughout the entire Central Chaco. The modern Florida Hotel in Filadelfia displays an archaic telephone, one of the original apparatuses and switchboards Dad convinced MCC to donate to the pioneering Chaco.

Education

From the beginning, education was essential to develop local minds and to maintain both the German language and Mennonite values. Education was entirely in German in the early years. Mennonite children still begin their schooling in German, but now all have easy access to Spanish secondary school and several local universities. For example, the nursing school that Mom and Dad established in 1943 is part of a university with a fully accredited nursing faculty, graduating more than fifty nurses every year.

Healthcare

The shack serving as Dad's hospital in 1941 has been replaced by three modern hospitals. Originally, medical assistance was available at no cost to members of the colonies and neighboring native tribes, but as medical services have become more sophisticated and investments in hospitals more formidable, this became untenable. Today the colony's taxpayers easily cover their share of medical costs, and a prepaid employee program exists through the Kooperative to help the ever-growing indigenous population pay for their care.

Economy

The Chaco Mennonite colonies, which have become a thriving economic force in Paraguay, are strongly anchored in the Kooperative system the Mennonite immigrants instituted almost a century ago. The economy is based on the production of beef exported to all corners of the planet from three modern packing plants, a dairy industry that provides over fifty percent of the dairy consumption in the country, and agriculture.

The population in the Chaco area today is a unique combination of 1) various indigenous groups, which constitute five different linguistic cultures and dominate the labor force, 2) the so-called Latinos, mainly Paraguayan citizens who have moved to the Chaco from east Paraguay, as well as some Brazilians, and 3) a minority group of affluent Mennonites, descendants of the original immigrants. Despite now being the minority culture in the Chaco, they continue to proudly maintain a closed affiliation within the colony system and a Germanic culture that dominates all areas of commerce.

Today's shopping centers, industry, and beautiful homes in the towns give the impression that this is an oasis where all difficulties have been overcome. But the inequalities are more threatening now than when immigrants and indigenous people all shared the same poverty. As one pioneer said, "We have managed to overcome the difficulties of survival faced during the first fifty years. Now we have the more formidable challenge to overcome the difficulties related to wise management of prosperity."

Personal Ties

Sometime in the early 1950s, when our family was uprooted from Mt. Lake to initiate the leprosy project at Km. 81, Dad invested money in a tract of land, which at the time was inaccessible Chaco bush. He figured correctly that the value would increase substantially and thought that maybe someday his sons would be interested in developing the land. My brothers John Russell and David and I have taken on that challenge.

For more than thirty years, I have stood with one foot enthusiastically on my Chaco ranch and the other not so enthusiastic as a family doctor in Asunción. Initially, I had lots of support from Dad, and enjoyed working shoulder to shoulder with him. Fortunately, my wife shared my dream, and our sons are now settled in the Chaco with their families, one an agricultural engineer, another a veterinarian, and a third a doctor for the indigenous. My blind enthusiasm has been replaced by educated application of science to the land my sons have learned to love and respect.

All is not bliss. As I write this in 2021, we are facing the worst drought since climate registry began in Filadelfia in 1932. We look to the horizon, hoping clouds will appear. And then, just as the early Chaco pioneers did again and again, we gaze at the Higher Ground, where we find the necessary foundation to keep going, knowing these difficulties eventually pass. In the end, we are pilgrims dependent on God's mercy. But while we're here, we might as well enjoy the great bounty this part of the world provides.

KM. 81 UPDATE

Dr. Wesley Schmidt – son of John and Clara
I have many fond memories of Km. 81 as it was in the 1950s. Dad and Mom worked as a team covering medical responsibilities, administrative duties, chaplaincy, and everything else. Today, the multifaceted initiative of these two pioneers has been formalized into many different departments, with people assigned exclusive and specific responsibilities for each area.

From 1975 to 1978, as a recent medical graduate, I was fortunate to step into Dad's shoes for three years, taking on the role of medical director at Km. 81. Just a few months ago, I accompanied the current Paraguayan health minister Julio Mazzoleni in an official visit to the station. I was impressed with the beautiful gardens, ponds, and paved sidewalks connecting the new buildings. Several fancy vehicles proudly bear the Km. 81 logo, and the modern establishment contrasts sharply with the poor surrounding communities.

I recall Dad's comment when he and Mom were writing their will, donating a large part of their possessions to different charities, that "Km. 81 has more money than they need." Nevertheless, they donated significant funds for medical activities of Km. 81.

In the 1950s and 1960s, Km. 81's sponsors were the U.S.-based MCC and ALM. Dad and Mom also received financial support from their families and from North American churches. The Mennonite colonies offered volunteer labor. Now the bulk of financial assistance comes from thirty-two Paraguayan Mennonite churches, united through the GemeindeKomitee. The early bonds with the Chaco Mennonite churches were wisely developed under Dad's leadership, tapping into the spirit that we are many and varied members of a community who all seek to carry out a service of love. Dad frequently quoted Menno Simons in his reports to sponsoring churches and institutions: Our main motive is that "the love of Christ compels us." Dad also believed it was important for Mennonites to give back to Paraguay for allowing them to settle there, maintain their culture, and be exempted from military service.

The medical work at Km. 81 can be divided into several areas. First is the leprosy treatment and training center. Treatment has now evolved from Dapsone to polychemotherapy, with three curative drugs for a maximum period of twelve months. Km. 81 has over 10,000 different medical records of patients who have been treated for leprosy over the years. Currently, there are about 200 hospitalizations per year related to inpatient treatment for the rehabilitation of disabilities caused by leprosy, and all return to their homes and families.

Patients also receive rehabilitation services, including physical therapy, occupational therapy, and rehabilitation surgeries, originally developed under the leadership of Dr. Franz Duerksen, who succeeded Dad as director of Km. 81 during the 1970s and 1980s. There is now an Education Center that serves hundreds of students and officials from all over South and Central America, as well as Mexico.

Other areas of service include programs for patients with pathologies that are accompanied by stigmatizing conditions, such as tuberculosis, pemphigus, clubfoot, diabetic foot, AIDS, and leishmaniasis. These conditions have elements in common with leprosy, and the learning gained from leprosy is leveraged to serve patients with these pathologies.

Finally, Km. 81 has a clinic and hospital for non-leprosy ailments, which Dad originally started to gain the trust of neighboring communities. The non-leprosy clinic today has more than 232,000 medical records of patients who have been treated over the years.

As a doctor, I can hardly believe what the small dispensary Dad developed—which had to overcome the extreme distrust of neighbors, authorities, and patients, using basic procedures with little available scientific evidence—has grown into. Dr. Carlos Wiens, current medical director of Km. 81, is a modern version of Dad, making the leprosy station his life's project. Today, it is a major leprosy referral center, recognized by Paraguay's Ministry of Health, the Pan American Health Organization, and the World Health Organization.

TRES PALMAS UPDATE

David Schmidt – son of John and Clara

As I sit here on my porch overlooking the valley, the lake, and the community on the far side, I can see the house on the hill that belonged to Mom and Dad and am reminded of their impact on my life and the lives of others living in and around the Tres Palmas colony.

Their influence on this community began long before the actual existence of Tres Palmas. While at Km. 81, my parents planned long trips to this remote region of east Paraguay to locate and treat leprosy patients. They became acquainted with Mennonites living in the area and formed a bond that would continue for the rest of their lives.

After leaving Km. 81, Mom and Dad decided to make their home in this community. And due in large part to their investments of time and money, Tres Palmas began to take shape. The economy at that time was centered around logging, but Dad presaged that for a colony to survive, it needed more than sawmill employees. He offered land he had purchased to others at reasonable prices and long-term payments to attract people to the area.

When the logging business began to falter, many were forced to find other means of livelihood. Farms began to appear, but life was challenging, and many left the community. Once again, my parents became passionately engaged in helping people stay and participate in the formation of the colony. Through the years, they actively partici-pated in the local church, where they had their usual place on the left side near the window.

My wife, Judy, and I came to Tres Palmas in 1974 as self-supporting missionaries to the indigenous Guaraní living in the area. When our oldest son, Anton, aged five at the time, saw his Grosspa attending to people in his small clinic, he declared "That's what I want to be when I grow up!" Anton is now a much-loved doctor in the Tres Palmas area.

Presently, the colony has eighty-seven members, with a total of 184 people living in the area. Tres Palmas is racially diverse, with Germans, Brazilians, and Paraguayans, often living in ethnically mixed marriages. Of the 8,900 hectares, 5,700 are cultivated, with soy, corn and wheat being the main crops. Farming is mostly zero tillage, and with modern equipment, averages two or three crops a year. The locals also raise cattle for beef and dairy, producing 12,000 liters of milk per day.

With both Spanish and German prevalent in the community, there is a functioning church for each. The German church supports the indigenous community nearby and the hospital with one resident doctor and five part-time specialists. They operate a 1–12 school which currently has 136 students, about half of which come from neighboring communities. The lower classes begin mostly in German but later change to a full Spanish program recognized by the Ministry of Education.

What most characterized my parents were 1) their faith in a God who was always active in their lives, and 2) the perseverance they demonstrated in overcoming seemingly impossible obstacles. Although they are now deceased, Tres Palmas is thriving and I'm living here because of their faith and perseverance.

LUCERO HOSPITAL UPDATE

Dr. Anton Schmidt – grandson of John and Clara

Quite a few things have changed since Grosspa first initiated the Lucero Hospital, where I currently serve as a family practice doctor. We offer consultations for prevention and ongoing medical care for every age. We provide gynecology and obstetrics services, as well as dentistry and orthodontics. In addition, we have a general surgeon on staff, who handles all general surgeries. We also have a birthing and neonatal room, as well as a nursing staff that is on call 24-7. The hospital has over twenty beds available in private rooms, as well as a shared patient room. We have a well-equipped pharmacy.

The hospital has new ultrasound and 3-D/4-D imaging equipment that we acquired from Germany. We also have an x-ray machine and a lab that does basic blood and urine analyses. For more complex analyses, we draw the samples in the hospital and send them to Asunción.

We provide services for four different demographic groups. The largest group consists of Paraguayans from our area. Second are Brazilians from several villages around Lucero. Third, we serve the Mennonites in Tres Palmas. Finally, we serve indigenous groups from several communities around us. Our geographic service area exceeds a seventy-kilometer radius around the hospital.

It was Grosspa's dream that Mennonites would provide medical services to this rapidly growing and underserved community. It has become a reality, thanks to my grandparents' perseverative pioneering efforts.

ACKNOWLEDGMENTS

We are grateful for the many contributors to the meticulous documentation of John and Clara Schmidt's life and work, which allowed us to confidently write their story. We thank Gundolf Niebuhr (Fernheim historian and archivist), Frank Peachy (Records and Library Manager at MCC in Akron, PA), Joe Springer (Goshen College Librarian), and Jon Isaak (Director of the Centre for Mennonite Brethren Studies) for making much of this documentation available to us.

Three physicians who served as medical directors of the leprosy work at Km. 81 after the Schmidts left in 1971, Dr. Franz Duerksen, Dr. Wesley Schmidt, and Dr. Carlos Wiens, provided helpful information about the work at Km. 81.

We thank Edgar Stoesz, former MCC representative in Paraguay and former chair of the ALM board, for his reflections. "John made many enemies…and Clara came along behind him and calmed things down," he recalls.

Numerous early readers helped us refine and streamline the writing, including Jeniffer Thompson, Terri Griffith, Goldie Nijensohn, and our two sons, Brad O'Connor and Stefan Fiol. We are especially grateful to our sister Mary Lou and brother-in-law Rusty Bonham for their significant role in shaping this narrative.

And for helping us craft the story, we thank our teachers and editors, Lisa Ohlen Harris, Tom Jenks, and Eric Witchey.

ABOUT THE AUTHORS

Marlena Fiol, PhD and Ed O'Connor, PhD are spiritual seekers whose writing explores the depths of who we are and what's possible in our lives. They have devoted themselves to supporting others in identifying and removing the barriers to realizing their dreams. They consider every blog, essay, video, book, or workshop an opportunity to share their insights with others, as well as learn more about their own transformational journey.

To learn more, visit MarlenaFiol.com.

AND FOR ANOTHER LOOK AT JOHN AND CLARA'S LIFE

(as told through the eyes of their daughter)

Marlena Fiol's Memoir
Now Available

NOTHING BAD BETWEEN US:
A Mennonite Missionary's Daughter Finds
Healing in Her Brokenness

EXCERPT

Beginning of Chapter 1:

In the dark squared-off pews of the German Mennonite church sanctuary sat my accusers, stern and silent, all eyes converging on me. I dropped my head and concentrated on the rectangular pattern of the tile floor. The closed church shutters kept out the fiery late afternoon Paraguay sun. The weight of the musty, trapped air was suffocating.

Pastor Arnold Entz, a short, balding man with stooped shoulders and a large belly stretching the seams of a black jacket a few sizes too small for him, ushered me in through a narrow door at the front of the church. We walked beside the choir platform where I stood to sing each Sunday and behind the organ that I had played for seven years, since I was eleven. A single, straight-backed, wooden chair had been placed next to the pulpit.

The pastor signaled for me to sit. I made my way to the chair without looking up. I had dressed judiciously for this meeting. My dark gray skirt hung well below my knees. My arms itched against the starched, long sleeves of my white shirt, buttoned neck-high. I had pulled my long, wild reddish-brown hair into a tight bun at the nape of my neck. I wore no makeup.

Pastor Entz addressed the rows and rows of pews in High German. Although Mennonites in Paraguay all spoke the guttural, mostly unwritten Plautdietsch (Low German) to one another, in church we spoke only the more dignified High German, which was a distinctly different language. For example, "church excommunication" in Plautdietsch is "Tjoatjebaun" while in High German it is "Kirchenverbot."

"We have called a special church meeting on this first Sunday in January to discuss your sins and to determine the consequences," Pastor Entz said, turning to me. Heavy silence. I swallowed hard to keep acid from rising in my throat.

...end of Chapter 1:

Slowly, I pulled my eyes up off the floor and stared out across the stony faces. There were hundreds of them. They were nothing but a blur until my eyes fell on my father. He sat alone, without my mother, near the door at the very back of the church. His shoulders were squared, and his chin was up. The rigidity of his straight back was formidable. He didn't flinch, just stared at me coldly, hands clasped in his lap. My dad was always clear about what was right and wrong before God. And he tolerated no wrongs.

Tearing my eyes away from my father, I saw Heinz Duerksen and Hans Penner (both on the Mennonite administrative committee charged with overseeing Dad's leprosy station) just two rows up and to Dad's left. They glanced at each other, and solemnly shaking their heads, looked back to where my father sat. My father had given himself completely to the treatment of leprosy in Paraguay. He was a hero in the eyes of the people in this congregation—or rather, I thought in dismay, he had been a hero before I brought him shame.

I wanted to flee. But guilt kept me glued to the chair. The congregants looked satisfied with themselves, as though they had just successfully completed an important task.

It was unanimous.

"You are no longer allowed to sing in the choir or play the organ for Sunday services," announced the pastor in a monotone, turning toward me, his large belly protruding with authority. "Now, let us pray."

"Lieber Vater im Himmel, wir danken Dir für Deine Gnade...Dear Father in heaven, we thank you for your grace ..." His voice droned on and on.

I heard nothing further. They had just taken away from me all that I held most dear about the Mennonite church. I loved the music. But it wasn't just that. I had been a soloist in the choir and the church leaders consistently had shown such appreciation for my organ playing.

How was I supposed to face these people now? I imagined the word "UNCLEAN" stamped in red letters on my forehead.

The prayer finally ended, and people rose to leave. I watched my father's rigid back as he strode out and disappeared.

Made in the USA
Columbia, SC
19 November 2021

49324239R00211